THE RATTLE OF WINGS

The things that pressed themselves against the glass had bodies bigger than a man's biggest finger. They were orange with yellow underbellies, and their finely veined wings stretched a half-meter from tip to tip. Each bug had four wings and six bristly legs.

It was difficult for Rafferty to think of them one at a time when the walls, the gardens and streets, the air itself, were already filled with them . . .

Other Books by Bill Ransom:

FINDING TRUE NORTH, Copper Canyon Press *

WAVING ARMS AT THE BLIND, Copper Canyon Press *

THE SINGLE MAN LOOKS AT WINTER, Empty Bowl Press

LAST CALL, Blue Begonia Press

LAST RITES, Brooding Heron Press *

THE JESUS INCIDENT (with Frank Herbert), Putnam/Berkley

THE LAZARUS EFFECT (with Frank Herbert), Putnam/Berkley

THE ASCENSION FACTOR (with Frank Herbert), Putnam/Ace

* Out of Print

JAGUAR

BILL RANSOM

ACE BOOKS, NEW YORK

This book is an Ace original edition,
and has never been previously published.

JAGUAR

An Ace Book / published by arrangement with
the author

PRINTING HISTORY
Ace edition / July 1990

Cover art by Royo.

ISBN: 0-441-70353-4

Ace Books are published by The Berkley Publishing Group,
200 Madison Avenue, New York, New York 10016.

PRINTED IN THE UNITED STATES OF AMERICA

10 9 8 7 6 5 4 3 2 1

for my sisters, Susan and Doreen

Acknowledgments

James M. Mathias, MD; psychiatry
Robert B. Olsen, MD; psychiatry
Robert Colfelt, MD; neurology
Karen Hart, physiology
The McCarron family, the O'Keefe family and Johanna Nitzke.

Portions of this story appeared in slightly different forms in the following publications: *The Kansas City Star, Portland Review, Willow Springs Magazine* and *Iron Country.*

Thanks again, Frank.

Bibliography:

Silver Departures, Richard Kehl
Landscapes of the Night, Christopher Evans
The Country Between Us, Carolyn Forché
Life During Wartime, Lucius Shepard
Gathering the Tribes, Carolyn Forché
The Origin and Treatment of Schizophrenic Disorders, Theodore Lidz
The Drawing of the Three, Stephen King
Ender's Game, Orson Scott Card
We the Divided Self, John Watkins
Here Among the Sacrificed, Finn Wilcox/Steve Johnson
On Nature, Daniel Halpernen
The Destruction of the Jaguar, Christopher Sawyer-Laucanno
Dreams and Schizophrenia, Benjamin B. Wolman
Chaos, James Gleik
Collected Works, C. G. Jung
Soul Catcher, Frank Herbert
Crow, Ted Hughes
Crows, Ravens, Magpies and Jays, Tony Angell
"Letter to a Sister Who Lives in a Distant Country," Daisy Zamora
"Prayer for the Soul of my Country," Otto-Rene Castillo
Maxims, Marcel Proust
The Psychoanalysis of Fire, Gaston Bachelard
Sigmund Freud, Pindar, Herman Melville
For Whom the Bell Tolls, Ernest Hemingway
"The Porter," Ernest Hemingway

Childhood

Calamity does not spring from the dust, nor does trouble sprout out of the ground; for man is born to trouble as the sparks fly upward.

—Job

A DOT OF blue light appeared on the back of his closed eyelids, and Zachary Lee felt the icy blade of fear knife into his belly. Though asleep, and chambered securely inside one of the stone temples of his ancestors, he felt the prickle of his hackles rise to danger.

A dream, he reminded himself, *it's only a dream*.

Zachary Lee was a scientist, a logical man, but the logic that had led him inside this tumble of stone would not help him now.

The blue shimmer grew a fascinating opalescence that made it seem more a fattening than an incredible speed. The speed did not reside in the shimmering blue spot, but in his dream that raced toward the very fabric of being at near-light-speed.

His mind had become a magnetic coil and his dream was a vehicle that bore him down the great curves of an infinite accelerator. Zachary Lee had discovered how to mount the ride, but he knew neither how to dismount from it nor how to control its magnificent speed.

Images from his life blurred past: his tiny lab in the back of a van, the magnetic drives and servos he'd invented, his daughter's green eyes.

The blue ahead clarified into a pair of translucent wings, butterfly wings, hypnotic in their flutter. He had seen that shape many times before, in his experiments with the magnetic disturbances throughout the territory of the Roam.

His pendulum and its stylus had traced a huge infinity sign on this stone floor just one week past. It had been one in a long series of tracings. His daughter called them "butterflies," and now he thought of them as butterflies, too.

His dreams had warned him of death, that he might become one of the cinder people. Zachary Lee was hunted by the Jaguar's priests, whose informers sniffed him out by day and whose dreams homed in on him at night. He had to sleep sometime, and even an intellect as great as Zachary Lee's had no choice, once asleep, except to dream. Dreaming was necessary for sanity, for life itself.

Zachary Lee had turned a priest's dream-probe to his advantage and gained access to the dreamways—the dreamways that led to the lair of the Jaguar himself, sadistic tormentor of a peaceful people. The Jaguar liked little surprises.

As Zachary Lee sped towards the butterfly it glowed and fluttered wildly and he knew he was approaching the threshold of something great. He slammed into it with a sensation that he could only describe as a kiss, but he had no time left to describe it, nor anyone to describe it to.

Had he lived, he would have recognized it from his experiments as a shock wave of sorts, a phase-transition of magnetism and light from one state to another.

This phase-transition reduced Zachary Lee's brain matter to zero and it collapsed inward in a hot white flash. What had been husband, father and genius inside that shrunken char of a skull had found an insertion in the dreamways, but the Jaguar was waiting to snuff him out. He did not have time to regret that he, a peaceful man, had darted a Jaguar priest for nothing.

The Jaguar saw to it that few survived the dreamways. Those few succumbed to his tyranny with the resignation reserved for slavery, cattle and other manifestations of cold fate. Zachary Lee had not been the first to seek it out, to embrace it. Many a Jaguar priest could have warned him, but of course they were part of the Jaguar's stable, part of the hunt. Treachery meant scrambled minds, cooked brains.

The Jaguar manipulated Zachary Lee's passion to help others and lured him across the curtain. The Jaguar killed Zachary Lee atop an ancient stone temple early that rainy morning, with no more feeling than a fire has for ash. What remained of Zachary Lee were the scatterings of a skeleton, the sand beneath his shrunken skull transmogrified to glass.

During the history of time or the drapery of the universe—they were synonymous, to Zachary Lee—only a handful had breached this curtain and survived. One of these was the Jaguar, whose crude experiments with the dreamways caused ripples in the fabric. These ripples formed great magnetic pulses that rent the earth and the atmosphere alike.

Zachary hunted the Jaguar's priests, then the Jaguar himself, to rid his people of a hard vendetta. He had no way of knowing, at the time, that it was not a vendetta but a trivial amusement that had gotten out of hand.

By the time he knew all, Zachary Lee had left behind a lovely wife, pregnant with their second child, and his five-year-old daughter, Afriqua Lee. He had discovered two weak points in the fabric, traditional crossing-points of the ages: the stone ruins of the southern highlands, and a lush river valley of the northern reaches. It was in the valley of the northern reaches that he took his private stand against the Jaguar, and there that he died.

The Maya Roam of Zachary Lee was a nomadic community of tinkerers, inventors. Their technological wonders powered their vehicles and the great cities of the world. Now the Jaguar's priests worked the great minds of the Roam as if they were gold mines or cattle, entering through dreams and robbing them in their sleep, leaving them depressed, insane, scrambled or dead.

Zachary Lee, who never struck a man in anger, had darted a Jaguar priest to put a stop to this treachery. The Jaguar priests had hunted Lee's body, but it was the Jaguar himself who cornered his mind. The Jaguar considered this sacrifice a waste, a shameful waste. He sniffed out this novice of the dreamways and burned him with a single slap from his figurative paw.

The final battleground for Zachary Lee was his own mind, and the victory went to the Jaguar. But before Zachary Lee's mind was reduced to a random collection of organic molecules, the shock wave of his butterfly kiss rent the great curtain of the universe and sheared the rock mantle of the valley on which he lay. The universe on all sides of the fabric reeled from the blow.

Progress is not immediate ease, well-being and peace. It is not rest. It is not even, directly, virtue. Essentially Progress is a force, *and the most dangerous of forces. . . .*

—Pierre Teilhard de Chardin, *The Future of Man*

EDDIE REYES WAS a quiet boy even before the earthquake and the explosion downtown. People spoke in those days of his mother's blue eyes that he got to spite his dark skin, and the absence of his father, but the real talk later always came down to the earthquake or the explosion. What they whispered of in this quiet valley was Eddie's mother, and what he had done to her, and though this with his mother was an equally long time ago, it clearly had changed his life.

Dark-skinned Eddie and his pale-skinned mother lived with her parents just a few blocks from the Daffodil Laundry, a sprawling brick building behind the tracks that split the valley into equal measures of town and farm. His father had been run over by a jeep while waiting for a flight home from the war. Eddie never met him, but he could pick him out in the picture of hard-eyed men lined up under the wing of their bomber.

Six men stood with their legs apart and their arms folded in their leather jackets. Eddie's dad was the only dark-faced man in the group. He wore his hat tilted back, and a cigarette drooped from the corner of his mouth. Painted on the side of the plane were four rows of bombs to show the missions they'd survived. Eddie counted sixty-two.

Every day after Eddie became five his grandfather walked him the three blocks to the cafe next door to the laundry. There they would meet his mother for a soda while she took her break. His mother was a small, thin-faced woman who laughed a lot, and Eddie remembered that even though she was skinny she was always sweating from the heat of her machine.

She worked a machine she called "the mangle," which steam-pressed things between a pair of huge canvas lips. Sometimes she let him work the foot pedal while she set the creases. When the mangle responded it hissed like a small locomotive coming to a stop right in front of him. Hot. Very, very hot.

Something about sirens and a hot, still day in spring would fix Eddie Reyes like a dead bug to a board for the rest of his life. It started with the earthquake that spring when he was almost six.

Eddie sat on the sidewalk taking a wind-up clock apart while his cousin drew around him with colored chalk. Eddie liked the feel of taking things apart and putting them together, even when he was six. His grandfather made him a small toolbox of his own and it was his grandfather who gave him the clock. Suddenly, one of the gears that he'd set aside, the brass one with the axle through it, began turning all by itself in the middle of the pavement.

Eddie and his cousin watched, amazed, as the colored swirls of chalk bulged up with the rest of the sidewalk and then burst apart. The long sidewalk behind his cousin shook itself out like a rug, and the street broke into huge chunks of concrete. The scrape of buckling concrete and deep-throated groans of unseated rock shook suddenly back and forth: *Bam-bam Bam-bam*. Then a hiatus of stillness burst in one long rip of twisted lumber and the crumple of nearby walls.

Eddie thought it was like someone picked up the earth and shook it like an old shirt, then tore it apart.

Neighbors ran from their houses into the shattered street, shouting names and warnings. Some screamed. Some dusted themselves off and looked at the sky, others looked at parts of themselves to be sure they were still alive.

"Power lines here, watch out!"

"Gas . . . !"

Some stumbled out squinty and stunned, as though seeing the sun for the first time. Mrs. Brown, when she found her husband underneath the fallen wires, screamed in fright and grief. Some screamed names of children that Eddie knew. More than once he heard his own name, and his cousin's. Neither of them moved, and he saw that her eyes watched over his shoulder as he watched over hers. He heard her wet breathing, the *sniff* of her runny nose.

Now the clear air carried shouts of pain, and when he was sure the earth would stay still, he stood up slowly. He wanted to run to his mother at her work, and he looked up the street towards the laundry.

Mrs. Gratzer grabbed Eddie and his cousin. She gasped, "Oh, you poor kids. You poor kids. You must be scared to death."

She was huge, and had each of them tucked under an arm like bags of grain. Eddie couldn't breathe because of her grip and the press of her sweaty apron against his face. He hadn't had time to be scared yet, but he was starting to get that feeling in his stomach, that fast-elevator feeling that meant big trouble.

Mrs. Gratzer teetered in the doorway as she toed the screen door aside. The explosion from downtown pushed the three of them over in a heap. It was more of a feeling than a sound, a sudden punch in his lungs that popped his ears and took his breath away. Eddie landed on top of Mrs. Gratzer, and his cousin started crying from underneath.

"Jesus, Mary and Joseph," she said.

When Eddie followed the course her gaze took, he saw the huge boil of black smoke from downtown sniffing the street towards them. Things in the middle of it *pop-pop-popped* like fireworks. A fountain of fire burst through the smoke, high into the sky.

"Mom."

He remembered later that he simply said her name just like that and his emotions went completely blank. His body dodged Mrs. Gratzer's grab by itself and scrambled through the rubble up the street.

Everything changed so much with the smoke and with buildings spilled into the pavement and the pavement broken, that Eddie almost got lost. He tripped over one of the railroad tracks, then followed it to what used to be the back door of the laundry. Most of the building was gone. Bricks and broken glass littered the street and everywhere people dug into them and shouted names. The center of the laundry was a huge ball of fire, unaffected by the spray from all the broken pipes.

Standing there that day, staring at the rubble, he was reminded of the mangle because of the loud hiss of steam coming from everywhere, not quite loud enough to drown out the screams. The mangle had been attached to the wall that was now gone.

Wide-eyed firefighters dragged hoses through the streetful of brick chunks and glass to hook up to hydrants that didn't work. Shreds of charred sheets and blackened rags of pillowcases tumbled in the wind that started up with the fire. Everyone seemed so pale.

"Mom!" Eddie hollered. "Mom!"

One of the women from the front office, Eleanor who wore the glittery pins, pulled him from the middle of the street to what was left of the sidewalk. Her glasses were gone and her hair on one side was melted to her head in a clump.

"Eddie, your momma's not here. Some people just carried her and Robert and Nell over to the hospital. Wait here with me for your grandpa. . . ."

Eddie twisted loose and splashed through the flooded alley to the street crowded with people making their way to the wreckage of the laundry. He ran through the front door of the Albers Feed Store and out the back, which put him at the back door of the hospital. It was the same hospital where he'd been born, where his mother had been born. He heard shouts from in there, and screams, and the sound of something metal crashing to the floor.

Inside the back door a pasty-faced nurse snatched his arm and hissed, "Don't you run in here. Now, you get right back outside."

"My mom . . ." he said, and tried to twist free, but it didn't work this time. No matter how he moved she knew how to hold him. She pushed the back door open with her hip.

"I want my mom!"

A pair of heavy double doors slapped open in the hallway behind them. The nurse pulled him aside, but not before he caught a glimpse of Robert, the retarded janitor, who held his bandaged hands away from the bulky bandages on his chest. His lips and nose were covered with little white pads. He cried in little howls. In the quick slap of the doors Eddie heard people hurrying in there, heard the clatter of steel against steel.

The nurse pulled him back through the door, then guided him down the hallway without loosening her grip.

"Someone in the front can help you," she said. "We're too busy back here and you shouldn't be in here, anyway. What's your name?"

"Eddie Reyes," he said.

They rounded the hallway turn and he saw his grandfather at the nurses' desk, at the front of a mob of people, wringing his old felt hat. His grandfather didn't say anything. His stare made Eddie feel smaller every step he took.

"They want us to go to the waiting room," his grandpa said. "It'll be a while yet before they know. . . ."

He didn't finish.

"Before they know what?" Eddie asked.

His grandfather's huge hand pressed against his shoulder blades, the other held the waiting-room door open. Eddie ducked under. The place smelled of coffee and cigarette smoke. All around the walls people sat on benches and cried or read magazines. The room was so full he could barely breathe, and people kept coming in.

Eddie's mother lived through that day, the next, and the next. The hospital wouldn't allow him to see her, and his grandfather said that she would be there for a long time. It scared him that they didn't tell him anything except that his mother would be all right. In their private glances between each other, Eddie could see that his grandparents didn't believe it. And when one or both of them came back from the hospital, they whispered to each other and they didn't talk with him.

Eddie walked every day through the Alber's Feed Store and out the back. From there he could see her room, her window, and sometimes the curtains moved. He thought then that she waved, and he always waved back.

For three months she lay up in that old building. The ivy outside turned from scraggly thin ropes to a lush green cover that shaded many of the windows up to the third floor. His mother was up there, her hands a vapor and her face a vague memory in the bathroom mirror.

One day, one of the nurses came out to make him go away.

"What are you doing out here?"

He didn't answer.

"You come here to see somebody, don't you? Is it your brother?"

"My mother."

"Oh, your *mother* . . ."

Third floor, he thought, *the window next to the rusty ladder.*

He said nothing.

"You know, there are other sick people here. They don't like it when people look in their windows. . . ."

He ran down to the park and stayed there until the gulls screamed upriver to the dump. He was hungry when he got to his grandparents' place. They fed him in quiet, as usual. The kitchen smelled like that nurse, and later his cold sheets tightened on him like her hand.

He lay there as wide-eyed as his pet rabbit, thinking about his mom, about the whispers and rumors. He had heard that she didn't have any hands or face anymore, but he didn't think it was true, because he couldn't imagine it and as long as he couldn't imagine it, it couldn't be true.

Eddie made people uncomfortable because he asked to see her every day. He didn't belong anywhere, anymore, it seemed. Kid games seemed like kid games to him, now. He belonged with his mother, he decided, and he decided he would see her on his birthday. That was five days away.

That night, and every night for the next five nights, Eddie dreamed of the sidewalk and the road breaking up in front of him, and a boy his own age watching it all in a blue halo from the other side, the *under*side.

In his dreams the sidewalk and the road tilted up to become a wall. When they split apart and the chunks rained down, the crack that was left open was an opening to another world. It was a long way off, like a tunnel, but Eddie saw light through it, blue light and another face looking back at him.

The boy at the end of the tunnel was more a shadow than a boy, but Eddie felt like this was his friend, his best friend, something he'd never had before. In the dreams, when he tried to get a look at the boy, the shadow always turned away, but not without hesitation, and a look back over his shoulder.

"What's your name?" Eddie hollered through the crack in one dream, but it came out a dry croak that woke him up, and he didn't catch the answer.

Reality can destroy the dream, why shouldn't the dream destroy reality?

—**George Moore,** from *Silver Departures*

THE GIRL AFRIQUA Lee washed clothes with her mother, in the ritual manner, downstream from the Roam's summer camp. They washed ceremonial clothes four times a year, at streamside, the way their ancestors had done for four thousand years. She washed only five garments, and already her back hurt.

"It's a reminder of the old days, before machines," her mother had said. "You'll see, it can be fun."

They called it "staking tent," a part of the stakedown ritual, and this began Afriqua Lee's first year on the stream.

She looked around her at the chatting women and listened to the political speculation that would govern the kumpania for the next three months.

It was Afriqua Lee's sixth spring, and she was mindful of the honor because staking tent was for eight-year-olds. It was because her mother was so pregnant that the bending over, even for ritual, was impossible. The baby was due tonight, with the moon.

"Prikasha," her mother said. "Bad luck. Prikasha and mirame."

Her mother scrubbed clothes across the face of her favorite flat rock, a white one. Beside her, draped across the bank, a man's shirt, pants and socks dried in the unforgiving sun. They had belonged to Afriqua Lee's father. Something had happened to him to make the whole kumpania sad, and her mother said he was gone to the highlands forever.

Afriqua Lee pushed her thick black hair out of her eyes and wished that she'd tied it back like Old Cristina had told her.

"Mama? What's 'mirame'?"

"Unclean. The way that blond gaji stepped over the shadow of your uncle in the city."

Her mother pulled out the neckline of her blouse and spat on one of her breasts when she said 'gaji.' It was her greatest display of disgust.

"That outsider woman will be bad luck for your uncle, for the familia, for the kumpania and probably even bad luck for the gaji. Bah. A woman should know better than to lift her skirts over a man."

Again she spat, this time into the stream. Afriqua Lee shook out one of her mother's red and blue dresses, the one with the quetzal birds in the hem, and handed it back to her. A few big splatters of rain battered the leaves, then quit.

That was when the stream moved.

Afriqua Lee pushed out her hands to catch her balance and fell face-first into the shallows. Her wrist hurt, but she had to push her face out of the water because it came up her nose and gagged her.

She tried to stand and fell again, this time across the white rock of the stream bed, which was empty of its stream, and crumbling. She heard her mother's heavy grunt as she hit the rocks beside her.

In that instant the stream bed beneath them ripped open lengthwise, and Afriqua Lee hung on to keep from falling through. The smooth wet rocks slid out of her grip, and the sides caved in towards her faster than she could scramble out.

"Mama!"

She slipped halfway over the lip of the ravine and stopped in a heartbeat. When she looked down, she didn't see more rock and mud. When she looked down, she saw a face.

Looking back at her in the sudden silence was a dark-haired, brown-eyed girl. Behind the girl, spread out in white trays, lay a feast of meats and greens.

"Afriqua Lee!"

Someone grabbed her wrist and pulled her back over the lip of the terrible hole.

"Afriqua Lee!"

It was Old Cristina, pulling her to safety, pulling her away from the brown-eyed girl and the incredible feast at the bottom of the world.

"Your mother . . ." Cristina gasped, "she's hurt. Are you all right, girl?"

"Yes, Romni. . . ."

Afriqua Lee saw her mother across the rip in the earth's hide, across what used to be the creek bed that had torn apart clear to the skirt of the sky.

She remembered thinking that none of this could be so.

Mama!

A scream snapped Afriqua Lee back to the present. Her mother screamed again, and it ended in the kind of frightened cry she'd never heard in a grownup before.

Her mother's left arm twisted around behind her, the elbow bent backwards. It was bleeding, and something white, like a piece of kindling, poked through. She lay on her back, half covered with wet stones. Her belly rose and fell quickly, and convulsed even after she coughed.

"Holy Martyr," Cristina whispered, and made the sign of the noose behind her back with her thumb and forefinger. That was when Afriqua Lee became afraid. Old Cristina didn't swear lightly, and the girl had never seen her making the sign of the noose. That was something for the other old women, the ignorant ones, or for the men who blamed luck for what Cristina called lazy bones.

"Jump to your mother and turn her on her side," the old woman said. "I'll get help. We don't want her stuck there if the water comes back."

Afriqua Lee made the jump—it was less than a meter—and cradled her mother's head in her arms. She was breathing very fast, and though she was dark-skinned, like Afriqua Lee, her lips seemed unnaturally pale. When she got her hands under her mother's shoulders to turn her, her mother cried out in pain. Blood crept out the crevasses of the stream bed beneath her feet.

"They're coming," she told her mother. "Romni Cristina is getting help from the men."

Getting help from the men.

To ask help of a man was to incur a debt to a man, and no woman of the Roam would allow such a thing; this the girl well knew.

Poor Mama, she thought, *she must be hurt so bad. . . .*

She stroked her mother's hair back from her forehead, and her hand come back bloody. She had nowhere else to wipe her hand, so she used her skirt. There were shouts from the camp, and now she heard cries of pain from there, too. It was when she glanced up, towards the camp, that she saw the first of the wings hatch out of the old stream bed.

Each creature crawled to a rock, stretched out its set of long, delicate wings and walked in a circle until it dried. Then they all rattled skyward and settled into the bushes and trees. By the time the wide-eyed men arrived to carry her mother back to camp, Afriqua Lee could see very little green in the trees. It seemed the whole landscape was a seethe of bronze. Though the bugs didn't attack her, something about the sound that the mass of them made frightened her more than the earthquake and the rip in the earth.

The wide-eyed men swatted the bugs and cursed them. Hundreds of bugs died under their feet by the time they made the hundred-meter trek from the streambed to camp. The camp, too, was aswarm with bugs. People struggled to right their tipped vans or their collapsed trailers. Martin had been building up the stakedown fire and fell into it. The hysteria in the camp had already shifted its focus to the bugs.

"The Romni Bari's tent," one of the men carrying her mother grunted. "The women can care for her there."

None of them had spoken after seeing her mother, and Afriqua knew this was a very bad sign. Old Cristina held open the door herself, and brushed everyone who entered with cedar branches. The bugs grabbed onto the branches, and Afriqua Lee saw them eat the greenery as fast as their strange mouths could work.

Like every mobile residence of the Roam, the old woman's van was called a tent. It was the biggest van, fitted with the glittery electronics that were testimony to her people's genius, guardian of their wanderings through these dangerous times.

A dozen guests could sleep comfortably in the Romni Bari's tent, though these days it was home to only three—Cristina, Delphi and Delphi's daughter, Afriqua Lee. Only the single men of the Roam still slept in real tents, like the old days, and this only if they were still unmarried at eighteen.

"Show Martita the coffee-maker, girl," Old Cristina said, and closed off the bedroom where they had taken her mother.

"The women will care for your mama," little Martita said. "You and I must make coffee and pray."

Martita, at forty, stood only a head taller than Afriqua Lee, and the girl, like others of the Roam, thought of her as a child, or as a doll that walked and talked. She pulled a step-stool up to the counter as the men clumped to the door.

"Jaguar priests aren't curse enough," one of them grumbled. "Now we have these damned bugs. City supplies will be wiped out; they won't have nothing to trade us. . . ."

"Maybe we can start a burn, between the stream and the bluff. . . ."

"Look," said another, "Rachel's goats eat them. . . ."

But it wasn't true. Afriqua Lee saw that the goats only ate the brittle wings. They left the bug bodies writhing to death on the ground. There were only the five goats, pets of the crazy woman, and they'd already lost interest.

Her mother shrieked from behind the door, then shrieked again, weaker. Little Martita guided Afriqua Lee towards the stove, with a gentle hand at her back.

The coffee didn't help. The baby came out with the cord wrapped twice around his neck and died. Her mother had already lost too much blood. She died, too. This was something Afriqua Lee did not understand until much later. What she did understand was that her mother and the brother she'd never seen went somewhere to be with her father. She couldn't understand why they left her behind.

By the time Afriqua Lee and Old Cristina stepped out into the new morning sun, the landscape had changed beyond recognition.

"Holy Martyr!" Old Cristina whispered.

The trees stood bare as winter, even the evergreens. The onslaught of the bugs had been too fast and there had been far too many of them. The men tried lighting a few fires, but it didn't do much good. The trees were stripped anyway, and for every bug they killed, a hundred took its place. Today, the surviving kumpania sat around the smoldering stakedown fire in a shocked and uncharacteristic silence.

Fitting tradition, and following the Romni Bari's instructions, the girl Afriqua Lee approached the fire with her mother's favorite veil. She threw it about her shoulders in the same careless manner that her mother used.

"My mother and my brother have wed the Holy Martyr," she recited. "Help me to celebrate their fortune. Who brings a goat to the feast?"

Tomas stood and dusted off his black work pants.

"I will bring two goats. With twice the dancing, we will have twice the hunger, no?"

A few of the blank faces stirred with smiles, and in moments the evening's wake was planned. It was the Roam's way to celebrate, not to mourn.

Old Cristina, the Romni Bari, spoke the morning prayer of joy. The children were dismissed from the assembly to their chores, except for Afriqua Lee. Now that she was alone she was an adult of the kumpania. She would settle into a tent with others and accept the ritual that governed her position. In her sixth year she was now her own familia and entitled to a vote in the assembly. Her tent would be difficult to earn. She tried to listen, but the talk in her head drowned out the talk around the fire.

"Amate, what does your radio tell us?"

"Rumor, like we hear among ourselves. But some facts, too. The bugs are everywhere, they eat everything that grows. So far, they do not eat animals, but maybe they will when they run out of everything else. There are no males or females. Either they are a hybrid, manufactured to destroy crops, or they have another form. . . ."

"You know they are *manufactured*!" Tomas spat out the large word in bitter syllables. "We all know the Jaguar does this, rips the fabric of the world and shovels in garbage to torment us. . . ."

Afriqua watched the firelight, nearly invisible against the morning. The flame-dance that dissolved the log in front of her lulled her into the dream-world. In the dream she conjured up the same face she'd seen inside the rip in the earth. This was a dark-eyed girl, someone she had glimpsed before in her dreams. She saw the girl's father in a dream once, and wasn't surprised that he had her own father's face.

When Afriqua Lee tried to dream her own father, she replayed the day that Amate brought the news that he had darted the archbivy of the Jaguar priests. His skull would fry before sunup, of this the adults were certain. Zachary Lee had set out to stop the Jaguar at all costs. He had paid the cost.

She cried out in her dream and woke herself. Someone had carried her to a bed in Old Cristina's tent. The click and hum of magnetic servos lulled her back to slumber.

Afriqua Lee was too exhausted to get out of her clothes before sleep caught her. She tried to dream the dark-eyed girl, but that pathway would not open. Instead, she dreamed that the Jaguar's men came to the Roam and branded the grownups Tomas and Maryka, and the child Nicola, on the back of their right hands.

Afriqua Lee felt the pain herself, as each one of them was marked. She would never forget the pain, the stench of their skin as the butterfly sign hissed into the backs of their hands. She saved herself in this dream when she made the branding-iron melt before it touched her own skin. It formed a beautiful silver glove nearly too bright to behold.

Now I have them by the dreams, a voice echoed in her head.

Afriqua Lee whimpered in her sleep, and woke herself. For a minute she didn't know where she was. She recognized the Romni Bari's tent, and lay back on her pillow.

It bothered her that a voice came into her dream without a face on it. As she slipped back to sleep, she felt Cristina's hand on her brow and heard her whisper, "It's just a dream, little one. Old Cristina won't let nothing get you."

The rain can make all places strange, even the place where you live.

—Ernest Hemingway, "The Porter"

MARYELLEN THOMPKINS MET her father a week after the earthquake churned the valley, the day he came home from the Army. Her first memory of him was the strength of his hands as he picked her up and hugged her to him. He held her much too tight but he was her father and she didn't know what she was supposed to say so she hugged him like her mother told her and he set her down.

"You're a strong little muffin," he said, ruffling her hair.

"My name's Maryellen."

"So it is."

His eyes were a deep brown, like her own, his breath smelled like cigarettes and the whiskey that her grandfather drank.

Her father opened one of his drab canvas duffle bags and pulled out a pink silk robe with red birds and blue dragons all over it. On the left side in the front, stitched in small green letters, it said *Maryln*.

"Do you like it?"

He sort of giggled and that surprised her. He was nervous, too.

When she didn't move to take the robe, he draped it over her shoulder and ruffled her hair again. Her mother took two glasses down from the cupboard and said to Maryellen, "Why don't you take it into the bedroom and try it on, honey? It's late and you should be getting to bed pretty quick."

Maryellen parted the blanket that separated the kitchen from their bedroom. Just then her mother slammed the cupboard door with a *bang* and screamed, "Oh, God!"

Her father started at her scream and he hit Maryellen with his elbow as he jumped to help her mother. Her nose started bleeding and a couple of spots got on her pink nightie, but she moved the robe in time to save it. The blood in her nose had a funny, salty smell.

"What?" her father asked. "What is it?"

His face had paled and his eyes were strangely wild. He jerked the cupboard door open and glared inside.

Her mother leaned back against the wall with her hand to her chest and started to laugh.

"I'm sorry," she said. "It was something . . . we have mice. It was a mouse or something; it jumped right at me. Maryellen, are you all right?"

Maryellen looked up from the linoleum floor, and the tears from the sting in her nose made everything swim in halos from the bright bulb over the sink. Her light mother, laughing against the wall, reached out a hand to her dark father, beginning a laugh. He put his arm around her mother and held her tight to him. She remembered that she was afraid but she didn't want to say so.

Her mother wet a dishrag and cleaned up the little dribble of blood from her nose and her best nightie. Maryellen picked up her new robe and took it to the bedroom to try it on.

When she saw the new bed that her mother put up, and the blanket that hung between the beds, she realized that she would not be sleeping with her mother.

Maryellen listened as she undressed to the *clink* of ice in glasses and the low drone of this stranger that was her father talking quietly in the kitchen. Sometimes a laugh barked out, or an equally disruptive silence. She slipped the robe on over the pink nightie with the blood spots, then sat on the edge of her mother's bed, listening as the low drone grew to long explosions of laughter.

Her mother laughed her tiny laugh with him and Maryellen felt for the first time that this room, that the little kitchen and even the bathroom, were not hers, and she felt for the first time that she didn't belong where she was and she had nowhere else to go.

The laughter in the kitchen stopped. Just the occasional running of water and *clink clink* of the ice in their drinks broke the quiet. Maryellen lay down on her mother's bed and was just beginning to drift off to dream when her father sat heavily and suddenly beside her, startling her awake. As he leaned down to kiss her forehead, she smelled the sweet taste of whiskey on his breath, the same taste that her grandpa had when he kissed her goodnight.

"You look pretty in that robe," he said. His strong hands stroked her hair.

"Thank you. It feels nice."

"Were you afraid of that mouse in the cupboard? When I looked, there was nothing there."

"No."

She shook her head and wanted to sit up, but she didn't want to stop his hand that brushed at her forehead and her hair.

"We have mice all the time," she said, "but not usually in the cupboard. Usually they're under the sink."

His eyes were brown, like her grandfather's, like her own. His weren't open very wide, and the white parts around the brown center looked red and sore. Those sore eyes looked straight into her own, and he asked, "Are you afraid of me?"

Maryellen glanced down at her small hands, dark, twisting her new robe into knots. She didn't know what to tell him. No one that she'd been afraid of had ever asked her that before.

"Well," he said, "join the club. . . ."

He caught himself with a breathtaking reflex as he nearly fell off the edge of the bed. She recognized that giggle of his, then, because they were doing it together.

"I don't want you to be afraid of me."

She couldn't think of anything to say, and she couldn't meet his eyes yet.

"Those teeth are coming in . . . look."

He fished in a shirt pocket and held out one of her front teeth in his palm.

"Your mother sent this to me; it nearly chewed its way out of the envelope."

"I thought the tooth fairy had it. She left me a quarter."

"Well," he chuckled, "wasn't it great that the tooth fairy gave it to your mom to send to me? Looks like you've got another one ready to go."

He picked up her chin with one finger and wiggled a tooth with another. His finger smelled like cigarettes, too, and was kind of yellow. She pulled away.

"Why don't you come out to the kitchen and show your mother your new robe? I'll set out a couple of traps for those mice."

She didn't remember that they put her to bed, but she remembered being afraid in the dark at the thrash and cries from her mother's bed across the hanging blanket.

"When you touch me there," her mother said once, "I feel a glow all the way out the ends of my fingers."

Echoes of her mother's whispers came to her many years later, in the mountains with a boy named Eddie Reyes.

Then a *snap* from the kitchen popped her eyelids open, and the three of them in that tiny room held their breaths and listened to a low, hoarse *hiss*. Then, someone or something hammered at the kitchen cabinets.

"What the hell is that?"

Her father, whom she'd just met, jumped out of bed and dazzled them all with a sudden burst of light and his nakedness. His dark body thrust aside the saddle blanket that divided the two rooms; a sheen of sweat glistened on his bare shoulders.

Her mother rustled through bedding for her nightie, and her father snatched something from their dresser.

The *thump-thump* of cabinet doors and *crash* of garbage bucket continued from the kitchen, punctuated with a low *hiss*.

Maryellen's eyes adjusted to the glare and she saw that her father grasped an empty beer bottle by its neck. He pushed the blanket aside and steadied himself against the doorframe as he stepped across the threshold.

Her mother missed a grab for Maryellen as she ran to the doorway behind her father. The sudden flare of the kitchen bulb illuminated a huge rat, brown and snarling, standing on its hind legs in the corner. It shook the mousetrap on its foreleg like a curse at her and at her father.

At first she thought he would throw the bottle at it. But her father dropped to both knees and snarled back at the rat. The bottle in her father's hand thumped the linoleum twice. Then he hit it so hard, he broke the bottle. The top half of the rat exploded with the bottle into a dark stain on the cabinet. The rest of it twitched and spilled itself slowly over the linoleum.

Her mother scooped her close inside her warm robe and she heard her father throwing up beside her. Someone banged at the front door. What she remembered best was the hot softness of her mother under her robe, the now-sour smell of whiskey from the floor and the metallic taste of fear far back on her tongue.

It was almost morning by the time they all got to sleep, and that night, in her dream, Maryellen saw for the second time the girl Afriqua Lee. What she remembered of the lingering dream was mixed up with her memory of the earthquake: At the grocery store behind their house a wall split open with a ripping sound, like someone tore a huge skirt. Sand poured through the top of the wall to cover the vegetable display. Maryellen stood in the frozen stillness that nightmares bring, while the sand dissolved in white light at the tips of her new shoes. Blue sky shone through the crack in the wall and, high overhead, a pair of green eyes framed by curly dark hair peered back at her. Those eyes seemed very frightened, very wild.

A name was called behind the girl, an older woman's voice called her twice before the eyes disappeared and Maryellen woke with a start.

What she heard on waking was the old woman calling: "Afriqua! Afriqua Lee!" What frightened her a little, and what she didn't tell her mother about, was the handful of sand at the foot of her bed. The air around it vibrated, flapped like a pair of wings, and without a sound the sand vanished in a flash of blue light.

Human beings are free except when humanity needs them.

—Orson Scott Card, *Ender's Game*

RAFFERTY WAS FIVE years old and playing with a circle of stones in the sun. He sat inside the circle of shiny riverstones when a spring shower caught him and he heard the first dry rattle of wings rise with the heavy wet spatter of the drops. Thousands of huge, bronze-colored bugs seethed out of the ground and unfolded their brittle wings.

None of the *things* attacked him, but when they flew they rasped out an unpleasant scrape against the air and when they landed on Rafferty their stiff, stiltlike legs scratched his neck and hands. The neighbor lady screamed, and other screams echoed down the avenue of high, bright buildings.

Verna Tekel, the neighbor, scooped him into the heavy folds of her body and grunted them to her house, praying under her breath all the way in all three of the languages that she spoke.

Her house was the dark house of mystery, forbidden to him and to the other children. Dark-eyed strangers came and went at odd hours, happy people for such a dark house. They parked colorful trucks and huge house-vans right in the yard that separated her house from Rafferty's place, right where the bugs now swarmed.

They lived inside the vans, and the walls of the outsides rippled with colored pictures, advertisements and news. Strange music rode the breezes from her house at night, music that stirred something in Rafferty, like the language she spoke stirred something. Other people made fun of it, always behind her back, but to Rafferty it sounded familiar. He usually knew what she meant.

A design had been burned into the back of her freckled hand, the number "8" lying on its side. He had seen it on some of the people who visited her, people whose darkness contrasted with her freckled, pale skin and light, close-cropped hair. When she had visitors, other neighbors stayed indoors and locked up. They hired these dark men to fix things or invent things or to tell them news of the outside.

Sometimes the brown-eyed men brought him presents, like the mechanical parrot that walked and squawked, or the wind-up lizard that skittered up the sidewalk. They always stood outside with their presents and waited on the sidewalk because his aunt wouldn't allow them near the house. The house had been his parents' house, and he overheard the grownups saying that if it weren't for his parents these people wouldn't be visiting the city at all. Sometimes, when they said it, it sounded like a great thing. Other times, it sounded like a curse.

When his aunt decided that they'd stood outside long enough, or when she realized that they were never going away, she would let him go outside and accept the gift. Each time, the men would say something to him quickly, softly, something kind about his parents whom they clearly had admired very much.

The Jaguar priests had taken them, they said. He would not know for years that they had died horribly. All he knew at five, going on six, was what his mother's sister told him, that they had gone to the southern highlands to teach these people and something bad had happened so they couldn't get back.

Verna muttered a chant in that singsong language as she fastened the screen door and the old-fashioned glass door behind it. Rafferty was dazzled by the thousands of bronze wings that glinted in the after-shower sun.

They pushed up out of gardens and gravel driveways, from grasses and from rocky hillsides. They unfolded their glittering wings and joined the bronze fog rolling across the valley. It was like watching fire disassemble a log. While Verna shrieked into her handset for help, Rafferty knelt at the living-room window and listened to the scrabble of hard little bodies against the walls outside.

The things that pressed themselves against the glass had bodies bigger than a man's biggest finger. They were orange with yellow underbellies, and their finely veined wings stretched a half-meter from tip to tip. Each bug had four wings and six bristly legs.

It was difficult for Rafferty to think of them one at a time when the walls, the gardens and streets, the air itself, were already filled with them and with the dry rattle of their wings. The window was acrawl with them. He remembered for years his fascination with the bob and pulse of the thousands of yellow bellies flattened against the glass.

Verna yanked him away from the window and activated the blinds. He noticed the inside of her house for the first time while she muttered in a tight voice and threw things into a bag. The house was nothing like he'd imagined.

It was one huge room, with couches along the walls and a large wooden table near the kitchen. Unlike the outside of the house, the inside was spotless. The walls were not walls, but the same kinds of installations that decorated the sides of the vans. Pictures that could change. These were jungle pictures, and somewhere in the room a box broadcast jungle sounds.

Bright-colored blankets with strange designs draped the couches. Rafferty was standing on a red, blue, and black rug that had more of the bold designs. He saw animals in the rug, and big-nosed people with helmets and spears.

When she finally took him out of the house he was rolled inside one of these blankets so that he could neither see nor hear. He felt her noiseless car swerve and lurch and slam hard when it hit holes. It stopped, backed up and turned. He couldn't count how many times this happened, and he got sleepy enough inside the blanket to doze.

Then the car lurched hard his way and tipped, kept tipping, tipped all the way over. When the rolling stopped, Rafferty woke up squashed in place with the blanket over his head. He was pinned so tight, his chest and back felt like they met. He could move his left arm and his head.

He worked the blanket across his face and saw that he was lying on the ceiling of the car. His head was lower than the rest of him and the back seat had popped out to wedge him in. Gurgles and gasps came from the front seat. He called out, but the noises only came farther apart and finally stopped. The roof of the car beneath him was littered with shards of broken glass, incense butts and pink plastic hair curlers.

Rafferty could hardly breathe with the seat jamming him in so tight. He tried to shove it away but it would not budge. He panted tiny, burning breaths from the effort, and a lot of small black spots in front of his eyes melted into one big one. He wasn't really asleep—he hadn't caught his breath yet—but he knew he wasn't getting out of there.

When he knew he couldn't get out, he had to go to the bathroom. He beat on the back of the seat but that made the spots come back, so he started crying but that hurt, too. Outside, the familiar rasp and tick of those bright bugs played against the metal of the car. By the time Rafferty had wet himself, the inside of the car was crawling with them. They didn't bite or sting, they just crawled over him with their stickery feet.

He was wedged inside there with them for three nights before he ate the first one. It wouldn't get out of his face and he could barely bat it away. He caught it by the root of its wings with his free hand, shook it once and popped it into his mouth. His lips were cracked, his tongue and throat swelled dry from thirst.

What happened between Rafferty and the bug was purely some kind of reflex. Uncle explained that later. Rafferty kept hold of the wings and spat out the legs because they were long and skinny and they stuck in his throat. He lost count of the nights after that, and thought of the rest of the bugs that he ate as corndogs. A scattering of wings and legs tilted in the wind under his head, little bronze-petalled flowers with dark brown stalks. He learned not to smell the incredible stench that rolled in from the front seat, and he learned to live with the mice.

Rafferty slept with the scuttle of feet across his face, learned that crying only made his throat worse, learned that sometimes there was no border between waking and dreams.

He woke up crying in one dream because the boy in his dream was crying. Rafferty watched him climb up and down a ladder outside a ratty-looking building with vines choking its sides. In another dream, the boy called his name, and it was so clear that Rafferty woke up with a start and said, "Here. I'm here." His voice was raspy and sore in his throat from his crying.

He had a lot of dreams, but they were strange and felt like they belonged to somebody else. He always woke up exhausted, with a pounding headache, and he would sleep then without dreaming for a while.

Out of a dream of drinking from the well behind the dreamboy's grandparents' house, Rafferty heard the heavy crunch of footsteps and the clatter of gravel against the side of the car.

"Verna!" a hoarse voice shouted, a male voice. "Verna?"

Someone pulled glass out of one of the windows in front.

"Oh, no," the voice whispered. Then it coughed a couple of times, and gagged.

When the man sat down outside the car and slumped against it, Rafferty listened to everything as though he perched on a tree limb above the whole broken scene.

Rafferty knew this: If he didn't speak, the man would leave and he would die there. He knew that without knowing much about death except for the brittle creatures that he snatched from the seat-back and stuffed into his mouth. That, and what his senses told him about Verna in the front seat.

He remembered he wanted to say, "Thirsty," but what his throat managed to hiss out was, "Hungry." The word sounded like the struggle of dry wings against steel. He repeated it, louder.

"Hungry."

Just as there is a solid geometry, so there should be a solid psychology for the cases where the calculations of plane psychology are not exact. . . .

—**Marcel Proust,** ***Maxims***

THE JAGUAR DIDN'T think about his life before he tinkered in dreams. He didn't want to, had no need to, refused. He was born to the dreamways by accident, and the unbridled wealth that he stumbled upon diverted him forever from the smelly mess that he had made of his life. His body anchored him to the world, but if all went well, he could break that link without sacrificing his life in the process.

The Jaguar couldn't remember his own body—the body of Lieutenant Marco Reyes—without considerable effort. He lived on the cusp of coma. The hospital room that housed his body contained the standard-issue mirror, but he rarely had the opportunity to use it.

The Jaguar recalled dark, wavy hair and narrow nose . . . no, the nose had been broken at his first debriefing . . . green eyes. Last time he saw a mirror, dark hollows surrounded those eyes. His face had been flaccid, like the rest of him, not like the ruggedness of his lean army days.

There were those from real life who wanted Lieutenant Reyes back in the world. He had become the Jaguar to satisfy the mythology of the world on the other side. The first dream he'd tracked across the curtain led to a Jaguar priest desperate for a god, so Lieutenant Reyes crowned himself one. Now the Jaguar was infinitely greater than the GI that his small-minded world had committed to the Soldiers' Home. The high-level stuff he'd scooped from the dreamways got him off the petty charges, but it also guaranteed that they would never let him leave the home alive. That was just fine with the Jaguar.

The Jaguar tracked dreams in his own world long before he ever discovered the other side. He had been the intelligence weapon that made the bomb happen for his own country while he'd single-handedly sabotaged certain resources in others. Those resources had been people, but that was not how the Jaguar saw them. They were a live drill to him, an opportunity to hone a skill from theory to practice. It would have been tough proving this at any official hearing in the world, since what he had done he had done through dreams.

His military record certified him as both psychic and psychotic, and that suited the Jaguar. It kept them off his tail except for the occasional ridiculous experiment.

He kept a model of the world in his mind, even now, and checked off contacts as he'd made them. It was an intricate webwork of light. Since he had nothing to do but explore his own mind and others, the Jaguar had no trouble recalling each of them. He stroked them with his mind, appreciative of such fine cattle. Milking them was no trick, now, though it had taken him years to learn.

Once he realized that he dreamed in other people's heads, it took the Jaguar very little time to learn to explore those heads. Memories looked like Tinkertoys to him, and he found that he could take them apart, rearrange them for fun. If he could recall the structure of a memory, he could reproduce it within his own mind when he returned. He mined vast stores of data without ever turning a page.

It was a short jump to manipulating emotions, the chemistry of the brain itself, and, eventually, the genetic makeup of the dreamer. The genetic experiments had a tendency to go wild, so he confined them to the other side of the fabric. Travelling the dreamways to the other side took a toll on him, so he set up a control by proxy and enlisted the Jaguar priesthood as his primary tool.

His subjects on this side disintegrated with alarming regularity, so he could not milk his local cattle too often.

He discovered the fabric, the thin gauze that separated this universe from another, by accident, and by accident he survived the plunge through its shimmering weft. The other side of that nebulous fabric was all that interested him now. He resented being called back to this one. Resented, and feared. He had almost forgotten pain.

This side, that side . . . he'd wrestled many a bout with the fact that the fabric didn't have sides. There never occurred to him a better way to describe it, and *this side* was what he was approaching.

Breathe.

The Jaguar calmed himself.

This side was too . . . sensitive. A screw-up here and they would unplug him, let his body die. Or worse, they would unplug him and make him live in the world. They knew him well enough to know that he wouldn't settle for that. The Jaguar had not been born to die.

He was God, streaming through the fabric of the universe, his albatross of a body caught in its net. If this body died, the Jaguar died.

He had been working on that one when he felt the prickle of awakening remind him that he had skin.

The other side.

There must be a way to live free of his body. He had been experimenting with his cattle on the other side. If something didn't break for him on this side soon, the Jaguar faced a share in the misery he'd created. He had had nearly ten years to figure it out. His mind might last through infinity. But . . . the body?

There was something of the ventriloquist and dummy about it. Now the Jaguar lived at the end of a thin tether to his body and that body . . . had better stay alive.

He had travelled too often from the same place. His cluster of perforations threatened the integrity of the balloon-skin of this universe, or that dimension. The Soldiers' Home wouldn't move him again; that would be too risky. The Jaguar priests had shown him other weak points on that side, but he didn't know how he could get near them on this one. He couldn't say anything about it, and he didn't know how many trips he had to go before the whole thing burst in a great cancellation of matter.

A rip in the fabric would spill the stuff of this universe into the anti-stuff of another. A flurrying of molecules would form a wobbly hole in reality, a wobbling flutter of blue that flashed white and annihilated every particle of both universes as they came to touch. This profited no one. The Jaguar maintained a healthy respect for profit.

Profit, to the Jaguar, was not so much coin of the realm but years. The Jaguar wanted to live forever, and knew now that he could master that trick if he played the dreamways right.

Dreaming on his own side of the fabric hurt him when he woke, but that pain was nothing like cracking the light-whip for the trip through it. On this side he was predator, sniffer of dream-trails. He followed fantasies to their dens and unravelled pathways between the neurons that formed those fantasies. Of course, he picked up a lot of facts on the way. When he was conscious, there were people who kept him alive in exchange for some of those facts.

The Jaguar called this "milking." He squeezed information from his cattle like some farmers coaxed out milk. He rummaged around in brains, he woke up, he hurt. And every time he woke to face Max, who had a nasty squeeze all his own.

Being wrenched away from the other side was a grinding pain, not a slick, neat slash. Riding the dreamways aged him; he had to make the most of every trip. Forgetting his infirmity was expensive, and he always had to keep the tally of his body correct.

He would live forever, but not if he couldn't free himself of his deteriorating body. More of his precious reserves had been shifted to damage control. The body was failing, that was clear. Free of this body, he could own the universes on both sides of the fabric.

The Jaguar borrowed *here*, paid back *there*.

He kept ahead of a slow game while his cattle snuffled around him.

Cattle, yes, he had thought of them as cattle right from the first. He never set out to like any of them; he just needed information to pay blackmail to his government and to buy time to pay his dues for crossing the fabric as the Jaguar. He milked his cattle, or they dried up. If he milked them too often, they went loco, fast, and they died.

He recognized their symptoms: nightmare, weakness, fatigue and insanity. The wrinkles would come later. He was an infant of the dreamways, and learned the subtleties of mind-sculpture at the expense of many a headache of his own. Then, too, there was the psychological challenge of knowing their dreams, their particular structure of thought.

Nightmares and fatigue made them afraid to dream. They got medicines to sleep a dreamless night and those medicines blocked him out. Some, in their inevitable madness, chose to switch off their lives. His supply of cattle dwindled.

The Jaguar countered by sculpting dreams to ward off their boredom. The ultimate exploration for him, now, was the textural variation in the tension between color and time. He took nightmare and unravelled it and recast it to beauty. He made his cattle want to sleep, beg to dream. Such effort was not without its toll.

People talk of their dreams, particularly if those dreams change their lives. One nurse sought counselling and had to be removed. Another talked about her coma patient, the wonderful dreams she'd developed since working with him. He'd sculpted her a perfect memory, not as a gift so much as for fun. It was in the Jaguar's interest that her recall never be tested.

She brought the investigators down on him again, and they brought Max, and that even got a nibble from the KGB, so he scrambled her brains to protect himself. It was good practice.

The nurse, whose name tag read 'Barbara,' woke suddenly from a nap in the nurses' lounge, ran straight down the hallway and dove headfirst through the sixth-floor window. One witness, another student nurse who had set up a tryst with an intern, remembered vividly the wild-eyed terror of her classmate who shoved past in her desperate sprint down the hall.

The Jaguar found self-protection a reflex. Like the excellent athlete, he exercised reflex to a hair-trigger. These people were messing with the man who had handed them the bomb on a platter, free, no strings attached. They'd better not prove themselves ungrateful; they'd better not become a nuisance.

If you have not seen the day of revolution in a small town where all know all in the town and always have known all, you have seen nothing. . . .

—**Ernest Hemingway,** *For Whom the Bell Tolls*

THE VALLEY WAS small, lush, crowded against the mountain by the monster city downriver. Farmers in the valley supported a small town on berries, beans and flower bulbs. Like any small town of any language, nearly everything about anyone was known by everyone. Invisibility, even for a quiet child like Eddie Reyes, was out of the question.

A clerk in the feed store watched every day as Eddie walked in the front door, past the brooder full of baby chicks, and out the open double doors in the back. Some days Eddie bought small red salt licks for his rabbits, sometimes a bag of oats, but usually he simply walked through. The clerk never asked about his mother, and Eddie never brought it up.

The clerk, Weldon, was one of the few men in town with a beard. It was blond, broad and bushy. Weldon was the tallest man Eddie had ever seen. He was strong enough to throw feed sacks and hay bales into trucks all day without sweating or slowing down. Many men made the feed store their base of gossip and conversation, but Weldon never joined in. He wasn't sullen; he was always busy and simply ignored them while they had their coffee at his counter or on his hay bales. Weldon was another mystery of the valley, one who smiled, worked hard and kept to himself. He had been arrested once for poaching deer out of season with a flintlock, and some called him 'Mountain Man' after that, but not to his face.

Sometimes, when Eddie hurried through the store and their glances met, Weldon would nod and then shuffle some papers, stack something or pick up his broom. Eddie was sure that Weldon could reach the rusty fire-escape ladder that zigzagged behind the ivy and up the back wall of the hospital to his mother's window.

His birthday dawned with the second Friday in June, and Eddie waited outside the feed store for Weldon to open up. The morning stayed gray, and the clouds squeezed a slow drizzle onto the shoulders of the town. The black rabbit under Eddie's coat squirmed against his ribs. It wasn't weaned yet, but it knew Eddie well enough not to struggle when he picked it up. He talked to the rabbit every day because he had nobody else to talk to.

A trickle of rain slipped down the back of his collar. Eddie shrugged and pressed himself farther back into the shallow doorway. The loose fender of Weldon's pickup rattled as it made the turn.

"He's coming," Eddie said.

The rabbit said nothing.

"Morning," was all Weldon said.

Weldon glanced at Eddie a couple of times while he worked the key into the old lock. He waited for Eddie to step aside, then unlocked the door. It was almost a half hour early, so he left the sign in the door that said 'Closed.'

Weldon fussed with his big coffee machine while Eddie leaned against the counter and petted the rabbit under his coat. Eddie was nervous, now, and so was the rabbit. It was breathing faster, and it poked its busy nose farther under his armpit.

Weldon put the lid on the urn, plugged it in and slid it to the corner of the counter beside Eddie. Then he waited. Eddie felt him waiting and when he finally glanced up, Weldon's eyebrows rose as if to ask, "Well?"

"I need some help," Eddie blurted. His bottom front teeth weren't quite grown back enough to stop a slight lisp.

Weldon smiled, and without lowering his huge, bushy eyebrows he asked, "Help with what?"

"That fire escape," Eddie said, and he nodded towards the back of the store, towards the hospital. Weldon didn't seem surprised.

"Now, in the daylight?"

"It's my birthday."

The rabbit scrambled a little to turn itself around. Weldon's glance flicked to the front of Eddie's coat, back to his eyes.

"If we're going to do it, let's do it now," Weldon said. It

came out as a long sigh. Weldon was already headed for the rear doors and Eddie hurried to keep up.

The big man jumped up, grabbed the lowest rung, and pulled. He dropped to the ground, but the ladder hadn't budged. Weldon jumped up again and got a better grip this time. He bounced himself on it twice and let go.

"Jesus," he said. His face was red and he was breathing hard. Weldon looked up and down the alley between the buildings, then patted Eddie on the back.

"Are you *sure* you have to go this way?"

Eddie nodded. "They won't let me in. You have to be fourteen."

Weldon mumbled something into his beard.

"What?"

"Nothing. Come on."

Eddie followed Weldon back to the feed store. Weldon took another key from his mass of keys and opened up the Coke machine. He unclicked the mechanism and a bottle of Coke dropped out. He put the machine back together, like a refrigerator, and opened the bottle. He offered it to Eddie and Eddie took a sip. He couldn't tip the bottle up without dropping the rabbit out from under his arm, so all he could get was a sip.

Weldon took a swallow, then said, "Watch this."

This time when he jumped, he grabbed the rung with his left hand and held the Coke in his right. He shook up the bottle with his thumb over the top, then sprayed the rest of the Coke into the hinge of the ladder. He tossed the empty to Eddie, got a good grip and bounced it a couple more times. The rusty ramp unkinked itself with a sharp screech. It was slow going, and not at all as quiet as Eddie had hoped.

Weldon was sweating pretty hard. Eddie had seen him work hard in the feed store and this was the first time he'd seen him sweat. Weldon bounced on it again but it wouldn't come down all the way.

"Can you jump and reach that now?" Weldon asked. He was trying to talk and catch his breath at the same time.

Eddie stood underneath, and the tips of his right fingers almost touched the rung. He nodded.

"Yes."

He looked both ways; there was still no one in the alley. Someone out front of the feed store was pounding for Weldon to let him in.

"What about this?" Weldon asked. He patted the bulge in

Eddie's jacket where the rabbit hid. Without waiting for an answer, Weldon picked Eddie up and set him on the fire escape.

"Thanks," Eddie said.

"Happy birthday," Weldon said. "Good luck."

He walked back inside the store.

Eddie didn't like the gratings under the steps of the fire escape. He could see clear through to the ground and it seemed a long way down already. He worked his way up the three floors through the ivy to his mother's window, trying to keep the rabbit calm against the thrash of his heart in his chest.

He spent a minute with his eyes closed, catching his breath. Through the ivy he glimpsed the shadow of a boy his own age dodge down the alleyway towards the mill. The lumber mill on the next block was three blocks long and they grazed sheep among the stacks of lumber. His glimpse of the boy showed him only someone his own age and size, someone like the boy in his dreams.

Rafferty.

The name from inside his head sounded perfect. This shadow had skirted him for a while now; it had even skipped through the edges of his dreams. In the last dream, Eddie looked down on the shadow-boy from the gnarled branch of a yew. From where he perched, Eddie could see the boy hiding down there, and someone circled towards him in the grass. Eddie looked down from the tree to see himself reflected in brown lake water: he was a crow. He shook his wings out to make sure. His heart was beating awfully fast, and whatever it was nearly had the boy.

Rafferty.

Again, the name had awakened him from a sweaty sleep, but Eddie had barked it in the brusque vernacular of a crow. Now he scanned the sky and treetops. There were crows, all right, but they all stayed put. The trees swayed, and a bit of a headache made him squint even though it was too cloudy for glare.

When he heard voices in the back of the feed store, he raised his mother's window and stepped through, between the curtains.

Eddie's mother must have heard the window, because as he slung one leg over the sill she gave out a little cry of surprise. She had already partly covered herself with the sheet she gathered between her stumps. A white patch covered one of her eyes. All he could really see of her, the way she huddled into her sheet, was her one blue eye surrounded by a swirl of pink scars to the top of her head where her hairline began.

Eddie's rabbit squirmed against his ribs.

His mother made that cry again and he realized it was his name. She glanced at the blue curtain that separated her bed from the rest of the room. It was closed. Eddie heard snoring from somewhere on the other side. His mother's blanket shifted, and on her patched-eye side her ear looked like a melted flower bud.

He pulled his other leg over and scooted off the sill into the room.

"Eddie," she whispered, and hunched the blanket higher, "I don't want you to see."

She lowered her head and he thought she would tell him to leave.

Then she sighed, and whispered, "But I've wanted to see you so *much*."

She talked through a tight throat, and her shoulders shook. She cleared her throat and lowered the sheet so that Eddie could see her eye.

"It's your birthday and you were born right here, downstairs. . . ."

She shifted herself over on her bed and patted the cover beside her. He listened before he moved for sounds of anybody in the hallway, but it was quiet.

"Six," she whispered. "You're six and you're such a little man already."

She was shivering, but he only noticed it after he sat on the bed beside her. This close, there was a very strong smell that he didn't like, and the rabbit didn't like it either, because it started scrambling under his jacket until it got out and onto the bed. It huddled against Eddie and worked its busy nose at his mother.

She rubbed his back through her bedclothes and nearly hugged him. But he sat still, not knowing where to look, and noticed how perfect and white his mother's feet were. They barely touched the floor and her toe-knuckles kinked white where she held to her balance. They were small feet, delicately veined in a blue very nearly the color of her remaining eye. They were wide, she'd told him, because she went barefoot as a girl.

"I brought this one so you could see him," Eddie said. "The whole litter is black-and-white, but this one is all black."

"Does he have a name?"

"No," Eddie said, "I thought you'd want to name him."

She started to reach out from under her sheet towards the rabbit, but pulled back.

"He won't bite," Eddie said. "He's the best one of the bunch."

When she moved, Eddie saw that one arm was much shorter than the other. One arm stopped just above the wrist, the other ended at the elbow. He couldn't stop staring at the dull lumps they formed against the inside of her sheet.

His mother said, "Put him here, on my lap. I can't . . . I can't hold him, so you'll have to watch out that he doesn't get away. They wouldn't care for a rabbit running the halls here, would they?"

Eddie picked up the rabbit and set it carefully in his mother's lap. He noticed that she winced a bit, and he realized how much of her was burned. Her back, where the gown fell open, looked as smooth and white as her feet, her backbone standing out like thick knuckles. She hurt her back at work just before he turned five and had to stay home and take medicines for a long time. They ate macaroni-and-cheese almost every night then, and Eddie would rub her back with smelly stuff every morning and night.

His mom would not take her arms out from the covers to pet the rabbit, but she sort of cuddled it there in her lap. She leaned one shoulder against Eddie and he kissed her beside her good eye. She would not show herself below her eyes, and forming some words seemed hard for her. He realized that she spoke in a whisper because that's all she had, not because she was afraid he'd be found.

Suddenly there was an elevator sound from the hallway, then dishes rattling in a cart.

"You'd better hide . . . oh, the window!"

Eddie hurried to the window and pulled it closed. He got up so fast he startled the rabbit, and it scrambled off his mother's lap and under the bed. As the food cart banged the door open, Eddie slid himself under her bed, too. The rabbit was gone; he couldn't see it anywhere.

A pair of white shoes filled with white stockings walked around the cart and toed up to the next bed first, then his mother's.

Eddie's rabbit had left a scatter of pellets and he was glad it hadn't done that while it was in his mother's lap. Wads of dust-balls hung from the springs at the head of the bed. Eddie's nose tickled and he rubbed it hard so he wouldn't sneeze.

"Morning, Mrs. Reyes," an elderly voice said. "Jeanie will be up from therapy in a minute to help you out with this. My, you're doing so much better than Doris, here. We've got a full house and I've got to run. Is there something I can get you before Jeanie comes in?"

His mother cleared her throat, and in her hoarse whisper asked, "Would you open the window? I'd like some fresh air."

"I'll have to ask doctor about that," the voice replied. The shoes squeak-squeaked back to the cart. "Infection is the hobgoblin of burn patients. We don't want you to come this far just to lose you now, do we? Doctor will be in this morning, too. I hear that he has some news from that burn center in California. You be good for Jeanie, now, and I'll see you at lunch time."

The door slapped shut behind the cart and they were left with the wet snores of Doris across the curtain. Eddie scrambled out from under the bed.

"That was close," he said, but before he could say anything else his mother shushed him.

"Eddie, you've got to get something for me from home and bring it here right away. Can you get home and back in the window again?"

He nodded.

"Yes," he said, "but the rabbit is still . . . oh, there he goes!"

The little black thing crept out from under Doris' bed, testing the air with its quick nose. Eddie started after it and it darted away.

"Leave it," his mom whispered. "They'll be here in a minute. Go home to the bathroom and get my back medicine out of the cabinet. You know which bottle it is? Okay. If there's anyone in here, then wait outside the window until they're gone. Can you wait out there without anybody seeing you?"

"Yes," he said, "the bushes . . ."

"Go now," she said, her voice louder, harder. "Don't stop to talk to anybody; don't tell Grandma or Grandpa. Hurry."

"But . . . the rabbit . . ."

"He won't go anywhere," she said. "Catch him when you come back. I need that medicine, Eddie. You have to do this for me. Now, go, they'll be here—"

Eddie heard the voices in the hall, and before he knew it he had raised the window, slipped outside and closed it. He waited a moment, listening to the therapist make small talk while she fed his mother. He sat under the window, knowing he should hurry on the errand for his mother, but unable to move because he wanted so much to see her face.

He looked once again down the alley to where it dead-ended into the lumber yard, and again Eddie thought he saw the figure of a boy about his age scale the far fence and disappear.

The metal treads of the fire escape echoed his steps down no matter how careful he was. Going down the side of the building was scarier than going up, but he kept hold of the ivy and that helped. The last jump to the ground pitched him forward on his hands and knees. He scraped his palms in the gravel, and even though they bled from the scrapes, he didn't cry.

He didn't shortcut through the feed store this time, but went the long way down the alley and around the lumber yard instead. There was something about the boy that Eddic had seen that made him hope he'd run into him.

In the years after his sixth birthday, Eddie would remember many details of this day. He would not remember the run home, nor how he managed to sneak past his grandparents. He did remember finding the big bottle of blue pills behind the cough medicine in his mother's cabinet, and he remembered the sting of the steel rung of the fire escape when he jumped up and grabbed it with his scraped-up hands.

This time, when he listened at the window, he heard hoarse barks of pain from his mother.

"That's it, Leda, we're just about done," the therapist said. "Let's try it one more time."

His ear was right next to the window now, and he could hear his mother's sobs and heavy breathing.

"No, please. Let me rest, *please*."

"We need to keep you moving, Leda. If we don't keep at it, your arms will just lock up like they did at first. Aren't you doing much better now than when we first started? I think so. You couldn't move them at all, then. Now look at you. Once more, now."

Eddie pressed his head against the cool brick of the wall and tried to shut out the dry, empty screams of his mother's scorched throat.

He watched a trail of tiny red ants make their way from a branch of the ivy onto the brick, then into a crack in the mortar. When he looked closer, he saw that thousands of ants used the crack in the wall as a kind of superhighway, some of them stopping to touch antennae with each other in their two-lane scramble.

Everything was quiet in the room now except for his mother's heavy breathing. He peeked over the sill and saw that the curtain had been drawn around her bed and he could only see the lumps of her feet near the bottom rail. He raised the window again and stepped inside.

She was lying on her back with a sheet up to her waist. Her head was flung back on her pillow, and she gulped great breaths of air through the angry slash that had once been her mouth. She didn't really have a face. From the middle of what used to be her nose on down, it looked like somebody had just pasted on skin, like the figures she'd helped him make out of newspaper and paste. She wasn't ugly, exactly, even though she didn't have lips anymore to cover her teeth. But he couldn't stop staring and he stood there, stock-still, until her breathing eased and she opened her eye.

"Oh, Eddie," she said, "I'm sorry . . . I didn't want you to see. . . ."

He left the window open and stood by her bedside with his hand on her shoulder. Presently, she lifted her arm under the sheet and touched his cheek. He knew he should say something, but he couldn't think of anything.

"Mom, I love you," he said, and kissed her forehead.

"Oh, Eddie, I love you too. This is such a mess."

He was going to let her rest some more, but she tried to sit up.

"Would you help me up?" she asked.

He reached behind to the smooth, warm skin of her back and helped her sit up. It wore her out again and she had to catch her breath. Her breath didn't smell very good when she breathed hard in his face, and he tried not to show it.

"I love you, Mom," he repeated. It was all he could think of to say.

She rested her forehead on his shoulder.

"I love you, too, Eddie. You have to remember that, because other people won't understand. But *you* know it, and I don't want you to forget . . . to forget me as I was, or to forget that I love you."

"I won't, Mom," he said.

She gathered herself up a little more and took a deep breath.

"Well," she said, "did you bring it?"

"Yes."

He took the medicine bottle out of his pocket and set it on the bed.

She held up her stumps and said, "I can't open it. You'll have to open it and get me some water. I can't use a straw yet, either."

He opened the big bottle of blue pills and set it on her tray beside the bed, and he poured a glass of water from her pitcher. The pitcher was big and heavy, and he slopped the water all over the tray. His mother didn't scold him. She didn't seem to notice. She took another deep breath.

"Okay, Eddie, I need to take them all. It's okay, because I'm supposed to take three a day and I haven't had any since I've been here, right? So I have to catch up."

"But Grandpa says that when you take medicine . . ."

"Does it look like it can hurt me?" she snapped. Then she immediately softened her voice.

"It's my back," she said. "It hurts so much I can't think straight. Now we've got to get this done and get you back home before anybody comes back up here."

He helped her by giving her the pills a small handful at a time, each of which she swallowed with a big gulp of water. Eddie didn't realize until then just how useful lips were, because she couldn't really keep the water in very well. Her mouth on the inside was cracked and dry. What was left of her tongue was thick and smooth; all the little rough spots had been burned off.

When it was finished, she lay back on her pillows, her arm linked in his.

"I'll get some sleep now," she said. "Thank you. You should run back home now. Take the bottle with you."

"My rabbit . . ."

"Hurry and see if you can find him," she said.

Eddie found the rabbit behind the other woman's wastebasket, in the corner of the room. It skittered away from him and when he made a grab, he got it by one back leg. He backed into the other woman's tray and it came crashing down on top of him, but he kept hold of the rabbit.

Footsteps came running down the hall and he ducked behind his mother's curtain. Her eye watched him, but she didn't say anything. He stuffed the rabbit under his jacket and clamped his elbow down to hold it. He snatched the empty pill bottle from the tray and stepped out the window just as the door to her room crashed open. He couldn't reach up to close the window and hold onto the rabbit, too, so he crept down the fire escape and hid in the ivy at the bottom until he was sure no one was looking.

When he jumped to the ground, the rabbit fell out from under his jacket and scrambled off into the weeds. Eddie looked back up at his mother's window, which was still open, then ran all the way to the trees by the river and didn't come home until dark. By then, his mother was dead and the whole town knew how it happened.

What great sleep there is for a childhood.

—**Gaston Bachelard,** *The Poetics of Reverie*

MARYELLEN WOKE UP when her breathing stopped. She fought the smother of wet earth that plugged her nostrils and choked off her breath. She felt like she was buried alive, or looking upward from under pond water at her mother's grieving face.

She gasped a breath.

"Come on, honey. Wake up, now."

She gasped another breath, pushed off the wet washcloth that her mother held to her face. She realized that she had not been drowned in a pond after all, and caught her breath.

"You had a bad dream."

Her mother's voice sounded funny, a long way off.

A dream, she reminded herself.

"I was drowning," she said. "Something held me underwater."

"You're here, now," her mother said. "Your father had a bad dream, too. It was a zoo in here," she laughed, "the two of you chattering nonsense. The Army hospital said they fixed that for him. They say you're supposed to let people alone when they talk or walk in their sleep, but the yelling was going too far. . . ."

Maryellen's mother sat her up in a chair and brought her a cup of tea with some toast. Maryellen tried to remind herself that she was home. She had a headache, the first headache she ever remembered. Her father and the dead rat seemed like dreams themselves, but she knew they were true. The sweat that matted her hair to her forehead was real.

"You just wore yourself out sleeping, poor thing," her mother said. "You must have been one tired little girl. Your daddy, all the excitement . . ."

A tone of uncertainty edged her mother's voice. Once more she wiped Maryellen's face with her cool, wet washrag.

"No," Maryellen told her mom. "I was playing."

"Playing?" She laughed again, that quick laugh. "Well, it sure looked like you were sleeping. Then thrashing. Who did you play with?"

"Afriqua," she said. "Afriqua Lee. She's got green eyes and curly, curly hair like that lady in your magazine. Do I *have* to go to church? I don't feel good."

Mom's lips pressed her forehead.

"You're not hot," her mother said. "You can go to church. Maybe you can catch a little nap there, if you want. Nobody'll notice. Say good morning to your dad and finish getting dressed."

Maryellen mumbled "Good morning" to her father without looking up, and allowed him a hug on her way to the bathroom. She wore her new robe, the pink material all shiny and much brighter in the daylight than it had been the night before.

She washed her face, and when the vivid dreams of the pond refused to go away, she was afraid she was going to throw up. She hoped she didn't, even if it would keep her home from church. When she shut the water off she heard her mother talking to her father.

"I don't know, Mel. She looked so *pale*, and you didn't see her eyes; they were so wild. She didn't even see me."

"You're the kid expert," he said. "This is all new to me. All kids have bad dreams. She's probably fine, but I'll stay home and take care of her. . . ."

"No, you don't. You've been gone so long that people here think that I made you up. I want to show you off for the whole town."

Maryellen straightened her robe and left the bathroom. Her mother swept her close for a hug.

"You look better now, babe. Do you feel better?"

Maryellen nodded. She didn't really feel better, but she didn't feel bad, exactly, except for the headache. She tingled, and just felt . . . *different*. Her body was there but she didn't feel like she was all the way in it.

"Good," her mom said. "I want to show us *all* off, starting today."

They rode the mile to church in her grandfather's black car with the running board. Her parents borrowed it for the day, and if the weather stayed good they would all have a picnic at Lake Kapowsin. Her grandparents lived just behind them through the bushes. They always walked to church, and usually they walked with Maryellen and her mother.

She loved riding in Grandpa's car but today she simply endured the ride to church, and the bouncing aggravated her headache. Fragments of her dreams whirled about her like candy wrappers in a dust devil.

Her new dreams were special dreams, much different from other dreams. They were much more like being awake than dreams, and the foreign world of Afriqua Lee began to feel as familiar as this one.

Afriqua Lee and her people lived in large, segmented vehicles, silent even though they were huge. Four or five of her grandfather's cars would fit inside the Romni Bari's personal van. Buses and vans of the Roam lit up all over, or took on the colors of the landscape, or created a landscape that had never been there. They left no track, and no sound escaped them, and they didn't stop for gasoline like her grandfather's car. There weren't many places to stop between the cities—places with people, that is.

When they came to the wall of a city, the sides of the vans advertised their wares. Members of the Roam sold expertise and information, delivered goods and messages. City people couldn't travel to other cities; she didn't know why. The Roam could travel to any city it chose, but it couldn't have a city of its own.

Some of the vans put on shows for children, to entertain them while their parents bought what they needed from the Roam. Maryellen saw one of these shows in her dream. It showed jaguars chasing monkeys through an overgrown courtyard of stone. The stories were picture-stories, different from the ones in her books.

The city in her dream, seen from the top of a huge pile of stones, walled itself in against the world. The wonderful vehicles of the Roam moved in a great procession when they entered and when they left the gates.

"Come on, babe," her mother said, and shook her again. "We're here."

'*Here*,' Maryellen thought. *Where is 'here'?*

She glanced over her mother's shoulder, out the car window, and remembered. Sometimes she sure fell asleep fast. The pipe-tobacco smell of the upholstery brought her back, and the tolling of the church bell across the street battered her headache. The day, too, was too bright for her head, and she squinted her way up the aisle. She squeezed into the pew between her mom and dad.

Each time they rang the bells at the front of the church a funny sign lit up in her mind. It was red, and flashed on and off just like the water-faucet drip in the plumbing store sign. This sign was a numeral "8" lying on its side. She had seen this sign in her dreams, on the backs of some people's hands. She had fallen into it at the beginning and end of her dream.

Her father woke her this time, as the pew emptied for Communion.

"C'mon, Muffin," he said. "I'm taking you out to the car."

He laid her down on the back seat and fixed his coat for a pillow. Then he sat behind the wheel but turned so that he could put his feet up on the seat and watch her, too. He rolled his window down and smoked, talking with her quietly. She watched, fascinated, at the slow swirl of smoke around his head.

"I could go to school on the Army money," he was saying. "I got a couple of job offers already, but I don't want to work for somebody else all my life. That's too much like the Army. I want to be my own boss."

He quit talking and Maryellen didn't say anything.

"Haven't you ever seen anybody smoke before?"

"What?"

"The way you're staring. It's like you never saw anybody smoke before."

"Oh," she said. "No. I've seen it."

The passenger door in the front opened up and her mother leaned her head inside.

"Dr. Trapp is coming," she said. "He was just a couple of rows in front of us, so I asked him to take a look at her."

Her mother reached over the seat and brushed back Maryellen's hair.

"How're you doing, babe?"

"Okay."

"Do you still have your headache?"

Maryellen nodded.

Dr. Trapp opened the back door and sat on the seat next to her. He felt her head and throat with his pale, skinny fingers. He made her stick out her tongue, and asked her the same things that he always asked her in the office. When he looked into her eyes, he hesitated, then he looked again.

"That's curious," he said. His angular face wore a puzzled expression as he sat back in the seat beside her.

"What's curious?"

A hurried tightness squinched her mother's voice. It seemed like she spoke while holding her breath.

Dr. Trapp was staring into Maryellen's eyes again, going from one eye to another. His eyes were blue, with flecks of gold. He didn't blink much, but when he blinked she saw the fresh scar where he'd had a mole removed by his partner, Dr. Jacobs.

"Her pupils . . . open and close at random."

"Like in a skull fracture?"

Her father's voice startled her, right above her head. He went on:

"I . . . saw some of that, you know, in the war. . . ."

"Well, Mel, her scalp's not tender, no signs of an injury. She'd remember anything that hit her *that* hard. I assume that you know of no such injury . . . ?"

"No," her mother said. "Nothing that other kids don't get—scraped hands and knees. Lately she babbles in her sleep, but so does Mel. Today she's been impossible to get to wake up. . . ."

Her mother's worried face appeared over the seat, then disappeared to talk with the doctor outside the car.

"Has she had any shaking, or tremors, or fits of any kind?"

"No," her mother said, "not that I've ever noticed."

"Does she fall asleep at strange times, or does this just happen as a result of her normal sleep?"

"No, no," her mother insisted. "She was just hard to wake up today, that's all. We were up late last night, but a few times lately she would sleep round the clock if I'd let her. She's not like that. You can see how hard it is to keep her awake today. And she's so *quiet*. . . ."

He opened the door again and wiggled her foot.

"Is your neck stiff, honey?"

She shook her head. She had her eyes closed because the light made her headache worse.

"Just the headache?"

"Yes."

He closed the car door, and it sent streaks of red shooting through her head.

"She has no fever, although she's clearly been sweating," he told her mother. "My greatest concern would be for meningitis, but this doesn't look like that."

"What could it be, then?" Again, it was her mother's worried voice that asked.

"I don't know," he said. "I want to see her tomorrow in the office. Call me tonight if she changes in any way for the worse, but bring her in tomorrow even if she's all better."

Maryellen slept most of the day away while relatives came to welcome her father home. The men laughed over their beers, and her father brought them into the kitchen one by one to show them the nicks in the linoleum and to tell the story of the rat. Each time, he pushed the curtain aside and looked in to see how she was doing.

All of the coats were piled on her parents' bed, and Maryellen's mom kissed her forehead each time somebody came or left. When everybody was gone and her parents sat in the kitchen alone, swirling the ice in their glasses, Maryellen felt a sudden, intense hunger. She padded out to the kitchen and wolfed down a huge plate of spaghetti while her parents joked with each other and tousled her hair.

"Better, huh?" her dad said.

"Yes."

"Probably just some kid thing," he said. "She got over it pretty fast."

"We can borrow my parents' car again tomorrow to take her in."

"She's better," her dad said. "She said so herself. We can't afford to pay him to tell us what we already know. Kids get these things; they get over them. . . ." He waved his hand to dismiss the whole thing.

"But, he said . . ."

"Right. He said to bring her in. He didn't say it would be free. It's going to take everything we've got to get out of this dump, and the sooner the better. If she gets sick again tonight, we'll take her. How's that?"

Her father's voice snapped the words out and his tone bordered on a growl.

Her mother rubbed her eyes the way she did when she was tired or when she just wanted everything to go away.

"All right," she said. "I'm tired and don't want to think about it right now. She's been like this off and on since the earthquake. Maybe it's just . . . nerves or something."

"Yeah," her dad said. "Nerves. So we'll see how she is in the morning. You ate a good dinner and got plenty of sleep, Muffin. That's all you needed, right?"

"I guess so," she said.

She felt like she was taking sides against her mother, and she didn't like that feeling.

The dream-work . . . does not think, calculate, or judge in any way at all; it restricts itself to giving things a new form.

—**Sigmund Freud**

DR. MARK WHITE approached the last summer of his two-year psychiatric residency on The Hill with relief. Most of his colleagues from medical school had chosen private hospitals for their residencies, to groom themselves into the network of suburban practice. Mark's appearance did not lend itself to suburban practice—executives and their wives did not want to trust their psyches to someone who looked like a lanky boy scout. His bright blue eyes and unmanageable brown hair furthered the image of a naive adolescent.

Mark decided that he would continue with public medicine in the fall, but he had kept that decision to himself. He was going to treat himself to some fishing first. This morning he had bought his first fishing license in six years, as a commitment to relaxation.

He had offers, all places like The Hill, but he had no plans beyond his residency. The offers had not been attractive. They had all come from overworked, understaffed state agencies. He had ignored his advisor's warnings about a residency at the state institution, and now he reaped the consequences.

"Rich people get as crazy as the poor," Dr. Bidet had advised him. "Psychiatric care takes time; it's not like a gallbladder that's wrapped up in a couple of hours. Time costs money—if it's *your* time, then it's either your money or somebody else's." He rubbed his fat neck and sighed. "I think you're an excellent physician, Mark. I'll recommend you wherever you choose to go."

Mark had never admired his advisor, a corpulent teaching psychiatrist with a very limited, very lucrative private practice. In therapy Mark had faced his distaste for the rich and fat, a 'reverse snobbery,' as Mindy once put it.

Dr. Mark White had chosen The Hill for unprofessional reasons. The hospital grounds, parklike and peaceful, perched on the ridgetop overlooking the valley. On a clear evening, standing on the helipad atop the fifth-floor roof, he could watch the sunset trickling down the Olympic Mountains as it pinked up the watery spaces between the San Juan Islands. Even the rain was a pleasure up there. Rather than washing the landscape gray as it did in the city, rain simply brightened the evergreen vista and freshened the air. If The Hill was not therapeutic for others, its location was pure therapy for Mark White.

His name tag read: 'Dr. Mark,' and he seldom wore white. He worked in one of the three corduroy sports coats: brown, gray or beige. By the time he started his tenure at The Hill he had already made his only tie, a black clip-on, last four and a half years. It was a going-away gift from his younger brother, who was delighted to inherit his room over the garage.

His tie was the last straw with Mindy, who made the issue of a state institution an ultimatum.

"I can't stand the thought of you working in an *asylum*," she said. Her nose wrinkled up in that gesture that he'd always thought of as cute. He now saw it as officious, and aimed at him. After all, he was the only one in the room with her at the time—not his patients, not the *asylum*. She was not wrinkling her nose at them but at what he had to offer her. It suddenly appeared far more pungent than it had when she'd met him in medical school.

Mark White had a firm confidence in the skills of his head and his hands. The year of psychotherapy required for his matriculation in psychiatry had not gone wasted. He had looked forward to The Hill, not down on it, and every time he saw Mindy picking imaginary lint off the arm of her chair he felt the gulf between them widen. She was digging a hole between them by the bucketful. He knew that nothing short of continental drift could save them.

Mindy had been his only intimate relationship, and he regretted his inexperience, particularly his inexperience in ending it. Even the best therapy only reached so far.

In the end, he didn't have to worry. She took charge of the ending as she had taken charge of their meals, or their selection of movies that she preferred to call 'films.'

"I respect your social conscience," she told him. "But I believe that money saves more people than good intentions. You should be an example for them to aspire to, not grubbing around among them."

He had simply smiled and taken her hand.

"You're being understanding," she said. Again, that wrinkle of the well-tanned nose. "*Being* understanding is not the same as understanding. You'll see what I mean. Someday, you'll need something or someone, and nothing will quite bring it off like money. That's why I'm going to Houston."

She flew to Houston as the first vice-president of the BankWest International Investments division and married the chief executive officer a year later. Mark circled it on his calendar after he received the invitation, but by the time the wedding rolled around he had already met Eddie Reyes.

In dreams begin responsibilities.

—W. B. Yeats

THE BOY RAFFERTY dragged stones to the uncle's grave to prop up the lid of an old toolbox that he'd inscribed with 'Uncle Hungry' in neat black letters. Above and below the name, and to either side of it, four clusters of translucent wings caught the rising March sun and licked the bleached backdrop of wood like cold flame. Rafferty dropped the young sack of his body down on the gravetop and watched a finger of sun pry apart the iron lips of the sky.

The wind that whipped around the corner of the barn was the last of the night wind, running for cover. The boy was tired, sweaty from the night's digging. The wind that had teeth in it last night passed him this morning without a snap. Along this side of the barn, the morning-sun side, a scatter of crocuses nodded their lavender heads. The uncle saved those bulbs an extra year before planting, just to be safe.

"Quiet as a grave," the older man might have said. Rafferty said it for him and added the quick snort that the uncle used for a laugh. Wind-sighs, the raspy rattle of loose dust off the stonetops, his crow on the barn roof stretching his right wing out—it was as though everything were waiting for Uncle to show up so they could get on with things.

Right after the hatch, inside the still, things were much more quiet than this. Those quiet days dragged into months, a year, two years thick with fear, with knives in the night and the heavy stink of rotting flesh from the barn and from the spring.

Visits from the Roam had been their only relief.

Rafferty fingered one of the bronze flutterings tacked to the box lid—a clump of brittle, translucent wings. Inside the barn, bushels of these wings filled bins along one wall. His uncle, or the man he called uncle, saved them from those first terrifying months of the hatch.

Nothing like it since, the boy thought.

The voice in his head was older than he remembered. Those bright buzzing things crawled out of the ground that day and they took wing after a spring shower. He remembered seeing the sun during that shower, and a rainbow. He remembered that glimpse of the boy, Eddie, whose blue eyes stared back at Rafferty from the crack in the world.

Later, the strong hands of a blue-eyed man unrolled him from the blanket and laid him on the slope outside the car. One of the hands had that same design of the "8" on its side that Rafferty saw on the neighbor lady.

Until that moment, Rafferty had had no idea how bad he smelled. The hillside around him was not the seething mass of bugs that he had heard a few days before, but there were still plenty of them around.

The air outside the car made him feel dirty at first, then clean again. The places that had stopped hurting in the car throbbed now that he was free. Even though the breeze had a chill to it, he lay still, and bathed in the luxury of clean air. He sucked at the water-bottle that the stranger offered him, and lay still.

Verna's brother felt Rafferty's head, his back, his arms and legs. The boy moved his fingers and toes when asked, and noticed, behind the thin man who prodded and pulled at him, that nowhere did he see any grass, any of the new spring leaves. Around them, as far as he could see from the hillside, the leafless and barkless trees shone pale in the afternoon's glare.

Rafferty woke up in bed, between smooth clean sheets, to cramps in his stomach and visions of those bright bronze bugs just out of reach. He smelled coffee and fried bacon. Bandages itched at his chest, back and shoulder. He had three Bandaids on his right shoulder. The bandage between his shoulder blades itched the most.

"Stop scratching."

The uncle's voice came from a doorway beside the foot of the bed. "Come and eat."

The boy found clothes stacked on a chair and put them on. Everything was blue and a little too big. Rafferty didn't think he had anything at home that was blue except socks. These blue socks and sweater were especially bulky, but warm. This was the first time he remembered having warm feet since the hatch. Now, sitting beside the cold grave five years later, Rafferty remembered that as the last time he had had milk from a refrigerator.

"This is the last of the bacon," Uncle had told him. "Those other pigs won't be ready to put down yet for another couple months."

Uncle had been right. That was the last time he'd had bacon, too, but this year . . .

"Bacon this year, buddy," Uncle said, but Rafferty didn't know how to get the bacon out of the pigs. In the five years since that morning at his uncle's table, he'd learned to eat that meal over and over in his mind. Then he'd learned not to.

Verna's brother sat across the table from Rafferty and sipped his coffee. He was balding, and when he sipped coffee the furrows in his brow opened and closed above the steadiness of those blue eyes. Rafferty could see now that the design on the back of his hand was a scar, and he wondered how it got there.

Uncle was always grinning. Rafferty knew that pretty soon he was going to have to talk. His plate was almost empty.

"What's your name?" Uncle asked.

"Rafferty."

He tried to get his throat to swallow a mouthful of dry fried potatoes. "What's yours?"

The uncle frowned. "I thought you knew," he said. "You said, 'Henry,' when I found the car. Call me Uncle Henry."

Rafferty felt himself blush. "I didn't say 'Henry,' " he said. "I said '*Hungry*.' "

Henry laughed and said, "Well, then call me 'Uncle Hungry.' There's going to be a lot of it going around."

A week later the first raiders came through. Uncle Hungry woke him up with a hand over his mouth, grabbed up some clothes and blankets and led Rafferty into the dirt basement. He slid something aside that looked like a piece of furnace and he put Rafferty inside a tunnel.

"Crawl ahead," he whispered. "Stop when you get to an open space."

From upstairs came the splintering of cupboards and shelves, the heavy thump of boot-heels, curses. Rafferty heard Uncle Hungry close the tunnel behind them, heard him stop several times. The boy picked his way through roots and fallen-in chunks of sharp rock. Suddenly the tunnel opened up on both sides. When the uncle caught up with him he switched on a red flashlight. Rafferty stared at a grotesque mechanical creature that squatted in the middle of the room.

Uncle nudged him out of the way and stepped over a case of bottles on the floor. He set the blankets and clothes on top of a stack of bottles, then he wedged the flashlight into some wing-colored coils rising out of the machine's head. Uncle jammed a big roll of pink fluff into the opening they'd just crawled through. He slumped into one of two overstuffed chairs and waved Rafferty into the other.

They sat inside a huge underground room full of sacks, bottles, crates and their two chairs.

"It's a big cooking-pot," Uncle explained, his voice low. "Called a 'still.' It cooks cereal, from those bags."

He pointed to some sacks stacked on a board beside him. Rafferty tried to imagine how many bowls of cereal you could cook in that still, and where you might find that many people at breakfast.

"Nobody can find us here," Uncle told him. "We'll hide out here until they're gone."

The room with the still was the quietest place that Rafferty had ever known. He heard all of his own breaths, and all of Uncle Hungry's. Uncle's stomach gurgled every few minutes and sounded like a conversation in another room.

"We have plenty of batteries," Uncle said. "We have a water faucet. Lots of cereal and sugar but no way to cook it without getting caught."

We, Rafferty thought. *He said that* we *have plenty of batteries.*

He didn't know how long he slept that first night in the still, but he remembered being so hungry when he woke up that his stomach cramped when he took a drink of cold water. They couldn't leave yet; the raiders were camped in the house.

"We can get out if we have to," Uncle said. "This other tunnel comes up between the manure pile and the barn. But then we'd just have to hide, so we might as well hide here." He stirred a couple of spoonfuls of sugar into the water.

"Here," Uncle said. "Drink it now. It'll stop the cramps."

Uncle Hungry figured later that they hid in the still for fifty-one days, living on that sugar and water and grain. Another party of raiders killed the first bunch, stripped them, carried off all of the rest of the food topside. It was summer when they came out of the ground. Rafferty couldn't tell where the sky and the earth left off, because of the dust.

In fifty-one days in the still Uncle Hungry taught Rafferty letters and spelling, reading, numbers and counting money. And he taught him something of the Roam, the nomadic people who had been his teachers. Rafferty taught Uncle the rope-skipping song, the song about stars, and a trick for getting gum out of his hair.

Uncle showed him the scar on the back of his hand.

"You see, I wear the brand of the Jaguar. That's because someone else has been dreaming in my head. The Roam can tell you all about it. We always let them stay here; they bring their caravan through twice a year. They put up in that flat spot down by the creek. That's how come I got this. The Jaguar's priests found me when I was asleep. I don't know how they did it. I had a dream where a bunch of fellas held me down and this fat, dark guy branded me. Verna had the same dream. Sure enough . . ." He held up the hand again, for emphasis.

"Why did they do that?"

"To keep track of me. They say I'll go crazy, or burn up from a flash of light in my skull. But I think that's just talk."

"Who is the Jaguar?"

"Nobody really knows. There are old stories, of course, but that Jaguar was a god, and a good one. This one causes trouble, no doubt of that. But these plagues, earthquakes, floods—it's just handy to blame everything on him. He has it in for the people of the Roam, for some reason. With the brands and whatnot, he's turned some cities against them—against *us*—but nobody knows why. It's against the accords, and we've lived by the accords for a lot of generations. Townspeople, where you lived, just want it to go away. They figure if they drive the Roam out, then the trouble will stop."

"But, the Jaguar . . ."

". . . is a man," Uncle said, "I'm sure of it. But he's not from around here. Nobody has seen him except in a lot of nightmares, including mine."

Rafferty thought of his dreams of Eddie, then, and he wondered whether Eddie worked for the Jaguar.

Someday I'll talk to him in a dream, he thought. *Then I'll find out.*

What he said to himself sounded brave in his head, but it didn't feel brave in the pit of his stomach.

A couple of times a day Rafferty or Uncle would pull the insulation aside and crawl halfway back up the tunnel to listen through a pipe that led to the kitchen. Farther up the tunnel, a few meters from the house, Uncle set a trap that would collapse the tunnel on top of anybody who touched it. Uncle told him how to unhook it, but Rafferty didn't ever go up any farther than the pipe.

They traded stories and, finally, secrets. Rafferty told Uncle about eating the bugs. The uncle laughed and said, "You won't be the last one that eats bugs, you'll see."

Uncle didn't make fun of him for it. He asked a lot of questions about them, including how they tasted.

"Like corn-dogs," Rafferty said. But it wasn't really true. He couldn't remember how they tasted, he just remembered trying to think they were corn-dogs.

Then the uncle told a story that made him cry. Rafferty didn't know what to do when a man cried, so he sat still, curled up in his damp chair.

"Verna and I, we had a brother," Uncle said. "He was the oldest. There was Floyd, then me, then Verna. We were three years apart."

Uncle talked in the low whisper that they had learned down there in the still. He cleared his throat and coughed.

"Floyd worked in the city for sixteen years. He started drinking. I told you about drinking, and what this still's for."

Rafferty nodded.

"My father's father built this still, kind of a family tradition. Well, when Floyd disappeared the first time, this is where I found him. I run the still when I can't get work; the Roam trades the booze for me. I won't drink it myself. The last time I found my brother, I found him here.

"He was drunk and had a rifle with him. That's the old-fashioned kind of gun with a long barrel. I figured he might be down here if he was on a toot, and I was right. He had these terrible dreams for years, and the only way he could stop them was to drink himself to sleep. Sometimes he had them anyway, and sometimes they came when he was awake. That was the worst part. And he would be sick afterwards. He said it was the dreams made him sick, but we all knew it was the juice.

"He sat here up against the still, holding the rifle across his chest and when I saw that, I was scared. I thought if he was drunk he might shoot me, and I could see he was drunk. I was so *scared*. . . ."

The uncle was a little shaky and his voice squeaked when he started to talk again.

"I said to him, 'Floyd, let me take that rifle back up to the house for you.' He wouldn't look at me. Kept looking off at the ground, batting at things that weren't there. Finally, he said, 'Henry, you go back to the house now.' Then I knew what he was going to do. I didn't know about the Roam yet, or the Jaguar.

"I waited there where the tunnel opens in. I don't know how long, just feeling my knees shake. Then I backed up the tunnel and was dusting myself off when I heard the shot. He was dead before I got back in there. And something about that really made me mad. I was thirty-two years old. He should've given me the rifle and done it another time. Or shot himself while I was looking. But this way I was a part of it because I didn't stop him. I *couldn't* stop him, I was *scared*. . . ."

That had been their twentieth day, and it was also the day that the raiders shot at each other in a fight. There were seven, then five, then there came the priests who killed the five and stole the food.

When he and the uncle finally surfaced that hot summer day, when they quit blinking back the insistent sting of the sun, the uncle and Rafferty pointed out to each other the local variations on death.

There was no sign of vegetation. The animals that lived were nearly dead. Starved and spooky, two thin Angus stumbled across the driveway, most of the hair missing from their hides. Featherless chicken carcasses littered the yard, stinking up the afternoon. Some had been eaten by something else. The bugs were still around, but not so many. Uncle pointed to a dead calf seething with the things.

"They ate all the greenery," he said. "Now they've got a taste for hair and hooves. Looks like they're fond of paint."

Uncle nodded towards the house and barn, the outbuildings and the fence around the pigpen that all wore the same gray expression.

The uncle stood in the middle of the dusty drive, hand shading his eyes. He had fifty-one days of dirt packed into his shirt, pants, hair and skin. His beard grew out mostly gray, like the outbuildings. Later, Uncle showed Rafferty a picture of some stunned miners rescued after a cave-in, and they looked just the same. Blinking in blackface, white around the eyeballs and lips too pink, the uncle brought his hand down and settled it on Rafferty's head.

"Let's wash up," he said. "If the pump's not working there's always the spring. Then we better figure out a couple of recipes for those goddam bugs."

Figuring out recipes was easy. The hard part was figuring out how to catch and keep a couple of tons of dead bugs. They dried the bugs under screens in the yard, then ground them into a meal that made "soup, cakes or steaks," as Uncle Hungry put it. The chickens and pigs thrived on the mash. The cattle preferred the bristly legs and crisp bronze wings.

Everything became a container. They electrocuted barrelfuls of the things while the power held out. Uncle put up a chicken-wire fence on stilts and covered the top with more chicken wire. He hooked this up to a wire that went inside the house. Whenever a cloud of the pretty bronze things came through on the wind he flipped a switch. Bugs dropped by the thousands as they were zapped on the wire.

Rafferty and the uncle shovelled the catch out onto the drying tables they'd made out of screens. It was Rafferty's job to turn over the trays of bugs and to catch any birds that came in.

The Roam came through in their odd gallery of trailers and vans, winding up the devastated road inside their wizardry and their bond. The bug-cakes fed everyone. Dawn enlightened the storytellers and thawed the musicians' fingers. Rafferty, though an outsider in language and custom, felt like part of the Roam. He could see why Uncle liked them.

When the power finally failed for good, Uncle rigged up the wires to some vehicle parts and put the parts on a bicycle. If Rafferty rode at a good, fast pace he could generate enough power to zap the bugs. Even though the bicycle had no wheels and never left the kitchen of the house, Rafferty dreamed himself cycling to the sea beside his friend Eddie. On these trips, he got to know Eddie, and something of the other world that was so similar, yet so very strange.

When it was Uncle's turn to cycle he daydreamed, too, Rafferty could tell. But he never knew where Uncle went.

After two years, raids on the place pretty much stopped but the uncle was careful with smoke and fires. He showed Rafferty how to make fires, how to tell what animal left tracks and where it was headed, where it had been and why. He taught him about weapons, and how to fight. Many of the Roam stayed on instead of following their usual seasonal meander, and they taught him what they knew about machines and about the Jaguar priests.

After they got out that first time, that summer afternoon, Rafferty and Uncle Hungry never moved back into the house. They salvaged what they could from the broken walls and they built up the underground room. The uncle piped in spring water beside the well water and they hid down there two more times. Both times they nearly got caught, but Rafferty didn't want to think about those times right now.

The sun slipped a shoulder through the clouds, and Ruckus, his crow, chattered to himself. Rafferty realized that he and the uncle could go days without saying anything more than "Morning." "Catch anything?" "Yep." "Nope."

With just a hint of wind and mutters of his restless crow in his ears, Rafferty felt something cold flip-flop inside his stomach. It was like that certain point in hunger, the point of reflex that made him gnash down that first bug, the juicy one that tormented his face. His mind kept replaying the shake in Uncle's voice that time underground when he said, "I was so *scared*. . . ."

Rafferty looked up at the loft window near the top of the barn wall. Uncle Hungry's green stocking-cap was perched on the sill.

What was he doing in that window? Rafferty asked himself. The sound of the thought was a shout, not a wonder. He tried to swallow around the strangle in his throat, and for some reason his thoughts kept turning to the Jaguar.

"Didn't he know he could fall?" he asked Ruckus.

A shift of cloud shut out the sun, and Ruckus ruffled his feathers. The boy Rafferty eyed both horizons of the road: sunrise and sunset. He spoke to the one yellow crocus beside the barn.

"Didn't he know he could fall?"

Rafferty was sure, by the shake in his voice, that he was scared.

We find a little of everything in our memory; it is a kind of pharmacy or chemical laboratory in which chance guides our hand now to a calming drug and now to a dangerous poison.

—**Marcel Proust,** *Maxims*

IN HER DREAM, Afriqua Lee met the brown-eyed girl in a huge open field undulating with thousands of tiny blue flowers. Their fragrance made her think of death, but these days so soon after her mother's wake all flowers made her think of death. The girl wore a pink robe, a vibrant pink that shimmered among the flowers. Her robe was stitched with a peculiar glyph and two plumed serpents, guardians of the Holy Martyr.

She must be a spirit from the underworld, Afriqua thought. All she could muster to answer the girl's wave of greeting was a nod.

"You're Afriqua Lee," the girl said, and beamed a smile that seemed very happy to see her. A tray appeared in her hands and she placed it on a low table that also appeared between them. The tray was gold, and the gold table-top levitated, feather-light, a hand's breadth above the flowers. A white tea set rested on the tray.

Afriqua Lee's heart double-timed against the fabric of her night-gown. The idea of an angel of the Holy Martyr speaking to her, even in a dream, was a truly powerful thing. Even Old Cristina would not take it lightly.

"Yes," she answered, "I am Afriqua Lee. And who are you?"

A comfortable breeze rippled the blue blossoms and fluttered the floppy sleeves of the girl's pink robe. The serpents on the robe did not have feathers but large, leathery wings that seemed to fly with the flutter of the fabric.

"Maryellen Thompkins," the girl said, and plunked herself down among the flowers. "We're having tea."

"Tea?"

"Yes," Maryellen said. "Do they have tea where you're from?"

"Of course," she said, and plunked down beside her. A cradle of sky-blue flowers caught her in their petals and held her while they leaned with the breeze. She studied this Maryellen Thompkins who was now pouring green tea into fragile white cups.

Maryellen had the same long, straight hair that Afriqua remembered her own mother having, except that Maryellen's hair was brown and her mother's was black, black as obsidian from that crater at Wind Mountain. Maryellen's eyes glittered a deep brown, and kept Afriqua's gaze without prying.

"Are you real?" she asked Maryellen.

"Yes," Maryellen said. "I'm real. The tea is pretend, though."

The thin cup tilted in her perfect hand, and Afriqua Lee sipped the green, aromatic brew. She felt her lungs hold that breath an extra beat to savor the freshness of the tea.

"It's my favorite," Maryellen said. "Do you have mint where you're from?"

"Yes," Afriqua said. "The familia drinks coffee. I do, too. But we get tea when we're sick."

"My mom gives me tea when I'm sick, too," Maryellen said. "Tea and toast. That's what I got this morning. I'm sick."

Afriqua felt herself frown, and the chill of a cloud-shadow slithered her spine.

"My mother . . . the earthquake . . ."

Maryellen's eyes widened and she set down her cup.

"Did she die?"

Afriqua Lee nodded, then looked up, hopeful.

"Have you seen her? Have you seen my father?"

"No," Maryellen said, "just you."

"I thought . . . if you were from the underworld, maybe you've seen them."

"The underworld? Where's that?"

"It's where you go after you die. Everybody knows that."

"Well, I'm alive," Maryellen said. "I'm still in the world. We call that place 'Heaven.' The underworld, that's a bad place and we call that 'Hell.' "

''Well, my mother wouldn't be in the bad place. Do you dream of other people?''

''Not like this,'' Maryellen said. ''It's more like I'm dreaming *with* you. Like I'm *really* with you but I know it's a dream.''

Suddenly, the girl began to fade. They reached for one another but it was too late. The girl, the pink robe, the tea set were gone.

Afriqua Lee shuddered again. The shadow that played around her from the gathering cloud roiled, indistinct, across the blue meadow. Once she thought it formed the silhouette of a jaguar, then a butterfly. How strange that a sign so fortuitous would bring her such a chill.

Some people expend tremendous energy merely to be normal.

—Albert Camus

BECAUSE EDDIE COULDN'T stop crying, they took him to Dr. Jacobs, whose office was next to the library downtown. After listening to their story and trying unsuccessfully to calm Eddie's hysteria, Dr. Jacobs made a call and had them take Eddie to the hospital on the hill. Everyone in town joked about that hospital and, because they feared it as well, called it, simply, "The Hill."

Eddie, for his six years known as the invisible boy, the quiet boy, turned over end-tables and scattered magazines across the office floor. He hid under the desk when they said he was going to a hospital and it took three of them to pry his fingers loose and get him out.

Eddie Reyes had seen his mother, and listened to her pitiful, painful cries from outside her window. He knew what kinds of things they did to people in hospitals and he didn't want them to get their hands on him.

But they did.

The hospital was a huddle of buildings inside a cyclone fence, in the middle of a large lawn. The hospital itself was a five-story structure backed against the hillside, with the two-story buildings spread out like hatchlings from its wings. A few very big trees broke up the expanse of grass. Outside the fence was a road, and there were woods across the road. A lot of flowers bloomed around the buildings, and Eddie's grandmother said she thought it was a pretty place.

"We don't get people your age very often," the doctor said. "The windows in here are for taller people, but if you stand on this little table you can see the whole valley."

The doctor seemed to want him to go ahead and stand on the table, but Eddie couldn't do that. If he put his feet on the furniture at home his grandparents would lock him in the closet all day, so he couldn't get his feet on anything. They would lock him in the closet if they heard that he'd put his feet on the furniture at the doctor's, that was for sure. They locked him in the closet almost every day for something. Eddie knew that the doctor didn't know that, but he didn't want to tell him, either.

The doctor cleared his throat.

"It's all right," he said, "you can come in without standing on the furniture."

The doctor found him a stool that rolled, except when it was stepped on; then it stopped. He told Eddie to call him Dr. Mark. They stood at the window and Dr. Mark showed him the river, the school, the wreckage that used to be downtown, and his mother's hospital.

"Most of the youngsters that we have here can't read or write like you can. You're a very intelligent boy. Your grandma says you're the best artist in kindergarten."

Eddie was not crying when Dr. Mark talked to him; he was too tired to cry. His eyes and his throat hurt and what he wanted most was a drink of water. They sat down side by side on a couch in Dr. Mark's office. Eddie balanced a box of blue Kleenex on his knees and twisted a wad of tissues in his hands. He couldn't make himself look up, because he didn't want to talk and as long as he didn't look up they couldn't make him talk.

Dr. Mark opened his office window and let in a breeze. Along with the fresh air came the cacklings of a pair of crows. He returned to the drab green couch and sat next to Eddie again, close, but without touching.

"Do you like baseball, Eddie?"

Eddie shook his head.

"Everybody likes to do something outside. What do you like to do outside, on a nice day like today?"

"Nothing."

"Do you play outside at all?"

"Sometimes."

"When you play outside on a day like today, where do you go? Where would you rather be than here?"

Eddie sniffed, then coughed a little cough.

"I like to go down to the river."

"Do you go fishing down there?"

"Sometimes."

"What else do you do at the river?"

Eddie shrugged.

"Sit."

"Do you sit and think, or do you just sit?"

"I think."

"What do you think about when you sit by the river?"

"Stuff. My friends."

"Tell me about your friends. Who's your best friend?"

"Rafferty," Eddie said, and saying it made him smile a little bit.

"Is Rafferty the same age as you?"

Eddie nodded.

"Do you play with him every day?"

"We don't exactly play," Eddie said.

"Is he in kindergarten with you?"

Eddie shook his head.

"Where do you see him, if you don't see him in school?"

"In dreams."

Dr. Mark paused for a few moments and wrote, 'Rafferty—imaginary playmate,' on a yellow pad.

"Tell me, Eddie, is this Rafferty a real person, or do you just see him in dreams?"

"He's real."

"Where else do you see him, besides dreams? Down at the river?"

Eddie nodded. "I saw him at the hospital. And when the street broke up."

"You mean the earthquake? You saw him then?"

"Under the street."

"*Under* the street? You mean, where it broke up?"

"Yeah. I looked down and he was down there."

"What was he doing?"

"He waved."

"And you saw him at the hospital, too?"

Eddie nodded.

"What were you doing at the hospital?"

Eddie pulled the Kleenex box closer, then pushed it out to his knees and balanced it there.

"You don't want to tell me?"

Eddie shook his head.

"Okay, you don't have to tell me. Let's see, do you have a pet? Is there a pet in your life that you can tell me about?"

"My rabbits. I have twelve . . . eleven rabbits."

"Is there a favorite one?"

"Yes," Eddie sighed, "but he got away."

"Did he have a name?"

"Rafferty."

"Rafferty," Dr. Mark said. "That's an unusual name. Did you name him after your friend?"

Eddie nodded.

"How did the rabbit Rafferty get away?"

"I dropped him and he ran into the flower bushes behind the hospital."

"Were you visiting someone at the hospital?"

Eddie teetered the Kleenex box off his knees and scrambled to the floor to pick it up. He sat back on the couch and didn't say anything.

"You live with your grandparents, is that right?"

Eddie nodded.

"Where is your father?"

"He died in the war."

"If he died in the war, then you probably never got to see him. Is that right?"

"I saw pictures. My mother . . ." He stopped, then bounced the box on his knees some more.

"Your mother has some pictures?"

"She has one picture. He's beside a bomber with his friends."

"And what about your mother? Where is she?"

He peeled little bits of cardboard from the opening where the tissues come out of the box. He didn't know where to put them, so he kept them in his hand. This time, Dr. Mark didn't ask him another question, he just waited. Eddie scanned the office and took in the desk and chair, the wall of books, the magazines. He really wanted to look out the window but the window was behind the couch. People's shadows stood outside Dr. Mark's door; he could see them through the funny glass. They looked like Rafferty the times that Eddie glimpsed him by the hospital.

"In the hospital."

"Is your mom sick? Is that why she's been in the hospital?"

"She got hurt. They wouldn't let me see her."

"But you found a way to see her. Is that right?"

He stopped peeling the cardboard and piled the pieces on the couch between them.

"Eddie, if I got some crayons in here and some paper, would you like to draw some pictures?"

Eddie didn't answer. He knew he wasn't in Dr. Mark's office to draw pictures, that they wanted something from him. He didn't want to get in trouble and he didn't want his mother to get in trouble, so he gripped his box of Kleenex and kept quiet.

Dr. Mark took the Kleenex box and handed him a pad of white paper and a box of crayons.

"Can I have that back?" Eddie asked.

"Sure," Dr. Mark said, and he set the box of tissues next to Eddie on the couch. Then he crossed the room to his desk and shuffled through some papers.

"Draw a picture of your family," he told Eddie. "Put everybody in it so that I can see who they are. Then, what I'd really like to see is a picture of your mom. Draw me a picture of her the way you saw her the last time, when you visited the hospital. When you're done with those, let me know. We'll take a pop break."

Eddie drew a picture of himself helping his mom run the mangle at work. She wore her favorite red blouse with the blue scarf around the neck, and behind them his grandparents watched from the window. His cousin played on the sidewalk outside the laundry, drawing on the pavement, and his uncle sat in his pickup at the stoplight, smoking. Eddie used mostly red crayon for that picture because the bricks were red, the light was red and so was his mom's blouse.

He didn't like the white crayon, so when it came time to draw his mother in the hospital he just outlined everything in black. He colored in the black rabbit, and his mom's little bit of hair way back on her head. He drew the window open, and the water pitcher on the stand, and the other bed behind the curtain. The rabbit was in his mom's lap. He made a round O for her mouth.

Even though her eye patch was white, he colored it in black with its string around her head so that it would show up better. He didn't know how to draw her hands with the bandages, so he just scribbled some black at the ends of her arms and hid one of them behind the rabbit.

He tried to draw the bottle of pills but it came out just a kind of a lump on the bed beside the rabbit. He drew the scars on her face with the pink crayon, but he didn't like that one either.

It didn't show up the same and he wished he'd drawn them in black like her hands.

When he was finished, Dr. Mark took the drawings with them and they went to the cafeteria for a soda, where Eddie explained the pictures to him. Eddie found it easy to talk about the pictures, and he told him everything that happened from the earthquake until he lost his rabbit.

"Eddie, your grandparents want you to feel better, but they feel bad, too. When someone dies, everyone who was close to them feels bad. I didn't know your mother, but I'd like to hear more about her. How do you feel about that?"

Eddie didn't answer.

"What happened yesterday at the hospital downtown?"

"I told you. It was my birthday. I visited my mom."

"You must have loved your mother very much."

"They wouldn't let me see her. . . ."

Eddie started to cry again, even though his throat hurt.

"You know, it's normal for people to cry when their parents die. Adults do it, too. You can go ahead and cry here."

Dr. Mark sat quietly across the table from him, his hands folded, and Eddie didn't feel like crying anymore. He only felt like crying when he tried to talk, and he wished he could explain that.

"Your grandparents are worried about you because they tell me you can't stop crying at home. They say you don't eat or walk or anything; you just cry. That's why they brought you to see me. They are worried about you—they didn't bring you here to punish you. Do you understand that?"

He nodded.

"They wouldn't let you see her, but you found a way to see her anyway. Is that right?"

Eddie nodded again.

"How did you do it?"

"The ladder outside."

Eddie's voice sounded strange to his own ears, and made him cry even more. He remembered how strange his mother's voice sounded when she tried to talk.

"You mean, the fire escape?"

Eddie nodded.

"What happened when you got to her room?"

"She was all bandaged. She couldn't talk very well. I showed her my rabbit."

"You brought the rabbit from home just to show her?"

Eddie nodded.

"Did she like that?"

"Yes, she liked it. My mom likes animals. Especially ones she can hold."

"Did you bring anything else from home for your mother?"

He told Dr. Mark about sneaking her back medicine out of the cabinet at home and taking it to her at the hospital. Dr. Mark told him that his mother must be proud to have a boy who could help her like that when she couldn't help herself. That was the part where Dr. Mark had to clear his voice a few times, and he adjusted his tie a lot, and he took a deep breath before he went on.

"So," Mark concluded, "the last time you saw your mom, she had taken her back medicine and she was feeling better?"

"Yeah," Eddie said. "Her back used to hurt her a lot. Sometimes she had to stay home from work. But always when she took her medicine, she was all better. When she had her medicine. Sometimes she didn't have it."

"Did Dr. Jacobs tell you what happened to your mom after you left her?"

Eddie shuffled his feet and nearly spilled his glass of ice, making it roll on the edge of its bottom. The doctor didn't seem to care.

"He said she went away."

"Do you know where 'away' is?"

"Yeah," Eddie said. "That's where Rafferty is. It's a very big place, bigger than the whole valley. And that's where my mom went."

"When you dream, and you see Rafferty, do you see your mom, too?"

Eddie shook his head. "No," he said. "It feels different when Rafferty's there. She's in a different place, I guess."

"Well, Eddie, I'm going to talk with your grandparents for a few minutes. We'll go back to the office and set up another appointment for a couple of days from now. I'd like to talk with you again, okay?"

Eddie nodded.

Dr. Mark took their tray and slid it into a big rack full of trays, and they walked the long hallway back to the elevator, and then rode the elevator up from "B" to "1," where they got off for the office. It was a slow elevator that clanked, not one of the fast kind that tickled his stomach. Eddie's grandparents waited on a bench in the hallway, and stood up to talk to the doctor.

"Okay, Eddie, you can wait inside and I'll be in to talk with you in a minute. I'll just be a minute with your grandparents, here. Then you can go home. You can keep that box of Kleenex, if you want."

"Thanks."

Eddie sat on the couch with the Kleenex, and closed his eyes. He could hear Dr. Mark talking with his grandparents through the glass behind him.

"He's doing better," Dr. Mark said, "but he hasn't realized that his mother is dead, nor what his part was in it. I would like to see him again after the funeral, but between now and then there are some things that need to be done. Can I count on you to help Eddie out?"

"That's why we're here," his grandfather said. "This is no picnic for us, you know. But we want to do the best thing for the boy."

"Good, that's good. I would like for you to tell him again that his mother is dead, and that she's gone away. You said that Dr. Jacobs also told him this, and I'd like you to take him back to Dr. Jacobs so that he can repeat it. Then Eddie has to see his mother before she's buried. . . ."

"No!" his grandmother interrupted. "No, we can't do that to the boy. She's so terribly . . . burned and . . ."

"And he's already seen her," Dr. Mark said. "He remembers her as being alive, as taking the medicine that always helped her before. To realize that she is dead, as best a boy his age *can* realize it, he has to see her. He should participate in whatever your family custom is. If you don't have one, adopt one. And he should see her laid to rest. . . ."

"She's being cremated," his grandfather said. "This isn't an open-casket situation, I hope you know . . ."

"I realize that, sir. But for Eddie's sake, he has to see her as a dead person. I'm sure that the funeral home would help you with this, and he should be in the company of someone who will let him touch her, talk to her, see that she's not breathing and not like a living person. Is there someone close to him who would do that?"

There was an uncomfortable silence behind the door.

"If neither of you feels comfortable, perhaps Dr. Jacobs . . . ?"

"I . . . I'll take the boy," his grandmother said. "I'll take him."

"Good. Then call me the day after the funeral to set up an appointment. I'll want to see him as soon as possible after that. He's had some hard times in his young life, but he's an exceptional boy and I'm sure he can come out of this all right."

The office door squeaked when it opened, something Eddie hadn't noticed before.

"Eddie, your grandparents are taking you home, now. I'll see you again in a couple of days. Okay?"

Eddie nodded. When he opened his eyes he saw that tears had dropped into the Kleenex box and dotted the tissues.

Eddie's tight throat strangled with his cryless sobs. He stared into the box of blue Kleenex, and the hole reminded him of the hole in the world that the earthquake made. He remembered Rafferty, haloed in blue on the other side. The hole opened up like a butterfly. Eddie wanted to run away with Rafferty. Then he could find the part of 'away' that his mother went to.

Eddie felt his fingers and toes tingle, and he concentrated on the Kleenex box when he tried to catch his breath. His ears rang too loud to hear, and he felt Dr. Mark's hand on his shoulder just as a fast-fluttering hole opened up in the box of Kleenex and he fell right in.

Every god that is dead can be conjured to life again.

—**Joseph Campbell,** *The Way of the Animal Powers*

THE JAGUAR FELT the hot blades of waking work at his flesh and suppressed a groan.

It's worse every time, he thought.

With that thought came a whiff of fear, a sour scent that he associated with his minions. His last awakening had nearly killed him. The subsequent debriefing had kept him on the cusp of death for weeks, a testimony to the skills of Max and the agency that paid him.

This waking would bring the Agency down on him again with their never-ending studies and the ubiquitous Max to probe his mind. Agency methods were of a particularly persuasive physical and chemical nature. Max enjoyed experimenting with a few tricks of his own. The Jaguar had beaten them before, but the Lee intrusion from the other side had cost him dearly.

The particle annihilation that crisped Zachary Lee had backlashed. Besides the momentary rent in the curtain of the universe, it had unleashed the Jaguar's genetic experiment prematurely and burned a little of his own brain, to boot. Certain access lines were cauterized, data frozen beyond reach. Genetics had never been his strong suit.

Goddam bugs, he thought. *It took me ten years to find one that dreamed.*

If he could alter a bug to specification, he could alter a human.

And then move in.

If they brought him as close to death this time as they did last time, the Jaguar was going to have to risk the move to another body, suitable or not. Like any good businessman, any good politician, he would simply have to minimize his losses.

The waking-blades were at him again, hot-knifing his nerve endings. A band began its slow crank around his skull.

Relax, he commanded himself, *just relax*.

Someone from the other side had worked his locks once; he would have to be more cautious. He'd felt the scratchings, the tinkerings at his secret door. He knew from experiments on his cattle that that door could be the entry to his most secret self—deeper even, to the lace garment of his being, his replicable core, his DNA. Lee had been the first to try it; the Jaguar was not foolish enough to believe that he would be the last.

The Jaguar had learned to round up his otherworld cattle by proxy. His loyal priests served as foremen and wielded his personal brand.

Branding was sheer terror—it created a psyche as indelibly scarred as the hide. The pain and terror of branding imprinted his cattle with the infinity image, the gate that he passed through to mount the dreamways. Imprinting an image in the mind installed a password in the psyche. Such an image gave a dream-burglar free passage to the brain and all of its regulatory mechanisms. Its neurons, its chemistry, the brain structure itself, were at his command.

The only one to discover that the image was more than an image had been Zachary Lee, and Zachary Lee was no longer a problem.

On this side, they had his body all wrapped and packaged. They watched over it day and night. Indeed, he had delivered himself into their hands, into this perfect place, for safekeeping, though none of them suspected as much. Waking to their studies and interrogations had never been a pleasure. He saw to it that he woke as seldom as possible. Lately they put the pressure on; they were getting serious. It was clear to the Jaguar that at any time waking could be fatal.

Once again pain, an excruciating, skull-crushing pain welcomed him back to the world. The Jaguar was unwilling to tinker with his own brain, choosing instead to suffer during his search for another. Now he began his cycle of slow, deep breaths to cut the pain, and he hoped that he would not vomit.

Sometimes he fooled them if he kept from throwing up. He

would pass through pain and play comatose until he regained hold on his precious sleep. The EEG betrayed him, as did the hardware taped to his eyelids. But staffing at the Soldiers' Home hospital was sparse these days, and occasionally he carried off the sham. Waking was always a horror.

The Jaguar kept a file of tidbits for the Agency, though, so they'd stopped being hard on him right off the bat. Hardball came later, when they made sure he was wrung dry.

They called it 'debriefing,' but he knew better. He kept high-ranking cattle in his personal corral—Belitnikoff, a lanky KGB colonel; Wu Li, a troubled physicist; Mitsui, of the Tokyo Exchange, and Livingston on the Federal Reserve. They were always up to something that Operations found tantalizing. Of course, his pryings caused disturbances in themselves, which developed some interesting product.

The Jaguar hated it. After his first breach of the fabric of being, he lost interest in the trivial politics of a measly little world. There were universes to conquer and he knew, in time, he could have them all.

He was a tinkerer inside a great machine. He had not yet met another tinkerer on equal ground on the dreamways. Zachary Lee had blundered and the Jaguar had been lucky. His life depended on keeping his body alive and the dreamways secure. Right now, his body was his foremost concern.

He had babbled to Max about the other side, about being the Jaguar, but it had been a fortuitous babble. Max thought he had taken him too far and broken his mind completely. It ended the debriefing, but not the threat. They believed in his domestic cattle because they could see them. They would no more believe in another universe than they believed in UFOs.

In his big breakthrough six years ago he had given the Ops boys specs to a classy little jamming device. He told them he got it from Wu Li. The truth was, one of his priests had handed him his first link to an engineer of the Roam, Zachary Lee. That link had provided a pathway that ran both ways, and Zachary Lee had found it.

The Jaguar had stumbled from a dreamway directly into the mind of the great Zachary Lee. Inventions, particularly information-gathering devices, information-gathering-jamming devices and magnetic motors had been Zachary Lee's contribution to the Roam. His political clout meant nothing to the Jaguar. Lee's charisma at the end proved nothing except that the Roam would not give up one of its own, not even to keep the Jaguar at bay.

He had told Operations about his limits, but it was not in their interests to believe him. They stole his own blood and gave it back, they duplicated hormones and subhormonic compounds, they knocked him out, they kept him up but never could they get him to duplicate his sleep of the dreamways. Nor could he.

It always just *happened*.

It was their job to remain suspicious, and he respected that. When it was their job to make sure he was holding nothing back, he would tell them everything. He knew that. It had happened before. Not for a while, but they did it before and he knew they'd do it again.

He allowed himself a flicker of amusement through his pain.

They didn't dare believe it—that a world coexisted beside their own. Amusement, again. The more he ranted about it, the less likely they were to believe it. And they would stop when he ranted, because clearly he had told them everything.

The Jaguar simply preferred to avoid them, and sleeping for months at a time had been perfect. He gave them less and less, pretending to burn out. It was not in their best interests to believe that, either.

He prayed that they would not find out just how little pain he could stand anymore.

I could stop it, he thought. *I could sever my pain centers.*

But he couldn't, no more than a surgeon could open his own chest and take out a lung. Self-tinkering was too dangerous to risk, and there was no one he trusted, in this world or the other, to go mucking about in his brain.

His priests were ranch foremen to him, each in charge of a herd. This kept the Lees of the herd from seeking him out. The priesthood was both security and early-warning system to the Jaguar. To get to him, the other side would have to get one of the priests. It had already worked once. The Jaguar kept close tabs on the condition of his priests.

A perfect, white pain slashed his cranial nerves, and another snatched him in the belly for a hard twist.

Breathe . . . ! he commanded himself.

It eased, and the weight on his chest eased up, too. He pushed the pain away from his face by imagining it as a handkerchief, a very light handkerchief that he could keep away by blowing slowly, slowly, through his pursed lips. . . .

They didn't yank me back!

Chemicals brought him out faster. This time it was his own body's doing. This time he had surprise on his side. He thought he might bear the pain that he knew was coming. The Agency didn't know he was waking, either. That had proven advantage enough before. They might not be watching, after all this time.

All this time . . .

It had been . . . *moments? months? years?* . . . since they'd juggled his blood chemistries drastically to raise him up. When it was chemistry, there was no wait for the rest of the pain. The waking was a full sprint down a very long straightaway of jagged glass every time they tinkered his blood. When he came out naturally, he roller-coasted back to himself, back to the same white pain.

When they woke him chemically, they received unreliable product and they endangered his life. His life was their project, their jobs, and this was an extreme that they seemed reluctant to breach. The unreliability of the product was not entirely his own doing, though he contributed to the disinformation whenever it suited him.

The Jaguar homed in on the Roam because he needed information, and the chief product of the Roam was information. They traded it to the fortified cities like farmers traded potatoes. Gadget production and repair were tangent functions that employed most of the tradesmen of the Roam. They were protected by the accords. Yet, in the occasional den of a city harm did come. That's why the Roam preferred the wild stretches outside the walls, and wandered them gladly.

The Jaguar had nearly ended all that, tinkering around with that world. Now he had all he could bear to worry about this one.

May you always wander in hunger. May you never eat to your heart's content.

—Curse of the Goddess of Roads

EVERY MORNING THROUGHOUT the muddy spring of her sixth year, the girl Afriqua Lee snapped awake from the split earth opening beneath her. Each time, she reached upwards for the iron grip of Old Cristina's hand that had saved her. And each morning she wept for her beautiful mother who was gone now, her laughing mother who would never be back. Lately she sought out her mother in the mirror, in the flare of her own nose or the sparkle of her green eyes. Her permanent teeth that were filling the gaps in front would duplicate her mother's white, even smile.

This morning, like so many mornings, she languished under the strong fingers of Old Cristina, who stroked her hair to tame the pounding headaches. She always hurt so *bad* after the dreams. She had so *many* dreams.

"Your eyes are so *wild*, girl, first thing in the morning."

Afriqua Lee smiled, and forgot to hide her mouth.

"Yes, girl, those teeth are coming. Your two in the bottom are coming back straight and the ones on the sides are wigglety already."

Old Cristina, the Romni Bari, always took time for Afriqua Lee.

"I used to have nightmares, but now I don't," Afriqua told her.

"You don't? That's good. Do you have nice dreams now?"

"Now I have a plane. A magic plane."

"What do you mean, 'a magic plane'?"

The strong old hands rubbed the girl's scalp, nearly lulled the headache away.

"It's like my magic ears. I can hear things, you know."

"I didn't know," the Romni said. "What kinds of things do you hear?"

"People talking. But my magic plane is the best. I take off when I get to sleep, and I'm flying, and up there there's a blinking star. A white star brighter than the rest, and it's blinking."

"Do you fly around the star?"

"No, I just point the nose of my magic plane and follow it. Well, we always fall out of the sky."

"That sounds scary to me. You don't get hurt?"

"No. I never get hurt. I follow the blinking star until it turns into a bright blue butterfly, and when my magic plane lands, it lands inside a dream. Somebody else's dream. And I can change it if I want to, so it's not scary. Unless I *want* it to be scary . . ."

"Why would you want it scary? To scare the person having the dream?"

"Yeah," she smiled. "Sometimes I do that."

"Girl, you're some dreamer yourself. Magic plane."

This morning, like every morning, bigshots came on business from the other kumpaniyi. Afriqua Lee sat at the table as Old Cristina's personal fetch. She learned the Roam's business in the world, as well as whom to bow to. At noon, when the bigshots cleared out, the older woman and the girl shared soup and green tea on their special table.

They sat in a glass alcove of Cristina's home, which was positioned for its view and for the personal privacy of the Romni Bari. During stakedown, the Romni Bari's tent was positioned first, and all the rest related to it according to rank, familia, privilege.

Their silent vehicles, their tents, interlocked at stakedown to form their own city, its walls a webwork of light-play and solar nets. At sunset, the Roam engineers threw the power to the high walls and adjusted the resolution. Anything inside the walls was now hidden behind an electrosonic camouflage. When they caravaned to the real cities, the sides of each van lit up to advertise the wares or skills of the owner.

Each time they went through stakedown, the vans repositioned themselves to reflect status changes over the past four months. Repositioning meant that Afriqua Lee and the other children had to learn a new way to school. She thought that life in the city must be pretty boring, if everything stayed the same all the time.

Old Cristina made tea for Afriqua Lee, but for herself she always brewed coffee. She was a large woman with a larger laugh, who swathed herself in bright scarves and billowy skirts to match. She walked with the roll of a seaman on leave, and Afriqua Lee would forever associate the smell of talc with Old Cristina.

Size was a mark of status among the Roam, and Cristina was a Romni Bari of size. Under her gray hair she stood eye-to-eye with most men, taller than some. She strolled the kumpania daily, with Afriqua Lee in tow. Old Cristina laughed a lot, in spite of hard times. Afriqua Lee liked it when she laughed without her teeth, her mouth a wet pink flower.

Old Cristina often told stories of the cities and the Roam, and many of these stories became important when the men came to talk morning politics. The girl knew some of the men from their dreams, but she didn't tell Old Cristina. Even before she saw the effects on them, and knew what it meant, she knew it was something like peeking in windows, something she didn't dare tell.

Through her own memories and dreams that she borrowed, Afriqua Lee remembered real homes in the city. In real cities, streets didn't change and homes stayed in one place. The Roam had chosen to take their cities with them, and the accords were clear. They had done this of their own free will. She didn't know what it meant, but it was on everybody's lips these days.

Afriqua Lee never understood why her relatives in the Roam called their homes 'tents.' They jigsawed themselves into the greatest city in the world in a full day of jockeying and levelling. It always seemed to the girl that stakedown was over in just a switch. She had only moved twice with the Roam. The Roam's portable communities were perfect, clean, silent. They brought trees with them, and small, potted parks with their flatbed gardens. The cities smelled horrible, but the Roam always had fresh air.

Afriqua Lee had lived her first few years with her parents in the city. Because of their Romni blood they moved a lot, even then. The drivable homes of the Roam were much nicer than any homes that she had slept in in the city.

The old knock-down and bolt-together houses were fun, and they took the longest to set up. A few of the younger single men slept in real tents at the fringes of the encampment and they decorated these with old-fashioned paintings and pennants. Old Cristina's long, sleek trailer with its light-play sides was a far cry from those.

Some of the young men loaned out to a city for two years, earning credits for themselves and for the Roam. The accords provided for women, but women seldom went. It was different for them, through the Roam. Few Romni, men or women, had lived on both sides of the walls. Her mother had. She, herself, had.

Everything, including the tents, plugged in for camouflage against the priesthood and its scouts.

A secure camp, like this one behind the gaje Henry's place, meant they didn't need to be on raider alert all the time. Those were the times the Roam cooked with their shielded electricals and banned the ritual coals, to keep the smoke down. At those times everyone whispered and nobody played ballgame in the square.

The first night after stakedown Afriqua Lee helped some of the older children drag in wood and branches for a high-risk bonfire in honor of Henry, the last of a gaje family who had helped and hidden them for three generations.

The grim aftermath of the hatch remained everywhere, even in this lush valley of their northernmost reach. In the nearby woods, thousands of trees stood shining in the morning sun, stripped of bark to their bare wood. The grasses and mosses that the familia had told her about were gone, blanketed over by a powdery gray dirt. It made her cough and sneeze, but she worked hard because she liked bonfires. It was her first time out of the compound since her mother died, and it felt good to her.

She had not known Henry, but the shy boy who lived with him watched everything from a window high in an old barn. She could see him in the distance from her perch in the Romni's alcove.

She wore one of the new blouses and skirts that Old Cristina had given her. Already the gray dirt had worked into the sleeves and the hem. She had learned to work the cleaners, though. Cristina told her that they worked just like the cookers, but she didn't see how. The clothes came out clean and the food came out cooked—that seemed like magic to Afriqua Lee. And she was glad she didn't have to wash clothes in the stream every day, like the old days. Once every four months was plenty.

She liked the stakedown ritual, when the women gathered at

the stream, but she would hate to wash clothes like that every day.

Old Cristina had bequeathed Afriqua Lee the garment of her own familia, the mark of her personal tent. It was a red blouse, blue shawl and black skirt, all with the iridescent quetzal trim.

"It's yours," the Romni told her in the thick accent of the Roam. She thrust the reed basket of clothing into the girl's hands. It seemed like everyone was giving her clothes since her mom died, as though she didn't have any of her own. But something in Old Cristina's manner told her that this was different.

Afriqua Lee fingered the black designs stained into the sides of the basket and the bits of red rag woven in for color. It was heavier than she thought it would be and she lifted a knee to catch it quick. She unlatched a thonged piece of bone and slipped the lid.

On top lay a very old, very intricate black veil woven with the history of the Roam. Beneath the veil lay the ceremonial clothing that the Romni Bari herself had worn as a girl. There were some everyday clothes, too, that she'd saved from a torturous childhood. Afriqua Lee liked wearing them—they made her feel taller, like Old Cristina herself. She liked the feeling of being taller, and the feeling of new teeth growing in the front.

"That monster what started this thing—that prikasha, Jaguar . . ." Old Cristina pulled out the neckline of her blouse, spat on her breast and snapped the elastic back. "We are onto him, yes. We have done him much harm. His stupidity killed many, it's true, but we have done him harm."

"How can we harm what doesn't exist?" Stefan asked.

Stefan was a cousin of Old Cristina's, and he was one of her political advisors. "The Jaguar is a myth. It's those priests, who *say* there's a Jaguar, who ruin the accords we fought for, who do these things. . . ."

"Yes"—Cristina swept her arm around her head, indicating the gray barrens around their encampment—"the priests would destroy the accords. But this . . . *this* is the doing of something more than a handful of spleef-whiffers. The Dark Ages. The plagues . . ."

"Henry said the government made the plagues. . . ."

"Don't interrup." Cristina waved a finger at Stefan's nose. "Don't interrup when the elder talk. Nobody interrup the Romni Bari. Got it?"

Stefan nodded and answered in a low voice, "Yes."

"Good. Yes. The plagues maybe was a government job. Lab says they are a *doing*. Or an undoing, by someone who is playing with some big fire. Not God."

Afriqua Lee's familia travelled the northlands every year from May to September, spending an extra month or so on the coast when hard times dictated.

Trips up and down the coast included boat-trading and selling, manufacture of small hovercraft, electronics and magnetics devices—each under the auspices of a different familia. Transportation, communication and repair were the way of life of the Roam, under the new accords.

"Buy 'em, sell 'em, trade 'em. Vera's magnometries and holographic art."

The sides of their many vans hawked their wares.

The Roam stored components and electronics gear in huge refrigerator vans with air conditioning and temperature regulation—all offshoots of their meticulous cleanliness.

"Peoples have good ideas, yes, and the accords start us out a good government. But those priests . . ." Again, Cristina spat. "Anyway, now somebody makes these bugs. Nobody can find who. Cities think awhile maybe it's the Roam. Now peoples be saying it's this Jaguar. Peoples dying every day, no place to bury in cities . . . horrible, girl, horrible."

Afriqua Lee had heard of the huge death-vans cruising the streets. The vans were for hauling away bodies.

"Did they want to kill *everybody* . . . ?"

A plump finger tapped the girl's nose and her eyes watered from the strong garlic smell it left.

"There is a Jaguar," the Romni pronounced. "I say it is his doing. He unleashes his priests on us while he brews a bigger pot of misery. I think he just likes to."

Afriqua Lee closed her eyes, saw something like a shadow with bright, blue eyes. She shuddered off the sudden chill, and slipped out the door to school.

Marie de Manaceine . . . kept puppies awake for periods from four to six days and found to her surprise that this killed them.

—**Christopher Evans,** *Landscapes of the Night*

IN RAFFERTY'S MEMORY of that bleak, muddy autumn five years ago, Old Cristina and the Roam materialized with the mist one morning, as they had appeared on this spot every autumn for centuries. They mourned Uncle Hungry in their raucous, spirited way and made a place for Rafferty at their tables.

Then, with the stiffening of winter, they ghosted away one night as suddenly as they had come. Teenagers of the Mopan kumpania rode cleanup for the Roam, returning the site to normal, covering their tracks. They would straddle their little scoutcraft and catch up to the Roam's convoy of giant vans by midday.

Pulling up stakes was a serious matter among the Roam. Many a generation had survived over several thousand years because the entire Roam could strike even the largest rendezvous overnight. At its peak, the Roam numbered seven million souls. As many as two million had shared rendezvous at one time and they became, for that three months, the largest city in the world. But when they pulled up stakes, they did it in one night.

Uncle's place settled into its winter silence. The familia disappeared every year but their influence lingered through all four seasons. Now that he travelled the dreamways, Rafferty found it possible to keep them with him, to learn from their greatest minds in his sleep.

Through his dreams Rafferty learned how to slip the walls of the dream and enter the mind of the dreamer. He could see, feel or know anything that the dreamer knew, one thing at a time. It took him three years to learn how to navigate in there. He thought of himself as a crow, sometimes, swooshing at treetop level through the canyons. Only these canyons were inside somebody's head. It was another several years before he realized the terrible damage he had done.

This year, by chance, he stumbled undetected into a dream of the Visionmaster, and got himself well-lodged with a passkey. Rafferty enjoyed frequent access to his teacher's mind during the nine months of his absence and made the most of it, retrieving puzzle pieces and reassembling them inside his own head later. Out of respect, or perhaps instinct, he left the personal stuff alone.

He'll be surprised, Rafferty had thought. *When he gets back he'll just be expecting some ignorant gaje kid. . . .*

The Roam had returned to a brighter Rafferty, one who frightened them but whose innovations and inventions dazzled them, as well. The Visionmaster did not return with them. The night before their return he had died in a headlong rush into a refrigeration van, screaming, "Bubble of life! Bubble of life!" He had been inconsolably depressed for months, despite his considerable talent with magnetrics and ions.

Rafferty's daydreams, too, sought out the dreamways, and many of his days were spent recovering from the surreal aftermath of those crippling headaches that plagued him more and more.

He'd begun to dream that Uncle would pull up with them to tell him tales of the highland jungles of their winter camp. He'd been captivated by the flips they'd showed him when he was only six, flips that showed broadleaf jungle and the stone monuments of their ancestors.

This year he determined to see it for himself. Since Verna had snatched him from the city, Rafferty had never been more than a half-day's walk south of the creek. The Tattoo boys turned the perimeter vans at Uncle's into a jungle for him once. They told him they'd tuned the picture so fine that he should be able to *smell* that jungle, but all he smelled was the garlic that roiled out of their breath.

The Roam appeared and disappeared each year for five years, and out of this he learned something of hope. Ever since the first time they left, Rafferty hoped with all his heart that they would come back, and every time they had. He supposed that

Uncle learned the same lesson when he was a boy, and it had been evident in his joy each time he'd seen them staking down.

Cristina and her Roam had set up their miraculous city in the twenty-acre meadow behind the barn. Uncle called it a meadow, and so did the Roam, but Rafferty had only known it after the bugs, so he called it the mud flats. He walked down there after the Roam pulled up stakes and found no tracks, no sign that hundreds of people had lived there for three months.

He revelled in memories of their bright-colored clothing and their music. Like Uncle, Rafferty shared their passion for gadgets and soon he had found himself apprenticed to the Visionmaster.

"It's something I wanted more than anything," Uncle had told him. "I never got the chance, but I learned plenty by watching, tearing things apart. . . ."

A hyperactive older man, the Visionmaster called himself the "Romno of Research," but Theo Kekchi was the Roam's official Master Tinker. He believed that everyone should know as much about everything as quickly as possible. Before the bugs, before the Jaguar, he had designed a homegrown bioelectronics system.

"It was like woodcarving," Theo had explained to Rafferty. "I just used smaller tools."

Theo Kekchi had designed what he called a "chemical chisel," a substance that he could coax the body to manufacture. This substance made the DNA of certain cells replicate wildly. During replication he attracted the DNA to a template which he had chemically introduced. It would re-form there, a dozen strands to a cell.

When the cell burst, guide-dog molecules enveloped the DNA, protecting it. Then Theo could transfer this DNA to any cell he chose, also chemically. In that manner, he insisted, he could build virtually any kind of creature imaginable, and many more that are not. He theorized that this was the method that someone had used to produce the plague of bugs.

Theo Kekchi chose the bioconductor for development and production, and it was fast rewriting the manuals on the world's technology. Though living tissue, it was free of the ethical question of creating a creature of more complexity.

Whoever had tried the same experiment with a few little bugs had it get away from them. Unlike the rest of the Roam, Theo had retained the highest respect for the attempt, while displaying the highest contempt for the experimenter's sloppy methods.

"Someone blew it," Theo had said. "That's how we got the

bugs. They knew how to scramble some proteins but they didn't know what they were getting. But how could they come up with it? How?" His fist banged the conductor vat. "Nobody's doing anything like I am in the cities. Somebody would have to be inside my head. . . ."

Rafferty knew *he* hadn't been the one messing around in there, not that time. He shuddered when he thought of the sick person who had invented the bugs. He didn't want to meet whoever it was in some dark tunnel of anyone's mind.

The bugs had ravaged half the world with their unquenchable appetites.

"Like *your* appetite, youngster," Theo had told Rafferty. "Never have I heard so many questions. . . ."

Theo started to make a joke, then shook his head.

"Listen," he said, "you keep that up, boy. You'll be Visionmaster yourself someday. Hah."

Rafferty would miss Theo, in person and in his dreams, and it would be years before he understood the mechanism of his teacher's death. It was one of many insights that would haunt him throughout his years.

Every year when the vans and trailers of the Roam wound their way to the farm, Uncle Hungry had been a truly happy man. He liked people all right; he just didn't like cities. That's where his brother had learned to drink. It troubled him greatly that it was his family that made the whiskey that ruined him.

Whiskey had been a family matter for a long, long time. The Roam had run whiskey for Henry's great-grandfather and kept the sales end of the business at a healthy distance from production. It was Old Cristina and Henry who agreed to shut down the still and go out of the liquor business. At first, there was a lot of grumbling in the Roam.

"You're shutting off trade incentives," they said.

"Bribery is bribery," Uncle had said, forgetting that bribery, too, was a longtime tradition of the Roam.

"Whiskey violates the accords," Cristina pronounced. "If we want them to stick to it, we stick to it."

There was no vote on the matter, and it didn't hurt business a bit. The Roam had information, and that's what cities needed. They'd get by on their raisin wines and spleef just fine, but they'd all be up a creek without the word.

When Rafferty first met the Roam, right after the hatch, it was the gray spring of mud and despair. Uncle took him down there when they came out of the still that time. Rafferty walked right to the wall of the camp and would've bumped into it, too, if Uncle hadn't stopped him. There was an invisible wall that his hand could feel, that shimmered with the image of an empty pasture. Touching the full life-sized picture, he felt something behind it, like a hum.

The Romni Bari's quarters and her component support vans set up in the south pasture with her immediate family beside her. A half-dozen buses and vans pulled in by nightfall, each taking its precise position from the Romni Bari's bus as dictated by family or tribal status. Rafferty didn't know this about the status until later. There, in the glare of his sixth summer, he soaked in their color, their wealth, their virtual impenetrability.

Five years later, in the mire of despair over Uncle Hungry's death, he pulled up his own stakes to join the Roam. He headed northward, at first, as Ruckus showed him the way through the Blue Mountains. Then they turned downcoast to his first winter in the sun.

When the boy first set foot to the road, Ruckus determined to lead him to the sea. Like all crows, like most people, he was sick to death of the dried bug meal that the humans called 'flour.' From the time the boy hit the road the crow had been dreaming of clams, mussels and ripe fish delivered up by the tides. He had never been there. These memories he, too, had stolen from dreams.

It was Ruckus who led him to the seacoast that year, and it was the crow who guided him on his forays into the outside world. The dreams were changing. Rafferty was drawn to the other side, and it was a good thing. When the dreams were on him, nothing else mattered. When they weren't, he couldn't always make them come. When he did, their landscape was empty and very, very lonely.

He always felt afraid and exposed during those times, the way Ruckus must have felt when he sensed a hawk. Only for Rafferty it wasn't a hawk, it was the Jaguar. Many a Jaguar priest had been snared while casting out solo on the dreamways. Sharing a dream was safer, but the company wasn't always that good.

Even Uncle had spoken of the Jaguar, and when he did, it was hissed through clenched jaws.

"Did us a favor, he did," Uncle had told him. "Thinned things out a bit, stirred up the gene pool." Rafferty could tell by the flat tone of his voice that he didn't mean it.

Rafferty remembered thinking of the Jaguar as a wizard in

black robes—he'd seen one in one of Uncle's flips—stirring a huge pot of blue jeans.

"The governments, they all blamed each other at first," Uncle had said. "But the infection that Jaguar turned loose didn't know anything about borders, skin color or prayer. It only knew how to stay alive by eating, and that's been plenty. Some say it was an accident. But he was at the center of it, and he's still going strong. Don't seem accidental to me."

That first autumn that Rafferty had returned with the Roam they had staked down the rendezvous as usual, but first the old woman had sprinkled dried petals on Uncle's grave. The toolbox lid was still there to mark it, and one tattered cluster of wings.

The Roam were a fastidious, secretive lot, and it was years before Rafferty was to understand the nature of their true product, the depth of their mystery. *Information* was their product, as well as misinformation, and in these desperate times nothing was more valuable.

Their fastidiousness required access to a lot of water, and their intricate structure required large open ground for meetings. Uncle Hungry's place was one of about two dozen that Rafferty was to visit over his next ten years with the Roam. They deferred to his ownership of it after Henry's death, though ownership was a very fluid concept in the culture of the Roam.

The official language of the Roam was a trading language they had concocted hundreds of years ago. But among the Roam there was a speaker for every language of every city in the world. Rafferty was good at gadgets, and Afriqua Lee had mastered language. Only Rafferty knew how she'd done it all along.

It was a while before they told Old Cristina. She made the sign of the noose behind her back and ordered them to stop it. She ticked off the casualties they had caused, all ending in madness or death. It was the kind of secret that even the Romni Bari couldn't keep forever.

The Roam brought music to the farm, and tents, and colorful wonders of the world. They stored wind power in air compressors. Large Barnard wind valves popped up all around the community. They sold components, power adaptors or compressor drives for storage and their marvelous devices. The Roam lived well without ever plugging in to power generators in the cities, but their thrifty nature demanded that they take advantage of it wherever they could.

When she left Uncle's place that first fall when Rafferty was six, Old Cristina had handed him a black basket. Two bone catches fastened the lid.

"Careful," she had said.

The basket wobbled when he took it, and whatever was inside moved. It moved by itself.

He set the basket down on the stoop and squatted next to it. A little bit of red ribbon decorated one side of the basket, and something inside pecked at the red ribbon. Rafferty undid the pins and eased the lid off.

A sorry little rag of a fledgling crow stared back at him; he could see himself reflected in the glossy eye. It opened its beak wide and squalled, wanting to be fed. When Rafferty made no move to feed it, the little crow made a stab at his fingers. He dropped the lid back down and heard it *thump* the little crow's head.

Rafferty snatched the lid off again and the little eye glared at him. The crow ruffed its feathers and fetched a halfhearted peck at the ribbon.

"Remember," Uncle had said, "don't be too good to him. If something happens to you, he's got to know how to take care of himself. Don't let him forget how to be a crow."

It was Old Cristina who gave the crow to Rafferty, and Old Cristina who had introduced him to Afriqua Lee.

By the time the uncle died, Rafferty had learned that no one truly owns a crow. He had learned as well that the uncle gave him roots, and the sickly young crow gave him something to care for. And Old Cristina had given him the crow. Between Uncle and Old Cristina he had pieced together the series of disasters that had led to their secret lives there on the mud flats in a small mountain valley.

There was little talk of family, even then; the first plagues had seen to that.

Rafferty and the uncle had netted the birds that swarmed around their drying tables and cooked them, mindful to let the crows go free. This because Ruckus kept watch from the barn roof. Sometimes he lured birds in by imitating their calls. He also learned that the boy would feed him his fill if he waited until the business was done. Ruckus was a patient bird.

Now, the telltale crows flocked around him in twos and threes. The first took to traditional perches in the scraggly snags that surrounded the barn. Others balanced on what remained of the house. Rafferty's crow, Ruckus, called out rank as the gentry appeared and reassured Rafferty with sidelong mutterings and pointed glances. The elder crows gathered with Ruckus along the sagging ridge of the barn and Rafferty knew Old Cristina couldn't be far behind.

There were a lot of crows this year, and, like himself and some young men of the Roam, they were early. Rafferty studied the skyline.

Nearly two months early.

The birds luffed the breeze, tucked their wings in tight and spiraled down to the dirt around him, unusually quiet for crows.

Thanks to Ruckus, Rafferty had caught up to the migrating Roam a month after Uncle Hungry's death, and Old Cristina had taken him in. He was eleven and technically a gaje, but the Roam respected Henry too much to leave the boy on a stone. Besides, the boy displayed the same skill with gadgets that Henry had and he made himself useful from the start.

They had been amused that Rafferty had loaded one change of clothing, some dried bug meal, a water jug and twenty kilos of Henry's best hand-tools into Uncle's old backpack. His first day in camp Rafferty repaired the refrigeration unit on the kumpania's grain van and saved what food stores they had. Besides, Cristina liked him, with that alone it would have been impossible to turn him away.

The night he caught them on the high road south was a starry night, typically cool for the highlands. The kumpania had been bogged down for days restructuring a bridge across a deep, bare ravine. The kumpania threw itself into frantic preparation for a night of music and dance, of hot food, bright skirts and bracelets flashing in the firelight.

The pump on the refrigeration van had been an easy repair, one that he recognized right away as a gasket problem by the whistling sound it made on the upstroke. The men of the Roam had concentrated on clearing the lines that held the refrigerant. They could see that the pump was pumping, but they couldn't see that it was sucking air and fouling the system. Rafferty made a gasket out of a piece of old shoe leather and, since he had such small hands, managed to replace it without dismounting and dismantling the entire pump.

"Clean up in my tent, youngster," Old Cristina had said, "then have some coffee. We will be all night celebrating stakedown."

Old Cristina's furrowed brow furrowed further.

"Afriqua Lee dreams as you do."

"I know . . . we know."

"Do not endanger the Roam."

"I won't."

He fidgeted from one foot to the other, keeping her gaze.

"How'd you know?"

"Henry. He was worried. He say you get headaches, sick, dream funny. My Afriqua Lee, she is the same thing."

She made the sign of the noose.

" 'The big zero,' " he said, quoting Uncle, the fervent non-believer.

"You sound just like your . . . just like Henry." She turned her head for a moment, and sighed. "Go clean up," she told him, and didn't look back. "The kumpania will think you're a gaje."

It was the first hot shower that Rafferty had had since Uncle died. He luxuriated in the foamy fragrance of the strange soap and scrubbed his scalp until it tingled.

He towelled down and, when he reached for his clothes, saw that they had been replaced by fresh trousers, shirt and jacket, all embroidered with the bright complexity of the Romni Bari familia.

The black, mid-calf trousers had a red stripe sewn down the outer right leg, and his cap draped two cloth braids of red, black and blue halfway down his back. He rubbed the steam from the mirror and checked his appearance.

Everything fit him well except the jacket, which was a little tight in the forearms. Rafferty was not a tall boy, but working with Uncle had made him strong for his age. His skin was pale next to the Romni's, and his nose narrow, but he found he could flare his nostrils acceptably with practice. His steady gaze, though blue-eyed, would also mark him a person of honor in the Roam. He squared his shoulders, and the jacket sleeves slid above his wrists. People of the Roam were small, and Rafferty already outsized many men.

Rafferty was unaccustomed to the effects of the suppressors, so he barely heard the tap on the bathroom door.

It was Theo's replacement, Stefan. He wore the colors of the Network, which Rafferty didn't know much about, but he knew that it represented a lot of power.

"I'm your sponsor," Stefan announced, and pulled him into the hallway. "It was Theo's wish. Nice suit. There'll be some ritual stuff, some language stuff and a vision thing. Not for a while; don't twitch. You're a shoo-in."

The being we do not know is an infinite being; he may arrive, and turn our anguish and our burden to dawn in our arteries.

—Rene Char

MARK WHITE WORKED with Eddie Reyes twice a week throughout the summer of his sixth year. When school started, Mark had hoped that Eddie would be taken up in the normal life of a six-year-old and that the dreams, the imaginary friends, would disappear as they generally did. It became clear that the small-town school was unwilling to let go its favorite gossip. The gossip, and the absolute unwillingness of his grandparents to relate to him, kept Eddie visiting Mark at least once a week throughout the winter.

Mark's work with the boy felt different from the start, and he had to admit that Eddie had caught him up in two ways—sympathy for the pitiful home life he led, and curiosity about the rich fantasy life that he willingly displayed. That was also the winter that Mark White fell in love. He would not regret the love, but someday he would regret the blur that it made of his work on The Hill and in the Soldier's Home in the city.

Late-night soul-searchings in his Spartan apartment reassured him that city life for the sake of career advancement was not acceptable. The tradeoff was too great. His frugal ways had allowed him to build up savings enough to buy a house in the coming year, and he'd decided to buy in the valley. He could dismiss, once and for all, whatever Mindy might think.

Mark White was the promising young professional in the valley. The town's patriarchs paraded their eligible daughters past him at the various obligatory socials. Though polite and, at times, even charmed and flattered, the young Dr. White remained painfully alone.

Actually, he was merely alone during that time. He became painfully alone only after he met Sara Lipko. Sara was a photojournalist who had received an Arts Council grant to work with disturbed patients in facilities throughout the state. She came loaded with books, jaw set, and wasted no time on the likes of Mark White.

"Most people in institutions aren't sick," she declared when they first met. She blew a lock of brown hair out of her browner eyes. "They're victimized by a system that's trying to perpetuate itself. If you didn't have any patients, you wouldn't have a job, right? They're drugged by people like you until they're confused, then led into hearings where it's proven that they're confused, and they're sent back to the lockup so the state can keep you in Porsches."

Hostile to authority figures, Mark noted. *Typical knee-jerk, low-grade liberal paranoia. Assessment: pain in the ass.*

That was on Monday in the day room at The Hill. Mark walked away in frustration and disgust, comforted by the administrator's assurance that Sara Lipko would be gone in a few weeks.

"I've got a Porsche oil cooler in my Volkswagen," Mark confided to a colleague in the cafeteria. "It cost me thirty-five dollars at the wrecking yard. Does that count?"

Still, he was as troubled at the thought that she'd be gone as he was comforted. She was, after all, interesting. And outspoken. And there was no question that she was beautiful.

Thick, shoulder-length dark hair haloed her Slavic face and high cheekbones. Her large brown eyes looked into his own the whole time they talked, and Mark noted that she wore contacts. Eye contact with patients was an important part of his life, but it took tremendous will to hold his own with this woman.

She was only a couple of inches shorter than he was—he guessed her at five foot eight or nine. His peripheral vision took in her bespangled, gypsy-type dress that dipped just enough at the neckline to pique his curiosity. She stood very close to him when she talked. There was no ring on her left hand.

Mark found himself doing something that surprised him. In spite of her brashness, and his uneasiness in her presence, he borrowed her personnel record from the office.

"I want to see who's going to be meddling with my patients," he mumbled to Sherry at the desk.

"When you read the records, you'll see that 'meddling' is not quite the word," Sherry said. She watched him over the tops of her spectacles as he tapped the folder in his palm, then turned to go.

"Will you be offering private therapy to the visiting meddler?" she asked.

"Fat chance," he said, and heard her chuckle as he closed the door.

On Thursday, Sara showed up for his volunteer day at the Soldiers' Home and he knew it would be impossible to ignore her. Her records had revealed a Guggenheim Foundation grant that had taken her into two wars in Latin America. Her most recent book on the subject, *Daughters of Fire*, had won awards from five countries and was up for a Pulitzer Prize. If he'd had any doubts about avoiding her, the Colonel dispelled them when he ordered Mark to escort her on his rounds.

"You're here on Thursdays, she's here on Thursdays," the sad-faced Colonel told him. "She's a goddam liberal pain in the ass. She can't be running around here loose, and you've got the light workload."

"How long will she be here?"

"Eight weeks. Make her happy. If the state won't send us money, at least they can send some entertainment. That's all."

That cold Thursday in February he might've walked away from her in the Soldiers' Home anyway, except that he'd just spotted an EEG that got his attention.

It was very much like Eddie Reyes's aberrant tracing, a dreaming event that he hadn't been able to duplicate. It revealed a rhythmic rise and fall that looked more like a respiration record than brain-wave activity. This EEG was coded for the fifth floor of the Soldiers' Home, the high-security floor. There was no accompanying chart.

He'd conferred with several older colleagues about Eddie, and the consensus on the EEG was "atypical, unidentified seizure activity." Clinical diagnoses ranged between multiple personality disorder and psychosis induced by sleep deprivation.

Mark had tried various medications to change sleep and dream patterns. The boy continued to be a contradiction—a patient who made good progress in therapy but whose sleep disorder was increasing to the point where it interfered with his life.

It must be organic, Mark thought. *There's some brain dysfunction that I'm not picking up on.*

But here in the Soldiers' Home he saw another EEG that matched Eddie's, spike for spike. He was instantly and completely distracted.

"I'm interested in dreams," Sara said. She scanned the tracing over Mark's shoulder. Her breath smelled like Juicy Fruit gum. "Dreams are where everybody lives, you know. Can you tell anything about them when you read those strips?"

Mark couldn't resist stringing her along.

"Well," he said, "it's confidential, you know. I shouldn't reveal anything personal about my patients. . . ."

"I can keep a secret," she said.

He nearly fell into her wide brown eyes.

"I believe you. But this violates a patient's trust. Would you want some stranger to know your innermost dreams? Even dreams that you don't remember?"

"Of course not." She smiled. "But I'm as much a voyeur as the next guy. I'd like a peek at someone else's dreams. Actually, I'd like a peek at yours, Doctor."

Mark blushed, then blushed all the more for catching himself at it.

"Scarlet is your color," she said, laughing. "You wear it well."

Sara, too, was blushing and that made him feel less awkward. He liked the flash in her brown eyes and felt closer to her, but still he couldn't resist leading her on.

"Here," he pointed to a series of squiggles, "he's not dreaming yet. Here's his transition state. And here, the dream starts. It's a pastoral dream—you can see the countryside here and here you see trees at the edge of a clearing. . . ."

"How do you know they're trees?"

"Well, see these tall, fuzzy spikes?"

She nodded, her lips pursed and serious.

"Bushes are squatter and fuzzier."

"I see."

She squinted, and moved closer to the EEG. She picked up a corner of it and her shoulder leaned into his.

"What difference does it make to the therapist whether the guy dreams of a tree or a bush?" she asked.

"Depends."

"Yeah? On what?"

He thought maybe she was getting wise to him.

"On the color," he said. "Some people only dream in black-

and-white. That's one thing. If they dream in color, that's another. And if they dream in color, *which* color they assign . . ."

"You're bullshitting me," she said, and snapped a finger against the tracings. "At least it's interesting bullshit. Are you going to take me to see this guy, or not?"

As it turned out, it wasn't that easy.

"Gotta clearance?" the surly ward clerk asked.

"I don't need clearance," Mark said. "I'm staff."

"For this wing, you need clearance, I need clearance, the President needs clearance. I just follow the orders; I don't write 'em. And there's no way the civilian gets in."

"That's ridiculous. . . ."

"I'm sure that Colonel Hightower will be happy to explain, Doctor. Technically, that tracing you're holding is a breach of security. Will you hand it over, please? It's not to leave this ward."

Mark hesitated, then responded to the firm, unemotional gaze of the mechanical sergeant and handed him the chart.

"Thank you, sir. I'm sure the Colonel will respond to your request for clearance. Ma'am."

The sergeant accorded Sara a nod, then returned to his desk as though neither of them existed. A pair of pale-faced Marine guards flanked the ward's locked double doors.

"We'll take it up with the Colonel," Mark said.

"You do that, Doctor," the sergeant said, and didn't look up.

Mark took Sara's arm in an automatic gesture to guide her back to the elevators, then realized what he'd done and dropped it. She hooked her arm in his.

"Well, genius, what now? Are we going to let some illiterate bozo keep us away from the man of our dreams?"

Mark laughed, and realized how little he'd been laughing lately.

"I'll talk to the Colonel. He likes having you around; it gives the place class."

"He *said* that?"

"No, but that's how he's using it for clout. If you like dreamers, I've got the perfect patient for you. How do you relate to kids?"

The elevator's doors slapped open and they stepped aboard.

"Great," she said. "I was one myself once. Why?"

"I have a very young patient on The Hill who has me somewhat stumped."

"What's the problem?"

"Imaginary friends," he said. "He doesn't have friends his own age, so he's made one up, complete with another world and society."

"Sounds normal to me," she said. "Maybe that means I'm next. How old is he? When can I meet him?"

"Hold it," Mark said, and put up a defensive hand.

They got off at the first floor and wound their way through the wheelchairs cluttering the lobby.

"I'll need to get permission for you to see him . . . a formality, don't worry. He's six, going on seven, and used to living with adults, so he's pretty easy to talk to when he gets going."

"Why are you being so helpful all of a sudden?"

She gave his arm a squeeze and Mark's heart rate picked up.

"You're a writer," he said. "Maybe you can draw him out more than I have, get him to verbalize more. You'll like him, and he's the kind of kid who could use some strokes. I usually see him on Saturdays because of school, but I'll see what I can do about Monday."

"I'd come in on Saturday, too," she said. "He sounds interesting. Dreams are interesting, and the whole mystery of sleep. Even *you* are interesting, Doctor, and I don't say that to embarrass you. It's my job to notice people and things that would interest other people. You're one of them."

The tour seemed a blur to Mark. He knew he'd covered most of the hospital, but all he could remember was her touch and the way she asked knowledgeable questions. She was someone who did her homework.

He returned to The Hill and riffled through the last workup on Eddie. He'd turned Eddie over to the staff neurologist, Brenda Colfelt, who ran him through the complete battery. That had been a month ago, and Mark was desperate for a long shot.

"I've put him through everything," she'd told him one day. "Until Saturday I got nothing. But there *is* something different, something that showed up just before he came to see you."

"What is it?"

"On his EEG. You say he has a sleep disorder, right? So I tested him daily for a week. Nothing. All within normal limits; the kid slept well through the tests . . . nothing."

"So what *did* you get"

"I'm coming to that. Relax. I thought you shrinks were supposed to be patient."

"Sorry. I've gotten myself more involved in this case than I intended. . . ."

"That's okay." She laughed. "I'm glad to see it. The granite statue has a heart . . . just kidding," she said, and put up a hand. "Okay, I had given up and was going to bring the charts down to you when he came in Saturday to see you. I saw him in the hallway and he looked disoriented, tired, listless—nothing like his usual self. He's a sharp kid, right?"

"Right."

Now Mark was no longer irritated; he was eager.

Brenda went on.

"He was early, so I asked him to come down to my section. He looked like he could barely stay awake, so I thought, 'What the hell' and set him up for a tracing. He zonked out right away, and I got this."

Brenda handed Mark the sheet of tracings.

That had been a month ago. Mark had never seen tracings like the ones she showed him. They documented incredible electrical disturbances that he normally would only interpret as seizure activity, though he had never seen seizure tracings like these. They were chaotic at a glance, but a second look showed the rhythm in the chaos, and the similarities.

"Tumor?" he'd asked Brenda.

She shook her head.

"I don't know what this is," she said, "but he checks out clean as far as that goes. You're probably right about the seizure. He appears to be in a post-seizure state of some kind. Obviously, he was coming out of it when he got here. If we can catch him in one of his special dreams, maybe we can find out more."

Mark had cut his caseload down; he wanted time to study up on this Eddie business. He could make money when he needed it by taking private patients. Staying on at The Hill gave him the hardware he needed to study Eddie Reyes, and the prospect of getting to know this Sara Lipko a little better.

A lot better, Mark thought. He felt a flush at his cheeks, and smiled.

We have, each of us, nothing.
We will give it to each other.

—Carolyn Forché, *The Country Between Us*

EDDIE REYES HAD done everything that Dr. Mark asked, even when it made him sad. Like visiting his mom in that cold room. They couldn't close her mouth very well without her lips, but they covered her hands with a blanket so no one could see that they were gone. Somebody had set some flowers by her head, the tall, blue kind that she liked. She lay inside a box with a lid, and Eddie cried to think that they would shut that lid down on her face. He hated being shut inside dark places alone, something that his grandparents did to him almost every day.

"We can't afford somebody to watch you," his grandmother had told him, "and we can't have you wandering the streets. If you tell anybody, they'll take you away and put you in jail. Then you'll be locked up all the time."

He never told anyone, not even Dr. Mark.

His grandparents took him to Dr. Jacobs' office, and there his grandmother brought out a little blue box from her bag and she set it on the desk.

"What's that?" Eddie asked.

She had said it was his mother in there.

"How did they get her in there?" Eddie asked.

"You wouldn't understand, Eddie," his grandfather said.

"But . . . how did they do it?"

He imagined that she'd been miniaturized, like a doll, and

laid inside. But then his grandmother opened the lid and he saw the gray pile of dust inside.

"Your mom was cremated," Dr. Jacobs told him. "Do you know what that means?"

Eddie shook his head.

"It means . . . it means that instead of putting her body into the ground in a box, her body was burned and the ashes are put into a box. . . ."

Eddie jumped up and started to cry. He saw his grandfather through his tears, ran over to him and pounded his fists into his grandfather's legs.

"You let them burn her!" he sobbed. "You let them burn her up!"

After that, Eddie became even more quiet and withdrawn. He visited Dr. Mark at The Hill three times a week until school started, then just on Saturdays for the rest of the year. He got to go to his first year of school in town, but he didn't remember much of it.

Dr. Mark tried a lot of medicines to stop the dreams that year. Most of the time Eddie didn't dream at all. He only missed the dreams about Rafferty, and sometimes caught a glimpse of him anyway.

Some of the medicines made him hurry all the time, and his heart beat really fast. Most of them made him forget things, like school. It didn't seem long to him at all before his birthday came around again. His grandparents promised him a trip to an uncle's place in Montana, if Dr. Mark would let him go.

A pretty woman who worked on The Hill, Miss Sara, became his friend at the end of the year, and Eddie looked forward to seeing her. She smelled good, and hugged him a lot, and usually gave him presents even though Eddie knew that Dr. Mark told her not to. Sara gave him a book on bugs, with color pictures, because of the earthquake dream he had about Rafferty. And she gave him a silver pin with a hook-nosed, smiling face on it like the ones he drew from the stone figures in his dreams.

Every time he told Dr. Mark about seeing Rafferty, Eddie got a new medicine. Eddie didn't like taking them because they reminded him of his mother's back medicine. One of them, a blue pill like his mother's, made him tired and made the days go fast, but it stopped the dreams.

As soon as he got to Montana that summer, the dreams came back but they didn't come as often, and they had blank spots. It was Montana where he learned that he could learn through other people's dreams. He worked hard at learning through dreams;

that way when he went back to school he would be really smart and people would like him.

Eddie quit taking the medicines because he wanted Rafferty back. The dreams through the butterfly wings were so different from regular dreams. Regular dreams didn't have the same people in them, people that you got to know and like. Eddie liked Rafferty a lot, and tried to dream him up whenever he could. Trying didn't seem to help. He felt like Rafferty dreamed him up, too, and it made Eddie feel like he had a brother somewhere.

Eddie's aunt read books about children with imaginary friends, and told Eddie it wasn't healthy at his age. He was afraid they would give him more medicine, and it wasn't something he could explain, so he quit talking about it altogether.

By the time he left Montana five years later, there were two girls who moved in and out of the dreams with Rafferty. Eddie didn't focus them as well as he did Rafferty. One was a friend of Rafferty's, who was also the same age as Eddie. The other was a shadow with Afriqua Lee, and he never saw her clearly. It wasn't until sixth grade that he found out why.

Eddie's grandparents both died while he lived in Montana, so when his uncle sent him back to the valley, Eddie moved in with Uncle Bert, his mother's youngest brother, who was single. He lived in a cabin on the shores of Lake Kapowsin, and wasn't home very much.

Eddie liked the lake, the cabin and the privacy. There weren't many families nearby, but splitting wood for the stove kept him busy, and he fished the lake a lot.

Eddie waited for his bus on the first day of sixth grade, hoping that the valley had forgotten him. For five years his grandparents had sent him to a Catholic school near his uncle in Montana. He had missed the special dreams that came so easily in the valley, and now he had them back. He found it harder and harder to live outside them. He liked Rafferty, and he was afraid that if the dreams stopped, then Rafferty would die.

It was as though Rafferty made him dream, whether he wanted to or not. Sometimes Eddie felt that Rafferty broke in on his sleep so that Eddie would get him out of some scrape. Like the time with the raiders, when Eddie saw them coming and Rafferty didn't. But that time Eddie got sick from the dream, sicker than usual. He slept for three days afterward, and it was hard for him to concentrate for a week through the splitting headache.

Eddie was sure he wouldn't want to live in Rafferty's world.

It was a hard life, harder than Montana. Even his dreaming hadn't changed that. Eddie barely remembered when he used to dream other dreams. Those were dreams that he could change. If he was going to fall off a cliff, he could just dream himself into a parachute and glide down. But these dreams of Rafferty were different, very different.

When his grandparents died and Eddie was returned to his uncle Bert in the valley, Eddie was afraid of public school. He'd heard stories from the Catholic school kids about how tough it was, and he couldn't really remember anything from that first-grade year except Dr. Mark and Miss Sara.

The nuns in Montana warned Eddie about how much trouble there was in public schools because of girls and knives. Eddie liked living in his uncle's cabin and he didn't want some public-school trouble to ruin it.

He and a half-dozen other kids waited beside the gravel road for their bus. The dark-haired girl's feet crunched the gravel hard, skipping towards him. She seemed skittery, too. Uncle Bert's early-morning coffee had left Eddie skittery as a bat. Not a familiar face at his bus stop, except there was something about this girl. . . . She reminded him of someone he'd seen in his dreams. Whenever Eddie remembered this day and the girl's footsteps, he knew that she'd walked towards him all his life.

The two of them stood out of time like the eye of a storm. Their ride on the bus, the school, the ride back, were all part of a long white shaft of noiseless space that lifted him and the dark-eyed girl in one slow whirl of light.

Her hair swirled out from her face as she balanced on the back of the bus-stop bench. She danced in a crazy circle faster, faster, until that split-second between balance and balance lost, when she dropped, petal-like, to the gravel right in front of him. The quick lift of her chin and nose dared him to say something. She studied him as closely as he studied her.

She kept her mouth shut. She shook her head and her hands against the early morning chill. This fall day felt more like summer except that the air crackled something like the girl's new leather soles on the gravel. Their bus turned the corner from the levee road and everyone but Eddie and the girl hurried to line up, boys on one side, girls on the other.

The bus hissed and crunched to a stop in front of the line of boys. Its door flopped open and the girl elbowed to the head of the line and stepped aboard, smooth as a swan.

"Maryellen Thompkins," a boy behind him mumbled, and spat. "What a bitch."

She stood in the back of the bus in the center of the aisle.

Eddie found an empty seat just behind the driver. Before he sat he looked full into her eyes. The bus driver told her, without turning around, "Siddown."

Maryellen swayed up the aisle as the bus pulled away, and she dropped into the seat next to Eddie. Neither of them spoke. He blushed when she gave the driver the finger behind his head, where everyone but the driver could see. Her slim dark blur faced straight ahead all the way to school, and all the way to school Eddie fought against Rafferty's pull into dream.

This presence that was Maryellen Thompkins felt good next to him. She felt familiar, in the same way that his skin felt familiar. She definitely reminded him of someone from his dreams, and the way she assessed him with her sidelong glances made him think that she recognized him, too.

That's too weird, he thought. *That's too weird, even for me.*

In class, after roll call, each person had to introduce themselves and tell what they did last summer. When his turn came, Eddie's muscles tightened up in fear and he couldn't turn his neck. Words staggered out of him and he felt like a snowshoe rabbit caught in an early brown thaw.

". . . Lodge Grass, Montana. It's on the Crow reservation. . . ."

Someone made a cawing noise in the back and Eddie flushed. The teacher shushed the culprit.

"Go on, Eddie. Class, pay attention."

"I helped my uncle work the reservation cattle. A kid named Gene Left Hand showed me how to bring in calves so the men could brand them. They used a Lazy-Eight brand. That's a figure-eight laying on its side."

Maryellen Thompkins' eyes snapped open suddenly. Her gaze locked on his and she sat way back in her seat, almost like she was pushing her desk between them. It was a test. The part about the reservation brand was a joke—it was really the Lazy-C—but the brand he'd seen in his dreams was the Lazy-Eight. Eddie's mouth was suddenly dry, but he went on, never dropping his gaze from hers.

"A creek cut through the back country, so we took packs and fish poles and sometimes spent the night. We fished all afternoon while everybody else rode back in. Talked about what we're going to do. He's going to ride rodeo."

Eddie glanced at the teacher to see whether he'd said enough. When he looked back at Maryellen she was facing the window more than the front of the room, but he caught another glance she threw his way.

"I hope that I can go back next summer," he said, and sat down.

As the next student walked to the front of the room, Eddie watched a pair of robins listening for worms on the lawn. He thought back on summer, on all the things he'd like to have told the class but didn't—all those things he'd like to tell the girl with the powerful eyes. The familiarity he felt with her scared him. The Lazy-Eight test scared him, too, but he was excited at the same time.

What if it's true? he wondered. *What if it's a place we both go?*

He thought then of the shadow girl that he'd seen with Afriqua Lee, and the hair on the back of his neck prickled his collar.

As a skinny little kid named Dwight stuttered through his summer, Eddie remembered the day he left his uncle Elmer's place on the reservation, when the dull bite of autumn slipped into the morning breeze. Near the road a light coat of dew held the earth firmly to the earth. Haze around the cottonwoods glowed a magic pink when the sun first touched it; then it faded slowly into blue as the day opened up.

The road in front of Left Hand's place was made a road by its name. It limped through the low grasslands near the river and reminded the few distant families that there was another world somewhere. Those who left for it were quick to return, or die. Those who returned did so quietly, and spoke of the outside seldom, and worked very hard in the dirt.

Some carried things back. Eddie's uncle Elmer brought some bright-colored paintings of tigers and matadors, but they cracked under the harsh Montana summer. Left Hand's uncle brought a car, but there were no gas stations for nearly a day's drive, so now it was just another chicken coop in somebody's field. One brought a case of bourbon and drowned in Left Hand's cistern.

Eddie stood still that last morning, watching a colony of red ants, then the hunting spiral of a young hawk. The dew lifted from the roadside and a slight northerly breeze kept the ants busy opening and reopening their hole.

Maybe they burrow down to the other world, he thought, though he knew it wasn't true.

Eddie worried about the other world, about Rafferty. He'd begun to think of the dark boy in his dreams as his twin and looked forward to meeting him there. Eddie was sure that Rafferty couldn't see him all that well, but he seemed to know when Eddie was around.

It works both ways, he thought. *I see him clear when I'm dreaming, but he's just a shadow when I'm awake.*

But it was a shadow he always recognized.

Eddie shuddered when he thought of the brands that he'd seen on the people in his dreams—on Verna, Henry and the others. A brand in Montana meant something—it meant the cow belonged to somebody.

Who thinks they own those people? he wondered. *Why would somebody let themselves be branded?*

Eddie had seen his share of branding in the past few months. He would not miss branding calves, but he would miss the excitement of it and the teamwork with the men. Castrated, inoculated and branded, the calves wobbled to their mothers, smelling of shit and burned hair. The laughing and swearing men had already wrestled the next one down. At the end of the day they drank and played cards, and sometimes they let Eddie and Gene play, too.

Sometimes when they branded rangeland cattle they carried several brands, one for each owner. They marked the calves with the brand of the mother, and Eddie's uncle, the foreman, kept a tally. His uncle Elmer didn't like this kind of work because there was the inevitable argument with ranchers over his honesty. Eddie's uncle made it a point to have at least one hand from each ranch hired on, but there was always one rancher who thought he was being rustled.

Eddie wondered about the men who owned the brands, who had other men burn their signatures into the flanks of bawling calves with red-hot irons. He only saw the men whose muscle did the job; he never met the ranchers. He decided early that, given the choice, he'd own the brand rather than do the branding.

Later, enlightened by his dreams of Rafferty, the Roam and the Lazy-Eight, the thought of any kind of branding disgusted him. He toed a little more dirt over the ant-hole while he waited for the bus that would take him back to the coast, back to the valley and public school.

The store farther down the road stood on the hill like a shoebox on a boulder. Onion-white and peeling, the front of the store was cluttered with hand-lettered ads and rodeo flyers. He and Gene walked up to it one day with their packsack full of empty bottles to trade for some sodas. The owner, a fat man with fish-belly skin pooching out from under his T-shirt, made them wait outside until he finished his newspaper. Then, he made them wait until he finished his lunch.

This was the summer he was to learn how to wait, how to hold time like his breath, and focus on ants or hawks or a thin swirl of dust covering his boot grain by grain. It was the summer he learned how to learn through dreams. He could visit the dreamways just about any time now, and if he wanted to pay the price, he could make changes in Rafferty's world. He wondered if that worked both ways. If Gene wasn't there to wait with him, Eddie always had his dreams.

When the wait at the store was over, Gene bought a cream soda and Eddie got a strawberry pop. He remembered that the owner brought the sodas out from inside the store, and they were warm.

"If you want, you can sit at our table."

The small, thin voice brought Eddie back to the classroom. The introductions were over. Either he'd missed Maryellen's or she hadn't given one.

"We usually sit by the window. My name's Larry."

Larry shook his hand formally and Eddie noticed that he had warts on his fingers. While they waited the last few minutes for the bell, Larry picked at his warts and stared across the room at Maryellen. She didn't look back, and for some reason this made Eddie feel better.

The cafeteria was the usual clatter of kids and food. Eddie unwrapped his lunch; the others filed slowly through the line.

"I hear you ride the same bus as Maryellen Thompkins."

The name was a branded calf bawling through his daydream.

"So?"

Larry frowned and picked at his warts. Then he asked quickly, "You ever been in a fight? I mean a *real* fight where one guy gets the other guy down and don't let him up, and keeps kicking him in the back and ribs."

"No," Eddie lied, "guess I never have."

"I have," Larry said. "The day I came to this town Maryellen Thompkins kicked me around on the playground at first recess.

There's always fights when she's around. We were only in the fourth grade then, but she was a lot bigger'n me."

Eddie turned his head away slowly, towards the bank of windows facing the tetherball court. Maryellen was alone out there, snapping the ball high and quick around the pole. The more Larry talked, the more Eddie could see why she did it.

"She's crazier'n a shithouse rat," Larry said. "You could whip her, I know you could."

"You don't know anything about me."

"I know she didn't shove you around at the bus stop. I have friends. I know she sat next to a boy instead of by herself for the first time since I been to this place. I know you lived on Loony Hill and you lied to me about fighting."

Larry snatched up his tray and took it back to the kitchen. The bell rang.

A gray sky pressed down on the playground until the pavement, the squat and squinty classrooms and the sky flowed together in one smooth sweep of low clouds and dust. The rest of the day circled tighter towards center, a slow-moving tetherball in a chill gray dream.

Larry took Eddie through the boiler room and into a small closetlike room in the back. Inside the closet there were three folding chairs, a makeshift table that dropped out from the wall like the bed that he shared with his cousin in Montana, a one-burner hot plate and a janitor. The janitor's back was to them as they walked up to the room, and he was emptying the last of the coffee from a camp-sized pot.

Without looking up the old man said, "Who's your friend?"

"New kid. Eddie, this here's my grandpa."

"Get the boy a cup."

It smelled strong and thick, so Eddie filled his coffee half full of cream and sugar, sipped it carefully.

"You boys supposed to be in class."

"We got out. I'm showing him the school."

The old man leaned in his chair and farted, poured most of his coffee into his saucer and drank off the top with a shrug.

The tetherball of the day wound tight against the pole, and Maryellen Thompkins sat next to him again all the way home. Bounces and rattles slewed the bus past tenements, cheap ranch-style developments and finally into the grid of barbed wire that marked, one by one, the straggly farms of the river bottom.

The only sound Maryellen made was clearing her throat occasionally, and she grunted once as the bus passed a Labrador on the back of a German shepherd. He saw no spark or excitement in the shepherd's eyes, only the dull luster of fatigue and need. Just as the bus passed with its forty cheering children, the Lab lunged once and dropped off.

Maryellen looked away as she grunted. Her face, dark and smooth and still, shone clearly against the blurred background of the bus. Eddie turned to look at her and caught a tinge of red that shadowed her high, tight cheeks. She faced him quietly, eyes wide with the sharp sting of fall or confusion. Above the crunch of gravel and rattle of loose sheet metal, they heard the tiny singing of the driver's transistor radio and realized that he and the kids and they themselves were waiting to hear what they had to say.

She slipped forward to the edge of her seat, folded her arms on the back of the seat in front of her and laid her head on her arms. On the back of her right hand, where he'd seen it in his dreams, she had inked an "8" on its side. Eddie swallowed hard. He reached over and traced it with his fingertip, but she didn't move.

The aura of Maryellen's plaid skirt rippled over his gray cords, the little scratching sounds she made amplified a thousand times over the murmur of engine, tires and waves of gray-faced kids. Eddie stared out the window at the damp pastureland. The ever-rising hum of everything drifted him back to his campsite in Montana, and the time he told Left Hand about Rafferty.

"Yes, you will see them," Gene had said.

"Them?" Eddie asked.

"The other side. Shadow-people."

Gene stirred the coals and sat back on his heels. It was a graceful squat that Eddie never mastered. His heart fluttered hard in his throat, and he waited for Gene to go on.

"Others walk beside us. They live and breathe just beside the cloth of this world, but they live in another. Not just one other world, but many others. Like the saddle between you and the horse. My grandfather says they are the worlds that could have been, that we are the world that is. In one of those worlds, Sitting Bull was President, maybe.

"Sometimes, when we're near worn spots in the cloth, we see the other side, and the other side sees us. Sometimes, they cross over, slip through."

"Can you talk to them?"

"I have heard that you can; I have heard that you can't."

"How do you know it's not a dream?"

"Because sometimes it happens when you're awake, right? And you *feel* different. . . ."

"Then you've seen it . . . you know what I mean?"

Gene shook his head and tossed a handful of green sticks on the fire. A thick, sweet smoke rose between them.

"I have not seen it, but I know what you mean," Gene said. "I know it scares the bejeezus out of the old guys. The Cheyenne guys say the first seven people crawled here through a log. The Navajo say we crawled from a hole in the ground. What's so mysterious about a hole in space?"

That which is fallow will one day be fertile again, and that which is valueless will grow to be priceless. Sooner or later you will dream a new dream and we will return to have our sport within it.

—Lucius Shepard, *Life During Wartime*

WHEN EDDIE RETURNED to his care after nearly six years in Montana, Mark dug deeper into the boy's family. Everything that he found pointed to a pattern of neglect that went back several generations. Inquiries about Eddie's father raised more questions than they answered.

Eddie had been told that his father had been hit by a jeep. This was the story that Mark had heard from Mrs. Wanden, the grandmother, the first time she'd brought Eddie to see him. She hadn't believed the story, and preferred to believe the rumor that he'd been killed in a tavern brawl.

Mark called Eddie's uncle, but Bert said he'd never seen the body and Marco Reyes was too crooked to die.

"He could con Death out of his robes, if you know what I mean."

The stone in the valley cemetery divulged his name, rank and serial number without elaboration.

Mark sent to the Army for a death certificate and files for one Lieutenant Marco I. Reyes. What he got back was a skeleton of a file that should have been as thick as the Bible. The file was remarkable for lack of information on Lieutenant Reyes, but it did list the cause of death as massive trauma secondary to being struck by an unmanned jeep. The death of Lieutenant Marco I. Reyes under a runaway jeep was dated three months before the war ended, which was, by coincidence, Eddie Reyes's birthday.

The file, thin though it was, still revealed that the lieutenant had not been a model soldier. He had received a hasty commission in that early-wartime shuffle that quickly promoted personnel who happened to be on active duty before the war broke out. He had half a hitch in by that time.

Since he spoke Spanish he had been shipped immediately to the Philippines as a member of a hush-hush Strategic Forces Organizational Unit. He was reprimanded eleven times for fraternizing with local women, which, Mark inferred from the convoluted reports, was Army lingo for pimping.

In under two years in the Philippines he had created an empire by trading protection, favors, weapons and supplies. Nothing was too big for Lieutenant Reyes to steal or to have stolen, including two thirty-foot dockside cranes complete with their tracks, trailers and the trucks to pull them. This latter had been accomplished through collusion with a Navy requisitions officer who, unfortunately for Lieutenant Reyes, had been under investigation for relatively unimaginative pilfering from supply ships. Reyes pilfered entire ships.

Once the investigation branched out to 'the Reyes operation,' nasty things began happening to investigators. They proved remarkably vulnerable to snipers, mines and 'disappearance at the hands of person or persons unknown.' Lieutenant Reyes was twice remanded to custody in the States for court-martial, and twice he received a stunning defense and was returned to active duty.

It was while on leave, pending reassignment after his second trial, that he met Eddie's mother. By Mark's arithmetic, Eddie had been conceived within the first days of their meeting. Their entire relationship had lasted two weeks; there was no evidence that they had ever legally married. Letters from Eddie's mother were not in his chart but were noted as being on file with other 'classified materials.'

Though not married, Lieutenant Reyes listed Eddie's mother and Eddie as dependents in his papers, as well as Eddie's uncle Bert.

Mark knew for a fact that no one had received his insurance, and there was no provision for its disposition in the papers he held.

Marriage doesn't matter, he thought. *They send the insurance to the name on the form, regardless.*

It was interesting to note that the lieutenant had suffered from a sleep disorder that had been noted early on in basic training. He often talked in his sleep, and had been reprimanded for oversleeping. On five occasions he had been sent to the dispensary, for disorientation, headaches and nausea after an oversleeping episode. He was judged fit for duty after each of these incidents.

The chart was a sketch, and Mark felt equal measures of fear and excitement as he read it. Nearly everyone in the psychiatric service had had a crack at Lieutenant Reyes, and no two diagnoses were quite alike. Like Mark's own assessment of Eddie Reyes, bets were hedged on every page, and it was clear that a good measure of treatment had actually aggravated the man's condition.

Depending on which doctor was to be believed, the lieutenant suffered from severe catatonia, narcolepsy, catalepsy, organic brain syndrome, schizophrenia, atypical seizure disorder or multiple personality disorder. The latter three, Mark knew, had been entered in Eddie's chart at one time or another in his own hand.

Lieutenant Reyes served as a bombardier in the Army Air Corps with the sixty-two missions that the boy remembered from the photograph.

And he still had time for his scams, Mark thought.

Lieutenant Reyes had been a spoiler all his life. If he couldn't win a race himself, he tripped others. Mark found himself relieved that the man was dead. He might've made an interesting subject, but at what cost?

Meanwhile, Mark was astounded at his reassessment of Eddie's intellect. The boy who had come to see him years ago had been a troubled six-year-old with the reading ability of an eight-year-old and an intelligence that tested within the range of high-normal. The boy who came back from Montana sent every graph off the scale.

He mulled over the matter aloud while Sara prepared her slide show for the American Association of University Women's annual banquet.

"Nobody gets *more* intelligent," he told Sara. "You can learn more information, but that doesn't make you more intelligent. Intelligence is a measure of the uses you make of information, not its quantity."

"Maybe there was something wrong with the first tests he took," she said. "He always seemed bright to me."

"Bright, yes, but not a genius by a long shot. And he goes to great pains to hide this intelligence, like he's ashamed of it. . . ."

"You know how kids are," she said. "He already gets harassed because of that business with his mother. If he's too bright at school, then he's *really* a geek."

"I don't know," Mark mulled. "Something feels wrong about this . . . eerie, even."

Sara set down the stack of slides she was sorting and shut off the viewer.

"What makes it 'eerie'?"

Mark cleared his throat and rubbed the back of his neck.

"Eddie claims he can learn through dreams," Mark said.

Sara shrugged.

"What's so remarkable about that? Those sleep-teaching experiments proved there was something to it. You can buy tapes now that . . ."

Mark waved off the possibility.

"It's not like that," he said. "He claims he learns by dreaming other people's dreams. He goes to sleep, starts to dream and somehow gets onto something he calls 'the dreamways.' When he's there, he contacts other dreams, follows them to the dreamer, and sorts through their brains like they're a library."

Sara laughed, then frowned and plucked at her lower lip.

"You're serious," she said. "Do you believe this?"

"I believe that he didn't just *become* more intelligent. I believe the tests were valid and administered correctly. I'm entertaining suggestions. Do you have any?"

After a moment she smiled.

"Yes," she said. "I get along well with him. He reads voraciously but he tries hard to talk like the rest of the kids . . . to blend in, be normal. Maybe if there were some way he could just . . . *talk*."

"He talks to me. At least once a week."

"I don't mean that," she said. "Talking with you or talking with the other kids, that's just a matter of coloration for a chameleon. I'd have him do what I make my writing students do. Keep a journal. Write down everything, especially dreams."

Mark shook his head.

"I don't think that would work," he said. "Eddie's getting so he doesn't want to talk about dreams anymore."

"All the more reason to write them," she said. "Besides, it's not like you to assume something won't work without trying it out. What have you or Eddie got to lose?"

Mark felt himself flush, and he smiled.

"You're right," he said. "Touché. Whatever's happening here, Eddie's the only one who can clear it up."

Adolescence

As we will never know what it means,
we will know what it cost.

—Carolyn Forché, *Gathering the Tribes*

THE LURCHING OF the rattletrap school bus aggravated the waves of cramps tightening Maryellen's belly. She slipped forward, folded her arms on the back of the seat in front of her and laid her head on her arms. From that angle, the pressure on her lower back let up and her cramps receded into twinges. Past the new boy, out the windows, the valley's brown fields ticked by, interspersed with swatches of evergreens.

Maryellen wanted to savor this Eddie Reyes. Not only was he different from other boys, he was different from other *people*. When he traced the Lazy-Eight on the back of her hand, she felt a relief like she'd never known. She felt safe, at home. Maryellen knew he knew about the dream world. How else would he know the Lazy-Eight brand? And why else watch her so intently when he spoke of it?

Maybe I'm not crazy, Maryellen thought. *Maybe I'm not crazy, after all.*

In the first moment she saw him at the bus stop, she recognized him. She didn't recognize him feature-by-feature; it was more of a connection through the eyes, a feeling that suddenly the two of them were specimens in the same jar.

Maryellen unfocused herself, and the bus melted into the up-and-down blur of a merry-go-round. To dull the persistent cramps, she replayed last night's dream of Afriqua Lee.

In the dream it had been early morning, and a fresh trickle of sun sifted through mist, the dusty window and Afriqua Lee's half-closed eyelids. The girl held them barely open to the light and made prisms out of her lashes. A pair of nightstalkers rattled around on the roof over her head, then screeched off to a nearby limb and were gone.

A snore, thick with age, rose from the hammock below her bed in the loft. Afriqua Lee pushed back her bright blankets to feel the refreshing chill of the northern reaches. She whiffed the return of greenery, fresh in the morning and fresh in the deeper shadows of the trees. The girl was surprised that Old Cristina still snored down below.

Sometimes Afriqua Lee would startle herself awake out of a sudden dream of the girl Maryellen, and then she would hear Old Cristina and her surreptitious sip of cold coffee from the glass.

The old woman always woke at dawn, and after cold coffee she'd walk the kilometer or so down to the river. There she sang the ritual welcome to the sun and smoked her one cigarette of the day. She emptied her ancient fishtraps—a joke among the young men—then lumbered back to fry her catch in meal. Even in the aftermath of the plague of bugs, her traps always caught fish. She cooked flatbreads beside them in the light-pocket, and by this time every morning their tent steamed up with the makings of coffee and hot, fresh fish.

The girl usually woke up when the old woman switched on the heat—it gave off a vibration that she enjoyed against her back. She stayed huddled and warm inside her covers until Old Cristina called her down. She enjoyed the waking part of the day, the threadlike connection to the world of her dreams and her dreamer, this Maryellen Thompkins.

But this morning Afriqua Lee woke first and something pulled her to go somewhere alone. Raiders still plied the scrub woods in these parts; she herself had seen what they could do. A girl her age had been peeled faceless by them, in an attempt to find her father. Afriqua Lee shut out the image. She smoothed her bedding and opened the skylight.

She crawled out onto the roof of the van. A damp chill started her skin shivering and she thought of going back inside for a coat. Her coat hung at the head of Old Cristina's hammock, so she rubbed her arms and hands instead and slid carefully down the cab to the ground.

She slipped behind the morning watch and neutralized the

alarms the way Rafferty had shown her. She walked up the road, away from the river, and warmed up right away.

The few weeds reclaiming the middle of the road hung their wet heads, heavy with dew, but she walked through them anyway so that she could keep the sun on her back. The years of barrenness after the hatch left her with an appreciation for anything green-growing, even weeds. Old Cristina claimed that now there was no such thing as a weed; anything that grew was a flower.

A trail cut off the road and wound back through the trees to a large, clump-grass clearing. Someone, years ago, planted apple trees in the clearing, most of them on top of a small rise that rolled up from the scrub alder at the bottom to a stand of young fir at the top. When she was younger she came to this place to climb the apple trees while her mother picked berries in the thicket at the bottom of the hill. In the fall, for many years, old-timers of the Roam hunted what game they could find in that old orchard. It was the only orchard for a hundred klicks to survive the plague of wings, though it suffered mightily.

Afriqua Lee came out of the scrub at the end of the trail where the sun had already lifted the dampness from the sparse grass. It would be a hot afternoon, hot enough that the idea of ritual laundry in the creek sounded good to her. She preferred fishing, but that was the old women's specialty.

The shady walk down the trail and through the wet brush exaggerated the heat of the morning sun. She slipped her heavy blouse and undershirt off over her head and stepped out of her layers of cotton skirts. She stood there, beside the alders at the foot of the hill, bare except for her cotton underpants. Women of the Roam exposed their breasts at the streamside laundry, but it was the most extreme prikasha to expose their legs. Afriqua Lee's had not tested the air in a good, long time.

It was only then that she felt the beginnings of a warm breeze curl up from the tops of the grasses, up the insides of her legs, up her belly and back and under her arms, tugging at her *here* and *there* until she dropped her underpants and walked most of the way up the rise. She lay back, spread-eagled, on a tiny patch of grass.

Sweat and sweet-grass prickled her skin and set waves of goose bumps rippling out from her clumped nipples, her small breasts, down her belly and thighs and into the summer morning. She slowed her breath, and as she did, she felt her body drip cell by cell into the scraggly comeback of fresh green that hugged the hillside. The deep blur of sky washed into white under her long, eye-watering stare.

She looked backwards, up the hill, at the apple trees above her. Upside-down they looked like roots and clumps of brush growing out of the sky. She imagined herself there as a child, even last summer, climbing in and out of branches, careful not to knock down the tiny apples just starting to swell at the tips of things.

For six years after the hatch, bad got worse and that thick perfume Death wears graced everybody's noses. They tried to outrun the plagues south, chasing rumors of food, and dodging shadows. That was at first, when there were still rumors and there might have been food, but not enough for a few thousand bellies. Six years after the hatch, the girl Afriqua Lee was twelve, more lithe than skinny, nearly black from the blaze of the southern sun.

What was once grass was trying to be grass again. Mist enrobed and softened the thin, spiky growth. Somewhere a distant bell marked the march of the sun now beginning in the mountains to the east.

Afriqua Lee held her breath again, heard the hollow rattle of an easy breeze through the weeds, the rustle of some small thing making its way through the tangle of sticks and rushes just below her feet, the deep aching pressure of the near side of silence. She thought she heard her name, a girl calling her name, and she sat up quickly, looked around.

Nothing.

She let her breath out slowly, noiselessly, and turned over. She stretched herself full-length on the hillside, arms flung out and her legs spread wide. The momentary tickle of the breeze over her damp back became a sudden, flashing itch that she shuddered off.

She pressed herself into the hill, into grass under grass. Pressed harder. Breasts, belly, thighs, knees, shins, arches of feet, toes. Tufts of grass flicked and burst as they unbent between the insides of her legs; small spears of new grass poked into her straggly triangle of hair. She breathed deep the grass and dirt; hugged the hillside tight, tighter. She felt the small red field ants discover her. One on the back of her left thigh. One, up her armpit, across her shoulder, then down the middle of her back towards her waist.

She turned and sat up. Familiar tensions began their slow seep from somewhere and she rolled down the hillside to the crumpled pile of clothes under the alders.

Maryellen Thompkins woke up in a start with a lurch of the bus. She leaned forward and pressed her forehead against the seat in front of them, not wanting Eddie to see the pain in her eyes. Though his eyes were closed she had memorized their color, a deep, deep blue.

The bus was nearly empty now. The half-dozen older kids were quiet for a change. Just a few second- and third-graders jabbered in the back. Her eyelids slipped closed again.

"You all right?" she heard Eddie ask.

She squinched her eyelids tight and didn't answer.

"You want me to walk you home?"

A tear filled the corner of one eye, then dripped across her nose. Another. She leaned against him slowly as the bus eased into their stop. Face down on his shoulder, she cried one hard, reluctant sob. As the doors slapped open she brushed a quick kiss against his neck.

"Meet you at the Lazy-Eight," she whispered.

To enter into the fabulous times, it is necessary to be serious like a dreaming child.

—**Gaston Bachelard,** *The Poetics of Reverie*

AS MARYELLEN STUMBLED down the steps and across the road, a dab of tear cooled under Eddie's jaw.

"Hey, Romeo, this your stop, too?"

Eddie looked at the driver for sign of an insult. No, the man only wanted to get home. So did Maryellen. And so did he.

The walk home, skirting the woods, felt a lot lighter than his walk to school.

I'm not crazy! he thought. *There's really another side!*

What excited him most was Maryellen herself, someone from the dreamways who actually had flesh and blood. One of Larry's rumors had been that both Maryellen and Eddie had tested so high that the school was considering moving them up at least one grade before the year got too far along. Whatever happened, he knew he didn't ever want to lose sight of her again.

During the walk home, Eddie felt as afraid as he felt excited. He didn't want to talk with his uncle, or with anyone but Maryellen Thompkins. His uncle didn't have a phone at the cabin, so talking would have to wait. And it would have to be very private. He was glad that his uncle's truck was gone from the driveway.

Eddie read his uncle's scrawl across the bag on the kitchen table: "Driving the Bakersfield run, back Thursday."

Eddie flopped atop his mattress and, after the usual dive through the flickering wings of the blue butterfly, he launched into his first face-to-face dream of Rafferty.

Eddie met Rafferty standing in the fork in a dirt road. The blue dreamway light was fading and the black spots cleared from Eddie's vision. Behind Rafferty, the left fork of the road led into the rockiest reaches of the mountain Roam. The right fork wound down to a lush valley, warmer than Eddie's, greener.

The landscape down the left fork had been stripped barren and blown clean to the surface of the stone. The hardiest straggly clumps of grass and a few gnarls of brush survived.

Upon the stone were the hook-nosed, large-lipped carvings of the priests of the ancient Roam. Hieroglyphs and finely etched renderings of animals surrounded them. Most prominent of these, and most often repeated, was the unmistakable snarl of a jaguar.

A barely discernible track led back to Rafferty's home. His faint footprints whisked off in a gust of wind.

We must be dreaming at the same time, Eddie reasoned. *Cool!*

Eddie heard the low chatter of Ruckus somewhere nearby, giving Rafferty the 'all clear.'

"We're both going to be sick tomorrow, you know," Rafferty said. He wore his best ceremonial regalia, complete with braided hat, jade ear-lobe plugs and embroidered tunic. His black trousers reached just below the knee, and a matching strip of bright embroidery decorated the outside of each leg. Eddie knew that each embroidery had significance to the Roam, but he didn't know what that significance was.

He did know that the outfit, and the dignity with which Rafferty wore it, made the boy look much older than his twelve years. Without the hat, Rafferty would be slightly shorter than Eddie, but the hat and his proud posture raised him up.

"It's worth it," Eddie said. "I've been sick for a lot less—like my algebra test."

Eddie reached out to shake hands with Rafferty.

He froze when he saw the pistol in Rafferty's hand—but Rafferty just laughed and gave it a spin. It flopped to the ground at their feet, a shuddering, silver fish. Rafferty tossed it to Eddie and it became a black rabbit that scrambled into the roadside brush. They both laughed.

"If we can do that in dreams," Rafferty said, "I believe we can learn how to do it for real."

"You're a freak on your side, too, huh?"

Rafferty laughed.

"Yes," he said, "a freak. There's talk about a trial, a kris romani. Some of the elders are afraid of us. We have had to take great care with the dreaming." He shrugged. "What matters is, we found each other!"

Rafferty silenced himself and stepped up to Eddie. This time it was Rafferty who offered his hand.

"I hoped to find you, someday," he announced. "To be sure that you're real."

Eddie shook it. A white shimmer pulsed from their grip, but the grip was warm.

"And you're real," Eddie said, "it's true. You're alive over there."

"Barely," Rafferty said, and laughed. "It's that kind of time."

"Isn't it amazing how much we look alike?" Eddie asked.

The two boys stood in the roadway for a moment and studied each other.

They shared the same dark hair and dark skin, the same dramatically blue eyes. They had mirror-image, lopsided smiles. Eddie's hair was shorter but as he watched Rafferty's shoulder-length hair, it shrank back to match his own. With a wink, he grew it back.

Eddie looked down at his sneakers and jeans. By willing it to be so, he exchanged them for beaded buckskins and white moose-hide moccasins, like he had seen at Gene's grandfather's house in Montana. His jacket was buckskin, too, with fringe at the elbows and the elaborate beadwork of the ghost-dance days. He left his head bare because he liked the feel of the sun on it.

"Is that what you *really* look like?" Eddie asked, "or is this what we make up for the dreamworld?"

"I'm not sure," Rafferty said. "Maybe we are monsters to the other. Maybe our minds make everything into something we can understand. I know that happens when I dream inside a language I do not speak. I think we just dream the *feeling* of the other person, and our minds fill in the pictures."

"They sure do a heckuva job."

"We're exceptional, you know."

Eddie laughed.

"Yeah, exceptionally loony. They lock me up for this stuff. Dr. Mark called you my 'imaginary playmate.' He said that most people stop seeing them when they start school. I'm abnormal."

"Be careful," Rafferty said. "We can make other people abnormal . . . by accident. By taking things out of them . . ."

"I . . . thought so," Eddie said. "Have you ever been inside my head? I mean, other places than the dreams?"

"No," Rafferty said, and his voice held the abrupt tone of honor affronted. "You?"

"No. Sometimes with other people, not with you. It didn't seem right, you know, like going through your stuff or something."

"You've paid the price for visiting before, haven't you?"

"Yes," Eddie nodded. "But only when I've made something happen, or tried to. One time I stopped three guys from grabbing you in a dream. It must have worked, but I was sick for a couple of days. Do you know what we can do and what we can't?"

"No." Rafferty shook his head and toed the dirt.

He reminded Eddie of himself, waiting for the bus at the roadside in Montana.

"I hoped that if we were both dreaming at the same time . . . that would be how we would meet," Rafferty said. "But I didn't know when you'd be dreaming. So I tried to remember all the times I've seen you and tried to match up. Today I started extra early. It worked just in time. I was ready to quit."

"Have you met others?"

Rafferty pulled at his lower lip, checked over his shoulder.

"Not this way. There's another shadow, a girl from your side. . . ."

"Maryellen Thompkins!" Eddie said. "I just found her. . . ."

"Yes, she is a dream of my friend Afriqua Lee. And there is someone else."

"Who?"

"The Jaguar," Rafferty said. "He is a great torment to our side. Old-timers believe he comes from your side, and now I believe it, too. He has to be from your side, because he can't be found here. Uncle thought it was a game; he's dreaming and doesn't know what it's doing to us. Maybe he doesn't believe we're real. . . ."

"Do you think we could find him?"

"We found each other."

Eddie clapped Rafferty on the shoulder.

"*You* found *me*, friend," Eddie said, and an urgency prodded at him. "I've been playing around with my grade point while you've been working."

"We need a sign," Rafferty said. "Something that is ours alone."

"I know some great codes," Eddie said. "We can set up a contact system. I met the girl on my side; I'll talk to her."

"Not a code," Rafferty said. "We need something simple. The Jaguar has his brand. It's a sign, and the sign is a key. We need our own sign."

"How about a square?" Eddie asked. "There are four of us, one to a side. . . ."

"Good," Rafferty agreed, "that's good. But if the Jaguar finds out, it's as good as his brand."

"We're a step ahead. We have our square and his brand, too. We can unlock his locks, but he can't get into ours."

"Don't be so sure," Rafferty warned. "He's been at this longer than we have."

A chill passed over Eddie, then another. He had the sudden feeling of something . . . sniffing. He saw Rafferty shudder, check the path over his shoulder, then shrug.

"Maybe four of us could track down this Jaguar."

"If he doesn't track us down first," Rafferty said. "Remember, the dream road runs two ways, maybe more. You live on his side; I'm sure of it. He doesn't want to foul his nest, so he experiments on us. If I'm right, it's you and the girl he'll go after."

"We'll just have to be careful," Eddie said.

"Very."

Rafferty laughed.

"*Are* there other . . . sides?"

"I'm not sure. . . ."

The light around them began its familiar flicker.

"I've been here too long," Rafferty said. "I can feel it already. The Jaguar's priests hunt us when we dream on this side; we're sure of that, now. We can't spend much time like this, or the Jaguar will find you. I think he knows when we cross the fabric. That's how he killed Afriqua Lee's father."

Eddie was suddenly dead serious. This dream-friendship was real, the bugs were real—the Jaguar might hunt him down, too. . . .

The flicker intensified, and began its fade to blue. Rafferty turned and started down the left-hand fork.

"Wait," Eddie called, pointing to the right. "Go that way. In my dreams, everything turns out okay if I take the *right* path."

Rafferty flashed him a smile and a wave, and was gone.

It was four years before they managed to meet again.

Eddie had dreamed so hard, he missed a day of school and suffered a booming headache. He was so disoriented, he couldn't remember how to make coffee, and his right eye didn't seem to work right. If it weren't for his bladder, he thought sure he wouldn't have come around at all.

. . . the dreams of our childhood . . . vanish from our memory before we were able to learn their language.

—Henry David Thoreau

WHEN EDDIE DIDN'T show up at school, Maryellen sulked all day. Her dreams had been wild, but not dreamway dreams, though they included the Roam. They were jumbled dreams, unfocused and full of fear, and she'd hardly slept all night.

She'd looked for Eddie at the bus stop, and when he wasn't there, a nausea got hold of her that she couldn't shake. It was the fear that he never existed, that she wanted him in her life so bad that she'd made him up, the way she was afraid she'd made up Afriqua Lee.

When Maryellen heard Eddie's name called with the roll, she knew that their meeting had been real. Still, the icy fear that joined the cramps in her belly didn't let up. It became a premonitory dread that dragged at her until recess.

She couldn't bring herself to come in from the playground, though it had been a long time since the games of her classmates had held any interest for her. She liked the tetherball. She could hit it and wind it, hit it and wind it around the pole and never have to talk to anybody.

Her teacher sent the principal out to get her away from the tetherball. By that time, the ball was spattered with blood and Maryellen had no skin on the knuckles of either hand. She couldn't find words when Mr. Hartung ordered her back to class, and she looked down in surprise at her legs that wouldn't move on their own. Without knowing why, she began to sob.

Mr. Hartung carried Maryellen to the nurse's room, which adjoined his office. While the nurse took her temperature and looked into her mouth with a light, the principal called her house. Her stepmother would answer the phone—the woman who now slept in her father's bed, the whiskey woman who dragged her tormentor son into Maryellen's life.

From where she lay on the nurse's cot, Maryellen could hear everything. But it was not her they were talking about. It was a bruised apple, a cracked sidewalk, a stray cat.

"Very well," Mr. Hartung said. "I understand. We will keep her here and let her rest. If you can get out of your meeting . . . Well, yes, but whether it's a bid for attention or not it's clear she needs . . . I see. Yes. We'll keep her here in the nurse's office, then. I think it would be best if she didn't ride the bus home today; she needs . . . Well, Mrs. Thompkins, I don't think today's the day to force her to do anything. She's resting well and . . . That's for you to decide. It is my opinion and the nurse's opinion that someone should pick her up as soon as possible and see her to a doctor. It is my judgment that she should not ride the bus home. She will be waiting for you in the nurse's office. Mrs. Thompkins?"

Maryellen closed her eyes to rest and immediately felt the blue flicker of the dreamways wash over her. She fell into the blue butterfly fluttering on the far wall and landed in the orchard hillside of Afriqua Lee's dreams.

It was bitter cold, and wind whipped the branches around like great skirts. Maryellen shivered involuntarily from the wind chill, though her own body rested in the nurse's room.

A small figure that reminded her of Eddie Reyes ducked into the shadows from the edge of the clearing. Maryellen started to call to him, but the voice that came out of her mouth was not her own. She knew at once it belonged to Afriqua Lee.

That was fast! Maryellen thought.

It was sunset on the other side, and Maryellen saw Afriqua Lee hiding on the hillside behind the cover of an old stump. The man who stepped out of the shadow of the trees seemed to be a piece of shadow that detached itself and floated forward. Maryellen took him for a raider at first, until she saw his Jaguar robe. He had not yet noticed Afriqua Lee.

His hair hung loose, almost to his waist. She had never seen such hair on a man before. A fringed pouch and a long reed hung at his hip. His bowed head was uncovered and his robe tied with a crisscross of leather strips. When he lifted his head Maryellen saw his beard, almost to mid-chest. She had never seen anyone in the Roam wear a beard.

The only sound was the *shuff-shuff* of his wrapped feet through dirt and scrub grass. He tilted his head back like an animal listening or whiffing the wind. He turned a full circle there in the clearing, nodding once at each quarter. When he stopped he faced west, looking directly at the stump that hid Afriqua Lee.

Maryellen trembled on the nurse's cot and drew her knees to her chest.

He knelt, removed the pouch from his waist and emptied it out in front of him. He brushed a flat spot in the grass and sorted out a flat board, an arrow shaft, a pile of small sticks, some dried moss and a knife. The knife blade was black, but it glinted on the last of the light like glass.

Obsidian, she thought. Old Cristina had shown Afriqua Lee some obsidian spear-points that looked just like his knife.

He began to make a fire. He caught the first sparks with his tinder. Behind the shadows there was a pile of dried, twisted branches. He scooped them into his arms and fed his fire, forming a flat-topped pyramid. Light was gone except for the fire.

The priest unhooked his reed. A cat, black as his knife, stepped into the firelight at the edge of the clearing, barely a spit from Afriqua Lee. The stranger's hand raised the reed to his lips, pointed it towards the cat, and puffed. It leapt sideways once, shuddered, then crumpled in its tracks.

He skinned the cat and rolled the hide off the carcass like a stocking, then put it into his pouch. He sectioned the cat into quarters, his knife moving almost by itself. Piece by piece he heated the meat and ate it, arranging the head and innards among the coals. Maryellen was surprised at how good it smelled as it cooked.

When he was done, all she could see were the bones neatly stacked, the skull and the softly glowing coals sputtering out in the clearing. He stood, still facing west. It was nearly too dark to see him now. He picked up his pouch, his weapon and his fireboard, and walked back into the shadows at the edge of the trees.

A door slammed, and Maryellen woke to the palsied anger of Olive, her stepmother. She yanked Maryellen from the nurse's cot and pulled her up until their faces met. Olive's breath stank of coffee, stale wine and cigarettes.

"You're doing your best to ruin this marriage, you little shit," she hissed. "You want attention? I'll give you attention."

Maryellen stumbled down the hallway, trying to keep up with Olive, who dragged her by the arm. From the school door to the car, Olive pushed and slapped her all the way. From somewhere deep inside her head, Maryellen heard a snarl.

You can't knit smoke.

The voice was Afriqua Lee's. It sounded more like advice than a warning.

. . . wisdom comes to us when it can no longer do any good.

—Gabriel Garcia Marquez,
Love in the Time of Cholera

RAFFERTY WOKE FROM his dream of Eddie Reyes to find himself bound and blindfolded. White flashes of some inner electricity coursed through his brain in time with his pulse, and his pulse hammered a tremendous spike of pain right between his eyes. He'd seen these flashes before, and felt the spike. Pain was the price he paid for treading the dreamways—pain, weakness, disorientation. . . .

Rafferty tested his bonds to make sure they were real. A blistering pain shot through his right hand. He was bent nearly backwards, his wrists roped to his ankles. The bonds were real.

Who . . . ?

"The little dream-ferret tests our work, Nebaj."

The voice, near Rafferty's head, spoke quietly, slowly with the thick tongue of a spleef-whiffer. Pungent wood smoke aggravated Rafferty's post-dream nausea. When he tried to wriggle away from it, a kick between his shoulder blades paralyzed him and turned the pulse of flashes inside his head into one blinding burst of light.

This time, when he woke up, he remembered the bonds and remembered not to move. This time the air smelled clean and a breeze warmed his exposed skin. Cramps in his back and chest made every breath a torment. This was what was intended by tying him up the way they did. Soon he would cramp enough to stop breathing altogether.

Nebaj, he thought. *Who is Nebaj?*

Someone of the Roam had spoken about a village called Nebaj. It was back in the days when Uncle was alive, one of those evenings around the fire in what had once been the south pasture. The men of the Roam told their stories to ready themselves for sleep. Rafferty, an insatiable listener even as a youngster, sat in rapture every night until Uncle carried the limp child back to the bunks.

One of the men had spoken of his childhood in Nebaj, far to the south. It was a mountain village, where the people wore bright cloth of their own weaving. It was higher than Uncle's place, and people there dedicated themselves to a spirituality that endured even the onslaught of the Jaguar's men. The Jaguar's men had come there to find someone who could interpret dreams, and had carted a score of villagers away. Some said they disappeared into the highland jungles; some said they were taken to the sea. Some whispered of blood sacrifice. The fact remained, none returned. According to the witness, their selection process had been particularly brutal, even for the Jaguar.

"Yes, Nebaj," the voice spoke again. This time it was close to his ear. "He wakes."

A dry, nearly soundless laugh rasped nearby.

A pair of hands grabbed the back of his collar and dragged Rafferty across flat sandstone to position his feet over the edge of a precipice. The hands loosened the bonds at his wrists. Rafferty unkinked himself and sat upright.

"Nebaj knows the pain of the dreamworld," the voice said. "You balance now over a very long drop. Relieve yourself, but make no other move or you will be pushed into the canyon. Make no mistake, Nebaj is practical, not merciful. Here, there is no mercy."

Rafferty did as he was told. As his painfully distended bladder voided its stream, he could not detect the sound of it striking bottom anywhere. The feeling, coupled with the blindfold and the recent journey into dreams, washed him with a sudden vertigo, and he pitched forward with a cry that sounded like something from his crow. He was caught short by the rope, looped at his waist. That same pair of strong hands pulled him back. In that moment, he heard an answering call from Ruckus, somewhere high above.

"Yes, Nebaj knows the waking pains of the dreamworld," the voice chuckled. "Our helpless ferret."

Rafferty's hands were trussed again, but this time they were not pulled tight to his ankles. His right hand throbbed as though all the skin had been scraped from the back of it.

The brand! he realized. *It's the Jaguar's men, and I've got the Lazy-Eight brand.*

A wind chime tinkled nearby.

No one sets up wind chimes in a travel camp, Rafferty thought. *They're confident that they are safe here, and they plan to stay awhile.*

Those hands, neither gentle nor rough, finished with their knots and leaned him against the cool of a rock face. The indentations against his back formed a pattern, a spiral, and he knew he must be in one of the hideaways of the ancient Roam.

From sunshine to shadow, he thought. *Feels like midday. I wonder how long I've . . . slept.*

His head throbbed but the flashes were gone, a good sign. His stomach growled over the nausea and he knew that the ravenous hunger would hit soon—the fierce hunger that attempted to catch his body up with the two- or three-day fast that his dreams had imposed upon it.

A fragrance came to him with the faint residual of wood smoke. The fragrance bloomed in his nostrils and thickened as the breeze died down.

Pom, he thought, *incense of the Jaguar priesthood.*

Rafferty had heard stories from the Roam of the bloodthirsty priests who cut out the hearts of their captives on crude stone altars and ate them raw. Pom was a preliminary to all their rituals, and Rafferty hoped, over the pounding of his pulse in his ears, that he was indeed a ferret unworthy of such high drama.

Other fragrances twined with the pom, herbs that Rafferty didn't recognize. The smoke came to him in little pulses of breeze.

He's fanning this toward me.

Rafferty heard a reassuring squawk from Ruckus, closer this time. The fanning paused, then resumed with the same hypnotic meter. Not only was his headache gone, but the nausea and hunger pangs had left him as well.

The smoke, he thought. *Whatever's in that smoke . . .*

His body felt very, very light. The man who fanned the smoke hummed a tune that Rafferty had never heard. It was a very soothing tune, one that he felt wash over his body like a wave of white light. When the wave broke, Rafferty felt no pain at all, from his bonds or his hand. He felt like a dry leaf floating on a pond of warm, white light.

"It's a trap!"

The sudden voice from the bottom of his mind clearly belonged to Afriqua Lee.

"Do not dream! The Jaguar scouts . . . !"

Rafferty altered his breathing. Where he had relaxed into great, sighing breaths he now let his chin drop to his chest and satisfied himself with the smallest, shallowest breaths he could muster. Soon the fanning came faster, and every muscle in Rafferty's body screamed for oxygen, but he held fast.

Rafferty pressed the back of his blistered right hand against the stone behind him. He concentrated on sanding off the fresh brand, merely twitching the fewest muscles for the slightest movement. The fanning stopped. He smelled a foul breath in his nostrils as someone inspected him for sleep. Rafferty allowed his body the sighing, smoke-free breaths that it craved.

The hands snatched him by the hair and slammed him face-first into sand.

"Ah, dream-ferret, abandon this foolish resolve. It will make you buzzard dung before nightfall."

The priest yanked off Rafferty's blindfold, and the white highland sun stabbed at both eyes, even after he squinted them shut.

The wind chime tinkled again, and when Rafferty recovered his vision enough to focus, he saw it hanging at a cave entrance behind the smoldering fire. Twisted stone carvings framed the cave. His eyes adjusted, and he saw that the chime was made of brittle white bones, dried and tempered by the sun.

One man guarded him; he saw no sign of another. That explained the bonds. Rafferty's guard busied himself over the coals of the fire, scraping them together carefully, then covering them with a mound of sand. Rafferty knew from travels with the Roam that this fire would keep for a day or more under the sand. This conserved precious firewood. It told Rafferty that the fire would not be used again soon, probably not until dark. He didn't know whether to be comforted by that or not.

Beside the firepit lay the branding iron with its wooden handle. It seemed such an innocent twist of metal, even elegant on the end of its delicate stem.

The hands of the priest were long and delicate as well, uncallused, with nails that rounded their fingertips. The greatest surprise was not in his hands but in his face.

This priest was a young man. Older than Rafferty, yes, but not nearly so old as his rasp of a voice. He wore the leggings and bright tunic of the highland Maya, with a cumbersome headdress and the thick ear decorations of mid-rank priesthood. They matched the dress of some of the carved figures. His feet were bare; their thickness and width made mockery of sandals. His face was very thin, and his clothing much too bulky to fit.

He looks like he's starving.

He was a handsome young man with glittery brown eyes, and Rafferty knew that the women of the Roam would court him mercilessly. While he, Rafferty, was mixed-blood and therefore gaje, this priest was of a different kumpania but his blood belonged to the Roam. He stirred something in a pot of water while he returned Rafferty's stare. The unmistakable aroma got his attention.

"Is that coffee?" Rafferty asked.

"It is."

Yes, the voice was the same. There was no sign of another person, no tracks other than the drag marks from the cliffside only a few meters away. The camp perched on a long ledge inside a canyon. It looked very nearly inaccessible to Rafferty.

The priest used a piece of stained cloth to filter out the dregs, then set a small cup at Rafferty's feet.

"For you. Nebaj likes coffee after a dream."

"I can't drink it with my hands tied," Rafferty grumbled. "Besides, how do I know it's coffee? You already tried to put me to sleep once."

Nebaj shrugged, picked up the cup and sipped the top third much more delicately than Rafferty would have imagined. In his time, Nebaj had learned the courtly graces. Rafferty wondered what convolutions of fate marooned him on this ledge in the high country.

"You see, no poison. You will sleep soon enough; it is what people do. When you sleep, you will dream. That is also what people do. When you set out on your dreamway, I will follow. That is what I do."

He reached behind Rafferty and undid the knots at his wrists, then sat facing him, sipping at his own cup. Both cups were crude red pottery, made for travel and disposal. Their only decoration was three hollow legs apiece, and inside each leg was a tiny ball that rattled when the cup was tilted and set down.

Rafferty reached for his cup and stopped, startled at the mess that the branding had made of the back of his hand. He had damaged it further himself with the scraping, but it was still just an unrecognizable mass of burn.

"There was only Nebaj to hold and brand," the priest apologized. "Your body fought though your mind was gone."

"Why . . . why do you do this?"

"For the Jaguar. It pleases him."

"Why doesn't the Jaguar just brand us in our dreams and leave our bodies alone? If he's trying to follow us there, what good does it do . . . ?"

"It is not for you that you are branded," Nebaj said. "It is for Nebaj."

"I don't understand."

"The Jaguar requires sacrifice. Nebaj must provide, out of three choices. One, follow a dreamway and mark whoever is encountered there. Two, pierce the tongue of Nebaj with a sea-ray spine and let the blood flow upon the burning pom. Three, pierce the penis of Nebaj with an eagle-bone whistle, then blow the blood upon the burning pom."

"I understand your choice."

Nebaj nodded.

"So why am I here? Why not just brand me and let me go?"

Nebaj laughed a near-silent whisper of a laugh.

"Ah, dream-ferret, you are a special find, indeed. There are priests hunting their lives away for the likes of you. You have dreamed yourself into the world of the Jaguar himself. Your meeting at the crossroads—who could have known the good fortune of Nebaj!"

"You mean, all these people who are branded are branded simply for dreaming normal dreams?"

"Yes, normal. It is a means of keeping track of those we have met in dreams. Very few ever glimpse the curtain. And now you have very nearly pulled Nebaj through the curtain with you."

He sounded proud, even awestruck. Perhaps this was a means to higher rank in the priesthood.

"But how did you recover, then get me here? Weren't you sick, too?"

"Yes, sick. There is a penalty to be paid, but the herbs help. Fasting, too, is a help."

"Why do you want me to dream again so soon? And why tie me up?"

Nebaj set his coffee down, then motioned to Rafferty to present his ankles. He proceeded to release him.

"Nebaj, too, must sleep," he said. "The ropes keep you from a needless fall into the canyon. As you can see, there is no way out except up, and up cannot be gained without a rope thrown down."

"So, there is someone else."

"In due time."

"What if I throw you over the edge?"

"Then the rope will never come."

"Am I dreaming now?"

"No. You know the difference."

Rafferty wasn't all that sure. He heard his crow call twice again, quickly—an attempt to get his attention. It got Nebaj's attention. When he turned and craned his neck to spot the crow, Rafferty hit him hard on the side of the neck like Uncle taught him to do.

Nebaj didn't go down. He sprang with a backhand to Rafferty's face and countered with a side-kick to his belly. Rafferty took the kick to catch the ankle. He gave Nebaj a spin and kicked his supporting knee out from under him, then punched the back of the priest's neck. Nebaj quivered and lay still.

Though the fight only took moments, Rafferty was reduced to a fit of uncontrollable trembling. He sat in the sand next to Nebaj and stripped off the priest's soiled tunic and trousers. He trussed the priest up in one of his own ropes and saved the longest length in case company showed up.

Company did show up. Ruckus landed on an outcrop next to the wind chime and gave the bones a curious poke.

"Thanks, Ruckus. You're pretty handy, for a crow."

Ruckus answered with his usual mutter, then fluttered to the firepit to poke for scraps.

Rafferty finished with Nebaj and dragged him inside the cave entrance, out of sight from above. He slipped the tunic and trousers over his own, and strapped on the helmet of rank.

Ruckus eyed the silver inserts that decorated the sides.

"You like silver, don't you, buddy? I'll give you all the silver in this helmet if you help me get to the top. See this?"

Rafferty showed Ruckus the rope. He held it up and let one end fall, then held it up again and let one end fall. Ruckus watched carefully, curious as always.

Rafferty anchored one end on a ledge with a rock and coiled

the rest of the rope beside it. He held out his arm, and Ruckus hopped aboard. Rafferty took him over to the coil of rope. He picked the free end up between his fingers, then let it drop free from the ledge. He re-coiled the rope, then did it again.

"Got it?"

This time, he coiled the rope and held Ruckus up to it. The crow looked at Rafferty, looked at the rope, then pulled the rope so that it fell free.

"Good boy, Ruckus. What a great crow you are. Now we hope that they left the rope topside, and that it's still attached to something."

Rafferty picked up a stone and stepped out from the cliff face as far as he could. He gave Ruckus a toss and when he was airborne, Rafferty threw the stone to the top of the cliff with all his might. It didn't fall back at him, so he was sure that he'd made it.

"Go on," he motioned to Ruckus, then shook the rope at him. "Go on up there."

The crow winged upward in a lazy spiral and disappeared above the rim. In moments a rope skittered down the rock face. It hung up just above the cave, and with considerable effort Rafferty was able to free it. He scoured the cave for all of the supplies he could find and bundled them into the priest's net bag. When he found the obsidian knife he paused, then placed it at the priest's bare neck. He held it there for a moment, two, and knew he could not kill him. Instead, he made a harmless cut across the throat, just enough to bleed.

There's your blood sacrifice, Rafferty thought, and stowed the knife with the rest of the gear. He left Nebaj a cup of water covered with the other cup, then scrambled up the cliffside to safety.

It is the egocentricity of adolescence that has specific pertinence to the development of these states and demands our attention . . . He now becomes capable of thinking about thinking . . . he can now plan from the possible to the real, and in so doing may never return from the mental realm of the possible.

—**Theodore Lidz,** *The Origin and Treatment of Schizophrenic Disorders*

EDDIE HAD TO bicycle up to The Hill twice a week for his sessions with Dr. Mark. It had been an easy choice because Dr. Mark let him come for free, and because Eddie liked the chance to talk with Sara. It was Sara who had shown him how to keep a journal, and Eddie felt that his journal kept him sane. Besides, after his meeting with Rafferty he knew that he'd have to keep better track of his dreams if he ever wanted to meet up with him again.

Dr. Mark was still on The Hill after nearly six years, and he saw some private patients in his home. Though Eddie was welcome there, a lot of the tests they did required the equipment on The Hill. The doctor still looked young in his face, but he had acquired some of the same slow, distracted movements that characterized the older patients. He didn't look like he got outside as much, either. Like the patients, his skin was beginning to sallow in spite of his youth.

At first, Eddie tried to say as little as possible about Rafferty and the dream world, but Dr. Mark had a way of leading the conversation. Dr. Mark was a good listener, and Eddie found himself talking about the dreams, anyway.

His biggest mistake, though, had been to mention Maryellen. For the rest of sixth grade, besides seeing Eddie on The Hill, Dr. Mark came down to the school for an hour a week to test Eddie and Maryellen.

Eddie was afraid that they might be separated, but both of them learned a lot from Dr. Mark about their dreams. The main thing that they learned was that they *were* different. Whether Dr. Mark believed it or not, they knew that nothing they read or that he told them about others fit their situation. Both of them read everything the bookmobile could find for them on astral projection, dreams, and on what Dr. Mark called "multiple personality disorder"—something Eddie read in his chart when nobody was looking.

"That's not the way it is with us at all," Eddie said one day in disgust. "I thought he was *smart*."

During that summer and the next year, Dr. Mark set up experiments, trying to get them to dream the way he wanted. He would give one of them a week's worth of envelopes, each dated and sealed. Each night one of them was to open the appropriate envelope before going to bed, concentrate on the card inside, then try to dream that picture to the other person.

The other person had a stack of cards at their bedside, and when a design appeared in a dream they would select that card, place it in a dated envelope and mail it to Dr. Mark. On Saturdays they met for results, and for more tests. The first week they scored a hundred per cent. The second week they scored a hundred per cent.

Maryellen's stepmother accused them of cheating. She forbade Maryellen to have any contact at all with Eddie Reyes. She tried to get Eddie removed from the school before the fall term came.

"Look what he's done to our little girl," she shouted. "Poisoned her mind, that's what. There wasn't any trouble before he showed up, and now half the school's loony. She's not crazy, or special. She's . . . *influenced*, that's all. He's like a little Hitler. Get him up on The Hill where he belongs. . . ."

Eddie and Maryellen listened outside Dr. Mark's office while her stepmother raged.

"Never mind," Maryellen said. "She's drinking again. She hates everybody."

"Especially me."

"Especially herself. She won't get you kicked out of school—don't worry."

"I know. Dr. Mark told me already. I'm glad we're getting skipped next year. You know, I think something big's going to happen."

"Something big? How big?"

"Like the earthquake. Like meeting Rafferty. I just have that feeling."

Eddie felt closer to Rafferty than he did to anyone on his side of the fabric except Maryellen Thompkins. Rafferty was in danger, as were the people of the Roam, and this danger came from a power that Eddie had never been able to identify. He tried the other side as often as possible, but the fabric only allowed him through a few times a year. And dreaming on this side hurt other people. He had to find out how he could help.

The next year his absences from school got worse, but even though he and Maryellen had skipped to eighth grade his scores hugged the high end of the scale. Maryellen took up photography and buried herself in her new hobby. Eddie buried himself in dreams. When the counselors saw that getting after Eddie for missing school didn't do any good, they went after his uncle Bert.

"It's not right, Eddie," Bert said. "You stay here. I don't ask anything except you stay out of trouble."

"I know. . . ."

"Listen. It's simple. They get money from the state when you're in school, they get nothing when you're not. Now, they can take you away, they can put you back on The Hill, or in a foster home where nobody will leave you alone for a minute. Is that what you want?"

"No."

"Then get ahold of yourself. I don't know what to think about this 'other world' you talk about. I don't judge what a man believes. But you're bringing the law down on my place. It's not right for a boy to daydream so much he forgets to eat, forgets to go to school. You get sick and pass out sometimes for a day, two days. You say it's the 'other world,' but one of the counselors says it's some kind of fit. If they think you're having fits, you know they won't send you to no foster home, they'll send you straight back to The Hill. Permanent. Remember, there are people in this town who are still out to get you. You get a grip. Find something to do that makes you concentrate."

"Uncle Bert, there are people who are *dying*. . . ."

"Don't give me that crap," Bert snapped. "I don't see no bodies. *You* see the bodies. And that's the problem. Boys your age should be dreaming of something else. Warm bodies, with tits."

Eddie's uncle took a long swallow of cold coffee and tossed the dregs out the front door.

"Listen," he said. "Look at it this way. If you go down the tubes, so do your dream people. Take care of yourself, and you can take care of them. Get it? And it'll make life easier on me. I hate it when the state takes up snooping. Your dad and I fought a war over that shit. Look what it got him."

"What *did* it get him?" Eddie asked. "My mom never talked about him—nobody talks about him. . . ."

"Maybe when you're older," Bert said. He wouldn't look Eddie in the eye. "But you take after him, boy, you surely do."

"How? How do I take after him?"

It was no use; his uncle stalked out the door for town.

Maryellen had her photography, so Eddie took up archery for concentration because he'd read that Zen monks did it. With his uncle's help he became the youngest member of the valley archery club, where he was a crack shot but still known as a loner. He got a job at the club repairing targets and equipment. By the time he was fifteen he fletched his own arrows and took up restoring guns of all kinds. By the time he was sixteen, he was making a wage at it. Maryellen's father was a drunk, but he was also a gunsmith, and Eddie thought this might help keep him closer to Maryellen.

Maryellen's father owned the only gun shop in town. He took an interest in Eddie at first, in spite of his wife's opinions. But the bond between Eddie and Maryellen became too much for him. He shut Eddie out of his life, and out of his shop.

"You two spend all of your time together," he told Maryellen. "That's not healthy at your age."

"It's the dream study, Dad," she said. "Dr. Mark explained it to you. If we can understand more . . ."

"If you can understand that I know what's best for you, that's fine," Mel said. "If you can't understand it, tough. You will when you get older. He's out of the shop. Socially, he's out of your life. Period."

"But, Dad . . ."

"And I can take you out of that study, too. Some of that stuff you're doing, it's voodoo stuff. Sometimes you're sick for days. . . ."

"But you can see the difference it's made. We're way ahead in school; they're talking about skipping us again. Here at home . . . we're helping other people, too."

"Don't talk to me about those imaginary people of yours. That's baby talk, and I don't see why that doctor lets you keep it up. Hell, Eddie's almost a grown man and he still believes that crap. How's he going to make it, thinking that way?"

"Dad, I meant, it's helping other people, *real* people, who have personality problems, nightmares and stuff. You know that. And we've . . . I've studied up on it a lot and written papers for school. . . ."

"That's why I let you do it. I'm not blind, you know. I just don't want to see you throw your life away on some dreamer. . . ."

"Dad, you forget. *I'm* 'some dreamer.' "

He walked away, with a dismissive wave of his hand.

"You're a photographer," he said, over his shoulder. "Stick to that."

Maryellen met Eddie at their usual spot down at the river. He was drawing squares in a sandbar.

"It's *her* doing, you know that," Maryellen told him. "My dad has to drink to put up with her, *that's* the problem. I can't believe he married that woman. . . ."

She cried, something she didn't do easily. It was a grotesquery of her musculature. In her struggle to not cry she displayed the bitter history of struggles that light has always fought on behalf of souls in darkness. The twin furrows between her brows deepened, reminding Eddie of his mother.

Eddie realized that those furrows were a sign of age, that he and Maryellen had already aged, before they had the chance to mature. It was one of those fates that life on the dreamways tossed out like dice. He hoped that it tossed them wisdom, as well.

Eddie knew that Maryellen's father didn't just start drinking because of his new wife. Maryellen's mother had been killed years ago, while Eddie was in Montana. Maryellen's father had been drunk then, and drove the car off the levee road and into the river. Maryellen's mother got halfway out the window before the river rolled the car. Maryellen had been at the babysitter's.

"Something's keeping us from the other side," Eddie said. "I think the Jaguar's onto us, blocking our moves before we make them."

"Or maybe we *are* crazy," she sobbed. "Do you know how crazy it sounds for you to say that. *Do you?*"

"Does that mean you won't help me anymore?"

Maryellen continued to cry, hunched over her wet hanky. She

wore one of those pink, fuzzy sweaters that shed like a dyed cat. Clumps of the stuff clung to the arms of his plaid shirt, a flannel material that he liked more for the feel than for the looks. He had hugged enough. It was time for talk.

"Well?"

Maryellen blew her nose, and Eddie realized that in the intimacy of the dreamways they had become like an old married couple. Familiarity, a kind of intimacy, but without the benefit of romance.

Romance was something Eddie didn't understand, but he knew he had no time for it. Still, when she blew her nose so unselfconsciously in front of him, Eddie had to admit to himself that he loved Maryellen Thompkins. It was the kind of thing that could ruin everything.

"I'll help you," Maryellen said.

Her voice was husky from all the crying.

"I'll help you because it'll help me figure all this out. And because I don't know what else to do."

"I don't, either," he said. "But we're not supposed to. We're just kids."

Maryellen looked at Eddie, one of those long looks that she could give, which was a cross between accusation and pity. The red rim around her eyes did not diminish their beauty, their fire.

"Kids!" she snorted. "Whatever we are, it's not kids. Have you looked in a mirror lately?"

Eddie swallowed. He'd had a hard look in the mirror just this morning, and the person who looked back had been a stranger. It was the eyes. They were still blue, but the mirror wasn't deep enough to hold them.

Even the damned love.

—**Stephen King,** *The Drawing of the Three*

THE JAGUAR LOVED to pry. When he was young and lived in the world, his hobby was burglary. The young Jaguar had not been a big-time burglar of diamonds and cash, though when he saw them for the taking, he took. He had been after the simple thrill of lifting a pair of lace panties from the floor beside a snoring couple, a watch from their bedside table, a comb from the vanity.

The young Jaguar would become so excited, standing over their sleep, that he had to unzip his pants and release his excitement in hot spurts atop their covers. Then, savoring the freedom of the nighttime streets, he ran wild down the sidewalks and laughed.

That was the young Jaguar, hitched to the world by his need. The Jaguar retained the need to pry. He no longer ran wild down the streets, but oh, how he loved to pry!

There had been changes in the Agency. The Jaguar no longer faced their inquisition when he woke. He still woke to the rock-faced, unamused, cold-eyed Max, but Max didn't hurt him anymore. The Jaguar understood that it was nothing personal, and that policies change, and that he should make the best of it while he could.

The new administration considered him a valuable national asset, and never did they use the word 'spy.' The old boys operated on greed and fear; they sent Max to punish him for his distractions. The young bucks understood the money meant nothing to him, that he was no good to them dead, that he was no good to them unless he woke up willingly. They let him play.

His cattle offered him thrills beyond limit. At first he had been content to rummage their memories, sort through the back drawers of their minds. He played and replayed their most private experiences. The memories belonged to the cattle, it was true, but the orgasms were his own.

Once, through the white pain of awakening, he felt his sheets being changed under him, and the voice of an orderly muttered, "I don't know where this guy goes, but he must come a half-dozen times a day."

Later, when the Jaguar perfected his tinkering, he thrilled to initiating action instead of memories. He directed his cattle in little dramas that played out in their lives to satisfy his boredom. He was merciless.

One trick had been to change the part of a husband's brain that housed his wife's name. 'Thelma' suddenly became 'Louise' to him, and the Jaguar sat back to watch the fireworks.

There were always fireworks; that was the point. But once the fireworks booth exploded in a shooting, and the Jaguar escaped just as the brains that housed him were blown into a set of venetian blinds.

Adrenalin!

Gods, how he loved that surge, but death had been too close that time. He wasn't sure that he would have died inside that brain, but he wasn't sure that he wouldn't have either. It was not the kind of experiment he wanted to prove on himself.

From that day on he entered only healthy cattle, and he tried to keep them out of trouble while they had him along. Getting them killed might be entertainment for the Jaguar, but getting himself killed was out of the question. For the first time in his life, he became considerate of the well-being of others, even if only while he shared their bodies.

He'd had a close one with Belitnikov, too, by whipping the man into a sexual frenzy that left his portly wife raw, his mistress limp and his heart in a tachycardia that took the Russian doctors a week to control. He'd very nearly lost a treasure for a little cheap sex, and he wanted to believe that he wouldn't do it again.

While he played, his priests pursued disturbances in the curtain. One young priest had been bested. Though he branded this wolf among his cattle, the wolf had not *become* cattle, and this disturbed him.

Does he cover his trail? the Jaguar wondered. If so, he would uncover it. The greater fear poked at his belly.

What if he's immune?

This had not occurred to the Jaguar before. The natural extension of that fear became: *If he's immune to my detection, there might be others.*

He didn't like that thought at all, because it felt so simple, so possible, so right. But it didn't stop there; it wouldn't leave him be. The thought had to nag him into: *There might be others on this side.*

There was a wolf among his cattle, and he didn't know much about wolves. He would have to learn, and learn quickly. There were two facts he *did* know, and both iced his spine: *Wolves hunt in packs, and they work together.*

If he couldn't track the wolves, at least he could identify and destroy his contaminated cattle. The Agency might be a help in this, but he didn't trust them, because he trusted no one. They would not destroy these wolves; they would cultivate them, corral them into cattle of their own. This the Jaguar could not abide.

Relationships with his most significant persons interfere with forward movement, create hopelessness and often terror, and initiate regression. . . . He is of the polar type who suffer acute disorganization under extremely stressful conditions, such as combat.

—Theodore Lidz, *Origins and Treatment of Schizophrenic Disorders*

RAFFERTY WATCHED THE woman and the girl from behind a jumble of rocks beside the trail. They worked their way along the base of the cliff, and the woman kept her gaze on the rough footing. The girl clung to her mother's hand and plodded on behind, the mother doing most of the work. They approached a butterfly-shaped discoloration in the cliff face, which grew more distinct in Rafferty's eyes as the setting sun reddened the rock.

The girl let out a weak shriek and dug her heels in, sobbing.

"Stop it, now!" the mother snapped. "I'm tired, too."

"I'm scared."

"There's nothing to be scared of," the mother said. "It's not even dark yet. . . ."

Rafferty's crow flapped up from the rocks and pulled for altitude. The girl shrieked again, and the mother shook her by the shoulders.

"It's just a bird, Anna. You scared it up by your racket."

"No, something else . . ."

The mother gave her another hard shake, and Rafferty checked his urge to step forward.

Maybe she felt me here, he thought. *She might be one of the sensitive ones, like Afriqua Lee.*

Then he caught his breath and reached for his weapon. A very large man walked out of the discoloration in the cliff behind the woman. The man wore a uniform-jacket with a lot of ribbons and medals on the front, and while the little girl blubbered he quietly took it off, still standing behind the mother, who was unsuspecting.

The man placed his coat about the mother's shoulders and she did not move. The child screamed and tried to pull loose from the mother's grip on her shoulders, but she was too exhausted to get away. Her shrieks and struggles quieted down in a few moments.

Rafferty noticed now that though he wanted to move, he could not. He knew he should be alarmed at this, but his mind remained absolutely calm. He heard faint calls of protest from his crow high overhead.

The man spoke quietly to the girl, but Rafferty couldn't hear what was said. The woman remained frozen in her hunched posture over her daughter, and the man removed a small tin from his back pocket.

The tin flashed in his palm as he flipped open the lid. Rafferty's crow squawked once more, louder this time, from somewhere behind him.

The man dipped a forefinger into the tin and it came out covered with a dab of blue. He reached out, against the girl's feeble protests, and rubbed it gently on the center of her forehead, in a sideways figure-eight. He did the same to the girl's mother, who then dropped her daughter's shoulders, pulled the coat tighter around her, and turned back up the trail.

Her eyes were a sleepwalker's eyes. Rafferty saw them clearly as she turned. She and the daughter waited beside the cliff face as the man turned his attention to Rafferty.

It didn't seem to Rafferty that the man had taken a step, but there he was in front of him, reaching out that forefinger with a dab of blue ointment. He was an indistinct man, but Rafferty was sure he was a man. Rafferty had no fear of him, though he suspected that he should. He realized, too, that he had not even breathed since the man stepped through the stone and out of the cliff.

The finger touched his forehead, traced two circles there, and Rafferty could breathe.

The stranger turned on his heel and Rafferty was compelled to follow. He couldn't remember any of the man's features, except that he was taller, dark and broad-shouldered. Though he had looked Rafferty straight in the eye, Rafferty had no memory of his eye color, or hair color, or the shape of his mouth.

The stranger stood beside the discolored portion of the cliff, and Rafferty's gaze was fixed by a blue glow in its center. The splash of blue flickered wildly on the rock, like two nightstalkers fighting in a sack. Suddenly the light widened to illuminate a passageway. The blue light loomed over the stranger's shoulder like a huge pair of butterfly wings.

He ushered the woman and her daughter through the passageway and into the cliff. Rafferty saw two silent flashes of light, and felt a rush of air from his nostrils. The stranger stood at the threshold and gestured Rafferty his turn.

Rafferty couldn't make his body *not* go.

He's the Jaguar!

At that instant, Rafferty crossed the threshold, and some blue vortex yanked him off his feet. He plummeted head-first into the cosmic peel. The northern lights streamed past, stood still, and he left them behind. Then, in a white flash, he left himself behind. . . .

"Rafferty!"

Afriqua Lee's voice—she had his collar, yanking him back. . . .

"Rafferty!" she whispered, and shook him again. "You fell asleep on the map light."

He smelled coffee, rubbed his face where he'd lain on his clipboard, and breathed a deep sigh. It was midnight, the Roam were nearly to their stakedown and he was supposed to be piloting the Romni Bari's tent.

"You jumped when I touched you," she said. "You must have been out. Are you all right?"

"Yes," he laughed, "thanks to you."

He sipped the coffee.

"Thanks to me? What do you mean?"

"The Jaguar almost had me. He'd hypnotized me or drugged me somehow, and I was going to be destroyed in a flash of light."

"How did I save you?"

"I fell through the light and you yanked me back by the collar."

Afriqua Lee sighed and massaged the back of his neck.

"Good thing it was just a nightmare," she said. "If the Jaguar messes with you, he's going to answer to me."

Rafferty sipped his coffee and didn't speak.

"It *was* just a nightmare, wasn't it?" she asked.

"I don't know," he said. "We'd better get moving."

If it was a dream, it was telling him something.

What?

That a woman tried to protect her daughter, and both of them were lost. That someone standing by was lost as well.

No, Rafferty told himself, *not lost. Trapped. And the others were the bait.*

He didn't like the association with the Jaguar, nor the notion of traps and bait. After stakedown he would bring this up again with Afriqua Lee.

Humanity does not ask us to be happy. It merely asks us to be brilliant on its behalf. Survival first, then happiness as we can manage it.

—**Orson Scott Card,** *Ender's Game*

AT SIXTEEN, EDDIE stared into his uncle Bert's bathroom mirror, trying to decide whether he should start shaving or not.

They'll grow if I shave, he thought. *That's what Dr. Mark said happened to him.*

Eddie couldn't decide whether or not he wanted to shave. It was the kind of thing that seemed like a lot of trouble, but the only other boy in the senior class who didn't shave was Dwayne. Dwayne wore eyeshadow and called himself 'Darlene.' Eddie reminded himself that he was two years younger than the rest of the boys in his class, but it didn't seem to help.

The dark fringe of down on Eddie's upper lip was only visible under the closest scrutiny, and today Eddie scrutinized closely. His lips were chapped because he'd had a cold and he'd been breathing through his mouth when he slept. The air of the river valley had been unusually chilly and dry all spring. The seagulls flocked in early this evening, and low, so Eddie suspected that it would rain tonight. It might help heal his lips.

They were not as full as Maryellen's lips, nor were they the pencil-thin kind that reminded him of windburned cowboys like his uncle Elmer.

Kid lips, he thought, and smiled. *Sixteen years under the belt but kid lips under the schnoz.*

His uncle Bert always referred to their family's distinctive nose as 'the schnoz' or 'the royalty.' It didn't jut out there like Old

Man Meyer's nose, but it had an unmistakable pride to it that did not go unnoticed.

Eddie saw in his drawn face, the darkness under his eyes, what the dreamways had done to him over the years. He and Maryellen were the youngest in their class because they'd skipped. Both of them looked older, even though he didn't shave yet.

He never thought of his as a hard life—he placed the blame squarely on his dreams. His mouth held fast to enthusiasm. His prideful nose tempered his adolescence with a maturity that was not at all common among his peers. Neither was it welcome.

Eddie liked his teeth. They never gave him any trouble and he was glad, because so far he'd only had to visit a dentist for a checkup and a cleaning. His teeth were as white and regular as his mother's had been darkened and irregular, but the dentist warned him, "Relax. You're under too much stress and your teeth show it. You clench your jaw and grind your teeth in your sleep. A kid your age shouldn't have to worry. Go fishing."

Eddie often wondered what his father's smile had looked like. *His eyes must have been brown or green,* he thought. *Grandma said I got my mother's blue eyes.*

He wondered what else he got from his father. The furrowed brow in the bomber photo was the same, the dark skin and dark hair, the same build that had started out lanky and was slowly filling out to muscle. The mystery of his father continued to haunt him.

There were a lot of missing facts, like the papers the military sends after a death, like the pension that his mother never received. There was one pressing fact—no two stories in his family agreed on how he died, or where, or exactly when.

He raised his dark eyebrows in sudden reflex, and tossed his head back the way his father had done in the picture. Eddie was clearly a close match, even without the hat.

His uncle Bert opened the bathroom door and they startled each other.

"Hey, Tiger, gettin' all slicked up?"

"Well, ah . . . just cleaning up, you know . . ."

"Maryellen called. She wants you to meet her down at the river. You better watch your step, boy. Her daddy'll have your hide. You know what they said. . . ."

"Yeah, yeah, I know. Did she say what time?"

"Four o'clock," Bert said. "You've got an hour, but goddammit, it's my turn in the bathroom."

* * *

The fishing shelter was nearly overgrown with the tall river grasses. Weeds were bent down in each step she'd taken ahead of him, and were well-trampled where she'd waited on her favorite stone. Atop the stone, in lipstick, she'd drawn a square.

He found her asleep behind the shack, her sleeping bag spread out on the grass. She slept to one side, as though she expected him to lie down beside her, so he did.

She wore his gray track-sweatsuit over a blue flannel workshirt, and tennis shoes heavy with new grass stains. Eddie didn't know how she'd got his sweatsuit, but he liked the intimacy of her wearing it. The afternoon was warm though overcast, and he thought if they were there long they might get rained on.

"Maryellen?"

She was sound asleep, her breathing very slow.

"Maryellen, it's going to rain."

Eddie looked up and down the riverbank, and saw no one. Summer fishing on the river didn't open up for over a month, and even hoboes didn't wander this far upriver. It was unlikely that anyone would stumble into their camp by accident, and his uncle was gone for the rest of the month to a job in Yakima.

He attributed his sudden sense of dread to the incoming weather and to his regret at not being able to find Rafferty in his dreams for nearly a year. Dr. Mark explained it as progress. Eddie felt it as a loss. There was something wrong.

"Maryellen?"

He shook her shoulder halfheartedly, not really wanting to wake her.

There was no doubt in Eddie's mind. She was too deeply asleep to be napping.

The square, he thought. *Maybe she's arranged a meeting.*

He lay down beside her and watched the clouds roll in. They wore the dark underbellies of a storm, but stayed high enough to clear the mountains and pass through. He would carry Maryellen into the fishing shack when the rains came. He didn't want to disturb her. If she'd gone to the dreamworld, she would probably be out for a while.

What will we do about her parents? he wondered. Her father was getting stranger every day. Mel Thompkins had taken to staying awake nights to check on Maryellen, and to keep him company during watch, he had his bottle. Eddie knew that

Maryellen's stepbrother was giving her trouble, too. He knew it more from what she didn't say than what she did.

Eddie took her hand and kissed it, then relaxed beside her for a quick nap before the weather hit. The last thing he expected was to cross the curtain in a blink to come face to face with Maryellen. And Rafferty, and Afriqua Lee.

For the first time, all four of them met in the dreamworld. It had taken Maryellen a week of planning, of scurrying messages through the dream-fabric. Eddie felt as though he and Maryellen dreamed now from inside the same body, they were so close.

It was sunny in the dream and the wind was still. The four of them sat inside a cedar grove; its evergreen fragrance ladened the warm afternoon.

A square of marble columns on a square of marble floor stood high atop a stone structure in the middle of the woods. The fluted columns supported a sill of marble. One of the columns was broken. Only a portion of its top and its base remained. There was no debris.

Inside the square stood a square marble table with four marble chairs. The surface of the table was inlaid with brass to form a sundial. It was contained within a brass square. Each chair had one of their names carved into it. Each name was bordered with the same brass square.

Each of them took the appropriate seat. It was like sitting in on a seance, only there was no medium, no observers—just the four of them in an atrium, sitting at a marble table.

Rafferty spoke first, though he appeared the most insubstantial of the four.

"Someone is after us here," he warned. "Don't give away clues about where you are. I was caught some time ago by a Jaguar priest. He nabbed me coming out of the dreamway. I am sure he knows about Eddie, possibly Maryellen."

Suddenly, for Eddie, the daily threat that Rafferty faced became real.

"They know there are two of us—males—one on each side of the web," Rafferty said. "We're a threat to them. When they're sure they've found us all, they'll kill us."

"But the priests can't cross into our world," Eddie said. "They can't come after me and Maryellen."

"The Jaguar is already there," Rafferty said, "I'm sure of it. But he may be weaker on your side of the curtain. He uses his priests here as a lens of some kind, or a coil, to boost his power and refine his focus. That's why they're so excited that we can communicate. Somebody is getting close to me over here. . . ."

Rafferty related his experience with Nabaj, and his dream of the woman and child in the canyon.

"The Jaguar has been much on my mind, too," Afriqua Lee said. "That is to his advantage on the dreamways. It would be better to invite him in, don't you think, and follow him to his den?"

"Only if we know more about him than he knows about us," Rafferty said. "Anything less is a trap we set for ourselves."

"Okay," Eddie said, "what *do* we know?"

"We know that a dream costs us dearly," Maryellen said. "Even that priest said so. The Jaguar probably pays his price, too."

"We pay out what we get out," Eddie said. "If he controls as much of your world as you think, he must either be asleep or suffering all of the time."

Rafferty frowned.

"If we conjure something, like the crossroads or this place, it keeps us down for a day or two. But this is small compared to some of the things the Jaguar's done—earthquakes, plagues . . ."

"Yeah," Eddie said. "He must be down for weeks after that."

"Maybe months," Afriqua said. "Or longer."

"How could you live that long, out cold?" Eddie asked. "You'd be helpless, you'd starve. And then there's the pain of the recovery time."

"Maybe he gets other people to dream for him," Rafferty said. "Like that priest, Nebaj."

"Maybe he's different from us altogether," Afriqua said. "Maybe he's an alien dreaming from someplace we haven't imagined."

"Maybe we're different from you," Eddie said. "But if he's from our side, he wouldn't be different from us. Unless there's a third side to the curtain."

"The pathways are open between us," Rafferty added. "Maybe he opened them, or followed us through somebody else."

"That would be like him," Maryellen said. "He wouldn't show himself. He'd get into the dreams of someone who could keep track of us. . . ."

"Let's start out assuming he's more like the four of us than he is different," Rafferty said. "He probably uses the Jaguar priesthood to intensify his power, something we haven't learned to do. But after a dream of his own he's helpless. So, *where is he?*"

"The priest says he's in their world," Afriqua said. "I agree."

"How do you know the priest wasn't lying?" Maryellen asked.

"The Jaguar's experiments with the butterfly kiss devastate us, not you," Rafferty said. "When matter from your side meets ours . . . *poof.* A flash of light, and it's gone. Brain tissue goes like that when he leaves residue from the dreamways. He's making our world miserable. Why would he want to live in it?"

"Logical," Eddie said. "And it's why we know less about what he can do. He doesn't do it here."

"I've calculated it out, and he must be near you," Rafferty said.

"How so?"

"When any of us plucks the fabric, it affects both sides of the curtain. Some places are more easily passed through than others, like your valley. Perhaps we're actually wearing a hole in the fabric."

"The two of you must be near him," Afriqua added. "Maybe you'll find him the way you found each other."

Rafferty added, "Or maybe he'll find you first."

" 'Near' meaning how near?" Eddie asked. "Ten feet, ten miles, ten thousand miles . . . ?"

"Probably the distance you could walk in a day," Rafferty said.

"But where is he?" Eddie asked. "Somebody must be keeping him alive when he's . . . sick."

"The Hill!" Maryellen broke in. "Eddie, he's got to be on The Hill! Or some place like it. At least when he's sick."

"Unless someone cares for him at home, someone professional. . . ."

Ideas are entities.

It was not Eddie's thought, but it rang in his head. It was like a messenger barging into a concert. Eddie felt as though someone were watching them from behind the columns. When he looked, he caught a flicker out of the corner of his vision and saw Ruckus ruffle himself on the ledge above him.

"Search for a catatonic who keeps coming around," Rafferty suggested.

"And we'll have him!" Maryellen said. "That's got to be it!"

"We could bait him," Afriqua Lee suggested, "but one of you would have to be the bait."

"And one of you would have to know how to spring the trap."

That was Maryellen's voice. Eddie couldn't see so well, anymore. A blue wash of light faded the scene, and her voice receded like a train down a tunnel.

"I've felt him snooping around, even now," she said. "We *could* bait him."

Eddie snapped out of the dream to a flash of pain in his head and belly. He was cold, soaked by rain. Light stabbed at his eyes and someone slapped his face. The sting rushed tears to his eyes. The blurred forms of several men stood over him. One of them, in uniform, slapped him and shook his shoulders and shouted questions at him. As usual, he was too sick to move and he couldn't make sense of their questions. One voice came in clear above all the others. It was Mel Thompkins.

"He's drugged my daughter," Thompkins shouted. "He's killed her. I want that boy to hang."

Even though we may, ourselves, have created an 'other' in our childhood, this other has not grown up, has become independent and autonomous, and like our child may no longer be under our control.

—**John Watkins,** *We the Divided Self*

"So," OLD CRISTINA said, "your dream is that strong."

Afriqua Lee shook her head to clear it and was immediately sorry. The pain between her eyes was so intense that her stomach flipped. Even the fragrance of fresh coffee from Old Cristina's light-pocket gagged her. After a flight down the dreamways, coffee had always been the only thing to bring her to her senses.

"I . . ."

It was no use; words only made things worse.

Cristina closed the curtains and refreshed the cold rag for her forehead. Afriqua wanted to tell her how there wasn't that much time, how the Jaguar had found his way to them, how his reach spanned two worlds and his spies were everywhere. She didn't have the strength.

Besides, where could they hide when their very dreams betrayed them?

"The Roam is moving," Cristina said. "The stench of Jaguar droppings fills the wind, closer by the hour."

Afriqua Lee heard the bustlings outside, the rattle of rigging and the cough of old engines coaxed out of their winter sleep.

"We are among the last," Cristina said. "The rest left last night for the highlands, the seacoast, the sand reaches of the Quetzal. Your Rafferty humiliated a priest and now we are paying for it."

"The Jaguar . . . we have glimpsed his tail through the curtain."

"While you pinched the tail, the paw struck down the Roam. The Jaguar priesthood has put a bounty out on every branded hand delivered to them, alive or dead, attached or not."

Afriqua sucked in a sharp breath and let it out slowly to ease the pounding in her head.

"But why . . . ?"

"To shame us into turning the two of you over to them."

Afriqua Lee was shocked at the horror of it.

Hands cut off . . . and it's our fault.

"Your father tailed the Jaguar and the Jaguar had him killed. How will you and your gaje Rafferty fare any better?"

"My father . . . tailed the Jaguar . . . alone. He was a fool."

"Who's going to help you? Rafferty? He disappeared weeks ago. And what's to become of us in the meantime?"

"Weeks?"

Afriqua lifted her head and dropped it back to the pillow.

"How long . . . this dream?"

"You have slept now four days. We thought you were lost to us. After the attacks on the Roam, there were those who would hand you to the priesthood. They demand a kris romani when we stakedown safe in the highlands. Well or not, you move with us tonight. Spies are everywhere. Do you understand the danger?"

Afriqua nodded and croaked, "Yes."

"Oh, girl. I don't think you have any idea. Perhaps that means you *will* skin this Jaguar. You will be safe while there is a Roam to protect you. That is my word as Romni Bari, as Old Cristina."

There are visual errors in time as well as in space.

—Marcel Proust, ***Maxims***

THE TYRANT SUN puddled a few weak mirages off the rocks ahead and Rafferty glimpsed a shadow zigzagging towards him. It was a rabbit, plump enough for these parts, and Rafferty stayed put.

All he carried today was his snake-stick and his knife, and he wore the heavy black cottons of a Roam technician. He walked the vision-walk that was required of every boy who would become a man of the Roam. He had been on the walk, in and out of dream, for over a month.

The rabbit darted his way, dodging from shadow to shadow up the draw. Rabbit was a powerful figure in the history of the Roam. Many leaders had taken the name Rabbit, and it was a rabbit that fooled the gods and allowed the Roam to win the ball game of fate. Rafferty took this as a sign.

Rafferty thumped the rabbit with his stick when it got to the bush at his feet. After the scrabble of dying paws on sand, he was left with the stillness of late sun on rock. The call of his crow buried itself in the sand and sky. Rafferty thought of storms, words and lives swallowed whole out here, and imagined the ragged edge of an owl's wing spread for strike. The image snapped.

The right side of the rabbit's head was crushed and its lone left eye stared hard at him, blue glaze flecked with bits of dust and gravel. Rafferty picked it up and the warm skin quivered under his fingers. He looked up and down the valley. Not a sound.

"Well, rabbit, what do you see?"

His dead voice bounced nowhere and sank into the walls of his own ears. He was reminded of the time, as a youngster, when he saw through the curtain to the other side, when he saw Eddie Reyes drop his black rabbit into the bushes.

"Tell them 'hello' for me," Rafferty told the rabbit.

Rafferty still wasn't sure what the other side was all about. Sometimes he wondered whether that might be where people went when they died, as well as when they dreamed. But only special dreams took him to the other side, and he couldn't always send himself there when he wanted. It was just as well; he wasn't sure how much pain his body could stand. He was sure that it was real, that Eddie was real, and that was enough.

His folding knife opened stiffly in his hand and he cut the rabbit's head from its body. He pinched the head tight under the jaw and carried it to the largest flat rock in the draw. He set it down facing east and sprinkled a handful of dirt over it. His body told him what to do. A mutter from his crow came to him on the breeze.

His knife moved in an old rhythm across the inside back legs, across the belly. He cut the front feet off and slipped the hot glove of hide off the body. A wisp of steam curled from the back of the rabbit where the scant fat lay between the shoulder blades like small ears.

A tall butte loomed out of the flatlands about a kilometer to the south. Rafferty rolled the rabbit carcass up in its skin and headed for the rock in a slow run. His feet kicked up sand behind him and worked his body smooth as dreams, smooth as the past itself. As the sweat came on and his temples tightened, he remembered all the long seasons, all the years of hunger that tracked him like wolves.

When he reached the butte he was barely out of breath but sweating heavily, a danger in the drylands. He hoped the exertion would bring on his vision so that he could take it back to the Roam. They would have to decide, then, to admit him or to drive him out for good. He did not want to think about what that might mean for Afriqua Lee.

He set the rabbit into a cut in the rock face above his head. Clumps of gray-brown fur stuck to the spatters of dried blood on his hands. He wiped them off in the sand. His thighs were damp with sweat, the heavy cotton pants stuck tight to his skin.

Rafferty picked bits of sage and dried grasses for his fire. He gutted the rabbit and ate the liver raw, something he'd seen Old Cristina do many times. It tasted sweet this way, about the texture of his own tongue. He wouldn't eat more—it would drive off the vision—but he felt the need to cook the rabbit just the same.

His fire took off, and he spitted the rabbit on a thick piece of sage. He propped it over the fire and relaxed against the rocks. Off in the distance he watched his crow lift off, finished with the offering of the head. The last of the sun let slip the gray-black shadows of twilight, and Rafferty saw the first nightstalker slink towards him about a hundred meters south. He picked up a few sharp, fist-sized rocks and piled them beside the fire.

He could've thrown them the skin, the guts or the carcass, and they would drift away like spots of fog, or dreams. If they knew him to be truly empty-handed, they would leave. But Rafferty wanted them to have to come for it. He was in that kind of mood.

Night came on fast in the southland, and by the time the rabbit was properly blackened, the first nightstalker crisscrossed the outside halo of the firelight and worked its way to the edge. Even in the bad light he could count ribs and patches of raw skin.

Rafferty's first rock missed the animal and didn't even raise a flinch. The next hit high on the stalker's shoulder. It yelped, jumped back out of the light, then circled in. This time, two more came with it. The first rushed head-on. The second and third flanked him evenly. Rafferty threw a quick one at the blur in the middle and snapped off a poor throw at the one on the left. He reached for another rock and saw the stalker on his right trot off, head high, a snake of rabbit guts trailing from its mouth.

Her mouth. In her high-headed trot across the light he saw her bone-thin back, her teats, and what was left of her nipples chewed and crusted thick with blood. The others ran her down.

When she turned again, robbed and snarling, she fixed his eyes across the fire and he knew he would need his knife. What he saw when he stared at her eyes was the strength that the terror of hunger can bring.

"So this is for keeps," he muttered. He crouched, facing the dark across the fire.

More than anything, she wanted him to go away.

Just go away and leave that sweet moist meat right there.

The others were busy with the guts, and Rafferty saw in the dreamway four half-grown kits whining in the dark behind her. They snarled in some sandy pit, wanting milk or meat but they would settle for her, this time, if she came back empty. They would not stop at her teats, and she had no blood to spare.

She jumped right across the fire, and Rafferty caught her under the jaw with his left hand, blocked her upwards and slammed his knife into her belly with his right. They barked together in surprise when his knife hit a rib and folded across his fingers.

He held her tight so that he could reopen his blade. It was all he could do to hang on to her chest while she bit up his ear and his face. Her hind legs raked open his shirt and thighs. She caught him under the left eye, high on the cheek, and pulled until he felt the top of his cheek sucked from the bone.

He dropped her and grabbed for her eyes, but she held on long enough to pull him down onto the fire. She spun, snatched the rabbit and snarled into the night.

Rafferty listened to the rustling and growling through the sage beyond the fire; then they were gone. It was a while before he could move again, and in the morning his crow brought him the remnants of the skull. But in the night, by the dying fireglow, Rafferty had received his vision.

In Rafferty's vision the Jaguar was not a jaguar at all but a fat man in a jaguar skin. He danced in circles on a red tiled floor, sweating and grunting, while a ring of white-frocked priests set out spicy meats and liters of fine wine. Rafferty watched from a high vantage point, as though he'd stolen the eyes of his crow.

In the courtyard of the dance stood statues of warriors in helmets, some in the thick-lipped, hook-nosed style of the Roam. They wore a battle dress that Rafferty didn't recognize, a bulky dress with no decoration. Outside the courtyard, sniffing the wind and snarling, a real jaguar circled the compound. It tested every gate and door, every window, every crack, and found it impenetrable.

Rafferty's feeling from the Jaguar-man was revulsion, and the odor that wafted up to his vantage point was not the odor of honest sweat but the stench of sun-bloated death. The jaguar outside the walls, though beautiful and well-muscled, showed the sharp ribs of hunger, and displayed, on his muzzle, the scars of repeated attacks against the impervious stones of the courtyard. On his flank he carried the butterfly brand.

As the Jaguar-man danced inside, the real jaguar threw itself against the glassy walls, only to fall back and rise again, more slowly each time. It rested at last, forepaws high against the wall, tongue lolling drool from the side of its jaw. Its green eyes fixed on Rafferty.

It is you.

The voice in his mind was unfamiliar, all-encompassing.

You, Rafferty, let me in.

The Jaguar-man danced with hundreds of ribbons in his hands, and he wound them around a great pole. Far on the horizon, at the ends of the ribbons, Rafferty saw the people of the Roam pulled closer, dragged helpless by the red ribbons piercing their chests, knotted to their bleeding hearts.

He woke to the dawn-thunder of the Jaguar's command.

You, Rafferty, let me in.

. . . all the iron and concrete
heaped into order
can't keep these single blades
of grass from breaking through
back into the world.

—Finn Wilcox, *Here Among the Sacrificed*

MARK WHITE LOUNGED in a hammock that his wife had brought him from Mexico, her encyclopedia of Mayan art open on his chest. He half-dozed and listened to the comforting rattle of her suitcases as she unpacked. This trip had taken her away for five weeks and three days. They had been in bed now, by his estimate, for thirty-four of the thirty-six hours she had been back. He was sleepy, a bit achy in the lower back, and very hungry.

Something niggled at him while he dozed. As he'd browsed the Mayan art book he'd had a clear and ongoing sense of *déjà vu*. He was particularly drawn to the jaguar motif carved in a ball-court wall, and to the figure of the hawk-nosed priest standing beside it. The name 'Eddie Reyes' had just sprung to mind, when the phone rang.

"Don't answer that," he called. "We're on vacation for one more day."

"Sorry," Sara said. "I told my editor she could call me today. If it's for you, I'll lie."

Mark had just found a comfortable position for his lower back when Sara came back biting her lip.

"What's up?"

"It's for you. I couldn't lie."

"What? The yellow press couldn't lie? Must be serious."

When she didn't crack a smile, he sat up and swung his legs over the edge.

"It's the sheriff's office," she said. "They have Eddie."

"Well, what . . . ?"

She motioned him to the phone.

"Attempted murder," she said, "of Maryellen Thompkins."

"Shit!"

After a quick assessment over the phone, Mark made two calls, one of them to Eddie's uncle Bert who, as usual, was never home. The other went to their hospital lawyer, Kurt Prunty, who agreed to meet him at the jail. Mark had been busy lately, too busy to catch up with Eddie. This wasn't how he'd wanted to do it.

Mark hurried into the new gray suit that Sara had bought him, and guzzled a pint-sized Coke to stop his stomach from growling. The fifteen-minute ride to the jail didn't help him to any more insights than he already had, but it gave him time to catch his breath and become Dr. Mark White.

He wrestled his old Volkswagen van into a tight spot in front of the county offices and ignored the 'expired' reading on the meter. The receptionist gave his rumpled hair a cursory raised eyebrow and handed him a message before opening the gate to the back.

"Call ER," was all it said.

"Did you take this?"

She nodded.

"It's the girl," she said. "They took her to the Emergency Room because they couldn't rouse her. They say she's real sick with whatever he gave her. The parents don't want you there. You'd better call first."

"Thanks. Call the charge nurse for me. Tell them not to give her anything until I get there. The girl has a sleep disorder and that's probably all that we're dealing with. I want to talk with Eddie first."

At the mention of Eddie's name the receptionist sat a little straighter in her chair and adjusted the slippage in her swept-wing eyeglasses. She buzzed the gate again without a word, and Dr. White let himself into the back complex that made up the valley's jail.

A young deputy led him into the cell block. When Mark asked him for a briefing, the tight-lipped deputy merely shook his head and kept walking. The cell block's deterrent to escape was confusion, and as many times as Mark had walked its hallways, he was still unsure that he could find his way out.

The jail was a labyrinth of cells, storage rooms and privileged areas for the trustees. The building had been a cannery, and decades of berry stains still darkened the floors. Less informed visitors assumed they were bloodstains, and most new prisoners were encouraged in that assumption; it made for easier handling. The jail seldom held more than three prisoners at any one time, but some enthusiastic contractor had talked the county into building thirty cells just before the end of the war.

The cells were filled twice, and on both occasions the valley was the center of national scrutiny. The first time, they held prisoners from the Japanese internment camp, which had been a hasty transformation of the local fairgrounds. The prisoners were all young men from the camp—American citizens who had refused to report for the draft. They were trying to make a point, but so was the country, so it sent them all on to the Federal penitentiary for the duration of the war.

The second time the jail was full, the dominant language was German. German citizens who had been captured in the Pacific and classified as prisoners of war were to be repatriated. The Government was so pleased with the way the valley handled the Japanese situation that they gave them the German situation. None of the prisoners had served in the armed forces, and many townspeople brought them traditional foods and played Bavarian music for them outside the walls. Most of the prisoners had lived in the Pacific to escape the German culture. Nevertheless, they displayed the appropriate gratitude for this relatively innocuous discomfort.

Mark had worked with the sheriff's office before, and regardless of personal feelings about his patients, the deputies had usually treated him well. Mark noted that his presence was bringing out an intense fear reaction in this rookie. When he saw Eddie, he understood why.

Eddie was curled on his bunk in a fetal position, face to the wall. The stains on his clothing, his blankets and arms, and the marks on the floor where he'd been dragged into the cell, were bloodstains, not berry stains. His left tennis shoe was missing, and the bottom of that foot had a large, drying bloodstain. A strong smell of vomit thickened the air.

"Jesus Christ!"

Eddie's breathing was so shallow that Mark could barely detect it. His pulse was undetectable at the wrist, but it was present in his neck, fast and very weak. His eyes were half-open and staring; both pupils reacted when Mark blocked off the light from the doorway. When Eddie was in his post-dream state, his pulse was always very slow and strong, his breathing very slow and deep.

"Call the ambulance," he told the guard. "He's in shock. He hasn't bled that much on the outside, he must be bleeding inside. He's going to the hospital."

"They've been called, Doc. . . ."

"Then leave us alone," Mark snapped. "You can think about doing five to seven for manslaughter if he dies."

The door slammed shut and the overhead light came on. It had been a long time since Mark had done a primary exam on a trauma patient, and he kicked himself for not bringing his bag.

Getting soft, Dr. Fat-Cat Shrink?

He got down next to Eddie's ear and said, "Eddie, Eddie, can you hear me?"

Eddie blinked his eyes and grunted.

"I need to find out where you're hurt," he said. "Let me know if I hurt you. Can you do that?"

Another grunt.

There was no vomit on the bed; it was all on the front of Eddie's shirt and jeans.

He threw up before they brought him here.

Most of the blood was on his clothes and it was nearly dried. The only fresh blood that Mark saw stained the bedding under Eddie's mouth and nose.

He bled before they brought him here.

In spite of himself, Mark watched anger put a tremble into his hands. He started his exam at the top of Eddie's head, moving his fingers through his hair, looking for bleeding sites. He found a small one on the right that had stopped; the hair was clotted around it. Eddie flinched from his touch in that area.

Mark checked the back of Eddie's neck and his spine, and was relieved when he got no sign of pain there.

"Can you wiggle your toes, Eddie?"

The bare left foot moved. The right foot moved.

"Fingers?"

His hands clenched and unclenched.

Mark reached underneath Eddie and slid his hand along his body where his right side lay on the bed.

"I'm checking you for bleeding here, Eddie."

He got a grunt of pain at the right shoulder, and on his upper right rib cage. The ribs there were mushy, and moved out when they should have moved in with his breathing.

Flail chest.

Eddie had instinctively done the right thing by lying on that side; it stabilized the fractures and probably saved him from lung damage. There was no pink froth at his nose or lips.

Eddie's face was something no mother would recognize. His lips were swollen purple, both eyes were blackened and swelling, and the right side of his face was nearly twice as big as the left.

"Did the police do this to you, Eddie?"

Eddie struggled with the reply, "Nuh. Nuh."

"Maryellen? Did Maryellen do this?"

"Nuh! Nuh!"

The cell door jerked open and the deputy stood back to let the aid crew in.

"I'm Dr. White," he introduced himself. "He's shocky, pretty mashed up on the right. No lung involvement yet, so go easy. My guess is that broken clavicle lacerated his subclavian and he's bleeding out into his chest. Get a blood sample for chemistries before you start an IV. I'll meet you there after I get a story here."

Mark told Eddie, "You're going to the hospital. I'll be there with you."

Eddie grunted, and gripped Mark's forearm tight. Mark took his hand and squeezed it back.

"They'll take care of you. I'll be right there."

Mark stepped into the corridor and pushed the deputy aside. Two other deputies, both of whom he recognized, hurried down the hallway towards him. Between them, looking grim, strode Kurt Prunty.

"You can do some fast talking to me, or you can do some slow talking in court," Mark growled. "He tells me that you guys didn't rough him up. Who did?"

"He was like that when they found him. . . ."

"Bullshit, Mr. Hubbard." Mark tapped a finger on the deputy's name tag. "He got that way in your presence or he wouldn't be in a cell right now, and you know it. He'd be in the ER where he belonged in the first place. . . ."

Kurt stepped between Mark and the deputy as the medics wheeled the gurney out of the cell and past them down the hall.

"What's up, Doctor?"

"One of our outpatients, Eddie Reyes, got picked up for attempted murder of one of my patients, Maryellen Thompkins. She's in the ER. I got here and found Eddie severely beaten, in shock with signs of an internal bleed." He nodded down the hallway. "That was him. Nobody's talking here, and I'm just getting pissed off, so I'll leave these public servants to double-talk you while I get some answers at the hospital. . . ."

"Now wait a minute, Doctor."

The only deputy with a mustache, Dusty, tapped him on the shoulder. "You just came busting in here, didn't ask anybody anything, and expect to have answers. Hubbard, here, is new and wasn't even on the scene. I, personally, was on the horn to the aid crew when you came in and I, personally, saw to it that you were called down here. So don't give me that crap."

Mark stuck out his hand and Dusty shook it.

"All right; thanks, Dusty. I need to get up to the ER. Fill Kurt in with everything you have and he'll meet me up there. Tell me this, though. How did Eddie try to kill her, and how did he get so messed up?"

"Drugs, we thought," Dusty said. "They were both there by the river in the rain, really knocked out. He came around a little bit but she's gone to the world. . . ."

"They do that, Dusty. That's why I'm their doc. It has nothing to do with drugs. Those two won't even take the drugs that I prescribe, and that's part of the problem. What made you think it was drugs?"

"Well, the girl's daddy, Mel Thompkins. He put in the call and met us down there by the river."

"He said, specifically, that it was drugs?"

"That's right. Said that she wasn't to be seeing him because they'd already had some hassle about that."

"So, he was the one who beat Eddie up?"

Dusty looked at Kurt, at Hubbard, then down at his shoes.

"Why don't you get on up to the ER, Doc? I'll talk to your man here. Don't worry, he'll get the whole story."

"Was it Thompkins who did it?"

"Shit," Dusty hissed. "Yes, it was Thompkins."

Mark thought it out on the five-block drive to the Emergency Room.

Thompkins found them and led the police to them. They would have sent Eddie to the hospital if he'd been found beat up. So

Thompkins must've beaten Eddie after the cops arrived. Why didn't the aid crew take Eddie, too?

Mark concluded that Eddie had been beaten while the ambulance was at the scene, while everyone else was watching Maryellen.

And besides me, Maryellen is the only one who knows that he was absolutely defenseless at that time.

They must have known a cover-up would be pretty feeble.

Good, Mark thought. *They'll get on Thompkins and give me some backup.*

The small Emergency Room was jammed. Besides Eddie and Maryellen, there were the usual half-dozen sick kids, sprained ankles, a chain-saw bite out of a foot, a very smelly old man in for alcohol detox and a drooling lady having a stroke. There were only two beds, so the stroke lady and Maryellen were inside. They had moved Eddie to the hallway just outside of surgery while they prepped him, and the rest of the people cried and cursed and smoked along the beige walls. Mark identified himself to the receptionist and walked in.

Mel Thompkins snapped him a glance that would kill but K.C., the emergency room nurse, seemed very glad to see him.

"I didn't get much of a chance to assess your boy," she said. "The duty doc is prepping him for surgery. As you can see, it's a zoo in here."

"You didn't take this job to be bored," he said.

K.C. was the only nurse that made Sara uneasy. She had enormous brown eyes and a quick smile. She was young, athletic, bright, aggressive . . . and made the wives who didn't know her uneasy. She was good at her job, and that made the docs look good, so they all talked about her a little more than their wives would have liked. She only dated boat builders, and claimed she was looking for Noah. This late spring afternoon her hair was a little damp from stressful work in a tiny room, but her eyes still said: "Hi, good to see you, come on in."

"Nobody's bored today except the patients"—she waved her hand towards the waiting room—"but that's why they call them 'patients.' "

K.C. launched right into her report without missing a beat, all the while watching the two cardiac monitors on Maryellen and the stroke.

"Your girl's a mystery. No neurologic deficits at all, reflexes brisker than normal, if anything, and pupils react equally and appropriately. No sign of trauma. Vitals normal, even healthy—not shocky like your boy. Blood studies so far say her electrolytes are fine; white count and crit are swell. Urine negative for sugar and proteins. Normal temp. Frankly, if it wasn't for all this confusion, I'd say she's just sound asleep."

"Thanks, K.C. She and the boy have both been treated for sleep disorder, as well as some other problems, and your guess is probably in the ballpark. Let's keep her until the drug screen comes in; then if she's still unresponsive I'd like her transferred to The Hill. . . ."

"Bull*shit*!"

Maryellen's father pushed K.C. aside and poked Mark in the chest. Mark noted the heavily abraded knuckles and the dried blood on his hands and shirt.

"It's *your* hospital and *your* studies that started this mess. The Reyes kid can't fool me like he can fool you. It's drugs; it's been drugs all the time. My girl was fine until she met him. I had a hunch they'd be meeting, even after I forbid it. So I called the law."

"How did you know where to find them?"

"I said I had a hunch, didn't I?"

"Pretty strong hunch, to call the law without locating them first."

"Are you calling me a liar?"

"Not yet," Mark said.

He slapped away the hand that poked his chest, and Thompkins winced in pain.

"I can see by your hands you've been picking your nose," Mark said. "You give me some straight answers and you might stay out of jail. If there's an attempted murder charge floating around here, it's your ass it's going to stick to."

Mark saw K.C. wink at him over Thompkins' shoulder. He took a deep breath.

Thompkins looked much older than Mark knew him to be. He had alcohol on his breath and the haggard, dishevelled look that went with the disease. But there seemed to be something more. . . .

Maybe he's got the same thing she has, he thought. *Maybe that's why he's been such a bastard all along. . . .*

Thompkins had got to blow off his adrenalin, so Mark knew he was headed for the maudlin stage.

"Did you think you could get away with killing him, right in front of the deputies?"

"I . . . I wouldn't kill him, even if he is a shit-pot. I wouldn't do that to my daughter."

Thompkins rubbed his beard-stubble, then moved to stand beside Mark so he could continue to watch his daughter. It gave him a good excuse to avoid looking Mark in the eye.

"I can't stand it, when she goes up there. She's *not* a loony, not like this Reyes kid. . . ."

"Maybe it's the word 'loony' that's the problem," Mark said. "We don't use it, ourselves, and for good reason. It scares people, they see how close they come themselves. And even when they need help they don't go get it because they're afraid people like you will call them 'loonies.' "

Mel Thompkins glanced at Mark, then back to his daughter. Mark remembered when Maryellen's father was still a handsome young man who cared for himself, who owned a small gun shop but was able to attract Maryellen's stepmother, generally considered a classy catch locally. Alcohol, bitterness and nagging had taken its toll. Mark hoped to spare Maryellen some youth.

"Have you ever had the kind of dreams these kids talk about?"

At that moment Kurt and Dusty pushed open the door, and Mark waved them back outside, indicating 'one minute' with his index finger.

"Well, not really," Thompkins was saying. "Today I was . . . taking a nap. I dreamed that this guy called me on the phone. He said something like, 'I'm calling from The Hill. Eddie Reyes got into our drug cabinet this afternoon and he's got your daughter.' I . . . had a few before I dozed off, and the dream was so clear that I thought maybe I *did* get a phone call. Anyway, I knew where they'd probably be, that fishing shack. Eddie's family used that spot for years. I don't know why I called the sheriff, like you say. All the way there I kept thinking how I'd look like an idiot if they weren't there. But they were . . . which makes me wonder for sure whether it was a dream or a phone call. Jesus Christ! they were just laying out there in the rain, soaking wet. . . ."

Mark picked up Maryellen's chart from the counter.

"I ordered a drug screen," Mark told him. "I suspect it'll be negative—you heard K.C.'s report—but I knew you'd want to be sure. I assume that's okay?"

"Yeah," Mel said. "Yeah, thanks."

"I'd like to get one on you, too, if you don't mind."

"What! Me?" Thompkins strode towards the doorway, but Mark didn't step aside. "You can't make me do it."

"I probably can," Mark said. "When you work on The Hill, you learn all kinds of tricks. And what I don't know, Mr. Prunty has covered. But that's not what I want. It's more important for you to tell K.C. exactly what happened with Eddie, so she can relay details to surgery. Dusty will want to talk with you as well, but, right now, saving Eddie's life takes priority. . . ."

Thompkins started to interrupt, but Mark put up a hand to stop him.

"It doesn't matter what you think about the boy," he said. "It's important to *your* future that we save his life. I'll let you know what's happening with Maryellen."

As K.C. took Thompkins aside, Mark pulled the curtain behind him so he could have some privacy with Maryellen. His exam verified what K.C. had told him, and verified what he'd already suspected. They were experimenting in synchronizing their dreams. Something must have gotten out of control. Mark had seen Eddie this far out of it before, but this was a first for Maryellen. It made the hairs on his neck and arms stand up.

What if they're right?

Mark had tried every theory, from brain dysfunction to hysteria, and still had no idea what was going on with these two. It was neither schizophrenia nor multiple personality disorder. It was real, observable, and absolutely out of the realm of the literature.

Well, Mark thought, *maybe it's time for some new literature.*

Stories go to work on you like arrows. Stories make you live right. Stories make you replace yourself.

—Benson Lewis, Cibecue Apache;
On Nature, Daniel Halpernen

THE EXPERIMENT STARTED in the day room on The Hill the first Monday in July. Eddie would write down his thoughts and dreams, and Maryellen would sketch. Between them, Dr. Mark hoped to capture a complete picture of the other side, and how they got there. He warned Eddie that going back to high school would be impossible unless the experiment worked. He did not say how he would know it was working.

Eddie had been around The Hill long enough to recognize the serious signs—short-term trials of various psychoactive drugs, dietary changes, control of visitors and environment. Dr. Mark's superiors were fed up. They wanted results, and they wanted them soon. Eddie felt the Thompkins family voice behind every move.

"They're doing this for you, you know," Eddie told Maryellen. "As far as this town's concerned, I'll always be the bad guy. They don't *want* me better, they want me *here*."

There had been a few *accidents* with Eddie's drug therapy, and adjustment to these accidents had been difficult. When it became possible to think through the mind-drool of the drugs, Eddie had accused Maryellen's father. The only result of the accusation had been a new notation at the bottom of his chart: "paranoid ideation."

Eddie thought he could forgive anything if Mel Thompkins had been a good father to Maryellen.

I'm better off alone than with a father like hers, he thought. Dutifully, he scribbled the thought into his notebook.

Mel Thompkins slapped her occasionally, marking her face and lips. More often, he screamed at her, loud enough and often enough that the police had been called to their house more than once. Worse, in Eddie's mind, was the stepbrother. Maryellen quit talking about him a couple of years ago, and by her silence Eddie inferred a problem. A big problem. A problem that he felt a father should solve.

I could find that bastard on the dreamways and fry his skull, Eddie thought. He did not write this thought down.

Some night on the dreamways he could wander Maryellen's brain, find out for sure.

No, he thought, *we don't snoop on strangers. I'm not going to start on her.*

Her father lived in his bottle these days, thanks to the stepmother. Each time Maryellen skipped a grade and her precious son didn't, Maryellen's home life deteriorated. Eddie could tell, because her attitude deteriorated, in spite of his best efforts to cheer her up.

Cheer her up!

How ironic. Now he'd landed himself a four-month commitment and Maryellen a stint in day treatment. Now they were supposed to chase down their dreams through the impenetrable fog of their drug therapy.

On his notebook cover Eddie had scrawled: "Trapped and drugged for his own good: Eddie Reyes, endangered species."

Maryellen had complained that she was a photographer, not an artist. Eddie tried to show her the bright side.

"One of us needs to be on the outside," he explained. "How else are we going to track down the Jaguar? Besides, how do you expect to photograph dreams? Get real."

"Get real, yourself," she said. "Look who's talking."

She couldn't help laughing at their situation.

She reminded Eddie of the time last spring when Eddie had taken her picture with the camera from the Journalism Department. They had arranged all of their classes together, except PE, in spite of her parents. It was their best protection in an increasingly hostile world. Their teachers harassed them about their absences. The students shunned them for their difference.

The greatest risk, the greatest crime of adolescence is being different, going against the crowd, appearing weird. Sticking together continued to be their only protection.

It had been a portrait assignment for Sara's journalism class, and Eddie had never seen Maryellen so self-conscious. It was always easy for her to use the camera, but tough to be the subject—even with him. He'd wanted her to relax.

"I love you," he'd said.

She ducked her head and laughed. She wanted to say it back, he could tell, and it would have been easy if she had been the one behind the shutter.

"I . . ."

Sklick

Maryellen laughed again, and hid her mouth with her hand.

In the print, he'd focused on her knuckle. He remembered hearing the *snap* of his film advance.

"Tell me," he said.

"I love"—*sklick*—"you. Oh!"

He cocked and focused as fast as he could. The wind blew some of her long dark hair into the corner of her mouth.

"Say it again," he said, and hunched down level with her eyes.

"I love"—*sklick*—"you. You're *crazy* . . ." *Sklick.*

"Again." *Sklick.*

"I love you." *Sklick.* She tipped her head back and laughed, trying not to look at the camera, a tear just starting—*sklick sklick*—at the edge of her eye, and they both doubled over laughing.

She got to go home every day; Eddie had to stay at The Hill. Every afternoon in the day room she told him how, alone in the kitchen each night, she ate as much as she could until she gagged. She put nothing away, cleaned nothing up. She did all of this in the dark, noisily.

No one got out of bed or called to her. Only her stepbrother knocked on her bedroom door, and it was against him that she'd installed the locks.

This Monday afternoon in July she came to the day room with her sketch pad, nodded self-consciously at Eddie, and dumped her things onto the table—blue purse, school folders with the figures colored in, a red book whose title he couldn't see.

He thought, *She looks as pale as a dark person can look and still be alive.*

The circles under her eyes gave her that haunted look that he knew the dream-killer drugs gave him, too. He'd seen it in her drawings.

Maryellen rustled through her bag for her pencils and sharpener. He stared off.

She began sketching him. In her hands he became lines that crossed shadows, shades of light and dark in a piece of nose, an ear, hair.

She spoke absently of fathers and noise, of war and the hardening of fathers. He watched his reflection watch her eyes trace his lips, the instroke curve of his jaw.

Maryellen sharpened her pencil, and the shavings tumbled out of the ashtray between them.

"They would have split up except for me," she said. "Ironic, huh?"

"I never liked her."

Her hands paused; then she straightened a ripple in her paper. She touched her index finger to her lips and stared down at her pad.

"Pardon?" she asked. "Your eyes—I was having some trouble there."

Eddie hated repeating things. He hated repeating things word-for-word and especially hated repeating things that were superficial anyway. Clearing his throat helped, so he did that.

"Your stepmother, Olive," he said. "I never liked her."

"It's mutual," she said. "Just the mention of your name in the house infuriates her. Sometimes I find excuses to bring up your name, like on the telephone or something, just to piss her off."

Eddie recalled the time he'd asked Maryellen to a movie two years back. It had been their one attempt at a real date. Maryellen came to the door, said she was sick and couldn't go. By her nervous hands he knew that it was Maryellen's voice with her stepmother's words. He pressed her for another time, knowing who stood behind her, freezing her throat, stopping her voice and opening the tears. When she began to cry, he turned away and walked stiffly to the car.

Then *she* came to the door, tucked safely behind the screen.

"I don't think that you should see Maryellen anymore."

He glared at her, waiting.

"Looking hateful at me won't do any good, either. I know you see each other at school, and I can't do anything about that. But I want her to see other people, other boys."

Still, he stared.

"Well, if you really want to know . . . if you'd do what you did to your own *mother* . . ."

"You ignorant pig!" he'd yelled, and out of some reflex grabbed for the door handle. The screen was locked, and he rattled it in his rage.

"He's going to kill me!" she shrieked. "He's going to kill me! You get him out of here. You *want* him to kill me!"

The humiliation of his own temper worked on him, and he kicked the screen door, ripping a hole in it. Eddie gritted his teeth so hard his gums ached, then jumped his bicycle and pedalled across the lawn and onto the highway.

He camped for three days on the river near Alderton; after that, behind his cousin's place. When he got back, the story was all over school, with the usual variations, but he was not arrested. His uncle gave him a token whipping and got him extra work at Ed's, to keep him busy.

Maryellen set her pad aside and rolled a cigarette. Her fingers were sure and quick at it now, in spite of the meds. Eddie noticed years ago that most people wrestled the paper around the tobacco and got a tube of empty paper or something that looked like a German shepherd crawling up a hose. Hers looked exactly like a Camel.

She puffed without inhaling and nodded, squinting the smoke out of her eyes. This smoking was new, something she'd picked up from one of the other patients. Dr. Mark didn't discourage her like Eddie thought he should. Eddie didn't know what to do when she was not drawing. He leaned his chair back and relaxed.

"Do that again," she said, and he glanced at her with that same glance he used when she asked him to repeat what he'd just said.

"You were real still there," she said. "You tend to move a lot."

"Makes me nervous, somebody looking at me all the time."

"There was a time when you didn't mind at all."

He grunted. It had been a long time since she talked about that.

"You weren't looking, anyway," he said. "You were staring."

"I was looking."

She shifted around in her chair, tapped her cigarette on the ashtray rim. He sat ramrod-still and didn't turn towards her. She went on.

"I'm drawing you here. I can't afford staring. Staring's non-productive. . . ." She broke it off with a sigh and a shrug.

"See?"

"I was *not staring*!"

She jabbed her cigarette into the ashtray, swallowed a long drink of water and picked up her pad.

"You were."

He barely mumbled it under his breath. Maryellen threw her pad down, her eyes suddenly hard and angry. Then, just as suddenly, they softened and her lips flashed him a smile.

He returned it with a giggle.

"Shit," she said. "This isn't very entertaining. We'd better get you out of this place."

Maryellen cupped her chin in her hand, and Eddie brought her some coffee from the pot against the wall. She stared past the wisp of steam into a stand of trees outside. Firs. He watched her pupils widen as her daydream washed between the other world and this one. The steady *clink clink* of her spoon outsang their breath.

We're old already, he thought. *Kids don't go through this crap.*

Eddie watched her eyes unfocus as she drifted through some memory. He tried to follow, but his meds wouldn't let him.

Each day that he woke up from a regular dream of Maryellen he felt healed. No twisted sheets of sweat, no regrets because drugs kept him off the real dreamways.

Eddie thought that maybe life was *really* a stage. Not a stage like Shakespeare meant, but a phase.

Mine seems to have fixed itself at a sort of cosmic puberty, he thought.

Dr. Mark told him he was missing being a teenager the first time around, so he might expect to go through it again sometime later. Eddie agreed that things intruded; he didn't argue that. More than ten years ago he'd survived the earthquake and the incident with his mother. This year, it was the beating that Maryellen's father had given him, and he chose to believe that since he didn't die he must have been reborn.

Eddie didn't get to see her much, except for the experiment, even though she lived so close. This week Dr. Mark had moved her to a neutral house, away from her parents. It was temporary, only until the end of the experiment. Eddie didn't trust her father's anger as much as he used to. The way he drank, it was just a matter of time until he lost it with her the way he had with Eddie. Eddie had seen the results of plenty of that kind of anger on The Hill.

Sometimes I don't think she remembers me, he thought.

When she went to the other side of the fabric, it was different for her. It was as though the trip back washed out something, filtered out some of the mesh of her memory. He didn't want to be lost like that. He hoped that what was lost was still there on the other side, for her to pick up later.

Outside, a summer rain kicked up a fuss against the windows.

Everything in the valley whispered *rain rain* from early fall to spring. The rain was in her blood like it pulsed in his, and, like Eddie, a thick press of damp leaves walled her away.

Her flowers, dried and crisp now, nodded from a pop bottle that they let him keep beside his bed. He got so tired these days—the medications made him tired—but he still liked remembering. The farther that a place was from his room, the easier it was to imagine it. Except the other side. Except for a few glimpses, they had blocked him from the other side.

Maryellen had brought him flowers when she came out of her . . . trance? coma? . . . and found out what her father had done. One was a tulip, a satinlike purple tulip with a few drops of water flecking its leaves. Its blue-blackness dusted its magnificent throat and shimmered on the back of his hand. That was a time when he didn't open his eyes much, when he explored his own depths eagerly. They couldn't give him drugs then because of his head injury, so he plunged through the fabric every chance he got.

He thought at first it was a war on the other side, but he discovered something even more horrible than that. It was a game. He always suspected the two were a lot alike because that's what it looked like in the history books.

He remembered that tulip well, because he wanted never to open his eyes. He thought, in the confused logic of a convalescent, that if he just kept his eyes closed for the rest of his life, then people would have to be nice to him. They would let Maryellen care for him because everyone could see he was harmless, and he could dream as much as he liked. She tried to talk him out of his darkness that time, but he stood his dark ground for a while.

"What's the difference, anyway?" he told her. "It's all just words. Just funny marks on paper or little waves in the breeze. We love and fight wars over words, and they aren't worth it. We write *war*, and the word is a thing that does not look like war, or smell like it. The word *war* doesn't wake people up at night screaming, their fists a pulp in the window. Words are liars in their very bodies. So are most people. So am I."

Maryellen was across the table from him, sketching. If he upset her, the clean, confident lines of her pencil didn't betray it. He didn't often upset her, which was why Eddie felt so easy talking in front of her like that.

"My father was allergic to war," she said. "He puked and they sent him home."

Eddie didn't like thinking about war. He'd seen his share on the other side and to see it was to share the feelings of those who saw it.

He'd seen what happened to Rafferty. Killing was easy and it settled things, but then it brought up different things. Thanks to Dr. Mark, and in spite of certain people in the valley, he'd learned to think of what happened to his mother as something other than killing. But she was dead, and his part in it tied her to him and tied him to death in a way that he couldn't explain. But Rafferty knew.

Maryellen was staring at him, then.

Eddie went back, in his mind, and scribbled down as fast as he could what he'd seen happen to Rafferty.

Rafferty had said to Afriqua Lee: "Tell her we put the girl and her kids in the van. We'll take them out with us. They'll make it."

Afriqua Lee translated. Rafferty held the back of the woman's neck together and pressed a wad of gauze in tight. Part of her skull and her right ear grinned out from under the tape. She blinked as Afriqua Lee shouted at her in some local whine, an Indian dialect he hadn't heard.

"Bien," she croaked back, and squeezed her eyes shut.

"We're down to moments," Rafferty told Afriqua Lee.

The woman started thrashing all of a sudden, a convulsion. Neither of them could help her, and nobody could help them if they were caught out there. The Jaguar priests were making a point of making an impression, and that meant that none of the men or boys would leave alive. The girls might live, but they'd surrender their hands.

Afriqua Lee helped Rafferty hold the wounded woman down

while he taped her arms and legs to her mat. She was a strong woman, pretty in the brown afterglow of the walls. Indian pretty, not skinny and starving like he'd expected. This country had fooled him like that. Rafferty remembered thinking he'd have bought her a drink.

She lay face up on her mat, rigid. Rafferty stretched a length of tape across her forehead and down the sides of the mat to keep her head still. She relaxed and her eyes opened. Now, with the tape and gauze all twisted up, her cuts were bleeding again and the hole in her neck clicked every time she moved.

"Ask her if she wants us to help her," Rafferty said, and showed Afriqua Lee the injector that Old Cristina had given him for this trip into the highlands.

Afriqua Lee spoke again, in the same rasp.

The woman nodded, in spite of her neck.

Rafferty injected her and she started to cry. Pretty soon the cry faded back, and as he emptied the last of their three ampules he brushed her face and her forehead with his hand. The cry subsided to a shudder, like his own. Then there was just the *shuff shuff* of her breath coming faster and shallower and the noise from the trucks loading up outside.

No animal sounds. The only voices were the few children. They had to move.

Her breath took on a gurgle, then a strangle. Her whole chest heaved tight against the tape; her eyelids slid open and she stared ahead, gasping.

Rafferty held her down to keep her from hurting herself. He held her down so she wouldn't hurt herself dying.

"Go on home," he told her. "Go home."

She twisted one arm loose of the tape and hooked it under his armpit; then she pulled. Her eyes begged him to come down with her into the dark, and she was gone.

Eddie's mind whirled with his own dreams, and now he had to fight off Rafferty's, too.

Today, Eddie thought, he should've stayed in his room and slept. It was one of those days again when sleep is just the thing.

Eddie was determined that love with Maryellen would be more than a dream. So much of what Eddie saw or heard he wanted to show her, on both sides of the fabric, but the way they had to live made that impossible.

A honeybee sipping from a drop of coffee on his spoon reminded him of her, of those things he'd like her to see. The delicacy of its orange tongue flicked out, sipped, flicked back. Beside it, one grain of rice stuck like an ant's egg to his chopstick.

Maryellen gave him those chopsticks a year ago, a lifetime before he had come to The Hill.

His hand finished the word 'Inevitable' in a scrawl.

As Maryellen was drawing, he remembered the little red ants that bite. There was a huge hill of them on the line between his uncle's place and her father's. Eddie's uncle claimed that you should drill your well where there's an anthill, that ants build over water. They stirred them up from time to time. Sometimes they'd drop a carpenter ant or two on top, just for the fight. The red ants smelled funny and bit, but at least they didn't eat holes in the house.

One time Maryellen's stepbrother scooped a handful of those red ants and stuffed them down the front of Maryellen's shirt. They had been thirteen or fourteen. She had a really nice figure even then, Eddie remembered, and the stepbrother was always wanting to get his hands on her. He tried all the usual peeks and taps and touches—a brush of arm *here*, a look over her shoulder *there*. He had graduated to grabs.

This time, though, she didn't push him away or slap him like she usually did. She very calmly took off her shirt, turned her back, unhooked her bra and brushed herself off. Then she put her bra back on, shook out her shirt, and as she slipped back into it she turned to him and said, evenly, "Don't ever do that again. Don't ever do *anything* like that again."

The meds made him wonder a lot, made his mind wander, but all of its ravelling seemed to lead to Maryellen.

Once, she had explained the differences between them. She explained that she grew up being hit and yelled at all the time. She got hit and yelled at less if she picked up certain subtleties in the people around her. He got abandoned for long periods of time, sometimes locked into closets or cars, and he learned to retreat inside, to shut off emotion and go away.

He breathed deep and settled into his chair again, the one overstuffed recliner in the day room. At this moment, during these moments of the experiment, the chair was his and no one challenged him for it.

"You seem so . . . afraid all of a sudden."

"No," he said. "I was just remembering, and remembering isn't always good."

She pushed her cup aside and picked up her pencil.

There was a time she would've picked up my hand.

"I read somewhere that it's our memory that keeps us alive," she said, and reached for her eraser.

"I'll bet that's true," Eddie said, and he believed it. "It takes time for messages to get from the body to the brain—I'll bet we don't even know when we're dead, because we have nothing to remember it with."

There was a strain to her laugh and he really wanted to change the weather in the day room. The *whish* and *scratch* of pencils complemented the rain.

He loved her, and didn't know what to do about it. He had to hunt down the Jaguar, and didn't know what to do about that. He had faith that everything would come clear if they just stuck together.

It had something to do with her focus, the intensity of her attention. He trusted insight, not instinct. Insight comes from *sight*, a conclusion of the senses—filtrate of the unprotected senses. Insight, the trustable unconscious, helped fill in the lapses in her focus, the eliminated detail of her subject. He suspected it was their mutual habit of focus that made him love her.

He glanced down at his notebook, where his hand had been moving by itself.

'There is no asymmetry,' he'd printed boldly. *'Remember the Butterfly Kiss.'*

He didn't remember writing any of it.

Her eraser nibbled at the paper, and she brushed the crumblings back without looking down.

Eddie saw that she was not drawing him, after all. She had used him as a model to draw one of his dreams of Rafferty, the one about the man with the blue ointment.

"I can understand dreams like . . . like our dreamways," she said. "That's happening while this is happening; it's parallel. But what about dreaming that happens in the future . . . ?"

He thought she got off track by thinking of it as 'the' future, but didn't want to get into it now.

Eddie always planted distance in the important things; getting close was too frightening. He focused on her drawing, and something tugged at him. There was Rafferty, who looked like Eddie, crouched behind a rock. There was the cliff face with the butterfly stain, the mother and daughter, the mysterious man holding his jacket around the mother's shoulders.

"That jacket"—he pointed to her pad—"that looks familiar."

It was an Army jacket with campaign ribbons on the breast and a bar on the shoulders.

"It should," she said, "it's just how your notes described what Rafferty saw."

"But you've seen their warriors on the other side," he said. "They wear old-fashioned stuff—sandals, shin guards, chest protectors. . . ."

"Yes," she said, "you're right. This is *our* Army. What do you think it means?"

"I think it means that whoever is on our trail is in the Army."

"Are you going to bring up that stuff about my dad again?"

"You made the connection, not me."

"It could be the Jaguar, you know," she said. "Maybe he was in the Army, too."

She continued drawing.

He didn't think she was listening now. He knew she needed a line of patter to orchestrate the rhythms of her hand.

Her gaze did not meet his. She focused somewhere near his ear and brushed his cheek on her way back to the page.

Eddie tasted the awful power of those eyes and saw how men could drown there. They were brown and wide, always wide. He was not uneasy, looking her in the eye, at being seen himself. Nothing that those eyes saw could embarrass him, no matter how deep the vision—of this he was sure.

"My leg's falling asleep," she said.

She stood and stretched, wiggling the toes of her left foot. She'd kicked off her sneakers under the table.

Eddie leaned back into his chair. He underlined his last scribble on the pad:

'If it wasn't for dreams we wouldn't see each other at all.'

Lovers need blessings. Their rectitude is not enough to counter the loveless process of the world. They must depend on the strength of the moment. . . . What the heart makes, the mind cannot destroy.

—Lucius Shepard, *Life During Wartime*

RAFFERTY WATCHED AFRIQUA Lee, knee-deep in the stream alongside a half-dozen older women, as she washed their clothes in a sunlit riffle. He knew how much she hated ritual washing, now that the Roam did not have the luxury of a permanent camp. The Jaguar priests and their raiders kept the Roam on the move, like a whipped nightstalker. Rafferty's chest puffed a bit to think that this time she did it for him.

Her skirt of the red quetzals was gathered and tucked at her knees, just clearing the water. She washed clothes as the rest of the women did, in the traditional manner, stripped to the waist, slapping out stains on flat rocks. Already the morning sun glared back at him from the water. It cast a white veil around Afriqua Lee, accenting her brown skin, her hair, the dark tips of her breasts that wobbled with her work. He knew that she knew that he was there, and so did the rest of the women. Tradition demanded that her gaze would not meet his own.

This was the very stream that had changed course during the earthquake that had killed her mother and brother. The Roam staked down at a new site, about a kilometer south of the south pasture of Uncle's place.

This year, Rafferty's special year, Old Cristina had led him to sites that he had never found as a youngster, that he was sure had been unknown even to Uncle. She prepared him as best a woman could for this day.

Rafferty stood across the stream from the women, facing the encampment of the Roam and, further back, the old settlement of Uncle's family. Behind him, what he had thought was hillside, Old Cristina had shown him to be a stone temple, covered with dirt and overgrown, but intact. It was only last night, when he stood atop it under the near-full moon with the old Romni wheezing beside him, that he realized the awful antiquity of the Roam.

Because he had come of age in the past year, Rafferty wore, for the first time, the red slash across the thigh of his dress trousers. The slash marked him an eligible bachelor of the Romni Bari's tent. Cristina gifted him with the honor, and warned him that this was a first. No gaje had ever carried such status to a Roam wedding. It was a validation of his standing within the kumpania, with the familia of the Romni Bari, and a statement of his intent to marry within the Roam. There would be objection, and it could be fatal. It had never been taboo to shed the blood of a gaje.

Most of the brush had grown back from the plague of bugs, and it offered good cover. He could not let it offer excellent cover. The women were supposed to see him, to mock him and comment loudly on his prowess, his clothing, his lineage. Only silence would indicate disapproval. It was only silence he had to fear.

"What lurks across the stream?" one prompted the others. "A bear in the bushes?"

"A blue-eyed bear," another cried. "Holy Martyr, save us from a devil-eye bear!"

Rafferty was encouraged; a fierce image was a good sign. Afriqua Lee did not look up from her wash, but pursed her lips and slapped one of his shirts against her rock. He knew all of the women at the stream, but he only had eyes for Afriqua Lee. One by one, he recognized their voices as, one by one, they validated his pursuit.

Silence would not stop him, after all.

"What is that between his legs?" This shriek from the thrice-married Sultana. "Does it furrow the trail when he walks?"

The women laughed themselves breathless at this, and Rafferty stepped out of the brush and onto the gravel bar across from Afriqua Lee. While they cackled themselves breathless, she worked on, unperturbed.

Some of the clothes were his own, and he recalled how Afriqua Lee had defied tradition that first night he had showered at Old Cristina's. Though just a youngster like himself, she had washed the clothes of a gaje, an unclean male. Even as a child she'd known her own mind. She never defended herself against the mutterings, never swayed, and proceeded to do the traditional things for him that a woman of the familia would do: washing, sewing, a stack of tortillas beside his door with morning coffee. He, tinkerer of the kumpania, returned her gifts with repairs, devices and clever inventions of his own. He had never so much as touched her hand.

"He has the heart of a jaguar, but trembles like a deer."

Pride welled in him at their acceptance of his suit. The formidable jaguar and the sensitive deer meant that he was the finest husband material.

"Perhaps it's a quetzal—look at the plumage!"

Indeed, he had woven the most iridescent feathers into his hair, thanks to the sharp eye of his faithful Ruckus.

Afriqua Lee washed his shirt as his heart pounded just meters away. Her hands had removed ten centimeters of red slash from the side of his trousers and stitched it to the diagonal across his thigh, just above the knee. When they married, she would replace it with blue, and thereafter each child would be represented above it with a red slash cut from the stripe at the side.

A suitor of the Romni Bari's familia would propose by offering his love a cloth braid of blue and red, and she would accept by unravelling the strands and weaving it into her hair. They would then take evening walks together in front of all the tents of the kumpania, and the children of the Roam would follow nearby, giggling and teasing.

Rafferty stepped into the stream.

A pebble plopped at his feet, then another. If Afriqua Lee had another suitor, then a dart would block his path. The stones were more of the women's foolishness, a mock protection of the girl being stalked. No dart plunged the waters at his feet.

"Run, girl, run!" they cried.

Afriqua Lee looked up at the skyline and around the treetops, carefully avoiding Rafferty, and inclined her head as though listening to a birdcall.

By the strictest standards of the Roam, Afriqua Lee had nothing to offer a suitor. She had accumulated no dowry, nor was there a male of her household available to offer one for her. An independent woman of sixteen was a liability, two years past her prime with neither promise nor arrangement. In truth, an independent woman of Afriqua's age was a rarity in the Roam.

She had proven herself an unusual child and an even more unusual young woman. Her beauty marked her desirable during quarterly gatherings of the kumpaniyi, yet she retreated to her van at the first sign of interest from the men, young or old. Rafferty had escorted her in her work as an interpreter in the cities, an agreement that had saved her honor and her life more than once.

A traditional wedding of the Roam was between a woman of fourteen and a man of twenty-five, an honorable spread by the Roam's standards. Rafferty and Afriqua Lee were both sixteen. That made him precocious and Afriqua Lee nearly an old maid.

Rafferty stepped into the current, the braid in his hand. The brush-birds continued to sing, and a buzz of insects urged him on. A school of fingerlings flashed away from his foot and the cold of the stream calmed the tremble in his right hand, where he held tight to the braid.

At midstream, she glanced up at him in spite of herself. He slipped once, twice, and flailed his arms trying to catch his balance.

"Look out!" a voice shouted.

Too late, she half-stood as he hit the water backward. She dodged the drenching wave but lost footing herself and plunged atop Rafferty into the stream.

The woman laughed so hard that men came running, thinking there was trouble. Through it all Rafferty managed to hold his precious braid out of water.

Afriqua Lee clutched his bachelor trousers to her chest and shook the water out of her hair with a *snap*.

"My hair!" she shrieked. "The Romni worked hours on my hair! Who would marry this muskrat of a woman?"

Rafferty held the braid in front of him like a shield, like the warding-off sign, and got his footing. His right knee throbbed, and he knew once he left the cold stream it would throb worse.

"I brought you the braid," he sputtered, his voice as formal as he could muster. "I, Rafferty, would marry this muskrat."

Ash does not suffer.

—*The Destruction of the Jaguar,* **translated by Christopher Sawyer-Laucanno**

AFTER HIS RECOVERY from the beating, Eddie had been released to Dr. Mark and he never went back to school. He spent the summer recovering on The Hill, where he submitted to the constant round of tests and to Dr. Mark's 'experiment.' Eddie threw himself into recording their thoughts and dreams, something he'd been afraid to do.

"What am I afraid of?" he asked Maryellen one day, "that they'll read this stuff and think I'm crazy? I'm in here because they're *sure* I'm crazy."

They filled notebooks and sketchpads; they scribbled thoughts and images on the nearest surfaces, including the day room's refrigerator door.

One Saturday afternoon Dr. Mark brought Eddie home to help him with the yard work. Sara had asked to see his notebooks and Maryellen's drawings. When Mark and Eddie came inside for their lunch break, Sara's eyes were aglitter with excitement. Books, papers and drawings were scattered over the oak tabletop, and Sara called them over.

"Look here, Eddie," she said, and pointed to one of Maryellen's drawings of Afriqua Lee's clothes. Next to the drawing, she had a page open in one of her big picture-books, a picture of some young Guatemalan girls. They wore identical dresses and headwraps. The stonework behind the girls in the picture was the stonework of the ancient Roam.

"Yes," Eddie said, and he said it with a sigh. "Yes, that's the Roam."

His hand couldn't help but caress the page. As he flipped through the book, he recognized a couple of the stakedown sites from his dreams of the southern highlands.

"So, Eddie," Dr. Mark said, "what do you think?"

"What do you mean?"

"I mean, do you think that you've seen pictures of these places before? Maybe that's how you've constructed . . ."

"You still won't believe me, will you?" Eddie said. He couldn't keep the anger and disappointment out of his voice.

"Eddie, I just asked you whether you'd seen these pictures before. It's my job to ask everything; you know that. If you answer my question, I'll answer yours."

Sara handed Eddie a big glass of Coke, even though she must have known that it got Eddie too nervous sometimes. He sipped it gratefully while he studied the pictures.

"No," he said. He looked Dr. Mark square in the eye. "I've never seen these pictures, these books or any pictures like them except in dreams."

"Okay, Eddie. Thanks." Dr. Mark held Eddie's gaze, and said, "Yes, I believe you."

While Eddie ate two meatloaf sandwiches, Dr. Mark talked to him about how other cultures repeat some patterns without ever meeting each other, how their art formed what he called 'archetypal patterns.' All of this was stuff that Eddie had read years ago in the quiet little library at The Hill.

"So," Eddie said, "what you believe is that I haven't seen those pictures. It doesn't mean that you believe me about the dreams. Is that right?"

"It means . . . yes," he said. "Yes, I believe you haven't seen the pictures. But I'm really not sure what to think about those dreams. They're real to you, and to Maryellen. You have a common language between you that I can't explain any other way. I would like to explain it some other way, because if what you say is true . . ."

"If what I say is true, then we're all crazy, right?"

Dr. Mark laughed.

"Yep," he said, "that about sums it up. Crazy or not, everybody will sure think so unless we can prove otherwise."

"Criminals are innocent until proven guilty," Eddie said. "But anybody who's the slightest bit different is loony unless they prove themselves normal. *That* seems pretty crazy, to me."

Aftereffects from the beating had changed the character and frequency of Eddie's dreams, and had brought on episodes of extreme disorientation. Mark had signed Eddie in at The Hill as a 'resident outpatient,' a vague category which would not show up on his record as an involuntary commitment.

That afternoon, when it was time to go back to The Hill, Mark asked Eddie whether he would like to stay with him and Sara.

"It's very unusual," Dr. Mark told him. "They tell you in medical school not to do things like this. Your uncle is gone too much, and The Hill isn't a healthy environment, no matter what the administration PR says. And we like you, Eddie, that's a fact. What do you think?"

Eddie thought that he was afraid. Not afraid for himself, but afraid for what he might bring down on Dr. Mark and Sara.

But he said, "Yes."

There was a meeting, with the lawyers and the state people and people from The Hill.

"He's all yours, Doc," Eddie's uncle Bert said.

Kurt Prunty, the hospital attorney, passed the paperwork from Bert to Dr. Jacobs to Dr. Mark and Sara for signatures, then collected it and jogged it into a neat stack before slipping it into his briefcase.

"Well, Mark," Kurt said, his hand outstretched, "Congratulations. You're the proud father of a sixteen-year-old."

Technically, now, Mark and Sara were his foster parents, but for the most part The Hill was still his home. Dr. Mark found him a job there, rolling carts and delivering envelopes, and he started to save a little money. He was glad. Now that he had a family he wanted to be sure he could buy them something for Christmas.

Eddie remembered that day dimly, but proudly. He never wanted to do anything that would make Dr. Mark sorry that he took such a big chance with him. But he wanted to see Maryellen—he *needed* to see her. He knew that she could help him find the Jaguar. Then this whole thing could stop; this craziness could stop. Until then, Eddie couldn't live with the idea that he'd abandoned Rafferty and the others to be hunted down like rats at the dump.

Maryellen had graduated with their class, with honors. Eddie had been so far out of it on The Hill that it was August before he realized it. He couldn't bear the thought of going back to school in the fall, even if they let him, so he took the GED cold, and passed with top scores. Now, in a big way, he felt free to hunt the Jaguar.

Eddie felt some changes in his dreams, changes that were out of his control. He felt as though the dreams were after him, and sometimes he sat up all night rather than risk a dream. He suspected that it was the Jaguar, and that if his guard was down, that would be the end of him. And if the Jaguar got to him, Eddie knew that he could get to Maryellen. He vowed that he would not become the bait that would trap Maryellen.

Dreams battered him constantly, and Rafferty was just a small part of the whole mess. Now there were days when Eddie looked forward to the same medication that he used to tuck into his cheek and spit out later.

He had dreams about bursting through the blue butterfly into the slathering jaws of a jaguar. He knew that they were only nightmares, but the impression was the same. He was repeating the sign, and the repetition would work as a brand eventually and let the Jaguar in.

The week before Thanksgiving, Eddie decided that he had to face the Jaguar down or die, because he felt his mind was dying, anyway. He didn't know whether he could muster the others or not, but he knew he could count on Maryellen.

"Let's go away together for a couple of days," Eddie said. "We could manage it, you know. Things are getting bad, real bad. I need to get away from here, pin down the Jaguar, and I need you to help me in case . . . in case things go bad for me, too. Besides, I want to be with you . . . you know. . . ."

A telltale flush crept out of her collar. He could tell by her eyes that she agreed, and his stomach flipped the way it had that first time they'd met, when he'd tested her by talking about the Lazy-Eight.

"Well?" he asked, and drummed his fingers on the table-top. "Yes or no. Going or not?"

"Yes," she blurted. "It's just what we need."

Neither of them trusted Maryellen's home phone or the phone at The Hill. If her father had not dreamed the phone call, then someone here was out to get them.

But if it was a dream . . .

Neither of them wanted to believe that the Jaguar had a hold on her father, and if they didn't talk about it, then it wasn't so.

One thing was clear. Somehow, somewhere, they'd made an enemy.

Eddie would work swing shift at The Hill and, at the appointed hour, Maryellen would drive up and they would disappear. He often slept at The Hill when he worked nights, so he wouldn't be missed for a while. Eddie didn't feel good about slipping out of Dr. Mark's place after all they'd done for him, so it had to be The Hill.

They needed a place, someplace isolated, and Maryellen had the answer.

"Olive has a cabin," she said. "It's up on the mountain, and nobody goes there this time of year."

"They'll look for us up there," Eddie said. "That's one of the first places they'd look."

Maryellen shook her head.

"They know that I can't stand her, or anything about her," she said. "They'd never think I went there. Besides, we're smart. We'll just make sure they think we're someplace else."

She waved a fistful of Disneyland brochures that she'd picked up from a travel agent.

"Are you kidding?" He laughed. "*Disneyland?* Who would think that we're the Disneyland types?"

"They already believe that we're permanently in Fantasyland," she said. "And don't criticize unless you have a better idea. Besides, the travel agent is a friend of Olive's. I made sure I asked her a lot of questions."

"How would we get there?"

"Fly, of course. Have you saved any money, working for The Hill the past few months?"

"A little."

"Well, I saved almost nine hundred dollars for college over the last three years. We'll draw it all out. We don't have to use it; they'll just see our withdrawal receipts and brochures lying around, and airline schedules. I bet it'll work."

"Betting isn't good enough."

"Okay," she said, "then we'll just have to make sure."

"Why don't we just take the money and go someplace else?"

"Because if we go anyplace commercial they'll find us, or somebody will find us. It'll be a license plate or description or some stupid mistake we make. . . ."

"Okay," he said, and rubbed his head. "We'll just have to make sure."

Dr. Mark and Sara fixed a real Thanksgiving dinner, something that Eddie hadn't seen in years. He volunteered for the Thanksgiving shift later that night, reminding them that on holidays the pay was double-time. Eddie felt a little guilty that neither of them questioned him at all.

A few other people came to dinner. Eddie knew them from the hospital—Dr. Jurgens, the gruff old drunk, and his wife, who was surprisingly pretty and the same age as Sara. The neighbor couple, the Martins, tried to make conversation with him from time to time, but their glances between Eddie and the carving knife betrayed their discomfort.

They probably think I'll go berserk and hack them all to bits.

At one point, when Eddie looked from them to Dr. Mark, Dr. Mark shot him a wink and a grin, and he felt a lot better.

"Like Kurt said, I'm the proud father of a sixteen-year-old," Mark said, and raised his glass. "Here's to a real family Thanksgiving." They let Eddie have a couple of glasses of wine, too, after making sure he was off his meds.

The others left and Eddie helped Mark and Sara clean up. It was the closest thing that Eddie had felt to a family since his mother died. He wished he could tell them what he had to do.

If they only believed me, he thought, *they'd know how important this is.*

"How's your writing going?" Sara asked. "Are you still keeping your journal?"

Eddie felt uneasy around her for the first time. It was the warmth of the family dinner, yes, but something more. He'd never tried to deceive them before, never deliberately kept anything from them or lied to them. It was especially hard to face Sara, so he concentrated on the dishes.

"Better than that," he said. "The *Herald* took my article on carpenter ants. Did you see it?"

"That was yours?" Her pleasure was genuine, as was her surprise. "But you didn't use your own name on it. Why not?"

Then she cleared her throat and recovered as only Sara could.

"Right," she said. "Dummy up, Sara. This *is* the classic small town, after all. I hope you got paid, anyway."

He liked that about Sara, her frankness. It's what he liked most about Maryellen, too, though Maryellen was a lot less talkative. Of course, with Maryellen communication went much deeper than words.

"Twenty-five dollars," he said. "My first sale. The hospital cashed my check even though it wasn't my name—Dr. Mark vouched for me."

Dr. Mark made coffee for the three of them. When Sara asked about his plans, he knew she was hinting at college. It was a perfect opportunity to set up their story, and all he could do to keep from squirming like a four-year-old in his seat.

"I'll go to college eventually, I guess," he said. He hesitated. "But first, I want to go to Disneyland. I've always wanted to go to Disneyland."

Dr. Mark laughed, which surprised Eddie. It was a good-natured laugh.

"Fantasyland, right?"

Eddie was uneasy, but Dr. Mark was having a good time and he liked seeing that.

"Of course. And it's what normal kids do. We . . . I'd like to do *something* that's normal."

Sara sang a few bars of 'When You Wish Upon a Star,' and told him about a photo job she'd done there years ago for a plywood company.

"You wouldn't believe the amount of plywood they use at that place," she said. "One of the little backstage wonders you learn about in the photojournalist business."

Eddie made it through the evening without making Mark suspicious, and managed to joke about Fantasyland a couple of times.

After work, while waiting in the orderly's room, the hours until morning snailed painfully by. Eddie kept himself awake by writing down as much about his dreams as he could remember, especially the parts that related to the Jaguar. He wrote in a fever, and it came to ninety-two pages in his notebook. He set it aside for Mark.

Eddie stifled a recurring fear that he would slip into the dreamways and be sick when Maryellen came to get him, and they would miss their chance together.

Eddie felt like he was holding a big dream off, and that was good. It would be there when he needed it. There was so much to be done on the other side. People of the Roam were suffering and dying, the fabric of the universe threatened to burst, the Jaguar's sour breath warmed his neck. But he knew long ago that he was hopelessly in love with Maryellen Thompkins, and right now their time together became his number-one priority.

One is surprised that a construct of one's own mind can actually be realized in the honest-to-goodness world out there. A great shock, and a great, great joy.

—Leo Kadanoff, via James Gleik in *Chaos*

AFRIQUA LEE TRANSLATED for the Romni Bari outside the gates to the City of Eternal Spring, the fifth city to refuse them entry in as many weeks.

"Because you are unreasonable, they have taken the hands of our children," the Councilmaster told her. "Because of you the Jaguar steals dreams and leaves behind madness. That was not in the accords."

"That is their crime, not ours," Afriqua Lee blurted, not waiting for the Romni's formal reply. True to tradition, the Councilmaster ignored her outburst and awaited word from Old Cristina. Though Cristina understood the language of the cities, she always insisted upon negotiating through her interpreter.

"What my impetuous daughter says is true," the Romni said, magnificent in her power-blouse and family braid. She repeated Afriqua Lee's indiscretion for the record. "That is their crime, not ours. They should be punished, not you, not us. We, like yourselves, are law-abiding people."

Afriqua Lee translated, forcing the anger out of her tone. The fatigue, the frustration, discolored her reason.

"What they want of you is a crime, it's true," the Councilmaster said. "But if what they want is two people, three people, ten people of yours, is it right that dozens of our children should be maimed to protect them?"

His colorful headwrap, piled high, gave him a stature that his biology withheld. The tassels hanging from his headdress attested to political successes before the accords, successes punctuated by the sacrificial slaughter of his opponents in the ritual ball game.

"If we do not know who they want, we cannot hand them over," Cristina said.

"And if they told you . . . ?"

"We would refuse."

The old woman's jaw jutted at the indignity, at even the implication of such dishonor.

"Are we to believe the mad dreams of a pack of ignorant spleef-whiffers?" she said. "You would not be such a fool. You would know that next week, next month, next year, they will come back with more accusations, another list of names, but this time one of them might be yours. . . ."

Afriqua Lee translated this as rapidly as Old Cristina wheezed it out. She had to ask the Councilmaster to repeat his reply, however, because she had been distracted by a fluttering of the Romni's eyelids and an increase in the heaviness of the old woman's hand on her shoulder. It was the first betrayal of the Romni's own exhaustion.

They are on us like a pack of dogs, Afriqua Lee thought. *Running us to death, snapping up the stragglers. . . .*

She attended to her job at hand. The Romni sought protection for her people inside the walls of a city, and Afriqua Lee spoke the languages of every city within the Roam. Afriqua Lee did not agree with this notion of sanctuary.

Then they would have us treed, she reasoned. *The walls would become a corral and we would be slaughtered.*

The Jaguar priesthood had its underground within every city, and that is how the branded children of the City of Eternal Spring had come to be so easily captured and mutilated. The deed had been done by a handful of their own uncles and cousins, themselves cattle of the Jaguar's fold.

Thanks to Rafferty, the Roam could now repair these mutilations, even though they could not yet prevent them. Afriqua Lee was relieved that the Romni spoke of this quickly.

"We have a device," Old Cristina said, "a development of our Master Tinker. It teaches a limb to replace itself. . . ."

"You would *bribe* us?" the Councilmaster sputtered in a rage. Afriqua Lee judged it to be a theatrical rage. "You would bring misfortune upon our children and then *bribe* us for entry . . . ?"

The Romni Bari raised a palm in protest. Afriqua Lee caught up with the translation, and the old woman spoke.

"Not a bribe," she said. "A gift. A permanent gift for your city, and any others who need it. Such a marvel cannot become property. Should you attempt to make gain from it yourself, its mechanism will be deactivated. We can do that from a distance; we do not need to enter your walls."

"A gift."

The Councilmaster's eyes registered suspicion, not gratitude. Excessive suspicion in such a one had been a survival trait.

Careful, Afriqua Lee thought. *Careful, Old Cristina.*

"Yes," the old woman said, "a gift. Such things are given freely, no? One should not expect anything from the giving of a gift except the pleasure of giving. Bring forth the device."

Rafferty stepped forward in his finery, dusty now from their forced migration and lack of rest. He presented the boxlike contraption to the Medical Control Officer of the City of Eternal Spring, along with a tablet etched with instruction in their own dialect. The tablet itself was a thing of beauty, etched by lightpen and written by Afriqua Lee.

The Councilmaster seemed more ill at ease, and beckoned the Medical Control Officer to his side. The two of them conferred with two portly advisors while another read through the instruction.

"How do we know it performs as you say?" he asked. "The tablet says it takes treatment every day for three months. We can witness no proof of it today. How do we know it's not a weapon to bring down our people or our walls once we bring it inside?"

The hot breeze brought a whiff of the City of Eternal Spring to Afriqua Lee's nostrils, and she nearly reeled from the stench. *Admission to these walls at any price is less than a bargain,* she thought. She much preferred the open spaces and the fastidiousness of the Roam to the stink that clung to the cleanest city.

"We have among us three outlander children," Rafferty was saying, and Afriqua hurried to catch up. "Their amputations were one, three and six months past. Medical Control can witness the stages of regeneration."

He motioned the children forward for inspection.

"The device is yours," the Romni said. "Test it as you will. We neither beg nor bribe admittance. If you know nothing of us, you know that we would rather die in honor than cower in shame."

The Councilmaster pulled himself up to full height and declared, "And if you know nothing of us, you know that for lack of your technicians, our pendulum comes to rest, our water ceases to flow, our light-pockets . . ."

Afriqua Lee translated the rest without listening. It was true. Without the Roam, the mechanisms of the city would falter. When mechanisms faltered, people faltered, laws failed. When laws failed, the order of a city became indistinguishable from the anarchy outside.

The afternoon had begun a familiar blue shimmer, and Afriqua Lee concentrated on shoving it as far back into her mind as possible. Exhaustion drove her to dream, and she could ill afford the exhaustion, must less a slide down the dreamways.

They are suffering this for me, she reminded herself. *Do what you can for them but do not pile stone on their burden.*

She watched Rafferty watch the skyline to the south. If the City of Eternal Spring turned them away, the elders had agreed that he should lead them into the ancient stoneworks of the wild highlands. It was a simple decision. They had nothing to lose.

Only Afriqua Lee knew how close Rafferty was to collapse. In two short years he had innovated devices the likes of which the world had never seen. Any other Master Tinker would be celebrated aloft on the shoulders of the Roam, but Rafferty's successes and his strange sleeping illness further distanced him from everyone except Old Cristina and Afriqua Lee.

Suddenly, from high overhead, came an alarm call from Ruckus. At the same moment, a shrill whistle sounded from atop the city's walls. The Councilmaster's formal carriage leapt backwards and through the gate with his entire entourage aboard. The gates hissed shut, and their locks snicked tight.

"Raiders!" Rafferty shouted, and Afriqua Lee half-pushed, half-carried Old Cristina to her van.

Rafferty barked orders into his handset. "We've been set up. Camouflage and scatter—we'll rendezvous in the highlands. Battle vans, camouflage and take positions. We'll give them a taste of the old Roam yet."

Afriqua Lee activated the camouflage on the Romni Bari's van and pulled into position beside Rafferty before he could activate his scrambler. Their camouflage absorbed their visibility, and the scrambler turned any electronic sweeps of the area into white noise.

The clumsy vehicles of the raiders trailed dust plumes and

noise as they bore down on the Roam's battlewagons outside the city's gates.

Gods, Afriqua Lee thought, *they are so many. . . .*

She activated the magneto blossom that Rafferty had installed atop the van and aimed it at the lead vehicle dead ahead. At one hundred meters she toggled the switch, and her target stopped dead, all of its circuitry wiped clean. She held the burst for five seconds, enough to thoroughly charge the metal of the vehicle and clump four more vehicles to it in a helpless mass.

Rafferty and his men concussed the enemy with sonic bursts and forced the first wave to withdraw.

Afriqua Lee listened to his orders over her headset, repositioned accordingly, and had time for one regret before the next wave swept in. Their wedding was to take place at the proper time, when they staked down in the highlands.

Damn tradition! she cursed. *Now I'll probably die a virgin.*

She yanked the proper levers, recharged the blossom and fired again.

What course after nightfall has destiny written that we must run to the end?

—Pindar

MARYELLEN KNEW THAT their time together would be more than a Jaguar hunt. She knew it would be more because she *wanted* more. She wanted Eddie, and she wanted him before the Jaguar crisped them down to char.

It seemed like it should be easy, giving herself to Eddie, but nothing about sex was easy.

This isn't just sex, she thought. *It's better than that.*

They shared an intimacy, through the dreamways, that surpassed anything sex had to offer. Still, they had been flirting with the notion without talking about it, and something had to be done.

Besides, she thought, *it's about time. And I can't imagine anybody but Eddie.*

Maryellen's friend, Jane Heynen, told her that boys didn't want anything to do with virgins because they were always crying and falling in love. But Maryellen was already in love, and so was Eddie. She didn't think it was likely that she would cry, but if she did, she figured Eddie could handle it. They'd been through a lot worse.

Should I tell him I'm a virgin?

She knew that he knew. It was something they had talked around, but not about. Had there been a clue in the dreams? The dreamways was a common history, but their daily dreams they'd kept private. Mucking around in brains caused psychoses—this they'd learned the hard way. Neither of them needed more trouble than they already had. All she knew of his personal fantasies was what he'd told her, which wasn't much.

What if all he wants is to go away for a couple of days?

Maryellen shrugged to herself, and smiled. She thought she could drum up some interest.

Maryellen had thought that sex was something that would just *happen*. She had never had a date, which Eddie well knew, but she wasn't so sure about Eddie, though he'd never said anything about it. Since he never had come on to her that way, she assumed he must not be interested.

That is, until she talked with her locker partner, Jane Heynen. Jane talked constantly, and most of her talk was absolute, bald-faced fantasy. Maryellen had thought many times that Jane would have been a perfect candidate for a one-year gift subscription to Dr. Mark. Whether Jane really knew anything firsthand about sex or not was hard to tell, but it certainly was her favorite subject.

Jane told her all about it. How Eddie had taken her for a walk down by the river, and kissed her, and how one thing led to another and before she could say no she was swept away in a whirlwind of passion. In fact, that was exactly how she'd put it.

"I was just swept away in a whirlwind of passion."

Maryellen didn't know what to say, so she tried the obvious.

"What if you're pregnant?"

"D'you think I'm stupid? I know how to take care of *that*."

Maryellen was sure that Jane was making it up. Jane's eyes glittered and the right one lazed outward the way it did when she got excited. Just the same, Maryellen's imagination conjured them down by the river, squirming and sweating together, *naked*.

"How?"

"Well, I don't want to go into the whole thing, but it takes a bottle of Pepsi and some paper towels."

"Pepsi!"

"Well, you could use Coke if you want, but it's awful strong."

Jane put up her hand to indicate that she really didn't want to go into details.

Maryellen knew she should've made the first move long ago, down by the river or up at the lake. But she didn't really know what that first move was. The matter never really came up. He'd kissed her a few times, sure, but neither of them became a whirlwind of passion.

Jane's half of the locker was stuffed with *True Romance* and *True Confessions* magazines. She'd never seen Eddie with Jane at all, and logic told her that it probably never happened. Or, if something did, it was not the way Jane described it.

Maryellen picked Eddie up at daybreak the morning after Thanksgiving, and they drove the hundred miles in her father's old Chevy pickup.

"My parents weren't suspicious at all," she said. "They liked all the talk about Disneyland; it's something *normal*. I was afraid they'd be up early this morning, but they drank quite a bit yesterday at dinner."

"What did you tell them?"

"That I wanted to be alone for a change, take a trip with my girlfriend Jane."

She stole a glance his way, but he stared off into the rain.

"I told them a trip would be a good time to decide about college. My stepmother's such a bitch, though. She always thinks I'm up to something."

"This time, you are."

"Yeah, and it's the *first* time. She makes me so mad I could spit."

The rain that washed out the dawn became a full-blown storm before the Elbe turnoff. Eddie was very quiet and drowsed off easily. For the first time since she'd known him, Maryellen felt uncomfortable with his silence.

She wondered what he must think of her, planning this weekend in cold blood, so matter-of-fact. They vowed to trap the Jaguar, and the nobility of that mission excused the subterfuge for their rendezvous.

Jane had shown her an illustrated sex manual and a cheap snapshot of a Latin couple astraddle a chair and one another. She knew Eddie better than she knew anyone, yet she was afraid.

What am I afraid of? she wondered.

That it would be like that cheap snapshot, came the answer.

Maryellen was very protective of her body. Both her father and stepmother hit her, and her stepbrother grabbed at her body whenever he could. That was how people touched her. She knew Eddie was different, but she was afraid, all the same.

There was so much she didn't have the nerve to ask him about, and she would never hop the dreamways and snoop.

If I don't have the nerve to talk to him, how will I have the nerve to go to bed with him?

At this point, going to bed seemed the easier of the two. And it wasn't going to bed that was the problem; it was sex that was the problem.

The closer the cabin, the slower she drove. It was mid-morning, climbing into the mountains, and her headlights were no match for the storm.

"It's the rain," she said, "I can hardly see down the hood."

"Want me to drive?"

"No, I can drive. I'm just being *careful*, that's all."

Eddie knew, when she emphasized being careful, that he should have brought some rubbers. He had thought a lot about this trip in the last couple of days, and most of that thought focused on their sleeping arrangements. They had not talked about it, and because they hadn't talked, he was sure she'd left the option open.

Eddie would have to get her to stop on the way, and there was only one town left between here and the cabin. He'd never bought rubbers before and knew better than to do it in the valley. Everyone would hear about it the next day. Not that anything could worsen their social standing.

If they stopped, she'd want to come in and he couldn't ask for them with her standing there, even if she was reading a magazine or something.

Eddie, you shit, you should've thought of this before.

He *had* thought of this before. That was the problem; he'd overthought it.

Eddie leaned over and kissed her on the neck.

"Thank you," she said, and took his hand.

A peculiar buzz rose in Eddie's ears, one that he'd felt a couple of times when he had been especially tired. He drowsed a little, daydreaming them already inside the cabin. A tumble of blue light flickered in the background, hovering like a pair of wings.

Eddie shook his head. The daydream could lure him off. He felt a strong pull right now; something especially bad must be happening on the other side, and he did not want this to be the time.

"I left a list at home with my things," Maryellen was saying. "Like a checklist for a trip, and gas station stops. I mapped out a great drive to Disneyland and it really looks like fun. Too bad my dad is so hard on you; it would be a good thing to do without having to lie about it."

The log dumps that marked the Morton city limits lined the roadway. Fat logs glistened like slender whales in the rain. After nearly two days without sleep, Eddie was rummy. It was hard to keep his head upright.

Maryellen pulled the truck into a parking lot.

"Why are we stopping?"

Maryellen pointed to the red SAFEWAY over the store.

"We need supplies," she said. "Stay here and rest."

She got out without looking at him and splashed her way to the store.

"I've got an errand, too," he said. "Back in a minute."

He slogged towards the Rexall up the street. It was a long slog.

Eddie stood by the magazine rack waiting for the lady clerk to leave the counter so that he could be alone with the pharmacist in the back. One old woman was buying Milk of Magnesia and a box of candies. The candy was wrapped in gold and red foil, on sale for seventy-nine cents. The pharmacist took off his white jacket, put on his coat and said to the lady clerk, "See you this afternoon."

"Good luck at the dentist."

"Thanks."

She turned her attention to Eddie, then, the dark stranger.

"May I help you?" she asked.

He couldn't think of how to put it right away.

"Well," she persisted, "can I find something for you?"

"I'm making up my mind about this candy," he said. "You could wait on that lady."

The old lady smiled, bought her candy and her Milk of Magnesia and left. The little bell tinkled the silence after her.

Eddie and the clerk were the only ones in the store. It was a dark Friday mid-morning, the day after Thanksgiving. Rain was pounding down very hard, he was in a Rexall in Morton with a lady clerk and he needed to buy some rubbers.

"Well, young man?"

He picked up a box of candy and a *Sports Afield* and put them on the counter. She rang them up.

"Will there be anything else?"

He sighed, inhaled deeply and said, "I'd like a box of Trojans, please."

The hand on the register stopped, stone-still. The fluorescent light in the middle of the store stopped flickering and not a drop of rain fell.

"Will that be regular, or tipped?"

His cousin always bought the ones with the tips. They filled them with hydrogen in chemistry class and bounced them off the ceiling.

"Tipped, please."

The hand, still poised above the register. The light and rain, holding.

"Will that be a box of twelve or twenty-four?"

He thought he might be getting the hang of it.

"How much for twenty-four?"

"Twelve forty-five, plus tax."

"I'll take twelve."

She totalled the bill, put the candy, the magazine and the rubbers into a sack. He paid her.

"Thank you," he said.

Eddie walked quickly to the door. Just barely, over the tinkle of the bell as it closed, he heard her say, "Good luck."

By the time he got back to the Safeway, Maryellen was already in the truck.

"Took you long enough. I thought you were going to be gone a minute."

"I had to get some things. Here, this is for you."

He handed Maryellen the box of candy and put the sack on the floor. He was a little embarrassed that he didn't get the candy for her, exactly. If he'd bought candy for her he'd have found something better. He hated candy, especially chocolate.

Maryellen put her lips to his ear, kissed him lightly and whispered, "Thank you. We're going to be fine."

Eddie pulled her over to him and held her, stroking her thick hair until a carload of teenagers drove by honking and yelling.

Eddie rubbed the fog from the windows with an old towel, kissed the back of her neck, and she drove them out of Morton to the southeast, through the heaviest rainstorm that either of them could remember.

They crossed the Cispus River on the forest service road that wound up to the cabin. At the other side of the bridge they stopped and got out of the pickup, to watch the churn of the dark water tear at the old log supports behind them.

"Water's right up there to the top," he said. "That bridge might go if this keeps up."

As he said it, watching the water laced with red from their taillights, he wished that the bridge would wash out and strand them up there. Alone and dry in their private cabin, cut off by this flood and the coming snows, they might hold out until spring. This was one of the few normal dreams he'd had—he and Maryellen, alone with their love and their wits.

"It goes almost every year," she said. "It might happen."

Rain streaked her hair and face. She seemed to be standing under the great opening of all the clouds.

He didn't want to say it, but he thought it had to be said.

"If you want, we could go back. We could do this another time."

"There is never another time," she said. "Besides, a washout would be doing us a favor."

In her dark face and eyes, as she stood under the gray sky in the dull red glow of their lights, he saw the same sadness and urgency that he felt in his own eyes, in his tight throat.

Eddie winked at her and didn't know whether she saw it or not, because just then she turned and stepped into the cab.

The thick-mudded ruts sucked at the wheels and tossed the old pickup side to side. Ahead of them, the indomitable rain rattled down on its way to No-Name Creek, the Cispus, into the Cowlitz River and through Mossyrock Dam, past Indian fishing shacks, beached nets, a woman crying at dawn on the tide-flats, past her muddy coat and gunnysack, north and west into the Pacific to warmer streams, the hot southern sun, to clouds and, next season, home.

"Why do we put up with all this rain?" she muttered.

She thrashed at the windshield with her towel.

"Because of the dreamways," Eddie said. "The fabric is weak here; we can kiss the butterfly and punch through almost anytime."

"You wouldn't leave it . . . live anywhere else?"

"No," he said. "When I go to the other side, that's enough for me."

A moss-stained cabin materialized through the rain. It was an old line cabin built out of thick cedar planks, and the roof on both ends hung over at least eight feet to cover the stack of wood just outside the front door. The wood looked crisp and dry.

"We're going to get wet," he said.

"We'll just have to move fast enough to beat the drops."

They peeled back the tarp and unloaded their packs. Eddie leaned against the tailgate in the rain. Rivulets began their creep under his collar, down his neck and back, down the crook of his arm to his wrists.

Maryellen hurried the bag of groceries up the steps, unlocked the door and set the bag inside. From the doorway she saw the vague outline of Eddie leaning against the pickup, head slumped forward, hands and packs hanging loose at his sides.

At first she thought he might be sick, or crying. Then she saw his head lift slowly from one side to the other, back and forth, as though he were warming up for a dance. Then he shook his head with a *snap*, like a dog, and his hair spun out and shot a thin, hard spray of water across her hands.

Eddie was fighting off the dreamways, that was clear. So was she. But Eddie had a distracted, haunted look that worried her lately.

Maryellen was grateful for the cabin. He would be safe here if he had to do battle on the dreamways. She believed that the two of them were hot upon the Jaguar, and she, too, wanted to close the gap.

Maryellen did not look at the dreamways the way Eddie did. There was no 'other side' for her anymore. 'This side,' 'that side' were parts of her, she reasoned, and anything that was part of herself was *here*.

"Well," he asked, "where's the stove?"

They wrapped themselves in their comfort of rain, filled their arms with firewood and stepped indoors.

Eddie followed her to the cast-iron heater and dumped the wood beside it. Maryellen went about the room lighting lamps while he looked for paper and a hatchet.

He rummaged through the scraps of kindling at the bottom of the woodbox. He didn't find any newspaper, but he did find the hatchet leaning against the shelf.

Eddie dumped the bag of groceries out onto the floor, crumpled the bag up and dropped it into the stove.

He lit the paper, closed the stove and stepped back.

Five kerosene lamps lit the room. A world of saddle blankets and antlers opened up around him. The cabin was small, but the high ceiling and open loft made it feel huge.

Beside the door was a sink, a small set of cabinets and a large water jug with a wood spigot at the bottom.

Maryellen jostled his reverie. "What happened to our fire?"

Eddie opened the stove, and a thick billow of smoke puffed out. The damp paper had smoldered away, but didn't catch.

"Must've been too wet," Eddie mumbled.

He splashed to the truck for the drugstore bag. When he came back he slipped the box of rubbers onto the counter beside the door, behind the water jug. He crumpled up the bag and a few pages of his *Sports Afield* and rebuilt his fire. Maryellen watched as he arranged each splinter and stick, everything just *so*; then she said, "Try this."

She held out a can of kerosene.

"My dad throws a cup or so on the kindling if he can't find any paper. Or if the wood's too wet."

Eddie reluctantly doppled some of it over his setup. He lit the paper and closed the door.

"Keep it open," she said.

He did, and waited for an explosion.

The fire caught with a slow *shoosh* and the dry cedar popped its heat straight for their bones. The psychology of the fire helped Eddie relax a little. He reloaded the stove and shut the door.

As though reading his mind, she said, "It doesn't explode as a liquid, only as a mist. Organic chemistry."

The stood together with their backs to the *pop* and *hiss*, daydreaming in a flicker of soft lamplight.

"That should keep us for a while," Eddie said. He wished he had something more to do.

"Yep," she answered. She had her back to the stove, to him, so he didn't see her suppress a giggle.

His uneasiness relieved her. She was thankful for it, wanted to tease him with it. He'd helped her be happy already, simply by not being anything like her stepbrother.

They faced each other across the stove.

" 'Organic chemistry'?" he mimicked, with a chuckle. "In whose body?"

"It just blurted out," she said. "Actually, it was a dreamway souvenir a few years back. I don't remember where I picked it up."

Eddie looked at Maryellen, confident as a church, and he wished for the right thing to say, the correct script. He'd picked up a few tips on the dreamways, but none of them seemed to apply somehow.

He suspected that people managed this nicely all the time, but he was at a loss. Something besides bed . . .

"Are you hungry?" he asked.

Eddie sorted through the groceries that he'd dumped out onto the floor and stacked them on the table. When Maryellen didn't answer, he turned and saw that she had her back to him and her hands to her face.

Shit, he thought, *she's crying. Goddammit, what've I done now*?

He held her tight from behind, his arms underneath her breasts, and he was going to say *What's the matter?*, when he saw that she was laughing.

"What's so funny?"

He held her closer, kissed the back of her ear.

"Us. This." She pressed her cheek to his lips. "The whole thing."

She leaned her head against his chest and held onto his arms. He clenched her tight in a bear hug, and nuzzled her neck.

She squirmed and played at getting away while he held her tight enough to keep her but loose enough that she could turn around and kiss him, long and hard.

"Hi," she said.

Eddie knew they'd just met in a world of their own making, quite different from the one either of them had left, quite different from the one that they visited in their dreams.

"Hi."

He watched her watch him. The fire popped beside them, and a fine steam rose from their damp clothes.

"Can you make coffee?" she asked.

"The best."

"The pot's in the sink, coffee's in that first cupboard, and water's in that jug beside the door. The water might be stale."

"You going someplace?"

"I'm going to the outhouse. In case you need it, it's around the other side of the cabin from the driveway."

When she left, he took four of the foil packages from his box of rubbers behind the water jug and slipped them into his pocket. Then he put the coffee together and set the pot on the stove.

He saw the footboard of a large double bed up in the loft. Every bed, chair and bare section of wall was covered with old saddle blankets with Indian designs. Both of his uncles collected them, too, and hung them everywhere.

Maryellen came in soaked again. She took a towel down from one of the shelves by the sink and rubbed her shaggy hair as dry as possible.

"If you don't get to it right away, it tangles real bad."

Her wet hair haloed in the lamplight and Eddie felt as though he'd been there, with her, forever. Nothing he could do now would be wrong, or misplaced, because now there was no wrong. They had the two of them, the world that they made in the warm cabin, and whatever words they might conjure to lift them through the night and their private days ahead.

Jaguar, you haven't got a prayer against us, he thought.

Maryellen said something, tangled up in her brush and hair, that he didn't catch.

"What?"

She pulled her hair back in a long twist and flipped it over her shoulder.

"I said, 'What are you thinking?' "

She draped her coat across the back of a chair and moved it close to the stove. Then she sat next to him on the small, badly worn couch. All this time he was wondering whether he should tell her what he was thinking, or whether he should try to make up something that would pass for intelligent, or romantic.

"I was thinking about the Jaguar, about us."

He watched her hands that were rubbing each other warm, and asked, "What were *you* thinking?"

"I was wondering whether things were going . . . well, whether things were going the way they're *supposed* to. And whether this would make strangers out of us."

He looked up at her eyes, dark and wide, and held their gaze in his.

She closed her eyes, and whispered, "I don't know where to start."

"It might be a little early," he said, "but we could take off our clothes and go to bed."

Eddie said it as calmly as he could. He felt he had to say it, and he had to say it soon, or his panic would bubble over and he'd get too nervous to say anything.

Maryellen walked over to their packs without missing a beat.

"We'll have to make up the bed. We can't keep any sheets or bedding up here because of the damp, so we'll have to zip our bags together."

He helped her untie them from the packs, then he carried them up the ladder and spread them on the bed.

"They won't fit."

"What do you mean, 'They won't fit'? It's a double bed."

"They fit on the bed; they just won't zip together."

"We'll manage," she said. "I'm sure we'll be warm enough."

She handed up their packs, then blew out the downstairs lamps. A light from the door of the stove played on the far wall, and the odor of kerosene thickened the damp air.

When she came into the loft, he was sitting on the edge of the bed, waiting.

"Well?" she asked.

"Well, nothing. I didn't want to start without you."

She sat next to him at the foot of the bed and began to undress him. First, his shirt-buttons. Then his shirttail and the T-shirt slipped over his head and off. As she unbuckled his belt and unzipped his pants her eyes never left his eyes.

His hands stroked her shoulders and the back of her neck. She pulled the back of his pants from under him, then down past his knees to his boots.

He wanted to say something funny, to joke with her about leaving his boots for last, but he didn't know whether it would hurt her feelings or not, so he didn't.

The slick cover of the sleeping bag was cold and slightly damp under him. The chill of the steel zipper cut across the backs of his thighs. His manhood, which he'd expected to leap full and ready from his pants, just lay there getting smaller with the cold. He was glad that the light was so bad.

She unlaced his boots and pulled them off. They *clunk-clunked* to the floor. Then she pulled his pants off his feet and pushed him down onto the bed, pressed full against him, her cold belt buckle icing his navel, her cold nose against his neck.

She turned and sat up, with her back to him. He unbuttoned her shirt from behind and pulled it off. She leaned back against his chest, sitting there in the nest of his lap. Eddie unhooked her bra and felt her breasts toss and wobble against his arms as she leaned forward to unlace her boots.

"You feel good," he said.

He kissed her neck and shoulders, down the small of her back, all the time keeping his arms around her middle, her breasts cradled on his wrists.

Maryellen undressed herself as he held her, then she lay back against him, not sure what to do with her hands. She thought the last time she had been held like this was underneath her mother's robe in the morning, before her father came home from the Army.

When her father drank, he hugged her or hit her, sometimes both. She got so she sacrificed the hugs to avoid the hits. Lately, if she didn't get hit she got no contact at all, except for Eddie. He'd never been afraid to hug her, even in school. Even in front of her stepmother.

"Cold?" he asked.

He felt her shiver against him, felt himself cringe against the snowbank of a sleeping bag at his bare back. Electrification of so much skin-to-skin paralyzed him with its exquisite pleasure. Eddie was afraid to be this close to anyone, even Maryellen. Getting close meant losing to Eddie, and he didn't want to lose her.

"A little," she said.

They pulled back the top bag and were just sliding under the warm flannel of it together when the coffee pot boiled over and steam exploded across the top of the stove.

"Jesus Christ!"

Maryellen scrambled out of the bag and down the ladder. She lifted the pot off the stove with his magazine and set it on the floor beside the stove.

She flowed in a soft blur, the light of the bedside lamp behind her and the ripple of fire from the stove in front. She had shown him sepia-tone photography once and she looked like that now, a reddish aura highlighting her hair from the fire. Her smooth legs muscled in pleasing counterpoint to the sway of her breasts.

Maryellen skipped the step-and-a-half back to the ladder and scrambled up. Her chilled dark nipples fixed him in their wobbly stare.

Eddie caught her around the waist and, as she leaned over him to blow out the lamp, he kissed her belly. His hands slid from her waist to her strong hips, then to her thighs, behind and up into her patch of crisp hair.

She lost her balance and fell on him, and one of the slats at the head of the bed gave way with a loud *crack* and they tumbled head down in a flurry of sleeping bags and smooth bodies.

"Is that what they call an 'icebreaker'?" she laughed.

Eddie kicked the sleeping bag off over his head and into a heap on the floor. He rolled over onto her, kissing her hard and deep, pushing his legs up inside hers. Maryellen tapped her tongue lightly on his, pulled her knees up beside his hips and felt him there, hard against her thigh. He tickled and tingled her until the tickle came out the tips of her nipples hard against his chest and out her toes. She heard herself sigh *Ah*, under her breath at first, then *Ah* and *Ah* as her hips and his hand danced their wet ballet.

Then he pulled away from her, kissed her gently and lay still.

"What?" she whispered, her mouth next to his ear. Her breath was shaky; it was hard to whisper. "What is it?"

Eddie didn't know how to start.

"Did I do something wrong?" she asked. "You can tell me."

Maryellen's hand swept his hair back, caressed his cheek.

"Oh, no," he said. He rolled away slightly. "You didn't do anything wrong. But . . . well. Well, I didn't know whether you were worried about getting pregnant, so I bought some, uh . . ."

"Oh."

"Well, I have some of them in my pants pocket, if you want me to use them."

She didn't want him to use them. Jane kept a few in their locker, more for show than for emergency. This first time she was willing to take the risk, just to feel him there inside her.

But here we are, she sighed, and recited the facts to herself. *This isn't a daydream, and I don't want to get pregnant.*

"Yes," she said, "I guess maybe we should."

Eddie rummaged through the pile of clothes for his jeans. She felt the supple workings of his thigh against hers as he squatted, going through his pockets, taking out the little silver packets, standing and turning to the bed, to her.

He'd never tried to figure one out in the dark or otherwise, but thought it might be easier if he could see what he was doing. The firelight flicker had died out, and holding the packet close to the window didn't help.

By the time he got one unwrapped, guessed which way it unrolled and sat down on the cold sleeping bag, his body quit cooperating.

It'll stretch, he thought.

He pressed between her legs again, and she shifted her hips so that she was more comfortable with the break in the bed. His strong hand moved against her, his fingers tickling in and out. Then something that was not his hand pressed hard against her *there*, pushing, pushing its way and not getting in.

She lifted her hips higher and felt his fingers on either side of it, and slowly, slowly it pushed and filled her until she thought she'd break, and then his hand slid under her hips, held her tight to him, and just as she felt the tickle opening up in her belly, he sighed *Oh* and *Oh* and pressed further inside her, then relaxed, out of breath, against her chest.

Maryellen kissed his face and ear and neck, rubbed his back with both of her hands, shifted her legs slightly to relieve some of his weight, and noticed, with the shifting, that the tickle was still there, only now it had a pulse. So she moved against him there a while longer, an hour longer, all night, tomorrow. Then Eddie moved away and lay beside her.

"Whew!" was all he said.

But he held her, and she liked that. His hand rustled along her belly, over and under her sweaty breasts, back to her belly. It dropped down into her hair, damp and matted, and traced circles around the tops and insides of her thighs.

She didn't know why, but she didn't want to touch him there. Maybe it was the dampness, the layer of slickness that she felt cooling on her own skin. Maybe it was the thing he was wearing. She pressed against him again, her back slightly turned, and rested one hand on his thigh and the other under his head.

Eddie jolted upright.

"Dammit!"

"What?" she asked, and jerked her sleeping bag against her chest. "What's the matter?"

"It's gone."

"What's gone?"

"The rubber," Eddie said. "It's gone."

He felt around their tangle of a bed.

Maryellen felt around, too, and hoped that he would find it first. Then she knew where it must be.

"I know where it is."

"Oh, yeah?" he asked. "Where?"

She sat up, cross-legged, with her back to him at the foot of the bed. The tilt from the broken slat made it difficult to hold her balance.

"Don't look, please," she said. "You'll embarrass me."

"I can't see, it's dark in here."

"Not that dark. Don't look, anyway."

She slid her fingers inside herself, swampy, her cheeks blazing.

"Here"—he touched her thigh—"let me."

"No, I can do it. . . ."

He heard it *thlap* to the floor.

"I'm sorry," he said.

He sat up beside her. The gusting rattle of rain slowed, rattled, slowed, and stopped. His hand still held lightly to the inside of her thigh.

"I *am* sorry."

"It quit raining," she said.

Eddie knelt on the bed in front of her, looked into her eyes that were huge and black in the low lampglow. Now that the rain stopped he heard the tiny liquid *click click* of Maryellen's eye blinks marking time. Her hand brushed the back of his neck, her eyes closed slowly and her mouth moved to his. This time, at the foot of the bed in the loft hot with the stove and in the stillness of the clearing night, the tingle in her belly exploded, and she answered his unasked question *Yes, oh yes* in his rushing ear.

Beyond

The dream is a natural occurrence, and there is no earthly reason why we should assume it is a crafty device to lead us astray . . . Nature is often obscure and impenetrable, but she is not like man, deceitful. We must therefore take it that the dream is just what it pretends to be, neither more nor less.

—**C. G. Jung,** *Collected Works*

THE JAGUAR HAD done a lot of sniffing with other people's noses, and the trail of a certain rustler became hotter by the hour. He left that task to his underlings. The Jaguar's energies were better spent on himself. Lately, he had invested them well, and now he would reap the returns.

He had isolated the chemistry of the butterfly effect and found that it was not only a chemistry but a pathway. When he linked his Jaguar priests, he witnessed part of the principle. It took him years to understand it.

Like a coil, an old magneto, and accelerator, he thought, *they work in series to extend my reach, my power.*

But the source of the power itself eluded him. At first, he was frightened by it, by the illness it gave him. Then, it was his salvation from the military, and, ultimately, his crown.

Why me?

He'd wondered this thousands of times over nearly twenty years. Now he knew.

His brain was different: he presumed it an accident of birth, but it could well have been from one of his many beatings as a child. At times it accumulated a chemical charge. When it discharged, it did so in a neural circuit of the cortex that flung him through the fabric. It also generated a bit of heat, and swelling, and the charge took time to build.

But I have it now, he gloated. *I can charge up that battery at will.*

One day the rustler would discharge, and the Jaguar would move in, and the problem of his pitiful body would be solved. He shuddered when he thought of how close he'd come to making a fatal mistake. Had he taken one of his cattle, one without the pathway, no amount of chemistry would have helped him back to the dreamways. The Jaguar might have become cattle to one of his own priests, and the danger had passed too close by to be amusing.

Maybe others tried this, and the historians called it 'possession.'

Except the possession was mutual—the body trapped the intruder while the intruder overrode the mind.

No exit—he shuddered again—*a living death.*

The Jaguar felt the shudder this time; his real body was coming around. The Thanksgiving holiday made it easier to mask his awakening in spite of their monitors and electrodes. He was saving up his charge in case his priests needed him.

They've botched things again, he thought. *If I have to rescue them this time, heads will roll.*

He corrected the thought, and allowed himself a sliver of a grin.

No. Heads will glow.

The hospital fielded a skeleton staff for the holidays. Most of the psych patients had been fed to lethargy, permitted leave or drugged limp. The Jaguar kept this waking quiet. He would rest awhile, safe from the medical-records clerk whom he knew to be the Agency's man. This was the sneak who reported back to the brass every time his electrodes betrayed him. The Jaguar was getting a handle on the electrodes, too.

Max still had a way of getting product, and the Jaguar had long since learned the folly of making it up. Max had a way of getting answers to questions he asked and to the more important ones that he didn't. As far as Max was concerned, the Jaguar wasn't asleep; he piloted a unique craft on a mission for his nation. Each time he returned, Max was at his bedside for the landing, for the . . . debriefing. Each time this unpleasantness was finished, Max gave suggestions, inquiries to make, orders. He never made promises; he didn't have to.

The dreamways pulled at the Jaguar now; he knew the clues: lapses of time, glimpses of shadows dancing behind the blue translucence of the great fabric of being. The valley itself was a great, green vortex, a spot where the fabric pulled itself into a funnel that drained into the other world.

When he wanted back on the other side, the funnel was reversed and he felt like a salmon battering its way up a fish ladder. This time, he had the feeling something had slipped past him, some quick shadow through the throat of the funnel, too quick for a glimpse or a grab.

The hardest part of playing possum was the natural stuff: bowel movements, personal hygiene, restlessness. The corners of his eyes were wired to betray his dreaming or to report his slip into his peculiar non-coma coma. Since full coma was nonproductive, they titrated his drugs to balance him below waking but above coma. No wonder it took him twenty years to figure out the chemistry of the butterfly in his mind.

He didn't know how he appeared when he was out. No amount of relaxation or self-reasoning countermanded his mother's toilet training, so simply letting it all go into the old man's diaper they gave him was the hardest of all. He had to pick up clues from the occasional orderly or nurse who talked to themselves while they worked.

"Weeks go by, you reglar as a clock, but you in trouble, now. One more shif like this and we gon do you a enema. But not on my shif, no sir."

The Jaguar hated hearing them talk about him, yet he slavered for it. It was all he knew of the self that was left of him on this side. Every once in a while a nurse or doctor would try to elicit a pain response from him to measure the depth of his sleep. One nurse, a burly veteran of Korea, enjoyed it so much that the Jaguar spent some of Max's precious time hunting him down on the dreamways and unplugging his brain axon by dendrite. Try as he might, he never got a chance at Max.

He must be reptilian, the Jaguar thought. *Only insects and oysters are tougher brains to crack.*

The techs didn't like their duty over the Jaguar. They cursed him, and he heard their curses. He heard everything, even when he was out, and what he didn't catch could be played back later from storage in some convolution of his brain that he had developed to help him catch up on this side. He knew what they felt, their revulsion. It must be a fearful thing to see a human vegetable wake up every month or two or three, talk to save its pasty skin, then fall back into the blessed relief of the dreamways.

The Jaguar hated the waking and the being awake, except now, when he needed the rest. He hated this side of the curtain, and he feared the other.

He recognized the psychoses that his dream-hunting brought out in his cattle. He relied on it, he cultivated it in those around him who failed to treat him right. Mercy was not a quality that the Jaguar cared to cultivate.

Always it was the race back to his skull, to rob every available cell in his mad rush to reconstruct the matrix that he'd seen in someone else's. The more complete the reconstruction, the more perfect the memory, the more the thing actually became his own.

The hospital's IV helped sometimes, depending on their own experiments, but most often it hindered. Even so, he couldn't live without it and he couldn't convince Max to make them leave him alone. Max didn't trust anyone, much less a resource like the Jaguar. The Jaguar was a prisoner, and it was a rare prisoner indeed who did not want to escape, wreak harm on its captors and turn the tables. Otherwise, they'd call him a guest.

He had been at this many years and, though he remained a novice, he had explored branches of the dreamways that Max believed to be pure fiction. Max didn't believe that the Jaguar had scrambled the genes of a bug on the other side and created such a marvelous hybrid, and the Jaguar hoped Max would live to regret it. If he had to leave this side, the Jaguar planned on getting even in style.

Escape into some poor wretch like Nebaj?

He shuddered. That was hardly an escape.

Straits aren't dire enough to consider that.

The spleef kept Nebaj on the other side, where he belonged. The Jaguar ran the other side like a fiefdom, with bursts of influence into his handful of priests, who plied the dreamways for him and ripened the climate for his eventual arrival. At times, their experiments went wild, but that, too, worked to his advantage. The Jaguar was good at playing to advantage.

He knew that others had crossed the great fabric; the evidence was too ample to ignore. Drunks did not cross, nor did the slaves of the drug-masters. It was no surprise to him that influences from this side (perhaps it was vice-versa; there was no way of knowing) had always come from cultures that used nothing more than dance and exhaustion as a medium.

The ancient Maya, the dervishes and others who ritualized exhaustive dance had left their mark on the fabric. The Maya touted a certain mushroom as their ticket to the dreamways, but the Jaguar knew this was a red herring. What actually transported them was their fasting to vision. The mushroom was for show when they came down the mountain to account the correct wonders to their people. It was the wise priest's way of keeping the dreamways to himself. With the mushroom came illusion, and the illusion satisfied the curious.

It was exactly what the Jaguar did with his own priests, his spleef-whiffing minions across the great sailcloth that powered the universe.

The Jaguar had one worry—that someone would catch him on the dreamways as he caught his priests, and shackle him forever to some chain gang. That was the danger of the hospital's drugs. That was a danger that he kept to himself.

To Max the Agency man, and to the Colonel, he was a freak, an anomaly, a one-of-a-kind. He cultivated that notion, all the while knowing there had been others, there would be others, there were others now, others who endangered him and over whom he had no control. He resented the fact that the hospital limited his ability to defend himself; he resented his worry, his healthy paranoia and the incursion of these others to his territory.

Perhaps he could escape into one of the invaders from this side, one whom his nose sniffed out in the valley. The uncertainty was too great, and his greater fear was to be trapped on this side, in an unacceptable body.

His relationship with the hospital was nearly symbiotic, and he had fallen into it by chance, but the Jaguar would have preferred something else. He would have preferred they'd never begun the experiments on sleep-disordered combat vets. Perhaps he'd have slipped through the cracks to a nursing home where he could ply the dreamways in peace.

The Jaguar would prefer to dream his life away. He would gladly donate his body to anyone who wanted it, though the few glimpses he'd had of it these days showed him it was hardly first-class material. He had seen a movie once of a huge brain that controlled the world. That was what the Jaguar wanted, to be a brain without the millstone of a body around his neck. And he didn't intend to settle for something as paltry as a world. He did not want to live in shackles in this or any other universe, and he did not intend to die.

So he had sensitized the fabric like a web, with himself as a great fat spider. In the web it was always sunny, just like in the hospital it was always gray. He felt ripples when his priests approached it, he felt the blows as someone else passed through. He knew they had to be nearby, as far as he knew there was only one weak point in the fabric and the valley was it. For ten years he had hunted the dreamways for them, and for ten years they had evaded his paw.

Nebaj knew of one, and pursued, and his blood would soon be sacrificed on the altar of the Jaguar's greater good. This, he thought, would lure the local rustlers out of the valley.

The Jaguar had found the father of the girl. Alcohol had battered the brain into mush, and this father was one of his poorest instruments. The Jaguar could not find her on the dreamways, but he found the father and that would have to do.

He felt someone bearing down on him. Someone sought him out as he sought them, and there were two of them. Their weakness was their time awake, when the Jaguar closed the gap and set his snares.

He'd thought of telling Max, but that would not work. Then Max would have another pilot, and the Jaguar's value on the Agency's tally sheet would plummet. It was an ominous thought.

For a week now, the Jaguar had nosed into Mel Thompkins, but this time he could not hold on. It was like stirring the coals of a hot fire—he would reach inside and poke, but he could not stay. A day, two days more, and he would have the place prepared for himself; he would be safe—if the hospital didn't catch him. A mere day from now and he could be free from the natterings of this pest.

If he lasted a day.

To experience *a dream and its interpretation is very different from having a tepid rehash set before you on paper. Everything about this psychology is, in the deepest sense, experience; the entire theory, even when it puts on the most abstract airs, is the direct outcome of something experienced.*

—**C. G. Jung,** *Collected Works*

THANKSGIVING NIGHT WAS a tough one for Mark White. He couldn't sleep, and it was more than simple insomnia or too much coffee. A heavy feeling of dread had its hooks into him, and he couldn't shake it. He didn't believe in premonition, but he did believe in the subtlety of subconscious clues. He rattled his subconscious the best he could, and precious few clues sifted out.

Maybe it was because the clue was too big. No matter where his mind raced, it always rounded the same turn; it always came back to Eddie and Maryellen. Other patients were patients, but these two were special.

As far as he knew, he was the only one who did not believe that they had fabricated everything simply to be special, to get attention. Yet he couldn't bring himself to believe all that the experiment had revealed.

What would it be like? he wondered. *What would it be like to be a kid, inside somebody else's brain, able to actually tinker with it as though it were a wind-up clock?*

Eddie's journals had described for him some of their limitations and a few of the dangers.

"We can't just go spying around in other people's brains, you know," Eddie had lectured Mark. "How we find somebody . . . it's an accident; I can't do it on purpose. At least, the first time I can't. After that I can find them sometimes, but not every time. We have to be dreaming at the same time."

"Have you ever dreamed inside my brain?" Mark asked.

Eddie shook his head.

"No," he said, and his face looked very sad for a moment. "Didn't you hear me? We try not to do it with friends. It's . . . prying. And it's dangerous." He thought for a moment, then added, "But if I do, I'll leave you a sign so you'll know."

So far, Mark had found no sign.

Eddie's notebooks included a warning: "It's a good thing I didn't dream many people on this side. It just gives the Jaguar a way in, a way to track us down."

This was something that Mark didn't find important at the time. He pursued what he perceived to be Eddie's paranoid fantasy, and sent him home with another prescription to help suppress the dreams. Mark felt uneasy even then. What he'd wanted to do was explore the dreams, establish clinical controls, study Eddie and, later, Maryellen. He'd kicked himself many a time for not fighting for an EEG on her while she was in the hospital, in the dream-state. Her parents had refused, and since he was more concerned with Eddie, he let it pass.

Damn!

He'd always taken on too many patients. Each fragment that he'd gleaned from their lives loomed larger and larger. He'd let things slip through his grip, which, tonight, suddenly crystallized in his mind as crucial: the EEG on Maryellen, the mystery patient at the Soldiers' Home whose EEG matched Eddie's, attempts to induce the dream-state in both kids instead of suppressing it with his drug therapy. . . .

That line of thinking wasn't productive now. Mark concentrated on what Eddie had told him about dreams.

Just at the threshold of dream, according to Eddie, "We are in the skin between worlds. Our time there is a fraction of a second, but for that time the dreamer passes through a fabric shot through with dreams and the paths that dreams take.

"If you meet somebody else's dream head-on," Eddie told him, "then you get that quick twitch that wakes you up. It knocks you back into your own skull. I guess it's like trying to put the wrong ends of two magnets together. I don't know why it's so different for us."

Magnets.

Mark had felt Sara twitch beside him just a short while ago, and he wondered where it was that she had almost gone. He resisted the temptation to snuggle up closer. He didn't see any reason for her to lose sleep just because he was restless and too lazy to get up.

"What happens to you?" Mark had asked.

"Blue light flickers very fast, but it's not the light going fast; it's me, somehow. I just dissolve inside and follow it home," Eddie said. "I don't know how else to describe it."

"Is it like TV? Do you just watch the other person's dream, or can you change it?" Mark asked.

Eddie shrugged.

"It depends. At first I didn't know I could *do* anything. It was like watching a movie, a Three-D movie, dreaming in somebody else's head. Usually I don't even know who it is."

"You mean, you're inside somebody's brain and you don't get a name, an image . . . ?"

"Well"—Eddie sighed a trying-to-be-patient-with-ignorance sigh—"it's awfully *big* in there. It would be like coming to Earth in a spaceship and expecting to find the name 'Earth' written everywhere. Have you ever dreamed your own face?"

Mark suppressed a snicker at the memory of that question. Here was a little boy setting him straight on the landscape of dreams. It had been ten years since they'd had this conversation, and Mark had to admit that he had not yet met himself face to face in a dream.

"The first time I tried exploring, I got my times tables for school," Eddie said. "I had to get out of the dream area and into another place. It's like wandering through a warehouse that goes as far as you can see. I just sort of ride around in there, take whatever turns look like they'll take me to what I want to see. Sometimes you know whose dream it is if you recognize the people in it."

"Is it like a highway?"

"Not exactly, but that's why I call it the 'dreamway.' I see bits of everything, hear things, smell things . . . it can be pretty awful, but I stay away from the awful parts. Like for the times tables, I found that one in with rhymes."

"This was a schoolmate of yours?"

"Yeah. I found his times tables. But everything inside a dream is made up of puzzle parts. When I get back to myself, I look around inside me for the puzzle parts in my head that match the ones I saw in his. When I get them together, then I know the times tables just like I'd memorized them myself."

Maybe it was because he was in the twilight between waking

and sleep, but Mark visualized for the first time what Eddie had been talking about. Then he realized what it could mean.

Molecules, he thought. *He puts together a molecule that encodes the information*.

That was how viruses did it, why not people?

The blood series that he'd done on both Eddie and Maryellen indicated some very peculiar hormonal variations, and in Eddie they coincided with his EEG aberrations. Both kids had a high hemoglobin, which didn't seem important. Until now.

Hemoglobin . . . iron . . . magnets.

Mark sat upright in bed and leaned back against the headboard.

If they've learned how to encode memory chemically . . .

The possibility, like many that involved the kids, seemed so great as to be impossible, preposterous.

But it's worth testing.

"Yet you stopped doing that, didn't you?" Mark had asked Eddie. "At some point you quit doing your homework the easy way. Why?"

Several students in Eddie's classes became behavioral problems. Then, as quickly as it started, it stopped. The talk centered around Eddie as a 'bad influence,' but investigation proved that the two students most affected had no contact with Eddie whatsoever. Everything pointed to sleep disorder as an underlying factor.

When this was mentioned at a monthly meeting of the valley's mental health professionals, Mark became curious. Eddie was in seventh grade then, and seeing Mark regularly. That was when Mark had asked him about it point-blank. Eddie smiled, obviously relieved.

"Then you *do* believe me!"

"I didn't say that," Mark said. "I just asked . . . well, if you do get into someone's head, do they know it? What does it do to them?"

"I don't think they know it," Eddie said. "But it's funny, I always thought I'd know if someone was inside mine. I've felt some nudges, you know, like from the other side. But nothing inside."

Eddie stopped, chewed his lower lip and took a deep breath.

"And?" Mark urged.

"And what?"

"Does it do something to them?"

Eddie squirmed on Mark's office bench and chewed his lip again.

"I'm not sure . . . I mean, yeah, something happens."

"Like with Lester and Philip?"

Eddie's face paled at first, then reddened. His eyes kept staring at some point on the floor.

"Yeah."

"Does it happen with Maryellen, too?"

Eddie's gaze snapped to meet Mark's. His lip and tone became sullen, and he hunched over bitten fingernails.

"You'll have to ask her that."

"I did."

"And what did she say?"

"She said I'd have to ask you."

A grin broke through the grim line that had been Eddie's mouth. He coughed, squirmed some more.

"Yeah," he said, at last, "it happens with her, too."

"And you two discovered it on your own, and stopped poking about in other students' brains?"

"That's about it."

"What about each other?"

"We've never done that!" Eddie snapped. "It's not right. But we've been inside the same people. That's because any time you go inside the dreamways, you leave a door open, or a marker. Like a key. It makes it easier for someone else to get in. It also makes it possible for someone else to find you."

"Someone from the other side?"

"Or from this one," Eddie said.

"How far . . . except for the 'other side,' what's the range of your dreamways?"

"I don't know," Eddie said. "I've seen some pretty strange things. It's hard to know whether I've been somewhere or I'm inside the memory of someone who's been there. I think we can go anywhere in the world, skipping from person to person. But the easy dreams are close by."

"What about language? Do you get inside somebody and find that you don't understand the language?"

"No," Eddie shook his head. "It's because there is no language in dreams except my own. I can learn a language on the dreamways, the way I learned times tables. But that's different. The dreams themselves . . . they're always in my language.

Dreams are different than poking around, but it's the dreams that get you inside to do the poking."

Mark watched Sara's sleeping face in the green glow of their bedside clock. Her full lips pursed slightly, as though she expected a kiss. Her eyes flicked back and forth under their lids, and he wondered what it would be like to meet her in the dream that possessed her now. Whatever it was, it took her far from their bed and this was the time that he felt so close to her body but so far from whatever it was that was *her*. Sometimes he felt closer to her when she was working in some other country than he did when she slept right next to him.

And that was the last thing he remembered until Sara woke him in the morning with her soft, stroking hands.

"You were restless last night," she said. "Is something bothering you?"

"Sorry."

He reached an arm around her hips and pulled her close, trapping her curious hand between them. "Yes, it's the kids. I'm worried . . . I don't know what worries me, exactly. Their situation, I guess. I keep thinking that there's a key somewhere that I've misplaced, and I'm going to find it right in my pocket."

Her playful fingers had aroused him, and she kissed him a long, hot kiss.

"You can look in my pocket," she whispered. "Maybe you'll find it there."

They made love that Friday morning as they often did when the world left the two of them alone—slowly, very wet and for a good, long time.

"Well," she said, later, "did you find your key?"

"No," he sighed, "but it was sure fun looking."

They lay still, cradling one another, listening to the percussion of rain on the roof and windows.

The phone rang, and Sara answered it. She listened for a few moments, then put her hand over the receiver and gave it to Mark. She looked pale.

"What is it?"

"They're gone," she said. "Eddie's left the hospital, and Maryellen's disappeared from her home. They say they found a lot of those Disneyland pamphlets in both rooms. The wicked stepmother would like to speak with you."

When Mark hung up the phone, he shuffled to the closet.

"I wish she'd call me *before* she calls the police," Mark grumbled. He struggled for balance, with one leg in his pants.

"So," Sara said, "they're off to Fantasyland, after all."

"I don't think so," Mark said, "and neither does the furious Mrs. Thompkins. It's too pat, too soon. It's what they wanted us to think."

"Are you mad?"

"I'm a little angry, yeah," he said. He pulled his T-shirt on backwards and had to reverse it. "It's a holiday; I'd rather spend it with you than tracking down the kids."

"That's not it."

Sara slipped her arms around him from behind and kissed his neck.

"You're mad because he lied to you. You're mad because you trusted him. You were starting to believe him, and now that he's lied to you, you don't know what to think."

"Oh, yeah?"

Mark turned in her arms and hugged her.

"How do you know all that stuff?"

"I live with a shrink," she said. "Genius rubs off. But I know Eddie pretty well, too. Kids open up for writing teachers; it's like being a cross between the confessional and Switzerland—neutral ground, and all that. He idolizes you, and so does Maryellen. Eddie must have a good reason for this; he knows what Mel Thompkins can do. He must think it's important, very important."

"Life or death," Mark said. "Because that's what he's up against if Mel finds him before the cops do."

"Then Thompkins is out looking?"

"Absolutely. And she says he took his rifle."

Sara muttered something under her breath and let Mark finish getting dressed. She sat in her flannel nightie at the dilapidated desk next to her dressing-table and tapped a forefinger against her pursed lips.

"So where are you going, Lone Ranger?" she asked. "Not chasing a madman with a rifle, I hope."

"I'll be chasing a madman, all right," Mark said, "but not that one. You've seen what the kids wrote about the Jaguar?"

"Yes," she said. "He's the bad guy who's destroying the fabric between our universe and another, right? The one who never has a face in Maryellen's drawings?"

"That's right," Mark said. "And Eddie's been convinced that

he's on this side, nearby, and that he's in trouble. Dammit! I've spent all this time looking for the symbology behind all this. . . ."

"What else is there?"

Mark looked her in the eyes but couldn't bring himself to answer.

"You think it's true?" she asked. "How could it possibly be true?"

"I'm thinking backwards now," Mark said. He sat on the edge of the bed and took her hands. "I'm just going to throw out a bunch of 'what-ifs,' and you stop me if my logic goes bad."

"Okay, masked man. Shoot."

"First of all, assume they're right. There's a Jaguar person somewhere near here who crosses to the other side and causes mayhem with the butterfly kiss, in brains and genetics and what all. Eddie says he must be like them, so he must go through terrible pain when he wakes up. His influence on the other side is nearly constant, so he must be asleep or hurting most of the time. Where can he get the physical care he needs under those circumstances?"

"A hospital?"

"Right. A hospital, maybe some kind of full-time home care if he's wealthy. He probably doesn't like life here all that much; he'd prefer to stay in the dreamworld all the time. Eddie said something else recently that bothers me."

"This whole thing bothers me. Do you realize how far-out this sounds?" She toyed with a basket of empty film cannisters.

"Of course," Mark said, and laughed. "It's my job to realize how far-out this sounds, and my job to make the patient comfortable enough to keep talking. I've been going at this all wrong, and now I'm trying to remember everything . . . ten years of everything."

"So what else did Eddie say that bothers you?"

"He said two things. One, that once inside somebody's brain you can actually alter their brain, their chemistry, their *self*. It's like a computer—you just have to know how to erase, restructure the jigsaw to form another picture—but until the person wakes up, you don't know what you get.

"The other thing is the scary thing, because I believe that this is what he's acting on. He said once that he thought the Jaguar was afraid of dying, and that he was looking for a way to live forever."

"Live forever!" Sara laughed. "Well, good luck. Ponce de Leon drank a lot of water and look what it got him. . . ."

Mark shook his head.

"I know, I know. But Eddie thinks it's possible to . . . stay in a brain, take it over."

"You mean, like, use a body until it wears out, then pick out another one?"

"Exactly. He thinks the Jaguar is looking for an ideal body on the other side, biding his time until he finds something perfect."

"Why wait? Why not just use any old body that you've got access to, then move into body beautiful when you find it?"

"The big question is, what if you move in and you can't get out? If you only get one shot, you want it to be a good one. And once he's safe on the other side, he can start playing with our world the way he's been fooling with theirs."

"All right, Holmes," Sara said, "those are the 'what-ifs.' What do they mean?"

"I think that Eddie and Maryellen are teaming up to make a move on the Jaguar, to flush him out or lure him in."

"Well, what do they do when they have this Jaguar by the tail?"

"They'd have to kill him, don't you think?" he asked. "Or get inside his brain and change him. He's got more experience than they do; I think that would be much more risky. If he turned the tables . . ."

"Mark, I'm a writer. Willing suspension of disbelief is my stock in trade. But that's on the page and this is reality."

Sara pulled his hands to her lips and kissed his knuckles, absent-mindedly. She wasn't through thinking it over yet, he could tell, so he waited her out.

After a few moments she asked, "You really want me to pretend this is real and give you an opinion. Is that it?"

"Yep. That's it."

"Well, I don't think either of the kids is murderer material, but you'd know more about that than I do. Do you think they're out driving around to all the hospitals in the area?"

"No"—Mark smiled—"I don't. And I think if they'd known where to go, they'd have rushed into it without all this subterfuge. That's why I think they're going the mind route, and why it's important for me to find the Jaguar before they do."

"Oh, Mark." The look Sara gave him was purest pity. "What are you going to do now? Visit all the hospitals, nursing homes and rent-a-nurse offices in the state? Region? Nation?"

"No," he said. "I think I know exactly where to go."

"I'm afraid to ask."

"The Soldiers' Home."

"It's a good thing you weren't in the military," she murmured. "They'd keep you there for sure."

"I'm serious," he said. "*If* all the what-ifs are true, then I have one shred of tangible evidence that there's a link between Eddie and the Soldiers' Home."

Her sadness-and-pity look was gone, and her eyes sparkled with their old fire.

"That paper . . . that patient you were so mad about when we first met . . . !"

"Exactly!" he said. "And I forgot about it because it was easier to forget than to fight. Easier than believing that another world is being dragged through disaster because of some power-hungry vegetable on a psych ward . . ."

"It's my experience with politicians that the ones who appear powerful don't try to prove it nearly as much as the ones who don't look it," Sara said. "If this person exists, he's probably power-tripping in this other universe because he's relatively powerless in this one. Right?"

"Agreed," Mark said. Then he shrugged. "It could be simpler than that. He could be playing a game in his head, unaware that it has real consequences in a real place."

"A mind game? That's your department, no?"

"Yeah," he chuckled. "The buck always seems to stop here."

Sara cranked some raw film into one of her canisters and snipped it off neatly, then loaded another. A stray shaft of sunlight escaped the clouds and illuminated her sure, slender hands.

"Maryellen has really taken to photography," she said. "I like seeing the two of them in school. They are excellent students, when they're there. Sometimes I wish I were a real teacher, full-time, instead of these special one-month consultant jobs."

"You'd miss the travel, and you know it," he said. "You'd hear about a coup in Costa Brava that you'd missed and you'd pout for a week. . . ."

"Stop it," she said, and tilted her nose in mock arrogance. "I do not pout. I think, I consider, I mull things over, but I do not pout."

"But my point about your travel?"

"Okay, touché. But working with kids every once in a while sure brings me down to earth."

Mark rubbed his eyes.

"I feel like I'm floundering in the basics," he said. "I have two patients hallucinating like mad, and I'm getting caught up in their hallucinations myself. . . ."

"Have *you* started dreaming their world, yet?"

"Not yet," he said. "But my dreams have been very strange lately, and there's a shadow around them. They've talked about this; it's a feeling . . . like being watched."

Sara clipped off her last cannister of film, tossed it into the basket on her desk with the others. She put her arm around him and kissed him.

"Tell me your dreams, you handsome devil. The doctor is in and everything is confidential. . . ."

"It's where this dream business leads that gets me," he said.

Mark knew now that he was more troubled than he'd let himself believe.

Thank god for Sara, he thought. *She always brings the best out in me.*

"Suppose it's true, what they say. The fabric between these two . . . universes . . . is a skin. Which is inside and which is out? Which is self and which is other? They claim they pass through this skin and back. They claim that 'out there' or 'the other side' is inside some other skin. The skin itself is the dream zone, where they pick up the scent and nose into some poor dreamer's skull.

"Going through the skin takes energy. Being out on the other side physically is . . . annihilation. It's particle-antiparticle stuff; everything goes *poof* in a burst of light. Dreams ride a shock wave. The return through the skin to this side is the waking phase. Hence the pain, the danger.

"If they're right, we're in danger ourselves, and from two directions. First, there's the 'other side,' as they call it. If some tyrant there figures out how to manipulate this side like the Jaguar manipulates that side . . . not pretty. Then there's this side. If what they say is true about getting information—imagine what the CIA or the KGB would do to get their hands on someone who could just tap into dreams, follow them to their source, mosey around in some president's skull for a while and shop for facts. . . ."

"It gives the phrase, 'I'll sleep on it,' a whole different meaning," she said.

Sara's hand caressed his cheek.

"What's up, Doc?" she asked. "Lost in space?"

He didn't answer, because a thought that had been in the back of his mind took form and suddenly sprang to the fore. When it sprang, it did so with full fang and claw.

"What is it?" she asked. "You're so pale . . . you look like you've seen a ghost."

"I just scared myself," Mark said. "Think about this. Think what it means if we're right . . . about the patient in the Soldiers' Home."

"Well," she offered, "it means that the Government is interested in him, and is interested in keeping other people from being interested in him."

"Yes," he said, and suppressed a shudder. "And wouldn't that also mean that they'd be very interested in two local children who exhibit the same symptoms?"

"Easier than believing there's another world."

"Right." He smiled again, and kissed her. "That, too."

"So," she said, "you've never come out and taken sides. What *do* you think about this other world business, these Jaguar priests?"

"I believe they're on to something," he said. "I don't know. . . . What if the Jaguar figured out how to harness those priests, like batteries in a series, or an electrical coil? What if he did that and blew a hole in the skin, and we're the weak point in God's skull? What if the kids beat him to it . . . ?"

Mark hugged Sara again, and whispered, "Sometimes, as a doctor, it's more expedient to assume that a suspected condition exists and treat it, rather than waste time getting tests back. 'To err on the side of life' is the medical term. That's what I'm doing here. We have everything at stake, *everything*. Covering all bases is mandatory when everything's at stake—that's the first thing I learned in medical school."

"And what was the second thing?"

"Marry an accountant."

Mark used the ten-mile drive to he Soldiers' Home to put

together an argument that wouldn't alienate Colonel Hightower. It didn't work.

The Colonel, as usual, was unrelenting, and Mark White checked the boiling point on his anger. He had always believed that anger didn't get anybody anywhere, but he was just beginning to see how, at times, it felt too good to pass up. The Colonel was still in charge, and he was fond of reminding Mark of that fact.

"Listen, White, I haven't seen you in years, and to tell you the truth, I don't miss you a goddamn bit. I know what you're after. That kid is your ticket to the big time if you write his script and he learns it. This is all choreography, media stuff, and I'm not going to perpetuate it from this office. Besides, it's a holiday, goddammit!"

"But, Colonel . . ."

"And communicating through dreams! That's *National Enquirer* stuff, not *American Journal of Psychiatry*. You're manipulating some artifact on a tracing and taking advantage of some troubled boy to make yourself a career, and I think it *stinks*. . . ."

Mark slapped the desktop.

"I can prove it," he said, hoping he could. He unclenched his teeth enough to keep his voice level. "Give me a shot at this guy—you can set up the double-blinds and we'll have scientific evidence. . . ."

"I promise you I'll have your job if you don't cease and desist *right now*. Is that clear? This patient is a security concern; you are not authorized . . ."

"I'm *asking* for authorization. . . ."

"There won't be any. Not for you, not for anybody. Any more on this matter and I'll have your license. You know I can make good on this."

"Okay, Colonel, okay. Let me describe your patient to you. If the description fits, you don't have to violate your security. But you'll know I'm right. If so, I can tell you what to do about it and the rest is up to you. I don't have to know."

"You really are crazy, White. Jesus!"

"Your man—or woman—has long periods of unconsciousness. When he wakes up, he's very, very ill. Whatever you've been getting from him in the past, he hasn't been delivering lately. At least, not to you. How'm I doing?"

"You've been reading too much science fiction, White. Now get out. . . ."

"You're going to lose him, Colonel," Mark said. "If I'm right, then one way or another you're going to lose him. What if he finds out a way to do for somebody else what he's been doing for you?"

"There's no way he could spring out of here short of an assault on the whole . . . goddammit, White, you're pissing me off! Now get the hell out!"

"Your language is getting nasty, Colonel. What are you afraid of?" Mark asked. "Who's got the kind of clout that can stop you cold?"

"You don't," the Colonel said, and stood behind his desk. He pushed his leather-covered chair away from his desk, making room for fight or flight. "Now get out."

Got you cornered, Mark thought. He pressed harder.

"This is CIA stuff, isn't it? You've got some loony in here mucking around with people's brains—doesn't that concern you?"

Then, before the Colonel could muster another outburst, Mark took himself up on a subconscious dare.

"You want my patient, too, don't you?" he asked.

"What do you mean?"

The Colonel was calmer now, shifty-eyed, pale as a shoplifter caught with watches in his shorts.

"You don't care what happens to your boy, do you?" Mark challenged. "He's not good to you if you can't control him. You know you've got my kid in the bag. You can sit back and see how this comes out, and either way you win. Rounding up new blood, is that it?"

"You have no patients here, Dr. White," the Colonel announced calmly, "and you are clearly a disturbed individual. What you are committing right now is criminal trespass. Shall I bring in the escorts?"

How much did they know? How much did I give away?

Suddenly, Mark White had a lot to worry about.

. . . in Chichen Itza
and in the north coast kingdoms . . .
let them prepare for the days
of stones and blood.

—*Destruction of the Jaguar,* **translated by Christopher Sawyer-Laucanno**

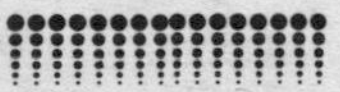

MARYELLEN SNAPPED AWAKE. A faint *splash-splash splash-splash* of tires through mudholes froze her breath in her throat.

"It's Dad," she whispered. She didn't know how she knew, but she knew.

She and Eddie had slept through what was left of the day. Maryellen turned to wake him up and felt another chill ice through her. Eddie was out cold.

A glint of headlights flickered through the trees.

"Eddie! Eddie!"

She shook him, and that didn't work. She scootched him up so that he was half-sitting against the wall, then slapped his face like she'd seen them do in the movies.

Eddie appeared rummy, but he came around with a groan.

"Eddie, somebody's here."

"Yes," he mumbled, "I'll be okay. A minute. It's . . . things are bad. . . ."

"Things are bad right here," she said. "I think it's my dad. Get dressed. You've got to get out."

Eddie took a couple of deep breaths, holding his head, then rummaged for his pants and boots, then his socks. Maryellen knew that his head must be booming, but he hadn't been able to go into the dream too far. She pulled her clothes on as best she could, stuffed her bra and underwear under the mattress and opened the window.

"Where you going?"

Eddie, too, whispered even though the car hadn't stopped yet. He moved with the slow confusion of a sleepwalker.

"No place," she said. "When he gets here, you wait up here. He'll come in the door, you go out the window. Step from the roof to the back of the woodpile and you're down."

The car lurched its way to the end of the drive.

Eddie wrapped everything of his that he could find into his shirt.

"My coat," he said. The words were mush in his mouth. "My coat's down there."

Maryellen slid down the ladder, raced across the cabin and back up the ladder with his coat.

In the bare sliver of light Eddie saw her close her eyes and breathe deep. He rolled his pack, his sleeping bag and his shirtful of odds and ends together and pitched them off the roof, behind the woodpile. He nearly followed them head-first, but caught himself on the windowframe.

Maryellen straightened out the bed, and Eddie lifted the springs and mattress while she slid one of the slats towards the head.

The engine shut off; the car door opened and slammed shut.

Maryellen kissed him quick, and he brushed his hand across her cheek. She scooped up the rubber and held it out to him between her fingers like a dead rat. He jammed it into his pocket, squeezed her hand and she hurried down the ladder.

Eddie stepped out onto the roof as her father's steps reached the porch. At the same time the door opened, Eddie pulled the window down as quietly as he could and crept to the ground.

In the aftermath of the dream and the rain, the silent landscape took on an alien quality that helped Eddie to pull himself together. His body didn't want to work well yet, and the blue afterglow of the dreamway still pressed heavy on his consciousness.

Mel Thompkins kicked the toes of his muddy boots on the doorsill. Maryellen opened the door for him.

"Hello, Dad."

She must have startled him. He reeled back against the woodpile, then caught his balance.

"Maryellen . . ." Her father glanced around, unsteady in the doorway. "Thought I might find you here. Where's the bastard?"

Mel breathed deep, like he'd been running or stacking wood, and she guessed that he must be drunk. She had no sense of time—it could be seven in the evening or three in the morning. Her heart fluttered too fast, and she took a deep breath to relax the painful tightness in her belly.

She wanted to say, *I'm looking at him*, but bit it back.

"I'm alone, Dad," she lied. "I came here to get away from all that."

Mel brushed past her to the stove, holding tight to the unravelled sleeping bag under his arm. He set it down next to the couch and she heard the faint slosh of a bottle from somewhere inside the bag. She turned the lamps up, put the coffee back on the stove and studied him as carefully as possible without making him uneasy.

Wet, black hair was strung down his face and his clothes were well-soaked. He must have stopped more than once to walk himself sober enough to drive, or to drink in the rain. He probably checked out the Cispus bridge.

"Why'd you come up?" she asked. She thought that going on the offensive would be her best protection. "I have to be a criminal to get some privacy for one day. . . ."

Mel shook his head; then he started to cry. He cried quietly at first, barely a sigh in the night over the stove. Then as Maryellen moved towards him, it became a tight-throated growl that put the hair up on the back of her neck and ran chills along her arms. The last time he cried this way was after he beat Eddie up. He'd spread newspapers over the living-room floor and got out a pistol to shoot himself. Olive had walked in and stopped him, and they'd kept the incident quiet. Maryellen thought that her father hated her stepmother, too, but couldn't make himself leave her.

Maryellen held him though it scared her, dampening herself on his coat and hair.

"He's gone, too. I got . . . a call . . . from the hospital."

"Well, he's not here. You can see that."

He continued to cry, his face cradled in the crook of her neck. She started to move to take his coat, but he held her so tight she couldn't get her arms free. It didn't feel like love.

"Dad, let me take your coat and build up the fire."

His crying slowed, but he still held her tight.

"I'll build up the fire and fix you a drink, okay? Then we can sit and talk."

He let her go, rubbing her head once like he did that first time when he came home from the war. He took off his coat, then put it back on.

"Chilly. It's chilly. You feed the fire?"

"I was just doing that, Dad."

She handed him a towel.

"Why don't you dry off while I get in some wood, okay?"

He held the towel out and looked at it.

"Dry off your hair, Dad," she said. She pulled on her coat. "I'll be right in with some wood."

She hurried off the porch to the outhouse. Eddie was there, all right. His shadow darkened the weathered planks. He followed her inside.

"I'm scared," she said. "He acts really drunk, but he doesn't smell like it. He's sure you're here."

Eddie kissed the top of her head and ruffled her hair, like her father had done.

"Maybe I'd better head out," he said. His tongue felt thick, his speech slurred. "Get to the highway, hitchhike back. If I show up, then . . ."

"He can track anything, anytime," she said. "Besides, you've got one foot in the dreamways. If he starts looking, he's bound to find something—then he'll find you on the road. . . ."

"What, then?"

"Stay out here. I'll try to get him to leave, but he's too messed up to go tonight. Maybe the rain'll cover our tracks. . . ."

"Maybe isn't good enough," he said.

"It's too late to cover them now," she said. "Chances are he'd hear you out here. I've got to get back inside."

Eddie's throat ached from the tight anxiety that he held there, and Maryellen stuck her head under his coat so that her father wouldn't hear her brief, frustrated cry. She hugged Eddie tight and laid her face against his bare chest. Her sudden weeping died as quickly as it had come.

"My father's crying. He *never* cries. He's in really bad shape. He doesn't smell like booze. I'm afraid."

"You think . . . the Jaguar . . . ?"

"I don't know. I don't know."

Eddie held her tight, the way her father had. She ducked her head outside but couldn't see into the cabin from there. He felt her nipples, hard in her cold shirt, nose against his belly.

"I love you, Maryellen."

His hands wandered up and down her back.

"I've loved you for a long time."

She stood on tiptoe and kissed him, her hands warm under his coat.

"I know," she said.

"You can count on me," he said, and slipped outside.

Maryellen ran to the porch and piled wood high in her arms. She kicked the cabin door open, closed, and hurried, off balance, all the way to the stove.

Her father sat on the floor in front of the couch, picking at the ties on his sleeping bag.

"Do you want me to get that, Dad?"

No answer.

"Dad?"

"I'm not deaf. No. Can get. I . . . can get it."

She opened the stove and bunched the few remaining coals together with a stick of kindling. She watched her father while she worked. Something about his disorientation seemed familiar. She blew on the coals until they caught, closed the door and opened the draft.

Mel had his sleeping bag untangled, and his bottle of bourbon stood on the floor in front of him. It was full, unopened.

"Get you a drink, Dad?"

She hoped now that he'd go to sleep and not feel like staying up all night.

He nodded at her, staring at the bit of fire reflected on the floor.

She poured some bourbon into a cup, then filled it with water from the jug.

"Water's getting low; we should save some for coffee in the morning."

He nodded again, and didn't look up when she handed him the cup.

"What's wrong?"

He shook his head, and spilled part of his drink on his bag.

"Is it me, Dad?"

He looked up but not to her eyes. He talked to her mouth or throat.

"It's just . . . don't know."

He set his drink down and started to cry again. "I have these nightmares. And all I want is to love somebody."

She kissed the top of his head still wet with rain and smelling strong of cigar smoke and sweat. He was not old. His black hair was just beginning to gray and it was as thick and smooth as her own. The only age he wore, he wore in his eyes.

The talk about dreams hit home. She thought maybe Eddie was right, the Jaguar had found him on the dreamways. Maybe Eddie could find out; he was already halfway there.

"Dad, I'll fill up the stove and turn down the lamp. I think I'd better go up to bed."

He wiped his eyes and nose on his shirt-sleeve and didn't answer.

"Don't forget, there's not much water."

She waited for him to say something. When he didn't, she climbed the ladder and started to undress.

" 'Night."

It was a whisper and she barely heard it above the hiss of the stove.

"Good night, Dad."

The bed was pretty shaky, but she drifted off to a fitful sleep, dreaming of Afriqua Lee and a long run up a dark hillside.

When Maryellen woke she was immediately afraid and knew it wasn't the dream. Her father stood over her, his darkness exaggerated by the dim light from the downstairs lamp. He stood, unsteady, staring down at her. In his right hand he held his rifle from the pickup. In his left, the opened box of rubbers.

He threw the box at her face.

"Where is he? *Where is he?*"

She sat up and pulled the covers with her. Maryellen knew that denial would only infuriate him more. The sight of the rifle in his hand frightened her too much to move.

"I don't know." Her voice was barely a squeak. "I sent him out when you came in."

He jerked at her covers, but lost his balance and fell across her. The bed snapped again and collapsed. She held his chest at arm's length, but his knee pressed harder into her belly until she let go. His body pinned her down and he pushed his face into hers. His whiskey breath nearly gagged her, but she was so scared she went rigid and couldn't turn away.

"I want him. You call him."

The bed settled again and he slapped her bare hip with the rifle as he caught his balance. The chill sting of the barrel froze every muscle in her body tight as ice. She strained to say *No No*, but the cramps in her neck paralyzed her throat into a tight whine.

She shook her head *No*, wrestled him off balance and slammed her knee into his crotch. He fell back off the bed and rolled slowly over to one side, then got to his knees. Finally, he drew himself up until he knelt on the floor and rested his forehead against the stock of his rifle.

In the hot breath after anger Maryellen shook so bad her fingers barely worked. They clawed her bedding to her chest, and she backed herself against the wall. She watched her father uncurl without a word and struggle his way down the ladder, the barrel of his .30-.30 *tap-tapping* the rungs after him.

Though in many of its aspects the visible world seems formed in love, the invisible spheres were formed in fright.

—Herman Melville, *Moby Dick*

EDDIE GATHERED UP his gear and picked his way through the mud along the tree-line behind the cabin. He made out the silhouette of a low structure about fifty feet back and headed for it.

He found an old lean-to woodshed that was nearly empty and fairly dry inside. He spread his bag out on the dirt floor among the bark chips and lay down, half-falling into dream, half-jumpy from the danger just across the clearing. Mel Thompkins was a gunsmith and the best shot in the valley. Eddie had no illusions about the man's intent, but running out would leave Maryellen to take whatever was meant for him, and that was something that Eddie could not abide.

Besides, he had to face the ugly fact that he couldn't run. He had already been hit too hard by the dream.

Tonight's dream had barely got its hold on him when Maryellen jarred him out of it. He was not quite out of it. This one was different. This time, the danger wasn't on the other side—it was right here.

Was Rafferty trying to warn me about this? he wondered.

He wrung out every scrap of memory that he could, but the whole thing was a jumble of broken images.

In the dream the landscape kept jumping around, flashing between Rafferty's country and the valley. In both cases Eddie floated up high, a soaring dream, following the roadways of both worlds on the wings of a guiding wind. He circled a temple of the priesthood and saw six of them, the young Jaguar priests whose dreams had aged the innocents of the Roam. He remembered what Maryellen had said about looking into a mirror.

This is what happened to us, Eddie thought. *The dreams made us smarter but they stole our years.*

The priests had chanted themselves into dream, and as Eddie gyred high above them he saw that an aura pulsed outward from their group like a powerful blue ripple in a dark pond. It moved like something electric, but looked like a piece of rainbow.

When the blue wave hit him he tumbled end-over-end in the sky, and when he righted himself he levelled off over his own valley. He recognized the hospital and the town straggling out like a hem torn from the skirts of The Hill.

The city sprawled at the mouth of the river ten miles past the town, and another series of blue waves pulsed skyward from there.

The Jaguar, he thought. *It's got to be.*

That was when Maryellen woke him. He felt a detachment from the dream and from the real world. He stretched out on his sleeping bag, not wanting to give in to the dream. It was important, this he knew, but so was staying alive. He was sure that Maryellen's father would kill him this time, doing the bidding of the Jaguar.

He's running scared, Eddie thought. *I must be getting close.*

The night edged itself into a gray dawn in the woodshed. A few crows muttered to each other in a nearby tree, and one of them squawked the morning rally. Eddie lay back on his bedroll and closed his eyes.

He crashed through the blue butterfly and soared the dreamways again. The valley spread out below him, misty from the river and the recent rain. As the blue pulse caught up with him, he wheeled about and rode it like a kite. Beneath him he watched the network of roads and streams unravel, and saw that he was being carried up the mountain, past the bridge which was now washed out, to the cabin.

The blue disappeared and the lift went out of his wings and he had to swim for it. He saw himself asleep inside the woodshed, and the small murder of crows that were on watch cackled him a welcome as he settled his dream-self comfortably on a dead branch.

This was new. None of the dreamways had ever shown him an aerial view.

It's Ruckus, Eddie thought. *Rafferty must be in trouble, too, and Ruckus is our link.*

Eddie couldn't move his real body, though he could see it from the dream-perch a dozen feet overhead. His dreamer saw Maryellen's father stagger around the corner of the cabin, rifle in hand, alternately stumbling and holding his head.

It's the Jaguar, Eddie thought. *He's been on our dreamways and followed us here. Now he's got Maryellen's dad. He's not drunk; he's dreaming.*

Eddie knew where Mel was going and what he intended to do. Once again, Eddie struggled to make himself wake, to move, to holler, but nothing came. The crows rasped their alarm, and looked to the dreamer on the branch.

Mel Thompkins stumbled to the entrance to the woodshed and could barely stand, much less hold his rifle steady. Eddie was surprised at the calm he felt, watching this man try to kill him. Another blue wave broke over the clearing and Thompkins fell to his knees. He leaned back in a clumsy squat, his eyes awash in a quizzical expression. He cocked the rifle.

Ruckus, Eddie thought. *It's up to you, Ruckus.*

Eddie's vision flashed to the stone temple and the circle of Jaguar priests. Ruckus raised the alarm, and within a few moments gathered two dozen, three dozen crows. They swept down on the faces of the sleeping priests, pecking at their eyes and lips, slapping their wings against their faces.

The dreamer on the branch raised the same alarm. The crows at hand knew the rifle for what it was, and they had scattered themselves higher about the clearing to see what the human would do. Now, at the alarm, they raised alarm themselves and, following the dreamer, flocked against the human and his rifle just as he lifted it to his shoulder.

We were going to die there,
I remember the moon notching its way
through the palms and the calm sense that came
for me at the end of my life.

—**Carolyn Forché,** *The Country Between Us*

MARYELLEN HAD NODDED off with exhaustion, and she dreamed a twisted night of secret meetings and frantic runs down dark, stony corridors. She was not on the dreamways, but she felt the heavy influence of the other side pushing her through the night. Every time she nearly caught up with Afriqua Lee, her father would kick open a door or bang on a window, screaming her name.

The rifle shot behind the cabin exploded her out of her dream and onto the floor. As she untangled herself from the blankets, a flock of crows behind the cabin squawked and screamed.

"Oh, God!" she said to herself. "Oh, no!"

It was just daylight, gray, but lighter than the black storm of the day before. Maryellen looked over the rail and scanned the cabin. Her father was not downstairs. She pulled on her jeans and shirt, scrambled down the ladder and out the open door of the cabin. She rounded the porch and saw him there at the entrance to the woodshed, kneeling with his forehead on the ground. Dozens of crows swarmed overhead, each one taking its turn to drop down and attack him before flying off.

"Eddie," she called, her heart pounding harder. "Eddie!"

Her father writhed back and forth under the onslaught of the crows, keeping his face to the ground. The moaning that came from his throat raised the hair on the back of her neck.

"Eddie!"

The crows made no move against her. She made her feet begin

the short walk to the woodshed. As she did, the birds settled into branches and onto the rooftops of the cabin and the shed. There were dozens. The branches crackled under their weight and they squabbled for position on the roofs. A few continued their harassment of her dad, though he showed no intention of rising.

She found Eddie in the shed, unconscious, bleeding from his nose. There was no sign of a bullet wound, so she guessed that he'd been dreaming.

She grabbed him under the armpits and dragged him to the pickup. Her father stayed still as she struggled past him. She kicked the rifle away from him, just in case.

Her dad's Chevy was crusted with mud; the windshield was shattered and a long scrape crumpled it from front fender to back on the passenger side. He'd parked it close behind the truck to block it in. She set Eddie down in the driveway and checked the ignition, holding her breath.

"Shit!"

The keys weren't there. They were in her dad's pocket. She looked up and saw that the crows had pinned him down again, and she didn't want to take any chances.

"There's a spare set with the truck keys," she told herself.

As she hurried to the truck a flash of fear came over her.

What if he took them?

He hadn't. She took the car key off the ring, moved the car out from behind the truck and tossed the car key into the woods.

Stuffing Eddie into the passenger side of the truck was too much for her. Pulling was easier, so she dragged him around the back of the truck, dropped the tailgate and pulled him by the armpits into the bed. Muddy water saturated both of them. Eddie's breathing gasped at times with the struggle in his mind. He grunted once, then lay in the bed, sprawled and still.

The ride on this road ought to bring him around, she thought.

Maryellen closed the muddy tailgate, jumped in and started the truck.

The more the patients deteriorate, the less sharp is the line dividing dreams from the waking state. Ultimately, in a severe deterioration the dream wins. . . .

—**Benjamin B. Wolman,** *Dreams and Schizophrenia*

RAFFERTY HAD NOT slept in three nights and four days, since he set up the trap for the raider forces at the City of Eternal Spring. Afriqua Lee, herself exhausted, remained at his side throughout the execution of his plan and their subsequent flight to the ancient stoneworks.

Who could be worthy of such a woman as she?

Rafferty vowed to make himself worthy. He had repeated public vows, as well. Old Cristina had defied tradition and married them as he piloted their van towards the stoneworks in the highlands. Rafferty fortified himself with another pail of the thick Roam coffee and watched a new dawn ooze from the tight fist of night. Though married, he and Afriqua Lee had yet to share a bed.

We will have our time, he thought. It was a thought he used to drive away the other thought, the one that said, *The Romni married you out of tradition because she didn't expect you to survive the Jaguar priests.*

There had been no priests in the battle at the city's gates. Rafferty smiled. He had been plotting the priests and their movements for two years. He knew that now they huddled together, fortifying their power with spleef and frenzy-dancing. He knew that they did not expect the Roam to hunt them down.

Today was the day. First, there was the camp to stakedown, scouts and guards to place, matters of the kumpania's survival to tend to. Festivities of a marriage between a tentless woman and a gaje dreamer would wait again, and so might their wedding night. Rafferty had started calling Afriqua Lee "Old Relentless Tentless" when she took over the controls during his battle conferences.

"The Romni . . ." Afriqua said, "she must be afraid, to marry us like that."

"Afraid that she's going to die?" he muttered.

"No," she said. "Afraid that *we're* going to die. This way we can skip the preliminaries in our next lives; we'll already be married."

He grunted his acknowledgment of this truth.

Their scanner picked out the subtle blazes he'd laid for their trail, and their machine heaved its way along the highland track, what was left of it. The others jockeyed their rides close behind, with the battle cadre strategically deployed throughout the column, flanking, and to the rear. Each escort rode a single-sling sprint, capable of a two-minute brush run of the fifty-vehicle column.

"Do you think the Jaguar can live forever?" she asked.

"I saw him in a dream," he said, "putting on the skins of other people's bodies."

"But, don't you think he would just be trapped . . . ?"

"I think I would be trapped," he said. "How can we know what tricks he has learned that remain beyond our ken?"

Rafferty checked the next series of blazes, and his security system that was linked to them—the 'white device.'

Surely they know of our win at the gates, he thought.

None of the Roam's communications-intercept devices had picked up messages from the city to the highlands.

The pulse knocked them out during battle, he thought, and his chest involuntarily swelled a bit. *The white device should keep them cut off.*

Rafferty was proud of the white device—his security and communications system—because it gave back to the Roam something of what they had given him. It was an impenetrable barrier to electronics from outside its perimeter, and a conduit for communications within.

"If this doesn't work," he asked, "will the Roam turn us over?"

"No," she said. "I witnessed the agreement at the kris romani. It was as the Romni said at the gates—if they come for one, they come for all of us eventually. We will stop it here or die."

"We will stop it here."

"Yes," she said, and her smile whitened a dark portion of rosy dawn. "We will. The Jaguar underestimates us. The Jaguar priests have never met the likes of the Maya Roam. And you have never met the likes of me."

"Truth of a truth," he whispered.

Rafferty set the galley for more coffee and took over the controls. They'd become so good at the switch that they easily opened up a lead on the rest of the convoy. They reined themselves in whenever the huntmaster clicked his radio twice.

Rafferty guided Old Cristina's van into the clearing that he and the hunting cadre had prepared the day before, and pulled into the special spot he'd made for her tent under the ceiba tree. The van's squeaks and rattles, and the thrash of loose rocks under its drive, were damped to silence by the white device.

Rafferty didn't move out of the pilot's seat. He leaned back, then sipped a fresh cup of coffee.

"Just in time," he said. "We're going to need a *lot* of this stuff—today *and* tonight."

Tonight, of all nights, he wanted to be free of the dreams.

The ancient Roam's track through the jungle had been crossed many times with raider trails. He'd watched Ruckus all day the day before when they rode scout. The crow crisscrossed the territory, mapping it out. Other crows called back and forth, so Rafferty knew that this was a good sign. Electronic devices might fail in bad weather, but a crow just keeps on ticking.

The hills of jungle that surrounded them hid dozens of stone ruins, and this flat spot had been an old stone plaza in a marketplace long dead. Rafferty and the battle cadre secured the Roam a position on the plaza, close to the stream. He marked corners for the Romni's tent beside a low platform of stone slabs that formed a kind of a dais. Visitors to the dying Romni Bari could wait here in style.

The priesthood's goons hunted them down, sniffing out some kind of trail on the dreamways. Rafferty felt it, Afriqua Lee felt it. The dogged pursuit of the Jaguar priests had already cost sixty deaths and two hundred wounded, the worst of it at the gates of the City of Quetzals. It had been a necessary sacrifice, to appear vulnerable enough to trap a careless raider force at the City of Eternal Spring.

"You have two among you that they want," the radio had crackled. "Leave them, and you are welcome."

It had become, by that time, a familiar refrain. The landless Roam could not be denied entry. That was the most basic tenet of the accords, forged over two thousand years of preaching and war.

Rather than demand entry on their legal rights and being seen as cowards, the Maya Roam turned and fought the henchmen of the priesthood. War, in the tradition of the Roam, signified a failure on both sides. It was not a pride; it was a shame. But a worse shame was to be bested in an agreement, and that's how they perceived the violations of the accords.

When it was over, Rafferty wanted to settle a score with the City of Quetzals, the City of Eternal Spring and the others, once the Jaguar business was done. Without the Roam to supply them, to repair them, the cities would die. Within city walls was law. Outside, except for the Roam, there was only wits, fists, darts and the blade. The Jaguar business would be done soon.

The question had been asked at the kris romani, "Should the young dreamers be put out?"

There was no question that it would buy off the Jaguar priests for now, but Rafferty was sure that there would be another time, another opening on the dream council.

Old Cristina squelched such talk at the kris with a lift of her massive eyebrow, but now Old Cristina was failing and there were power moves rippling throughout the Roam. It was evident everywhere—swaggers, backtalk, the arrogant parking of tents out of position.

Already at dawn, before Rafferty downed the last of his coffee, the camouflage net was spread, the dust of their path damped down, the white device block-and-relays switched on in the mobile tents of the Roam. The site would be invisible electronically as well as physically. Within moments of the last arrival, no one on a nearby lookout would guess that there was a camp, or that the camp housed the last thousand souls of the great Maya Roam.

The old woman had collapsed after their last flight, from the walls of the City of Eternal Spring, which brought them all into the southern highlands. She sweated though she was cold, and she cried out from time to time. Her right arm curled uselessly beneath her and a steady drool slipped out of the slack right side of her mouth.

The flight had been strong because the Romni Bari had been

strong, and now it was falling apart. Rafferty thanked the stars that they had made the southern reaches, and the jungle. If worse came to worst, the Roam could scatter and hide here.

The regrowth of highland jungle beat back the best of the Jaguar's plagues. It was scraggly country, for a jungle, but the traditional hiding places served them well, and there was food to be had for the hunting.

Rafferty had watched Ruckus ruffle himself into his hunting dance as the Roam positioned their vehicles for the streamside encampment. The crow was sorely tired of dried meat. As soon as Rafferty had set up his van and seen to Old Cristina, he took Afriqua Lee by the arm and whispered, "Get your darts; meet me at the stream."

"I will meet you here," she said, "for all the Roam to see." She squared her dusty shoulders. "We are a team, you and I. If we choose to break tradition and hunt together, it's time they got used to it."

Rafferty grinned.

"Right. If they don't like it, they can leave their plates empty. More for us."

Women of the Roam did not hunt, but Rafferty had seen how well Afriqua Lee popped a dart. Besides, he needed cover as he activated their defenses, and there was no one he trusted more. They would show the Roam a new partnership, a new tradition. It would take a new tradition to outwit the Jaguar and his priesthood.

Afriqua Lee stepped from the Romni's tent, parked beneath the sprawling ceiba tree, and he thought that no woman in this world or the other could possibly be as beautiful.

She had borrowed one of his hunting scarves to tie back her mane of curly black hair. It was a black scarf, as all of his were, adorned with a small embroidered border of green quetzals. The green intensified when she wore it, and electrified the green in her eyes.

Rafferty never wanted to lose a moment of his life together with Afriqua Lee. The matter had been aired at a kris romani, during a trial of two traitors to the priesthood. The Roam feared their dreams, what their dreaming had brought down on their heads. Most of all, they feared the offspring of two dreamers, but the challenge to their marriage was beaten by the Romni Bari. The grumblings didn't cease with the gavel and the token sacrifice of blood from the tongue.

Ruckus squawked his impatience, and lifted off. Rafferty and Afriqua Lee shrugged into their bandoliers of darts and charges, and followed.

"The green-eyed girl goes hunting," an old woman called after them.

"Watch out for the trouser-snake," another called, her cackle swallowed by the white device.

Rafferty darted a large paca, eight kilos or more, a dozen paces from the camp. He motioned Afriqua to wait, then hurried back to hang it by a leg and bleed it from the Romni Bari's ceiba tree.

"Start on this one," he told the onlookers, "there will be plenty tonight. Musicians, get your strength up."

Many of the men dropped their setup squabbles to gather up their darts and traps.

Good, he thought. *Now they'll remember how to hunt.*

Rafferty had spoken once at a meeting of the kumpania, saying that their custom of trading with other communities was too dangerous, their route too predictable.

"They're not very smart," he told them. "We can trap the priests if we think of myself and my bride as bait. We'll go a season early to the highland stakedown. It's heavy jungle and at its hottest, true, but we know that they'll be there, drumming up an ambush for us. Let's not disappoint them."

Now it was time to turn the tables. Rafferty sensed the priesthood close by, plying the dreamways, growing stronger.

Now was the moon of hard decisions upon them. The priesthood had begun its cycle of revenge and punishments in their pursuit of the dreamers. They had alienated the Roam from communities of their traditional route. Citizens who once awaited the Roam with jobs and stakedown spaces now met them with hard stares and locked gates. No matter that worldwide law took their side. It was a hungry time.

Afriqua Lee bounded across the camp in her long strides, another paca across her strong shoulders. She dumped it between the feet of Alma, the quick-tongued old woman.

"I thought a little hot meat between your legs might cool you down," she said, and turned on a heel to join Rafferty.

The other women shrieked and laughed at Alma's surprise, then hurried to admire the plump animal and to help her dress it. By then, Rafferty and Afriqua Lee were already hunting the stream, setting out perimeter scouts and activating their defense.

As the morning wore on, they activated two white devices buried in switchboxes. These insured the Roam a wide radius of strategic cover. They needed one more switchbox farther upstream.

Rafferty took a reading on the locator signals and checked the status of the 'protect device' modifications that he had built in to all units. Everything checked out. He planted several of the smaller, more potent protection units by themselves along their trail. The battle cadre could follow easily with their hand-held sensors, and these sensors would not trigger the protection devices as long as the scouts entered the correct code.

A precaution.

"I saw tapir tracks," Afriqua said. "Up here, where I shot the last paca."

His gaze followed the direction of her pursed lips to a limp silhouette hanging head-down, out of reach of animals from below. The jungle beyond the dead paca walled them away from the extreme highlands. Trails throughout the region were notoriously rocky and steep. They were getting close to the stoneworks, where he anticipated finding the priesthood. There had been no sign, physical or electronic, that they defended their position.

They don't believe it possible that we survived, he thought.

Rafferty heard a call from Ruckus, but ignored it when he saw the fresh tracks at streamside. They spanned more than a hand, and a bit of dirt crumpled into one as he watched. It was damp earth, and they still filled with water. He sniffed, and got nothing.

"It must've climbed out here"—he pointed up the bank—"and probably went up that slope."

Rafferty planted the last of his protection units at the base of the backline switchbox. He activated the switch and received confirmation from the battle base at the Romni's tent. The return signal included coordinates for his nearest scout and cadre—less than a kilometer behind them.

Good.

Three hillsides sloped up from the other side of the stream. Each was overgrown with broadleaf ferns, choked out at the base by thick underbrush. Brush was a favorite place for tapir to hide. The villagers called it a 'mountain cow,' but it didn't look like any cow that Rafferty had ever seen. He'd seen one a few seasons back, on a trek through the southern highlands. It sniffed the air once with its flexible nose and trampled off into the thickest brush. The brush would knock a jaguar off its back, and made a dart shot nearly impossible.

"Do you think our charges are heavy enough?" she asked. "Tapir hide is mighty thick."

"Load green," he said. "I pressed them myself; they're all heavy."

"But, still . . ."

"Still"—he smiled—"don't shoot for bone. It's best if we flank it and we both get a shot."

They tracked the tapir through its brush trail and found dozens of paca dens along their way.

We will eat well here, he thought. *It will give the Roam a chance to pull together.*

He hoped that he and Afriqua Lee would still be a part of it when it did. She made that tiny clicking noise with her tongue just when he noticed a peculiar odor on the breeze. Before he could register it, the wild-eyed tapir burst from the brush ahead of them. Its path had dead-ended into a stone wall, and it retreated towards them, two hundreds kilos of churning fear.

It worked just as he'd said. They stepped aside and let it charge between them. Then they turned as one, and each placed a dart between the tapir's ribs. Inertia carried it another dozen meters before it crumpled without a squeal.

In the stillness that followed, Rafferty heard Ruckus again, somewhere above the jungle canopy. It was his alarm call, and then his flocking call. In the same moment, dozens of crow voices responded.

Afriqua Lee started towards the dead tapir, but Rafferty stopped her with a hand motion and put his finger to his lips. Once again, that odor on the breeze.

Spleef, he thought.

He remembered Nebaj, and the constant smell of burned spleef at his camp, mixed with the thick incense of copal that the Roam called 'pom.'

Now Afriqua Lee smelled it, too.

Something about the regular angularity of the three hillsides registered with him.

Temples, he thought. *So, we've come that far. . . .*

Ruckus sounded his distress call again, and was silent.

Rafferty motioned for Afriqua Lee to follow him back up the trail. The stone wall was not a cliff face but a wall of cut stones.

One layer of stones had been delicately carved into skulls, no two alike.

Stoneworks littered the jungles of the southern highlands, former ceremonial centers and cities of the old Roam. This one was the oldest, the temple of the gate of Xibalba. Talk of it frightened the old folk, and they had been vocal in their fears about the stakedown here.

Maybe they were right, he thought.

On the left the stonework abutted the dirt hillside. Rafferty followed the wall to the right, working his way under the overgrowth, and Afriqua Lee followed. He saw that she'd switched to a multiple-fire magazine in her weapon. It didn't carry the punch, but it fired twenty darts without reloading. He made the switch himself, and Afriqua Lee smashed a scorpion on the wall next to his neck.

He flashed her the sign of the Martyr for 'thanks.'

Another half-dozen paces and they encountered a steep stairway. The wall continued on the other side of the stairs and disappeared into the brush. The odor of spleef was much stronger here, and the granite stairway was neither overgrown nor dirty. Someone had recently swept it clean. Rafferty raised his eyebrows and indicated the stairway.

Afriqua Lee shrugged, glanced around, then pointed her weapon up the stairway.

Rafferty smiled.

I love you, he thought, and hoped that she felt it.

Crows gathered in twos and threes in the jungle canopy above the steps. Their raucous cries squawked louder as he and Afriqua Lee approached the top

The only sounds were the crows, the rustle of trees in the breeze and the stream about a hundred meters away. They crept to the last set of stone stairs on their hands and knees, and peered over the top with their weapons ready.

Six Jaguar priests sat in a column of smoke-twined sunlight at a stone table set with chairs and pipes for seven. Rafferty recognized an aged Nebaj among them. Spleef-smoke and pom lay over the scene like hot mist. Dozens of crows took their turns attacking the somnolent priests, flapping at their faces and pecking at their eyes. The priests did not even fight back out of reflex, but stirred towards waking. The small guard troop busied themselves flailing at the crows in defense of the helpless priests. The stubborn crows kept it up.

Dream, he thought. *It's got them.*

He wondered what it meant that he'd been in a stone place before, a table and chairs much like this. . . .

He glanced back at Afriqua Lee, who arched a quizzical brow.

"This looks familiar," she whispered, "Maryellen's dream, the marble columns and the marble table and chairs."

"But this is granite," he said. "And we're not dreaming."

She rubbed the stone step, just to be sure.

A series of *put put puts* exploded the rock beside her and sprayed fragments into her face. She fell and tumbled down the steps. Rafferty snapped off a low, fast shot and blew up the guard's knee. A clip of darts unloaded from the raider's weapon into the sky; then he threw it away in frustration and grabbed at his wound with a shriek.

Afriqua Lee followed her roll down the steps with a pair of quick shots that knocked one raider over backwards and broke another's arm.

Body armor, Rafferty signalled. *Watch out!*

She popped an orange marker into the heavy ferns where the first raider fell, and positioned herself behind cover. Rafferty finished a quick sweep and she swept once herself. She saw something black drop to the stone plaza behind Rafferty's back.

Afriqua Lee signalled *Ruckus!* to him, and pointed.

Rafferty laid his weapon down and picked up the limp bundle of black feathers. He frowned, then set the dead crow on the top step of the gray stone temple.

He signalled back, *No, not Ruckus.*

The crows stepped up the fury of their mysterious attack. Rafferty scooped up his weapon and scanned the sky for Ruckus. He spotted the crow's ruffed-up silhouette high in a tree that bordered the ruins.

He looks sick, or . . .

Suddenly, the crows' attack made sense.

"Ruckus on the dreamways," he muttered in amazement.

Rafferty heard cries in the brush beneath him, the flat-toned discharge of hunting darts and heavy *thuck* of full-combat explosive tips.

"It's the Roam mopping up the raiders," Afriqua whispered. "What about those priests?"

"What about them?"

The crows were wearying, but they had forced the lethargic priests to come around. Clearly, the ones who managed to come to consciousness would awaken in extreme, searing pain. Rafferty knew that pain all too well, as did Afriqua Lee.

"They're not going anywhere," she said, "but are you sure they can't . . . you know . . . *dream* us dead or something? And what about the Jaguar—won't he come looking for his little pets?"

"If we stop the priests, we stop the Jaguar," Rafferty said. He leaned his back against the vine-covered stone of the temple.

Rafferty sucked in a deep breath. No one was sniping their way. A few wild shots from across the acropolis snapped off branches, intended for crows. Those were silenced by the battle cadre of the Roam. From Rafferty's vantage point at the rim of the acropolis, the six priests made easy targets.

"No," he whispered, "they can't hurt us. We need them alive if we're going to learn anything, but it's more important to stop the Jaguar."

He hand-signalled the cadre to go in silently. Presently, two of their men crested the acropolis, then four; then a dozen of the Roam circled the priests and trussed up the somnolent captives without a fight.

"Easily done," Afriqua Lee laughed, and they joined the others who were already trussing the lethargic priests. The skinny Nebaj was one of them. As the sleep-disorientation left him, the young priest's face contorted into absolute fear.

"This is the power center," his voice rasped, "you can't do this."

"Your power days are over," Rafferty said. "Besides, you're just the instrument. We want the Jaguar. . . ."

"You don't understand," the priest hissed, his voice thick with the influence of the dream. "He protects himself . . . you are killing us. . . ."

A flash of light vaporized both of the priest's eyes, and in the same instant his skull was engulfed in white-hot fire. Within seconds the peculiar fire consumed all of the priests leaving only their porcelain bones, each inside its own halo of blackened stone.

But Crow Crow
Crow nailed them together,
Nailing heaven and earth together—

So man cried, but with God's voice.
And God bled, but with man's blood.

—**Ted Hughes,** *Crow*

MARYELLEN WRESTLED THE wheel, and her pickup slued down the muddy ruts of the driveway. A hump of black muck scraped the truck's underbelly and tugged once, twice as the back wheels spun. She gunned it and lurched astraddle the ruts, nursing the pickup along in the early morning drizzle, barely faster than she could have walked.

"Please let the bridge be there," she prayed. "Please let the bridge be there."

She didn't know what kind of god to pray to anymore. There seemed to be so many and, in the end, they all looked so petty and so human.

The cabin was still visible in the rearview mirror when she could no longer tell the driveway from the muddy outflow of the stream. At this point the drive crossed an old logging road, and she was sure that the water beyond was too deep for the pickup. It didn't matter; it was also clear that the bridge was gone.

She pounded on the dashboard.

"Dammit!" She pounded again. "Dammit!"

She swiped at the tears that betrayed her frustration.

"Think," she ordered herself. "Just think for a damn minute."

A shot slapped the side mirror off the truck in a spray of glass, and instinct made her pop the clutch and crank the wheel to the right. Her tires spun smoke and hot muck. The old truck wallowed for an eternity before it grabbed enough traction to make the turn into the woods. Maryellen stayed as far down in the seat as she could as she guided the truck up the steep grade.

A spider web of logging roads crisscrossed the hillsides around her. Most dead-ended in the hills; two led out.

Which two?

The rut she was on led upstream, and she knew that another bridge crossed only about a mile upstream. It was higher, and in a deeper part of the canyon, so maybe it would still be good.

But if she went back to the valley, what would she say? That her father wanted to kill them?

"It's not his fault," she whispered, and prayed that it was true.

She glanced over her shoulder and saw that Eddie was curled up into a tight ball, bouncing in the bed. Back as far as she could see, there was no sign of her father or his car.

One of these roads runs all the way to Oregon, she thought.

Going back to the valley meant bigger trouble; that was clear. If they tried to run and hide, they'd be caught. The pickup would give them away on the highway. If they could stay in the hills, below the snow line . . .

She remembered a trip with her father, coming back from Portland, when they'd tried logging roads all the way and got through. She had been eleven then, and had slept all the way.

Which ones dead-end?

She couldn't remember. Maryellen had fished here with her father a few times, but never far from the cabin. She never seemed to know how they got where they got—it was one of the mysteries of her father. He knew these hills as well as he knew his rifle, and she didn't know them at all.

"No," she said to herself, "we've got to get to town. He'll just track us down out here."

Maryellen reminded herself that she didn't know her father any better than the roads—at least, she didn't know this maniac that he'd become.

The Jaguar.

She shuddered with the chill that his name conjured in her spine. She knew this had to be the Jaguar's doing. He hadn't been able to get inside herself or Eddie, but he'd found a way to her father. The Jaguar had broken through in his long hunt, and it was his breath from her father's mouth that sent the ice down her spine. He must have known they'd planned to hunt him out to free Rafferty and the Roam.

"He found us, Eddie," she said. "Now what do we do?"

She approached the lip of a gravel slide that nearly filled the bare track of a road and stopped the truck. She leaned her forehead on the cool steering wheel for just a moment.

"Too many people falling apart," she said. "I should have known."

Maryellen knew the secret of classmates falling hysterical in second grade. Her dream-burglaries, her petty trespassing, cost her classmates sleep, and the lack of sleep changed them. Maryellen and Eddie had figured it out separately, but by then incredible damage was done, much of it to themselves.

In school, or family, or with her few friends—the same wierdnesses, the same personality changes erupted when she'd been dreaming inside their heads, and so she'd stopped. Taking their sleep made them crazy. And being crazy hurt them—she knew that, now. Maryellen remembered how her father looked last night, how hollow-eyed and driven he'd looked the day he beat up Eddie.

The dreamway insanity—it had to be the Jaguar's doing. Maryellen had learned not to make the people closest to her crazy. Eddie had learned the same hard lesson. So, for that matter, had Rafferty and Afriqua Lee. Maryellen knew that she hadn't been dreaming her father's dreams. Eddie would have confessed to her out of principle if he'd linked up with her father on the dreamways.

That left the Jaguar, whoever he was, safe in his bed somewhere, trying to kill them by using her father as skillfully as her father would use his rifle.

He, and his rifle, were somewhere behind them, and she knew better than to think he'd give up a hunt.

The slide left a pile of gravel in the roadway from the uphill slope on her right. The slope dropped away about a hundred feet to her left before it disappeared over the lip of the canyon and into the foaming roil of the stream. In the open, halfway up the misted hillside, the roar of the swollen river drowned out her pickup's noisy engine.

The bridge is good!

Just a short distance past the slide, the road dipped down the slope to meet the wooden bridge that squatted with its skirts in the current.

Maryellen looked back again at Eddie, limp as a bag of laundry beside the spare tire. She considered bringing him into the cab, then thought better of it.

"You'll have a better chance back there," she said, as though he could hear. Talking to him made her feel less exposed, and not so much alone.

She took a hard look at the churning river, and swallowed. Nobody would have a chance down there. But if she didn't admit it. . . .

She put the truck in compound low and nosed around the lip of the slide. She had to drive off the road, downslope of the slide. The wheel spun out of her hands as though snatched by a giant. The hood of the truck dropped away and the back end of the truck lifted into the sky. It was the slope plunging away with the road.

The old truck rolled once, twice, then skidded to rest in some scrub firs and brush at the brink of the canyon.

Maryellen had grabbed the wheel in mid-roll, out of reflex, and held tight at arm's length until the last of the loose gravel stopped skittering past her. She was conscious of the greater roar of the river and the fact that she sat on the ceiling of the upside-down cab. The ravenous stream ate at the bank just a few feet away.

How long . . . ?

A crow sounded its hoarse alarm somewhere nearby, then another, a dozen.

"Eddie!" she whispered. "Oh, Jesus, Eddie!"

Maryellen crawled out the broken windshield and fought for balance as the gravel shifted under her. She crawled under the upturned bed, but Eddie wasn't there. There was no sign of him near the truck, so she scrabbled the slope on her hands and knees, calling his name. The sound of the river swallowed everything.

It was the crow that found Eddie first, face-down in the gravel, half-buried. The right side of his face looked smashed where he lay on it, and the gravel was bloody under his scalp where a chunk of it peeled back to expose his skull from his right eyebrow to his ear.

He was breathing, and when Maryellen tried to move him to a more comfortable position, he let out a terrible moan. His right shoulder was lower than it should be, and a piece of metal from the bed of the truck protruded from his right elbow.

"I'll get you out of here, Eddie," she whispered. "I promise, I'll get you out. . . ."

A crow dove at her so hard that its wingtip brushed her hair, and she flattened over Eddie out of reflex. Looking up from the hollow, Maryellen saw her father huffing out of the tree line above her. She scrunched down even farther and was sure he couldn't see them behind the gravel and the brush.

The sky was full of crows, as were the branches of the trees where the road came out of the woods to cross the slope. Her father batted at them with his rifle barrel and, in spite of their attacks, stopped cold when he reached the slide. She watched his eyes follow the tire tracks, the fresh gravel slide and the raw scar that the truck had made.

He scanned the slope once, and his gaze went back to the truck. He took a couple of hesitant steps, glancing back down the road and then across the slide to where the road picked up. He straightened his shoulders as though he had all the time in the world, then began gingerly picking his way down the slope to the truck. He held his rifle as ready as his balance would allow.

Eddie moaned again, and stirred, but Maryellen pinned him down with her body and muffled his mouth with her hand.

He can hear us up there, she thought. *Once he gets below us, the river will be too loud.*

Her father passed within twenty feet of them, but his attention was on the truck and his precarious footing.

When he gets to the truck, he'll track me back here, she thought. *What can I do?*

She searched the gravel for a fist-sized stone, and in a moment had a pile of about a dozen set within reach. She knew it was no match for his rifle, but it was all she had and she felt she might get lucky.

The crows had at him in a renewed attack, forcing him into a barely controlled run down the slope. At first Maryellen thought he would slide right past the truck, over the edge and into the river. She had been holding her breath, and now tried to catch up in short, silent gasps.

He slid right up against the bed of the pickup, rocking it slightly. He scanned underneath as she had done, then checked the cab. The crows kept at him, and he batted at them again. When he turned from the cab, his eyes followed her tracks up-slope. From where she lay, she was sure that he couldn't see her yet. He was downslope—that was to her advantage. She gathered her stones in close.

She trembled so bad she was afraid she couldn't throw at all, and she held her breath again when he leaned against the pickup and sighted at her down the barrel. She hugged Eddie and herself as far into the gravel as they could get.

Eddie cried out, louder this time, but she didn't try to shush him. With the din of the nearby water, it couldn't carry far.

The shot went wild, or perhaps he'd been aiming at a crow. It was a puny little *pop* drowned out by the river. She grabbed a couple of deep breaths and risked a peek.

Her father and the truck were both gone. A dark, damp scar of mud was all that remained.

Now, instead of being afraid of her father, she was afraid *for* him.

She thought that maybe it was a trick to get her out in the open, so she hesitated to expose herself. She was well upslope, and had a wide view, and saw no sign of him. The crows, so thick and aggressive a minute ago, now circled lazily overhead calling among themselves.

She crouched on her knees and felt the tremor of another huge section of bank giving way. She made her way to within a few yards of the slide.

The undercarriage of the truck was all that she could see, wedged in some rocks about a hundred feet downstream. Mud and brown water churned through the burst-out windows and door. There was no sign of her father.

"Daddy!" she called. *"Daddy!"* But he was gone.

And it was her father who saved them or, at least, her father's body. A forest-service road crew found him wedged between logs in the wreckage of the old bridge, and mounted an upstream search for survivors.

They found the upturned pickup and told Maryellen later how they found her and Eddie. She had built up a nest of branches under Eddie to keep him off the mud and gravel. She carefully tore the right sleeve away from his injured arm and bandaged his head with it enough to stop the bleeding. Eddie cried out sometimes, whether she moved him or not, but his breathing stayed strong.

She thought of starting a fire to attract attention, but the cloud cover was still low and she didn't have any matches with her.

Nobody up here, anyway, she thought.

But she knew she had to keep Eddie warm and she had to get him dry, so she decided to hurry back to the cabin.

"I'm going to cover you up, Eddie," she told him. "I'm going back to the cabin to get some blankets, and stuff to start a fire. I'm going to cover you up with branches. If I can find the keys I'll bring the car. I love you, Eddie."

She was pulling cedar boughs from branches when she saw the forest-service truck across the river. She was numb by then, and never did remember flagging them down. The rest of the day was a blur.

The road crew had a first-aid kit, blankets and coffee. They wrapped Eddie up, improvised a litter out of a tarp to get him off the slope and into the back of their truck. He cried out once, when they wrapped him in the blankets; then he was still.

They had only two blankets, and she insisted that they use them both for Eddie.

"You need one as bad as he does," the crew chief said. His name was Bob and he had red hair, and looked barely older than she was. His blue eyes looked scared and his face was so pale that his freckles looked like paint splatters.

"You're wet, cold, and up here with just your shirt and jeans," he reasoned. "You wouldn't want him to wake up asking for you and find out that you'd died of pneumonia, would you?"

"He needs them," she said. "He's fighting very hard right now, and he needs all the help he can get."

She refused to ride in the truck's cab, too.

"I'll ride in the back with him," she said.

The crew chief and his two men glanced at each other then down at their boots. Bob cleared his throat and scratched his nose.

"Well, uh, there's another problem, miss," he said.

"What's that?"

"Well, we just have the one truck, and there's your father's . . . your father down there. We need to get him out, too, in case the road on this side goes. And there are animals. . . ."

One of the men cleared his throat.

"I'll stay," the man said. "You can call from Ashford for another truck to come get me. You can take these two straight to the clinic at Morton. I'll stay with her father. If the river comes up any more, I'll pull him to high ground. This way, it'll only take an hour or so."

So that's what they did. They stopped once beside a small,

crumpled figure under a blue tarp. The crew chief lifted a corner of the plastic for her and placed a hand on her shoulder.

She hadn't told them about the rifle, the shooting, about the demon that had tormented her father into chasing them. She let them believe that they'd all been in the pickup together, and that she and Eddie had been thrown clear while the truck went over with her father. She wanted to believe it so bad that she cried when she saw him, battered and bloodless, free of dreams. She was glad for the chance to see him dead. It made him her father again, someone she was supposed to love, and did love.

The crew chief led her away.

. . . the handful of pollen
that always waited in ambush
to upset your lives
and the celestial track of the wind
shall rise from pure love
to save the soul of the earth.

—**Otto-Rene Castillo,** "Prayer for the Soul of My Country"

EDDIE WAS AFRAID when the blue pulse caught him, afraid in a way that he had never known before. He had thought of death, imagined it, feared it the way he thought most people did, and in that fear simply refused to think of it. Unlike most people, Eddie had been inside dreams of death, visions of death, and witnessed it through other people's eyes all too often on this side and the other. He had browsed memories of death, eavesdropped on it, learned to shut it out when he sniffed its telltale stench in the crannies of someone's mind.

This fear was not of death.

The blue riptide of purest power swept Eddie away with the beastly horror of life without being. Possession was its name, and the Jaguar its handler. The Jaguar had found him at last, and Eddie knew that if he had a soul, he was in the fight of his life for it now.

The Jaguar must have smelled his fear; it made him careless. He pressed Mel Thompkins hard to kill before Eddie could muster an escape. Interference from the other side spoiled his connection, spoiled everything, and he didn't dare jump Eddie's skull for fear that Thompkins would succeed while he was inside.

Eddie felt this uncertainty and knew what it meant. The Jaguar would rather have him dead than possess him. If Thompkins killed Eddie while the Jaguar was inside . . . Eddie would die, but the dreaming mechanism of the Jaguar would go with him. So Eddie took advantage of the Jaguar's hesitation. He jumped the dreamways, sidestepped the Jaguar and backtracked the blue pulse into the Jaguar's brain.

It was not pleasant.

The Jaguar had had a busy ten years, and so had the hospital. Drugs dulled the synapses and made travel as tough as a swim through cold molasses. Eddie wanted a crack at anything that would shut him down. He didn't want to kill anyone—he had suffered enough for the incident with his mother—but he vowed he would kill the Jaguar if he could.

What he really wanted was to shut down the Jaguar's dream center. The activity there was so high that it sounded like surf crashing the shoreline.

Eddie decided to scramble everything. He started with the road beneath his feet, the walls of the Jaguar's mind that loomed around him. He wanted to push on, towards the power center that pounded out its blue-on-blue waves. This road was criss-crossed with others, some of them curving upwards and into the side canyons of the Jaguar's mind.

No time, he thought.

Out of the churning mess of images that surrounded him, Eddie snagged some pieces and concocted a little animal like the whisk-broom dog in *Alice in Wonderland*. He set it sweeping along one of the roads and watched the road disappear. One information route was down.

And a hundred million to go, he thought.

Eddie had swept bad memories from more than one mind when he was younger, thinking he was doing the dreamer a favor. He had acquired a premature maturity along with the information he'd sought, and with this came the unspoken ethic that had guided him since—take nothing, leave nothing.

There was much he could have learned that would help him now, but at what cost would it have been to his innocent dreamers? He'd refused the lessons that transcended observation, lessons that he sorely needed to defuse this Jaguar.

Defuse!

The consciousness that was Eddie inside the Jaguar ridiculed the euphemism. What he sought was the quickest route to either of two locations: the medulla and its life-support center, or the link to the higher brain that allowed the Jaguar to dream, to reason, to be human.

But the Jaguar had spent ten years looting the cortex of every subject he'd ever entered, and Eddie had never seen anything like the clutter of the Jaguar's brain.

He had expected it to be dark because he thought of the Jaguar as dark, but the incredible power lit everything. Light did not diminish the confusion, the helplessness that Eddie felt amidst it all. Perhaps it was better to stumble in the labyrinth among monsters than to face the real thing, bathed in light.

If I can duplicate the puzzle, I can take it apart, he thought.

Dissolving images was a lot harder than putting them together. The bonds, once formed, did not intend to part. They linked up with others, which changed them as an additional ion changed a molecule. Not only did they change, but they gained weight, bulk, and became unwieldy. If the mind couldn't lift it, it couldn't use it.

Eddie raced along, praying that his route carried him deeper towards center, and as he sped through the Jaguar's brain he linked together the thousands of puzzle ends that he passed. He didn't know what changes he was forcing on the man's brain, but change was guaranteed.

It couldn't be worse, Eddie thought, and prayed he was right.

It was hard to keep going, hard to remember his mission. The Jaguar's mind was the richest onslaught Eddie had ever experienced. Eddie's uncle had trouble building a fire because he had to read every sheet of newsprint that he crumpled. Eddie knew, now, something of what that meant.

He entered a section of the Jaguar's brain that felt . . . strange. And he was frightened but not by its strangeness nor by any threat from the constant barrage of images. No, what frightened him about the area he now entered was its incredible familiarity.

Elsewhere, he let the constant stream of faces, chatter, objects, smells and places flow through him. There were sensual images that tempted him even outside his body. This was different. These were not stolen images, polished and new-looking in a way that he could never explain to Dr. Mark. These were the real thing, memories of the Jaguar himself, pieces from his life.

What stopped Eddie, what frightened him, was the image of the bomber with the hard-eyed young men jostling each other under the wing. The name on the side; he could read it clearly: 'Sweetheart.' Behind the name, in four neat rows, the bombs. He snagged the image in spite of himself and heard a gravelly voice call his name.

"Reyes," it said. "Reyes! Get yer ass over here. We ain't got all goddam day and yer face ain't all that pretty."

Eddie felt himself inhale a thick belt of raw cigarette smoke, felt the acidic churn of a quart of cold coffee in his gut as he walked under the wing of the plane. One of the men poked his ribs.

"You'll be a daddy by the time you get home, yeah? Don't see how any woman could sleep with the likes of you. Christ, you kept me up all goddam night again last night with that talking and screaming."

"Army's going to take care of it," he heard his thick voice say. "They got me in a special program when I hit stateside."

"Hold still, you yahoos," someone said. The Jaguar tilted his hat back, dragged on his cigarette one more time and the shutter snapped.

Eddie unplugged himself from the image, stunned.

It's a trick, he thought. *How did he . . . he must have got inside, I didn't know. . . .*

But he knew better. If the Jaguar had found him once, he would have him now. There would be no need to send Mel Thompkins with his fancy rifle. The memory was real, not a replicate of some innocent dreamer, his father.

The Jaguar *was* his father.

Eddie reached out for another memory, farther back in the line, and found himself looking through a bombsight at a railroad bridge. The sudden barrage of noise that came with it hurt his ears, and when he jammed his thumb down on the release the sudden upward lurch of the plane emptied his stomach.

"Bombs away!" he heard himself wail; then the plane veered right, pivoted for a moment on one wing and somewhere they took two hits that tumbled them over. He vomited again and gripped the bombsight in both arms as though it would save him when really it was Hugo's mastery at the controls that got them right.

Eddie backed out, moved down the rack, pulled out another memory.

This time the Jaguar was on a bus, pulling into a station, and all around him the men on the bus were out of their seats, yelling, stomping their feet, hanging out the windows. The Jaguar sat, watching his hands tremble. Deep scratches marred his wedding ring. His nails were bitten back to their angry red beds and he had chewed the skin away from them, too. Out the window a small woman jumped up and down in the front of the crowd and waved her shiny black pocketbook. He knew that it smelled like Juicy Fruit gum, like her breath. Under her little gray hat with the stylish chunk of blue veil he saw the woman who had no idea who he'd become.

Five days, Eddie heard the Jaguar's thoughts on that day, *five days and we ship out*.

Eddie had to pull the plug on that one; he couldn't stand any more. He couldn't stand the beauty of his mother in her youth, of what the Jaguar had made of her, of him. He couldn't tolerate the Jaguar's beautiful memory of her, so he shattered the pieces.

Against his better judgment, Eddie memorized the puzzle that held that memory for replay later. It would make up in part for all the pictures of her that nobody had saved for him.

Eddie had wanted to scrawl, "You're my father!" all over the walls of the Jaguar's brain.

It couldn't be—his father was buried in the valley; Eddie had been there with his mother, had set flowers on his stone.

Mark White had approximated a father, though Eddie thought of him now as a cousin.

But he was inside the Jaguar's brain, and the truth was clear—the Jaguar was his father. Then he realized the greater truth, the tragic one.

He knows.

For a moment Eddie was paralyzed with the enormity of that fact—he knew Eddie for his son, and set out to destroy him, anyway. It brought home to Eddie the magnitude of his danger, and his responsibility.

Eddie knew that it didn't matter who the Jaguar was. What was important was stopping him from destroying hundreds of lives in two worlds—maybe even the worlds themselves. Maryellen was a part of that world, and now, for that, he would not let it go.

The pulse beat faster, harder, and stuttered into an irregular pounding that unleashed the stench of fear around him.

Eddie's little scrambler was starting to work; the whisk-broom program must have found the corpus callosum and followed it to the medulla. The house of the Jaguar was coming down. Eddie raced nerve pathways to keep ahead of shutdown, and all around him those pathways were sputtering out.

What happens if I don't get out? he wondered.

After what he'd found, he knew he didn't want to spend another moment in there.

He scrambled through the sandy-floored warehouse of the Jaguar's brain and unlocked bins, unplugged cables, switched switches and signs. He linked the tails of as many puzzle pieces as he could as fast as he could and got the hell out of that place. He was barrelling full-steam towards the deafening roar of the blue waves when a searing white flash ripped into his own head. He saw nothing, felt nothing, heard Maryellen calling him as if from across loud water, but he couldn't answer.

The Jaguar was an addictive-obsessive. Like a chemical or sexual addiction, the power of the dreamways, the power over thousands of lives, had him hooked, stronger than any drug. And the Jaguar had had the best drugs, the finest brandies, before he flew those dreamways. That was the sand drifting shut the back streets and suburbs of his mind.

Eddie remembered little of his descent into the Jaguar's maelstrom. Now, in surgery, he got a taste for what invasion felt like. They went down into the bone of his head. Even asleep there, limp and cold on the steel table, Eddie heard them grinding away, sawing. The whine of the steel brush and steel drill ripped inside way far down and took chunks of him out.

He wasn't afraid, alone in the dark. *Alone* was something familiar to him.

One good thing about being left alone, he thought. *You learn to take good care of yourself because you know you're all you've got.*

Eddie felt himself lighten, as if a burden were lifted, as if someone flung wide the drapes in a dark room. He remembered that his grandparents had locked him up many times in the closet, and sometimes the pantry. They couldn't afford a sitter. They had done the same to his mother, and now Eddie understood something of why she had fallen for the Jaguar. Even after the longest day and night in the closet, the sound of his grandfather's key in the lock always made Eddie's heart leap, always made him feel *lighter*. He forgot the jailer, and welcomed liberation.

Needles pricked his face and forehead and his skull. The tail of the thread that closed him in tickled his nose and his cheek as the doctor pulled it across, knotted it and tied the rest of him down good and tight. He was good and tight in there, running and re-running in an endless loop of grainy movie, jerky in spots but continuous and demanding as the tides, as his bladder or the faint harmonics of dying stars.

He knew right away that the dreamways were lost to him forever.

Eddie woke up to a ripping pain that seared his shoulder. He gasped, too pained to cry out, and opened his eyes to a young, blond nurse saying, "I'm sorry. God, I'm sorry I didn't mean to bump you."

She steadied a chain-link apparatus that held his arm up in the air, and Eddie caught his breath in gulps and gasps.

"Slow, deep breaths," she said. She fumbled with the chainwork of the traction device and blew her blond bangs out of her eyes. Her breath smelled of coffee and fear; her cheeks blanched. "Oh, I'm so sorry. Are you awake, now?"

Eddie managed a grunt. The red flashes in his head and the pain in his shoulder ebbed back to wherever it was that pain came from.

"Good," she said. "Dr. White is here, and your friend. I'll get them. I'm so sorry about the bump."

Pain was something he never quite understood, like the gray sky filling the window behind her. Eddie tried to say, "It's okay," but what came out was another grunt.

. . . with the last sun or in the first rain
we will gather the fruits of hope.

—Daisy Zamora, "Letter to a Sister Who Lives in a Distant Country"

ONE WEEK FROM Thanksgiving they buried Mel Thompkins with military honors in a plot that was only a few paces from the markers for Eddie's mother and grandparents. It was one of those gray, high-ceiling days with the occasional shot of blue through the clouds. A hundred paces from the cemetery gate Mark White waited on 2-West at Valley Hospital to see Eddie through his third surgery, a scalp repair. Compared to the skull and neck fractures, this was mere cosmetics.

"Y'know that she's covering up for her old man," the sheriff said. He'd surprised Mark by meeting him in the waiting room after the funeral. "I suppose it doesn't matter much, except it does. Unfinished business bothers me. Doesn't it bother you? Never mind—you're a shrink; I don't want to know what that says about me."

The sheriff rubbed his nearly bald head, then stopped, suddenly self-conscious.

"It says you like things tidy, orderly and complete," Mark told him with a chuckle. "Excellent qualities in a peace officer. And, yes, unfinished business bothers me."

" 'Peace officer.' " The sheriff chuckled. "I suppose that's true. I've always been more interested in keeping the peace than enforcing the law. What bothers me about this unfinished business is the motive. Why would Mel go after that kid like he did?"

"Lots of fathers can't handle the boys their daughters date."

"But most of them can, Doctor. And most of those who can't don't go after them with baseball bats and rifles. Am I right?"

"Yes, but . . . look, he's got a long history of abuse connected with drinking. . . ."

"There has never been a complaint until the incident at the river," the sheriff said. "I can't do anything about that. After the first incident, he was remanded to counseling. Only made things worse. . . ."

"Who did he see?" Mark asked.

The sheriff shrugged.

"Somebody at the Soldiers' Home. Only showed up the once, but nobody notified us. He didn't want you or anybody in town; he claimed you were all on the kids' side. . . ."

"*Somebody* had to be," Mark said. "Look at them. . . ."

"No," the sheriff interrupted, "*you* look at them. Look at the trouble that's always been around them. Kids in their class flip out, their teachers have nervous breakdowns, two neighbors hang themselves, a teacher walks into the river with rocks in his pockets. . . ."

"You're just falling for neighborhood talk. . . ."

"Bullshit, Doctor. My job, like yours, depends on knowing when people are being straight with me and when they're not. You're not."

"What makes you think *that*?"

"The Soldiers' Home," the sheriff said. He tapped the thick sheaf of records with Eddie's name on them. "Colonel Hightower claims you're conducting some unauthorized research that threatens a confidential project of his. He's sending some Federal people down to talk with you."

"And if I told you that I suspect that it's the Colonel's research that's responsible for all this . . . ?"

The sheriff shrugged.

"Well, I like you, Doc, but the sheriff in me only believes hard evidence. Got any?"

"Maybe."

"There's no 'maybe' about hard evidence, Doc, just maybe you'll show me, maybe you won't. Right? When you've got it, bring it by. I can help you with these feds, but I need cooperation, too. Are you still seeing the girl every day?"

Mark nodded.

"She still singing the same song?"

"Yes. It was an accident. He had the rifle because he owned a gun shop and he always had a rifle."

"When—*if*—she changes that story, you'll let me know, won't you?"

"She will," Mark said. "Thompkins and his wife abused her, the stepbrother terrorized her sexually, her father tried to kill her and her best friend . . . it'll take her a while to believe that she's safe from him. Seeing him buried will help."

The sheriff's expression softened.

"You're right," he said. "No hurry."

"Do you really think that these kids killed Mel Thompkins?"

The sheriff shrugged again, dusted his hat on his pants leg and stood holding the doorknob.

"I've seen everything," he told Mark. "Call me."

You haven't seen anything, yet, Mark thought.

He listened to the receding *thuck thuck* of the sheriff's boot heels down the hallway.

The consciousness that Eddie regained was severely impaired, but, for the first time since Mark had met him, he seemed happy. Mark wondered how Eddie would handle the memories as they came back to him—*if* they came back—and how he would be received by the people of the valley.

Maryellen stepped through the doorway and Mark manufactured a smile for her. She looked terrible in her eyes and slouch, but she looked refreshed with clean hair and Sara's red jacket.

Maryellen had been witness to some terrible things; what she had left of her youth would not be easy to salvage.

"Hello, Dr. Mark," she said. Her voice was low and husky, her eyes red and red rimmed from crying. "Is Eddie out yet? Can we see him?"

"They're just now moving him from Recovery to his room," he said.

She hugged Mark, and didn't let him go.

When Maryellen spoke she had her face pressed to his chest.

"I've been on the other side," she said. "The Jaguar's finished, like Eddie said, but it's not like he thinks. It was like, with the priests. The Jaguar burned up. He burned alive from the inside. . . ."

She gripped his arms and cried silently into his jacket. Mark held her quietly.

"After his mother"—she sniffed—"after *that*, what will this do to him?"

The cocky OR nurse that Mark had learned to like, Billie Merritt, waved to him from down the hall and indicated that Eddie was settled in his room. She waved an envelope at him.

"Let's go see Eddie," he said. "He'll be fine. Maybe it's a mistake. Maybe your dream was speaking symbolically."

"These dreams don't do that." Her voice was flat, disappointed.

Mark led Maryellen to the recovery room and seated her beside Eddie. The envelope that Billie handed him was blank.

"It's from your wife," she said. "She came by about a half hour ago and said you *had* to see it. She didn't leave you, did she?"

Mark didn't answer. He had already opened the envelope. He unfolded the memo from Sara's news service just as it had come across the wire: "An Orting volunteer firefighter was treated for burns received Thanksgiving weekend while trying to extinguish a fire on a patient in the security wing of the nearby Soldiers' Home. Fire Department refused comment on the mutual-aid response, dispatched as '. . . a man burst into flames at the Soldiers' Home . . .' which adjoins their district. Identity of the patient is unknown, and the Department of Defense ordered personnel at the scene to remain silent until their debriefing ends, presumably early this week. . . ."

Eddie may ask sooner than later. Mark took in a long, slow breath and let it out, equally slowly. He did it again. Sometimes it paid to follow the advice he gave his patients. He finished the memo, and heard a groan from Eddie's gurney, then a cough.

Maryellen sat right next to Eddie's head. She wore the red jacket and carried a bouquet of blue irises because she wanted Eddie to see her first thing. She sniffed a bracing whiff of the flowers, took a deep breath and flashed a smile at Mark.

"You look great," he said, and slid the privacy curtain into place for them.

It was hard to tell how much of Eddie's thick speech was due to the drugs and how much to the head injury. He was overjoyed that Maryellen was there and didn't let either stop him.

"Bootful," Eddie managed, "you bootful."

"You look good, too," she said. "You look happy. Are you happy?"

"Feel good," he said. Eddie scooted his head over to a patch of sunlight on his pillow, and winced. "Hurt. Yeah, hurt. Buh feel good."

"Everything's fine," she told him. "Everything worked out. You did the right thing."

He looked puzzled, trying to remember.

"On the other side, they're going to be okay, too."

"Good."

She took his hand and kissed it.

"I love you."

"I luth you, too."

"You 'luth' me?" she joked. "That's better yet."

When Mark White got home that evening he burned the last piece of hard evidence—an aberrant EEG from Brenda Colfelt's office that demonstrated the mystery blips. He was sure that the Colonel had done the same with the set he'd glimpsed nearly a decade ago at the Soldiers' Home.

Sara watched him burn the records, and listened to him piece through the puzzle out loud.

"It's either their imaginations going physical, or physical changes are causing the imagination to slip into conjugate fantasies—*then* the hormones, *then* the neurovascular changes to . . ."

Sara shushed him.

"Do you believe . . . ?" she asked. Her gaze was dead serious. "Eddie said this comatose patient is his father? And that his father is this Jaguar who mind-controls people . . . ?"

Mark sighed. "I'm a believer. And this *incident* at the Soldiers' Home ties it all up. Also, there's a stone in the valley boneyard with his father's name, rank and serial number on it. His military records corroborate the mother's story that he was hit and killed by a jeep on his way home from the war. But I'll bet the linen there's no body in that grave or, if there is, it doesn't belong to Lieutenant Reyes."

"Are you going to dig him up to find out?"

"That's my ace in the hole with the feds," Mark said. "If they come nosing around, I'll give them something to nose. Whether the hole's empty, or filled with a stand-in, we win."

"This is a *great* story," Sara said. "Why . . . ?"

Mark put up a hand to slow her down.

"We don't want it told, either," he said.

"Why not?" she asked. "God, Mark, this is bigger than us, the kids. This kind of government experimentation, using people for guinea pigs . . . Mark, they might have *others*. . . ."

Mark dusted his knees off on the hearth and sat beside her on the sofa. The paperwork had started a perfect fire.

"If Eddie's right, that's all over," Mark mused. "Maryellen is probably the only one who could find out for sure."

"Eddie . . . defused . . . the Jaguar—you're sure about that?"

"I'm sure."

"I felt something once . . . something huge barrelling down on my dreams one night," Sara said. "I used that nightmare trick you taught me and woke up when I saw it coming. Do you suppose that was the Jaguar?"

"I have experienced something like what you describe," he said. "I suspected the same myself."

"You don't think it was the kids . . . ?"

"No," he said, "I don't. They're good, bright kids. We've practically grown up together, I feel good around them. This feeling of impending doom does not feel good."

Sara nuzzled his neck and tried to sound flip.

"So, Doctor, you admit to gut feelings?"

"Always have," Mark whispered. He fell back on the couch and Sara fell with him.

Eddie defused the Jaguar, all right—Mark was sure of it. It was the butterfly kiss that killed him. And Eddie saved that 'other side' that the kids talked about. It would be easier for Mark to deny that he believed those things. If he didn't believe them, then Eddie would be just another casualty of hallucination.

Mark kissed Sara's forehead, a little cool with worry, then her cheek and neck.

"Can you tell me how things are going to be for the kids?"

"Eddie's the easy one," he said. "His dream-meddling mechanism—it's fizzled out on him. It's a blessing, I think, though who knows what we've lost. At least what's left of his mind will be his own."

"That leaves Maryellen."

"Right," Mark said. "And they don't know about her. We want to leave it that way."

"But will *she* leave it that way?"

Eddie had wrestled the words out to ask Mark the same thing. Mark worried at it himself. He still had no answer.

After his chilly reception at the Soldiers' Home, Mark had executed the first records purge of his career. He wiped every reference to Eddie that he could find, but he left a fistful of standard EEGs and a pile of normal labs. Enough, he thought, to brush off the Soldiers' Home. Attention focused on Eddie and now it didn't matter whether they tested him or not—for Eddie, the 'phenomenon' was over.

We have to keep them thinking it's Eddie.

There was a time when Mark had regretted not fighting for an EEG on Maryellen. Now it might be a blessing.

Diverting the Colonel from the kids hadn't turned out to be easy, but nothing about these kids was easy. But it felt good to admit that he liked them.

The mystery patient that Mark had wanted to study no longer existed. The Soldiers' Home showed him the room—repainted, empty—and allowed him free access to the files, also gone. So was Colonel Hightower, the two guards, the ward secretary. This had been a special security wing, with only one patient.

Who won? Mark wondered. And that other thought, the nagging one that Sara put in his mind wouldn't leave him alone—*Power*.

He hoped Maryellen had the courage not to use it.

Could sex make the difference? No. The quality of innocence was something else. It was tangled with intent and sensitivity.

—Frank Herbert, *Soul Catcher*

THE DEEP DISH of night held Eddie down in its cold bowl. He imagined himself a fleck of rice in the black bowl of night. Somewhere, along the rim, Maryellen slept and dreamed her woman dreams that sometimes reached to him.

Once, it was as though she commanded his presence in a dream. Not as a participant, but as a witness. This time the dreamways led them into her stepbrother's brain. Eddie could tell that she wanted to scramble Chris like Eddie had scrambled the Jaguar.

She tried to give Chris a chance, but he didn't know any better. She hated him for what he had done to her and it did her no good to fight it.

She ambushed Chris's brain on the dreamways, and tested him with a few images from their past. He became aroused immediately, an arousal so powerful that it challenged her bid for control.

Is this why she did it? Eddie wondered. *Does she think I can rescue her in there?*

Eddie sensed her fury growing, the culmination of years of rage and fear. He saw the replays: Chris's incessant grabs at her breasts, her buttocks; his hands and feet on her legs under the table; her weekends locked in the bathroom while he cajoled from the other side of the door; the times she woke to find him standing over her bed, stroking himself.

He daydreamed the two of them back-to-back breathing the

stars and a cold half-moon. Her imaginary back felt strong and warm, the integrity of their skins indecipherable.

The night was their bed. They pulled each other close and didn't let go for anything but daylight. This was the woman who abandoned sleep in her dreams and dreamed Eddie home. He knew this because he'd met her there and loved her more than dreams or night could tell.

Comes from hell
you can't scare him with ashes.

—**W. S. Merwin,** *Asian Figures*

THE MORNING AFTER the funeral Maryellen's stepmother divided up her father's things into cardboard boxes with different people's names on them. Her stepmother took his pictures and family albums, even the ones with Maryellen's mother in them. She never saw a picture of her mother again.

Saddle blankets and Indian rugs disappeared into what was left of her memory. Along with them went his guns, holsters, belt buckles and his marksmanship trophies. In her own box all Maryellen found were his camera, some letters he'd written her and her letters to him.

All of the pictures but for the first one were taken at the cabin. That one was their Thanksgiving dinner the week before.

In the Thanksgiving photo she wore the white cashmere sweater that her father had given her for her birthday. She was daydreaming, staring at the table with her hands in her lap and a full plate of turkey steaming in front of her.

Her stepmother, Olive, stirred her drink at the end of the table. Behind her, one of her African masks leered down from the wall. The flash washed out the back of Chris's blond hair like a halo. Maryellen had pushed his foot off her leg twice since they sat down to eat.

Maryellen wouldn't have to worry about him anymore, and no one else would, either. She had taken care of Chris's sex drive on the dreamways, while she napped beside Eddie in the hospital.

Her father had shot the rest of the film from each window inside the cabin. From the kitchen counter he had worked around each wall, ending with a shot of their mud-spattered truck from the loft window, the one over her bed.

That night everything caught up with her. She was afraid to sleep and too tired to stay awake. Mark found her sitting on the floor and sobbing in the hallway outside Eddie's room. He convinced Olive to let Maryellen stay with them until Christmas.

She moved her things into Mark's study until Christmas, but she spent most of her waking hours at the hospital with Eddie. She spent some of her sleeping hours there, too. One of the night-shift nurses always let her sleep on the spare bed instead of in a chair.

Maryellen returned to her house the day it was sold. Olive and her horrible son were moving to Oregon.

"I'm not going," Maryellen said.

"Fine," Olive said. "You don't have to."

Olive had taken up smoking. She tapped her long filter-tip on the table-top, end-over-end, *tap tap tap tap*, then lit it and tilted her head back but did not inhale.

"There is some money," Olive announced, her matchbook on the table-top *tap tap* end-over-end, "for your college. If you want to stay here, I can put it into an account for you."

She rolled the ash of her cigarette delicately into a saucer.

Maryellen didn't have anything to say. She watched her stepmother's hands, nervous and thin, their blue veins stark against her pale skin. Maryellen's hands curled in her lap. Behind her hands, inside her warm abdomen, she imagined she felt a quickening.

"You have a week to find a place," Olive said. "We have to be out by the first of the year." She drank some of her pink wine and dragged on her cigarette.

tap tap tap tap

Olive poured herself another glass and gulped down half.

"Someone will have to be responsible for you," she said. "I'll get a lawyer to do it if you don't know anyone."

tap tap tap

She gulped the last of her wine, set down the glass and finished her speech.

"Your share is twenty-five hundred dollars. Chris and I don't have any money to spare; this move is eating me up. I'll put it in the bank Monday. You'll probably need a job."

Olive finished her cigarette and stubbed it out in the saucer. She brushed all the little pieces of ash off her black sleeves and off the table-top. Maryellen looked past her, out the window towards the river and Afriqua Lee.

"If people think you're crazy, nobody'll rent you a place or give you a job. Snap out of it."

Then she was finally alone. She found what she'd known all along—that breath came easier, and even temporary secrets were safer when she lived alone.

All the shadows of evening began their slow melt through pink to gray. Out the window a crow lifted off, his wings bowed and slow. Maryellen glimpsed his quick eye looking back, bright in the last of the sun.

"Nevermore!" she hollered after him. "Nevermore!"

Christ, she thought, *I bet they hear that all the time.*

About the Author

Bill Ransom has worked extensively in Central America as a medic and firefighter, and has included his findings in journalism and short fiction. One of these, "Learning the Ropes," was a 1986 selection in the Poets, Essayists and Novelists/National Endowment for the Arts Syndicated Fiction Project and appeared in *The Village Advocate* and *The Oregonian*; another, "What Elena Said," was a 1988 Syndicated Fiction Project selection for *The Kansas City Star* and *The Village Advocate*. He is presently at work on a screenplay of these experiences, *Daughters of Salvador*.

This novel, *JAGUAR*, is the continuation of a short story, "Uncle Hungry," a selection of the first Syndicated Fiction Project in 1983 which appeared in *The Kansas City Star*.

In 1979, 1982 and 1985 he collaborated with Frank Herbert to coauthor three novels: *The Jesus Incident*, *The Lazarus Effect*, and *The Ascension Factor* (Putnam/Ace).

He is a past recipient of a National Endowment for the Arts Discovery Fellowship and a nominee for both the Pulitzer prize and the National Book Award.

Bill Ransom, formerly an Advanced Life-support Emergency Medical Technician and firefighter, now writes full-time from his home in western Washington.